I0819660

EARLY PRAISE FOR

THERE'S ONLY ONE SIN IN HOLLYWOOD

"Deliciously witty and packing enough erotic heat to make sensitive souls clutch their pearls, Rasheed Newson's superb second novel brings us Xavier, a rising superstar determined to liberate queer Hollywood from a culture that demands silence and acquiescence. In studio boardrooms and backlots twinkling with VIPs named Poitier and Belafonte, unknowns try to become legends and heroes struggle to be heroic. **Newson writes in Technicolor—wow, are these pages alive!**—and knows where the bodies are buried. Love, fame, war, religion, political freedom, big dreams, and big money—***There's Only One Sin in Hollywood* is a quintessential Hollywood novel and an LA classic for our times.**"

—Laura Warrell, author of *Sweet, Soft, Plenty Rhythm*

"In Rasheed Newson's *There's Only One Sin in Hollywood*, inhumane history snares all lovelorn seekers, transforming fixers and actors into potent dreamers who frequent and abandon their fates with disastrous and extraordinary resolve. Propelled by a haunted, jaunty narration that makes a lively case for the necessity of memory, *There's Only One Sin in Hollywood* illustrates and innervates the queer midcentury. **This novel is an erotically charged, violent masterpiece of love.**"

—Kyle Dillon Hertz, author of *The Lookback Window*

"Newson's sophomore novel is a cinematic voyage into the decadence and inherent tragedy of old Hollywood. As characters jockey to Trojan horse a queer narrative within the undertones of a war hero's biopic, we the readers are morosely confronted with how little has changed in the past sixty years. Newson anatomizes lesser known cultural history while simultaneously inventing such beloved, gorgeously flawed, and veristic characters, one is stunned to remember it's fiction. In thematic homage to his debut, *There's Only One Sin in Hollywood* mixes readers a salacious cocktail of love, ambition, legacy, and activism. **This is the story Hollywood hoped would never see the light of day.**"

—Jason Yamas, author of *Tweakerworld*

"Rasheed Newson delivers another triumph and staple of queer literature with this noir-style, page-turning novel that captures both the regretful and hopeful timelessness of the gay struggle. **If Hollywood has only one sin, I hope this book is part of its salvation.**"

—Byron Lane, author of *Big Gay Wedding*

"Living up to its provocative title, Rasheed Newson's *There's Only One Sin in Hollywood* offers **a deft and deliciously decadent excavation of Black queer history. Sexy, sly, and with a piquant sense of humor**, Newson's prose handily shuttles you between glittering postwar Hollywood backlots and dimly lit lurid cruising spots in Griffith Park—all while making a period piece about a fixer stuck between two worlds feel impossibly urgent and fresh."

—Manuel Betancourt, author of *Hello Stranger: Musings on Modern Intimacies*

"Unabashedly erotic, irresistible, and heartbreaking, *There's Only One Sin in Hollywood* exposes the hidden gay world of the movies—the connections, dealings, and dramas of its Black figures—with panache and authority. Sparkling with real-life and invented Hollywood stars, and threaded with a complicated love of the movies, Rasheed Newson's second novel is an American tale of the first order. It will grip you until the last page."

—Richard Mirabella, author of *Brother & Sister Enter the Forest*

"*There's Only One Sin in Hollywood* is a study of juxtaposition—**an equal parts dark and dazzling drama** that's both a celebration of a bygone golden age of film and a memorial for the missing scenes that never made it from the cutting room. And it's a lesson for those unfamiliar with the difficult choices that those of us who identify with its characters have made before, during, and even after their time-capsule tale; a needed reminder that far too often, you can be Black, you can be queer, but the choice of how much safety you're willing to compromise in choosing one or both is, sadly, timeless."

—Aaron Foley, author of *Boys Come First*

THERE'S ONLY ONE

ALSO BY RASHEED NEWSON

My Government Means to Kill Me

SIN IN HOLLYWOOD

A NOVEL

Rasheed Newson

FLATIRON
BOOKS
NEW YORK

This is a work of fiction. All the names, characters, organizations, places, and events portrayed in this work are either products of the author's imagination or used fictitiously.

 For information, address Flatiron Books, 120 Broadway, New York, NY 10271. EU Representative: Macmillan Publishers Ireland Ltd., 1st Floor, The Liffey Trust Centre, 117–126 Sheriff Street Upper, Dublin 1, D01 YC43.

www.flatironbooks.com

Designed by Leah Carlson-Stanisic

Library of Congress Cataloging-in-Publication Data

Names: Newson, Rasheed, author.
Title: There's only one sin in Hollywood : a novel / Rasheed Newson.
Other titles: There is only one sin in Hollywood
Description: First edition. | New York : Flatiron Books, 2026.
Identifiers: LCCN 2025040593 | ISBN 9781250406149 (hardcover) |
ISBN 9781250406156 (ebook)
Subjects: LCGFT: Fiction | Queer fiction | Novels
Classification: LCC PS3614.E688 T47 2025
LC record available at https://lccn.loc.gov/2025040593

First Edition: 2026

10 9 8 7 6 5 4 3 2 1

CONTENTS

PART I

PART II

PART III

PART I

A LETTER FROM A PROJECTIONIST

October 1, 1971

To Mr. Jim Kepner,
At seven years old, I was the terror of the Emerson Palace Theater. Every Saturday morning, when the disgruntled ticket taker raised the red velvet curtains of the box office booth and saw me standing at the front of the line, he'd curse under his breath. I'd smile at him anyway and plunk a dime onto the counter. Nothing pleased me more in those days than being at the movies.

The Emerson Palace was the only movie theater for Negroes in Rufusville, Ohio. It had a single screen and three hundred seats and ran short action serials and slapstick comedies for children on Saturdays, from nine in the morning until two in the afternoon. The package of film shorts lasted roughly an hour, then repeated, and a ticket cost ten cents no matter when a kid showed up. I always stuck around for the full five hours, in the front row of the theater.

Republic Pictures' *The Adventures of Red Ryder* (1940) was my favorite that year. Once, when Red was in the driver's box fighting to rein in six wild horses, a low-life gunman leaned out of the stagecoach window to fire a coward's shot into our hero's back.

I hopped onto my seat and shouted, "Look out, Red!"

Several boys laughed at me. An usher shushed me. My older brother yanked me down onto my ass. But thank goodness I'd said something. Red turned around just in time to thwart the gunman. Relief and pride surged through me. That was when I knew my connection to the movies was stronger than others' in the audience: The stars on the silver screen could hear me. I could save them.

From then on, I spoke up more often, but the tolerance for my outbursts wore out once I grew louder and began blocking views of the kids in back of me. At ten years old, I was put on notice. The following Saturday, I cupped my mouth with my hands and booed when the enemy submarine appeared on-screen during *Freedom Comes High* (1944). The usher grabbed me by the ear and dragged me out of the theater to the cheers of the other children. In the lobby, I cried for forgiveness, but the usher ignored my pleas. He marched me toward the entrance. I was about to be cast out from the cool darkness of the movie palace into the burning light.

"Why you hassling that boy?" asked an elderly gentleman in a checkered navy-and-gray three-piece suit.

The usher tightened his grip on my ear. "Boss said I could boot him," he explained, "if he can't sit still and quiet."

"I won't say another word," I swore to the elderly gentleman, whom I recognized as the theater's projectionist.

"Let him loose," he told the usher. "I've got a place for him, and if that don't take, I'll show him out."

The usher shoved me toward the projectionist. His name was Mark Allenson, and he'd held his perch above the audience since the Emerson Palace opened in 1916. Trim and slight, Mr. Allenson was known as a confirmed bachelor. I once overheard a teenage boy refer to Mr. Allenson as a "pansy," and while I didn't know what that meant, there was no missing the disdain with which the boy spat the word.

But even as a child, my mind was my own when it came to passing judgment on people, and I liked Mr. Allenson straightaway.

Not only had he stopped my expulsion, but he didn't scowl at me like other old Black men were wont to do when I caught their attention. He carried himself in a courtly manner, and there was serenity in his deep voice. I followed him up a set of stairs that had been off-limits to me as a customer. At the top, we turned left and entered the projection booth.

I felt flutters in my chest. This was the inner sanctum. I considered it a revelation that the moving, talking pictures that enthralled me gathered their magic from the toil and skill mustered by a lonely alchemist in a five-by-eight-foot room. Mr. Allenson took a seat on a metal stool. I stood with my back pressed against the closed door. I'd never felt a sense of reverence like I did laying eyes on the clunky 1934 Super Simplex 35 mm carbon arc projector. The beguiling machine was aglow, spinning and whirring while a reel of nitrate film ran through it. A second Super Simplex projector was on deck, loaded to take command at the changeover.

I rolled up my sleeves. It was warm in the booth despite a low-speed electric fan that Mr. Allenson kept running to circulate and cool the air. Heat had the power of a lit match, and nitrate film could be as flammable as kerosene. So, the booth's walls were made of brick; its door was metal; its floor was linoleum; a fire extinguisher remained on hand in one corner; a deep sink jetted out from the back wall; and a full bucket of water sat in the sink.

The precautions were in place because of two gruesome tragedies: the 1897 inferno in Paris at the Bazar de la Charité, where nitrate film went up in flames, and 126 people died; and a fire that broke out thirty years later during a run of Hal Roach Studios' *Get 'Em Young* at the Laurier Palace Theatre in Montreal with more than 200 children in attendance. Seventy-eight kids perished. The cause of the Montreal calamity was debated, but Mr. Allenson knew there was no arguing about the ever-present dangers of nitrate film.

As a result, Mr. Allenson forbade smoking in the booth. He insisted that the projectors be given time to cool down after five hours of rotational use. He refused to run movies if the temperature outside reached one hundred degrees or higher. After the final showing of the day, prints were stored in the palace's chilly cellar.

That first day in the booth, I stood at the projectionist's window watching the children's package on repeat for the next three and a half hours. I was mesmerized by the godlike distance of my new vantage point. The dust that filtered throughout the expanding beam of light appeared to be carrying the images to the screen. Once the movie filled the frame, I found that I could now swallow it whole because the picture no longer loomed over top of me. Peering down on the crowd's heads, I caught the delay between the action on film and their collective response in the theater. There was always a moment of perfect silence between a joke and a laugh, a gunshot and a gasp, a happy ending and applause.

When the showing ended at two o'clock, Mr. Allenson told me to return next Saturday at 8:30 AM sharp and I did. When he let me into the Palace for free, I thanked him for his generosity but quickly discovered that he wasn't extending charity. He ordered me to climb down a ladder into the cellar and retrieve the reels for the animation shorts *Donald Duck and the Gorilla*; *Bugs Bunny Nips the Nips*; *Goldilocks and the Jivin' Bears*; and *The Barber of Seville* of the *Woody Woodpecker* series, along with the theater's copy of Laurel and Hardy's short film *Thicker Than Water* and the latest *News of the Day*.

The ladder was splintered and wobbly, and they could have hung slabs of meat in that cellar, it was so frigid. A cluster of spiders kept busy spinning elaborate webs. A naked, 110-volt incandescent light bulb burned continuously, giving the cellar a yellowish color. I found the reels stacked on steel shelves no taller than my waist. I brought up the day's programming from the cellar to the projection booth. Mr. Allenson checked my work and rewarded me with a shiny penny.

"Watch me," he instructed.

He took the reel for *Donald Duck and the Gorilla* and threaded the nitrate film into the projector's feed, through its rollers, and into its film gate. His tapered fingers coaxed the film into position with an efficiency that made the operation look deceptively easy. I should have studied his movements with my full concentration, but I got spellbound by the little paintings on each frame. One tiny frame was almost like the one before it until the small adjustments created the illusion of motion. Each frame a masterpiece.

Once the reel was threaded, Mr. Allenson began looping the film above the gate, which had to be done precisely to ensure the projector didn't jam while it ran. He explained that a jam could cause a tear in the reel, and a tear would bring a halt to the showing while the projectionist spliced and taped the film back together. The other peril of looping was that if the loop was made too big, then the picture would fall out of sync with the sound. The projectionist's job was an art and a science.

With the reel loaded, threaded, and looped, Mr. Allenson ignited the carbon arc light and turned the focus on the projector until the picture on the screen was pinpoint and crisp. He turned to me. "Got it?" he asked.

"Yes, sir," I lied.

"Good boy. Go on and load up Laurel and Hardy on the second projector."

I made a hash of it, loading the film on the reverse side. But Mr. Allenson didn't fuss at me. He guided my hands with his own, encouraged me even when I'd done nothing to earn it, and found excuses to plunk pennies into my pockets. Being only ten years old, I couldn't fathom why he was being so patient and kind with me. No one else in my life was patient or kind with me.

Without filling out an application, sitting for an interview, or formally accepting the position, I became the projectionist's apprentice at the Emerson Palace Theater. Mr. Allenson paid me with his own money anywhere from five to ten cents a day depending on my performance. It took me several weeks to become proficient at loading, threading, looping, focusing, rewinding the reels by hand, and cleaning the reel with an alcohol-based solution and a cashmere swatch.

I took to the work so eagerly, I didn't notice how it steadily consumed my waking hours. In addition to the children's showings on Saturday, I ran to the palace after school on Tuesdays to help stock the new film prints for the changeover on Wednesdays, when new movies made their theatrical debuts. As I grew up and Mr. Allenson grew older, I assumed more of the projectionist duties for first-run movies on Friday and Saturday nights, and I operated solo for the revival screenings during the Sunday matinees. All told, I ran at least two hundred short and feature-length films a year.

From the metal stool in the projection booth, I absorbed movies with a keener eye than the paying customers, because I had to spot the yellow circle when it flashed in the upper-right corner of the print. That yellow circle was a warning that the end of the reel was nearing and that the second projector needed to be cued up to take over. Miss it and the hypnotic trance of the film was broken. The audience was startled into reality. The yellow circle could appear anywhere from ten to fifteen minutes into a reel. Catching the quick cue was the final skill I had to master before Mr. Allenson would let me work on my own. The yellow circle was subliminal to the average moviegoer, but once trained, I would never fail to see it whenever I watched a film on the big screen.

At the same time, arthritis was warping Mr. Allenson's fingers into curved stone. By the third year of my apprenticeship, he took hold of my arm every time we climbed and descended the stairs to the booth. We didn't discuss his frailty and ailments. Mr. Allenson died in his sleep on the day after Christmas in 1948. I learned from his obituary that he was seventy-two years old.

The Wednesday after Mr. Allenson's ashes were interred, I was fired. Since I wasn't a legitimate member of the projectionists' union, a seasoned moving pictures machine operator out of Cincinnati, in good standing with the International Alliance of Theatrical Stage Employees, relocated to Rufusville and took over the job. I returned to the audience, handing over my dimes for tickets.

My exile from the projection booth cut deep, and I longed for my lost privileged view. I cared for movies and nitrate film and stars and reel canisters and picture-to-sound sync with an uncommon devotion. Mr. Allenson had initiated me into the rites of a projectionist, and I'd found my calling behind the scenes. I loved being an invisible hand.

My subsequent journey to Hollywood six years later was not direct, but when I accepted a role in the backstage business of the Dream Factory, it was a natural fit for me. I spent time as a security agent for Skyline Motion Pictures, but in the trade papers, I was what's called a *Hollywood fixer*.

During my colorful tenure, I rescued my share of stars. There was a song-and-dance lothario who knocked up and ran off with a mobster's daughter. I brokered an apology, a hefty reverse dowry, and a Vegas wedding.

One cold night, I dove into the LA River to fish out a drunk swashbuckling idol from behind the wheel of his blue convertible Duesenberg. The next day, he didn't recall the accident and demanded to know why his pocket watch was missing. He insinuated that I'd stolen the timepiece.

In defiance of the law, I mugged a spurned girlfriend who was taking love letters to a gossip columnist to out the archetype of film noir vamps as an insatiable lesbian. I cut the strap on the snitch's purse, dashed off with her bag, and burned the letters.

The most delicate situation was a musical comedy ingénue plagued by a male stalker. I set up a mousetrap using the ingénue as bait in her own home, and I disarmed the knife-wielding perp on the kitchen floor. It turned out the stalker was her brother-in-law.

At dinner parties, family and friends used to beg me to name-drop and boast. They enjoyed the insider's thrill of listening to substantiated Hollywood gossip. They wanted a closer look at the stars than what was given to them on the big screen. Often, I'd oblige them, since I had countless stories of philanderers, addicts, closet cases, and blackmail victims with famous names.

I have one story, however, that matters too much to be squandered over cocktails or reduced to a rambling anecdote between courses. I need to thread this one out, frame by frame, so that for once you can see the raw footage.

It began in the spring of 1954, when a Black teenager quit his factory job in Gary, Indiana, and hitchhiked to Los Angeles. Persuasive women who frequented pool halls and vigilant men who loitered in the lavatories at drive-in movie theaters had filled his head with the notion that he was handsome enough to be in pictures. He wanted to see if they were right and if he had the stuff to be an actor. So, he stole himself a new pair of blue jeans, and with nothing more than sweet talk, he hustled a virginal beautician into relaxing his hair into waves. Riding shotgun in Fords, Packards, and LaSalles, he silently rehearsed a James Cagney monologue from *The Time of Your Life* (1948), and he dropped the slight twang in his accent before he'd crossed Missouri.

No one welcomed him when he reached LA. He spent his days outside the Paramount studio gates waiting in line for cattle call auditions and learned from other hopefuls where he could go in the evenings to get free acting lessons. He managed to land enough work as a background extra in crowd shots to pay for a room by the week at the YMCA, and in his acting workshops, he straightened his posture and discovered how to project his voice.

While he turned in his leotard costume after ten hours of posing as an "acrobat" in a Martin and Lewis comedy (*3 Ring Circus*), the casting director Peter Lowery spotted him, called him over, and told him there was more than one way to land a part. He was game. So, Lowery gave him the address to a cliff-side house in the Hollywood Hills and instructed him to arrive promptly at nine o'clock on Friday night with a bathing suit. He decided for himself that his dark skin looked best against powder-blue swim trunks. What no one knew was that he was seventeen, claiming to be nineteen.

That first invitation led to others. In the beginning, no one bothered telling him who hosted these private parties or how they were connected to the industry. Such details were deemed dangerous in the hands of young prospects with questionable staying power. What was important was that he was a quick learner. He turned up on time and plied his charm indiscriminately; he didn't pick lemons off the owners' trees; he drank champagne when it was handed to him; he didn't wander through the mansions unattended; he dove into the aqua-green pools when asked; and he didn't resist the graceless touch of guilty white men.

George Cukor took a real shine to him, which was a minor shock because the revered director had never cared much for colored boys before. That all changed on a dime when Donald Wells, an MGM film executive, just to be cheeky, singlehandedly desegregated Cukor's Memorial Day celebration by inviting the newest Negro stud to be causing a stir among a select circle of men. Eyebrows raised at Cukor's Beverly Hills estate when the young man from Indiana strode to the edge of the pool and began to undress. Prejudice lost to lust. Cukor asked his Black guest, "What's your name?"

"Ruben Singleton."

"No," the director said, "that won't do. Let me think on it." Hours later, at the end of the party, Cukor put his hands on Ruben's wet, bare shoulders and told him, "Xavier C. Barlow. That'll suit you. Strength and power for an exquisite buck—almost beyond belief."

To be fair to the director and other onlookers, Xavier's physique did challenge the eye to accept what it was seeing. He stood six foot three. His shoulders were broad. His chest tapered into a thirty-inch waist. He filled out the back and the front of his swimsuit, and his legs were muscular and defined in stark contrast to the pale chicken legs of the others on display.

His casual air made him even more attractive. One could believe in those early years that he was an innocent. His older, white, male admirers certainly needed to imagine that Xavier wasn't aware of his beauty. They reassured each other that he didn't know the value of what he was seemingly giving away. Heaven forbid they be forced to acknowledge that they were the ones being used. That the young Black beau didn't have a hard-on for them. That he was getting the better end of the exchange.

Since his untimely death, the gossip rags have packaged Xavier's life story as the latest cautionary tale—a variation on Marilyn. He was astute and forward-thinking, but they've stripped him of his cunning and his brilliance. It's a sickening travesty. Xavier was not some gorgeous buffoon destroyed by fame, drugs, sodomy, and Hollywood.

I've spent four years mourning Xavier. The bond between us was never conventional. Off and on for nearly a decade, it was my duty to keep his nose clean. At first, he unnerved me with his boldness. He challenged me to admit who and what I am.

And I fell in love with him.

It's not an easy truth to admit or live with—even after all I've seen and done. Part of me wants to take back my confession and tear the page I'm typing on into confetti, but my fear is a meaningless reflex. I no longer have any excuse to hide. Lung cancer will kill me before Christmas comes around. Then there will be no one left to tell Xavier's story, and it deserves to be preserved. That is the purpose of your archives after all.

I hope you will accept this manuscript into your collection. It is my candid recollection as to how Xavier's life and mine intertwined to form a tragedy. I can think of no other way to damn the men who have Xavier's blood on their hands. Maybe when you finish reading these pages, you will also find me guilty of ushering my beloved friend to his grave. So be it.

Respectfully,
Aaron Toussaint

1

EASY LIVING

My first Hollywood party was a jazz bash thrown to honor Dorothy Dandridge in July of 1954 at the Dunbar Hotel on Central Avenue. I got pinned against the wall to the left of the bandstand as four hundred Black people crammed into a supper club room meant to hold half that number. Collective body heat and cigarette smoke made the air foul and steamy. I loosened my tie and unfastened the top two buttons on my white dress shirt to keep from sweating through my collar.

The jostling and jockeying didn't stop for a moment. Elbows poked my ribs. Ladies' hats smacked my face. My toes got stepped on so much they went numb. Yet I had to count myself among the lucky. Outside the hotel, the fire marshal barred at least a hundred cursing-mad Negroes, who stomped on the sidewalk and waved invitations in vain.

Pressed against the wall, I felt out of my depth. I was twenty-one years old and newly discharged from the navy. I knew diddly about business and squat about managing, and here I was riding Lieutenant Horace "Hornet" Dixon's coattails as his business manager. Worse still, I was recognizing a side of Horace that unnerved me, and I was starting to chafe under his command.

Onstage, Pearl Bailey sang her signature tune, "Takes Two to Tango." I spotted Harry Belafonte, standing in the wings, hungry for his turn in the spotlight. Lena Horne had a seat at a front-row table, and Count Basie had a room in the hotel. No doubt they would be called up to perform. To say nothing of the stars I couldn't see among the crowd or the ones who might be ushered from their limos through the kitchen to the stage for one number and hustled back again in less than ten minutes flat. Even a Hollywood novice like me could tell something special was brewing. We were in for a barn burner.

I figured Dorothy Dandridge would be coaxed to perform a song or two once she arrived. An empty chair next to Lena awaited her. I thought it odd that the party had begun without the guest of honor, but those versed in the ways of show business saw nothing amiss. It took acts of God to delay a curtain.

Twentieth was bankrolling this tribute to Dorothy because she was starring alongside Harry in the studio's musical *Carmen Jones*, due for release that fall. Hopes were high that Dorothy would not only snag an Academy Award nomination but win, becoming the first Black woman to be crowned best lead actress. Such a distinction would practically obligate every Negro in America to buy a ticket to see the film, maybe more than once. The estimated box office receipts could dwarf *Gone with the Wind*. So, the bigwigs at Twentieth prayed Dorothy would receive that Oscar more fervently than Dorothy did.

Not willing to wait for the movie to open in the theaters, Twentieth decided to start Dorothy's drumbeat to victory in the Dunbar. Major Black stars were chauffeured to the hotel and offered a suite for the night. Minor Black stars shared limos. I got an invitation and had to find my own way to the event, and I only made the guest list because I was the business manager to a war hero that Skyline Motion Pictures, at the time, planned to use for a movie based on his life story. Skyline and Twentieth were known in the business as kissing cousins; during World War II, they split the cost of making and releasing dozens of movies together.

I wasn't even dressed the way I wanted to be. Horace had insisted that to avoid any confusion that might occur if we both wore our uniforms to the party, I had to put on a gray suit while he donned his dress blues. Of course, arriving in uniform got Horace noticed and ushered to a table next to Ruby Dee. He didn't even glance back at me as the room quickly grew packed and rowdy, and I got swept farther away from him. From a side angle, I watched Horace smoking L&Ms and drinking whiskey neat all cool and unbothered like peace blanketed the earth.

I averted my gaze. That was when I spotted a slender, pretty man with honey-brown skin cut through the crowd, making his way to the front tables. Although I didn't then know his name, he received the deference of a man of note, but that wasn't what made him stunning to me. This middle-age Black dandy swanned over to Lena Horne's table with his fingers interlocked with those of a white man (the only white man in the room). They were obviously gay and lovers, too.

Lena greeted them both with kisses on their cheeks. The Black man curtsied and bowed his head to her before taking his seat. His hands danced daintily as he talked, and Lena treated him like he was the cat's meow. I waited for someone else to have a hostile reaction. Nothing. Later, I'd learn the Black man was cabaret singer Jimmie Daniels.

From where I stood, he might as well have been a leprechaun. That was how astonishing he appeared to me. I'd simply never seen anyone behaving like he was in public. Watching him, I must have forgotten to breathe and got lightheaded. Nowhere I had lived before Hollywood would have allowed a Jimmie Daniels to continue existing.

The crowd applauded Pearl, who concluded her set with a brassy rendition of "The Birth of the Blues." She called Harry out for his numbers, and the women went crazy for him, and Belafonte wallowed in their adoration like a pig in slop. He wasn't to my liking. He irked me with his double-edged strident persona, too ingratiating when he sang and too uppity when he spoke. He started in on "Matilda," and I decided I'd rather go empty my bladder.

I wormed my way through heaving bodies until I caught sight of the men's restroom on the ground floor. To my dismay, the line outside the restroom door snaked down the hall, and it was slow moving. I tapped a hotel bellhop and asked him where I could find another lavatory, and for a fifty-cent tip, he gave me directions to facilities in the basement.

By the time I made my way down the stairs, I really needed to relieve myself, and I hurried along, and I thanked my lucky stars that the way into the basement men's room was clear. Once inside, I was a little taken aback by how bustling the joint was. Men, in and out. Men minding their own bodily affairs. Such was my first impression.

The men's room was shaped like an L, with the entrance at the top of the letter. There were three sinks underneath a wide mirror to the immediate left and three more to the immediate right. The long corridor was lined with stalls on one side and urinals on the other. The end of the corridor turned left, where a dead end offered three urinals and two stalls.

Mind you, I wasn't paying too much attention to the restroom's layout when I walked through the door. The stalls and urinals along the long corridor were not only occupied, many had people waiting to replace the men currently making use of them. I turned into the dead-end section, and of the three urinals, the one in the middle was free. I walked up to it, unzipped, and relaxed into my flow. I stared down at my cock mindlessly, waiting for my stream to end.

Then the guy to my right tapped his foot faintly, twice. His black Stacy Adams wing tip didn't even make a sound against the mint-green-and-yellow tile floor. I was assuredly gay, having had sex repeatedly with one man, but I'd never cruised before. However, I picked up on the signals as if they were innate, and I responded as if I'd been taught the code. My eyes took in the fresh polish of his shoe, moved up along the crisp crease in his charcoal slacks, and settled on the open front of his dress pants, where he squeezed the base of his cock, presenting his balls and his hard-on like a prize.

My heart galloped faster than a whipped thoroughbred. The taste on my tongue turned to copper. I pivoted my body toward him, confirming my interest to this daring gentleman whose face I had yet to appraise. I looked up, taking in his chest and broad shoulders. His height surprised and aroused me. And his face—a collage of striking features both masculine (the square jawline; the hooded eyes) and feminine (the deep dimples; the long, curled eyelashes)—beguiled me.

I didn't realize in that moment I was exposing myself to Xavier C. Barlow and that he was exposing himself to me. Even if we had introduced ourselves, our names wouldn't have carried any weight. We were two nobodies. Queer strangers on the make.

Xavier began to stroke himself. I followed his lead, masturbating gingerly. A stout man standing in front of the urinal to my left coughed. I was startled, but when I glanced at him, he motioned for me to step back. I was blocking his view. His pants were fastened. He just wanted to watch us.

But I was hesitant to put on a show for him. The stout man had broken the trance Xavier had cast over me, and I suddenly felt very aware of being in a busy men's restroom with what I presumed were red-blooded heterosexuals who in an instant would transform into gay bashers if they discovered there were pansies in their midst.

I let go of my cock, and I was about to straighten up when Xavier reached over and began jerking my erection. I gasped. His grip and pace were better than my own. I closed my eyes. The sensation was too good to resist. Xavier had me back in a hypnotic blur. Panic drowned out by pleasure.

It was a purifying high, a sin worth the damnation. I realized what I was doing was illegal and dangerous, but it awakened desires and needs that I'd neglected. I opened my eyes. This didn't feel wrong. I craned my neck up to look at Xavier's face, and he reassured me with a wink. Then he nudged his head downward, and the message was clear. I extended my arm and started jerking his impressive cock.

We kept bringing each other to near climax, then backing off. I wasn't familiar with the term *edging*, but we were practicing it. One of the stalls behind us cracked open, allowing someone a better view, and a bald man peeked around the corner of the L to spy on us for a minute or two. I was in mindless bliss.

Thank goodness the other men in the gay section of the basement men's room kept their wits about them. An unseen man in the other stall behind me whistled sharply. He was the lookout, and when he sounded his warning signal, Xavier let go of me and stepped in close to his urinal. The stout man headed for the exit. I stood awestruck and too far back from my urinal to be innocently using it when Horace rounded the corner. I tucked myself away right as he found me.

"Aaron," he barked.

"Man, I had to piss so bad I nearly busted," I explained as I fastened my pants as quickly as my trembling hands could manage.

Horace looked around in disgust and scowled at me. "You about to bust, and you came all the way down here?"

"It was a madhouse upstairs. A bellhop told me this one would be less crowded."

He leaned close to my left ear and lowered his voice. "Damn it, Aaron. You better not—"

"Lieutenant Dixon, what an honor to meet you," Xavier said with what sounded like genuine awe. He'd made himself presentable and flashed that endearing smile of his. "If we weren't where we are," he continued, "I'd shake your hand."

Xavier laughed at his own joke, and I chuckled a little to fake camaraderie, and not wanting to seem standoffish, Horace grinned and nodded as if he'd enjoyed the jest.

"I know that's right," said Horace. "Find me in the hall after you wash up, and I'll be glad to shake your hand and sign an autograph."

"That would be mighty kind of you," Xavier replied as he pinched my ass before walking past Horace and me. "You're our Black ace, and you do us proud."

Horace beamed, and he wasn't faking the joy. "Thank you, brother."

Xavier saluted and walked over to clean his hands in the sink. I tried to slide by Horace, but he grabbed my right arm.

I attempted to put him on the defensive. "Are you drunk?" I asked.

He was straining to keep his temper in check. He didn't want to cause a scene. Fortunately for him, there wasn't much foot traffic in the dead-end corridor. Did perfectly straight men have an inborn sense that prevented them from venturing into fairy territory?

"What was you down here so long for? Why was your Johnson out?"

"You know some other way to piss? Jesus. Did you come in here just to see about me?"

Horace was possessive for sure, but when called out on it, he could never cop to it. "I got you a seat at the table," he said. "I looked for you upstairs, and you've been in the men's room going on fifteen minutes."

I couldn't argue with time, especially on account of how I'd lost track of it. "I'm sorry, Horace. There was a line down here, too. It was a big holdup."

He didn't believe me. "Let's get to the table. Lena's about to sing."

Backed by Count Basie on the piano, Lena set the house aflame with "I Feel So Smoochie." She left a suggestive pause between the words *so* and *smoochie* that had the audience in pandemonium. The bodies bumping and thrusting into the back of my chair kept scooting me forward until the edge of the table was up against my stomach. Horace and Ruby Dee were in the same predicament. The crowd wasn't gonna give an inch, so Horace and I pushed our table toward the stage, buying us another song or two of breathing room.

When we moved the table, an enterprising young actress seized an opening to better her position. She slid in shoulder to shoulder with me, propped a wooden apple box to stand longways on the floor, then sat on it as if she had a legitimate spot among us. I took no offense with her cutting in. Who was I to reprimand her? Hell, I was impressed by her gumption.

She, however, had no way of knowing my stance, so when I turned to look at her, she immediately pleaded her case. "I understand perfectly well how unseemly this appears, but I give you my word, I'm meant to be one of Miss Dandridge's personal guests. I was in the cast of *Carmen Jones*, and if Miss Dandridge were present, she'd attest to what I'm telling you."

She was a prim and proper beauty with her hair cut short and a ballet dancer's figure. She spoke in a confident and elegant way that folks where I grew up called *queenly*. She was only eighteen years old, but there was nothing childish about her. She wore an olive-green Dior dress with white satin evening gloves—the embodiment of a sophisticated lady. She also had spirit in spades.

I liked her. Besides, Horace didn't have anything to say to me once we reached our seats. He kept his eyes glued to the stage and shared his small talk with Ruby Dee. I welcomed having a new temporary companion.

"You're all right with me," I said.

She nudged me gently. "Thank you, darling."

"What's your name?"

"Diahann," she said. "Diahann Carroll."

"I'm Aaron Toussaint. Nice to meet you."

"Likewise."

I grinned at her. "Were you really in the movie?"

"Yes. I wouldn't lie about a thing like that." She patted my hand. "Blink and you might miss me, but I am in the movie."

"I'll keep my eyes peeled for you."

Lena ended her run with "Stormy Weather," and Diahann and I stopped talking long enough to join the crowd in applauding. Lena began teasing the audience with the promise of a surprise guest.

I playfully needled Diahann with another question. "I gotta know. Did you bring that apple box from home?"

"Don't be ridiculous," she said. "I nabbed it from the hotel kitchen."

We laughed as Lena continued to heap praise on the surprise guest.

"Is she bringing out Dorothy?" I asked.

"Oh, Miss Dandridge won't be leaving her house tonight." Diahann explained with just enough emphasis to be certain I caught her drift, "She hasn't been feeling like herself the past few weeks."

"I'm sorry to hear that."

"It is a pity. She's such a talent. Nonetheless, the party couldn't be canceled nor go on as a flop, which is why Twentieth had to fork over a king's ransom to bring out the grandest of grandes dames."

"Who?"

Diahann whispered in my ear, "Lady Day."

I covered my mouth with both my hands to stop myself from crying out. She was the greatest jazz and blues singer ever. Full stop. End of debate. She achieved the pinnacle not on account of the pitch or clarity of her unique voice but due to her unrivaled ability for making those who heard her feel the emotions of her songs. "Good Morning Heartache," "God Bless the Child," and "Strange Fruit" are enough to prove her genius. I'd listened to all her albums, but I'd never seen her live.

From the stage, Lena said, "How I wish I could sound like her. Ladies and gentlemen, please put your hands together for the one, the only—Billie Holiday!"

The second Billie walked out from the wings, it was like a bomb went off. The roar was hot, deafening, and sustained. It shook and frightened me with its raw, unchecked power. The hysteria of a mob electrified the air.

With a coy smile, Billie entered the spotlight, stood before the microphone, raised her hand, and said, "If y'all quit all that racket, I'd be happy to sing for ya."

Four hundred fell silent. I placed my elbows on the table and rested my chin in the palms of my hands. There was Lady Day, radiant in a gold-sequined sheath dress, and with big gardenias in her hair. To witness her easy command and shimmering brilliance, I'd have believed she was a Black goddess—almighty and eternal.

Count Basie played a vamped intro to "Is You Is or Is You Ain't My Baby," and Billie had her way with that hit, changing the lyrics to put the question to a man and bending the notes to her fiery mood.

Then she curtailed an offering of applause by going straight into "Easy Living," and she sang it so slowly, investing each word with melancholy. It was a display of her magic because I found myself hearing the lyrics anew. What I'd always taken as a declaration of love sounded through her intonation like an attempt at self-delusion, and a worn lie at that. Billie's version forced me to ask if I bought the song at face value: Could being a fool ever be fun?

She closed with "Strange Fruit." When I tell you grown men and women cried, I mean they wept. Horace dabbed at his eyes before his tears got a chance to run. Undoubtedly, he was thinking about his father. I used my silk pocket square to dry my cheeks, remembering a beloved older cousin who was strung up in South Carolina. Seemed like everyone mourned someone while Billie broke our hearts. One exception was Diahann. Dry-eyed, she leaned forward and studied Billie's stagecraft.

The audience honored Billie with a thunderous, rolling ovation. She blew them kisses. What came next would be shaped into Hollywood lore eight years later. That night in the Dunbar, it was just a haphazard photo opportunity. Lena, Count Basie, Ruby Dee, Harry, and Pearl joined Billie at center stage. The *Jet* and *Ebony* photographers stood on top of a front-row table.

With impish glee, Jimmie Daniels hopped up and perched himself at the feet of the major stars with his legs dangling off the stage and said, "Don't miss out, kids!"

His message was lost on me, but not Diahann: a photograph that would run in all the Black magazines and newspapers was about to be snapped, and if aspiring stars got themselves in the frame of said photograph, their faces would grace all those magazine and newspaper pages, too. Free publicity. Fame by proximity.

Diahann tugged at my arm. "Come along and help lift me up."

I pulled at Horace. "Move it. Skyline will want you in on this."

The three of us hustled over to the edge of the stage, where I hoisted Diahann up by her tiny waist. She was lighter than a sack of groceries. Then Horace and I hopped into our places, but we weren't the only ones who answered Jimmie's call. Another half dozen wannabes scrambled forth to pose below the headliners.

"Everyone else stay back!" Harry shouted, and no one dared to defy him.

Jimmie was in the middle of the bottom row with Diahann to his left, me to her left, and Horace to my left. I looked down the line as the photographers steadied their shots. To Horace's left was the tall, alluring man in a charcoal suit and Stacy Adams wing tip shoes. I faced forward. The double white flash from the cameras' bulbs was blinding. My expression in the photo was wide-eyed and stricken. Everyone else smiled.

Once the photographers had gotten what they needed, the party broke up in a hurry. Diahann didn't stick around to say goodbye. Xavier didn't shake Horace's hand or collect his autograph. In fact, despite everything that was said and written later, Xavier and Horace never crossed paths again after that night. The sum total of their interaction was in the men's restroom and onstage for that damn photo.

2

OBLIGED THEM WITH LIES

Hollywood wouldn't have become a part of my life if I hadn't soldered myself to Horace during our time in the navy, and I never would have enlisted in the navy at the start of the Korean War if my old man and my brother hadn't tried to kill me when I was seventeen years old and returned home on a Friday night from watching *Treasure Island* at the Emerson Palace Theater.

Mind you, I'd suffered attacks from each of them before under the roof we shared in our shack on Bridel Road. Those were one-sided fatherly smackdowns and brotherly brawls that only my mama could stop by hollering at them until the devil was chased away. Our last bout on the hottest day in 1950 was altogether different.

My old man prided himself on street-corner boasts. To hear him tell it, he'd never been sick a day in his life, or cried under any circumstances, or lost a fistfight, or been cheated out of money. He was short and wiry in build, but hot-tempered enough to keep other fellas from testing him. In his dreams, he possessed the silver screen swagger of Paul Muni in *Scarface* (1932). As it stood, my old man lacked much of what counted in the world, which was why he guarded his reputation so fiercely. His epitaph could have read, *You best think twice before crossing Benet Toussaint.*

He didn't have a head for money. He couldn't read or write, and before I was born, he got hired at a refrigerator factory but was fired within a week and wouldn't tell my mama why. By the time I came along, he was shoveling horseshit out on a ranch in Rufusville, Ohio, ten miles east of Cincinnati. Our family would have been better off if my old man had let my mama, who had some schooling, be a store clerk or, at least, take in wash. He said no wife of his would labor. Hence why we dwelled in a drafty shack with a frigid shower that drew its water from a well. (In the winter when the well froze solid, Solomon and I showered at the school gymnasium.)

Four years older than I, my brother, Solomon, took after our daddy in looks and disposition. He was mean even when there was nothing to gain from it. His favorite movie was *Crime School* (1938) starring the Dead End Kids. The Warner Bros. morality drama was meant to warn the public about the oncoming scourge of juvenile delinquency; my brother considered it instructional.

Solomon bullied me relentlessly growing up, and I made myself an easy target. I was meek and prone to crying, and to make matters worse, I pestered my brother by following behind him because I was drawn to his friends. Especially brawny Keith Wilson. My desires were still a complete mystery to me, but Solomon must have dimly sensed the crushes I had on his buddies. He'd get furious when one of them patted me on the head or draped an arm over my shoulders or uttered an encouraging word to me. He saw how overjoyed such minimal affection made me.

I struggled to make friends of my own. Not only was I unathletic, I didn't care to follow sports. I'd rather read than race, and I'd rather watch movies in the dark than read. Other kids viewed me as quiet and emotional, unstably so. No one missed me when I retreated into the Emerson Palace Theater.

My mama, Edith Mae, didn't question how I was spending my time so long as I didn't cause trouble. Married to a brute and nursemaid to a hoodlum, she was relieved that I wasn't a nuisance. I pitied her. My mama had brains, a winning personality when she let it show, and she was beautiful in the mold of her favorite star, Nina Mae McKinney. And she sold herself short for men beyond saving.

Mama thought Solomon was a good boy putting on a gruff front to please our daddy. She considered me sweet and sensitive, maybe a touch too much. My old man, of course, held his own estimations. He adored my brother and deemed me a sissy. He was the opposite of Mr. Allenson. My old man met any whining or crying on my part with the back of his hand. I tried to be invisible around him.

Girls flocked to Solomon when he became a teenager. He shot up a foot taller than our old man, and he maintained a devilish pencil mustache. Fathers knocked on our front door complaining that they'd caught Solomon necking with their daughters in parked cars and inside woodsheds. My old man pretended to be concerned, but he pressed Solomon for details. He egged my brother on if a pretty girl happened to stroll by when we were out on our town's main drag.

I was jealous. Puberty didn't light the same flame in me when it came to girls, and I was desperate to feel that fire. Like every other boy in my class, I could see that Yolanda Murphy and Justine Carson were the knockouts in our grade. But I didn't feel more than that. When I danced with Justine at a church formal, I attempted to will some excitement into my body. I squeezed her hips, and I held her close until the chaperone, Mrs. Brooks, told us to separate. Nothing in me stirred. I was fourteen and frightened and baffled as to why I didn't get revved up over the opposite sex.

My old man and Solomon ventured a guess. I was called a sissy often enough at home as a child that I answered to the slur when either of them used it to get my attention. As I got peach fuzz on my chin and reached a gangly five foot ten, I continued to admire and stay underfoot of boys a few years older than I was; I was their crew's errand runner and mascot. Whenever Solomon saw me fetching for those guys, he'd accuse me of being their cocksucker. Even during those fumbling teen years, girls sensed my absence of passion and dropped me after a few dates. When I returned home at decent hours on Friday and Saturday nights, my old man muttered, "You must be a bona fide faggot."

I chose to act as if I didn't hear him, because the case against me mounted daily. The sight of Quincy Green sparring against Ralph Webb in the gymnasium; or Niles Ashford jitterbugging in tight pants; or Willie Holmes absentmindedly adjusting his cock while he told a dirty story in the pool hall; or James Chandler sweating as he sang the blues full-throated were provoking the reactions that I'd prayed would be inspired by women. I didn't seek these flashes of arousal, but I couldn't extinguish them either. It was starting to feel inevitable that one horrible day, a merciless man would follow my gaze, detect the pant in my breath, or notice the involuntary way my tongue licked my lips when I was lust-struck, and I'd be damned. I needed to shield myself from exposing my nature. Except, at seventeen, sensible answers alluded me.

So, I lied. I made up a girlfriend. I said her name was Darlene Brown and that she lived in Dovencourt, which was two towns over and reachable on the bus line until midnight. I padded the fabrication by traveling to Dovencourt, finding a pretty girl my age, and paying her two dollars to pose as my honey in a photo booth. She hugged me tight and smiled into the lens. We were the essence of puppy love in the four-frame strip.

I wanted Solomon to force the story out of me. So, I wore cologne when I went out, and I came home around eleven o'clock at night. I strutted like I had a secret joy. My mama and the old man didn't seem to notice, but Solomon invaded my privacy just as I hoped he would. I stepped out of the bathroom one morning to find him plucking the photo booth strip out of my wallet.

"You little sneak!" he cried. "Aaron's got himself a little girlfriend, and from what I can tell, she ain't been kicked in the face by a mule!"

My old man grunted, still skeptical. Mama didn't look up from her morning cup of coffee, but I could tell she was smiling.

Solomon continued, "Dumb chick musta caught the hooves in the back of her head if she mistaken this punk for a man."

"Stop it now," Mama said.

My old man laughed.

I snatched back the photo booth strip and my wallet. "Stay out my business."

With delight in her voice, Mama pried, "Don't be like that, Aaron. Let me see the picture and tell us somethin' about the girl."

I obliged them with lies I'd prepared for their ears: how Darlene's family was new to Dovencourt, having migrated north from Georgia. I said I couldn't remember what city in Georgia her people hailed from, because I didn't want to appear too rehearsed with answers to every question. I volunteered nothing, making Mama chisel loose each nugget of information.

I made Darlene sixteen and claimed that she wrote poetry. Solomon assured me that I'd lose Darlene once I tried to get to second base with her. Then he headed to his shift at the slaughterhouse. My old man didn't say a word either way about my new girlfriend. Mama insisted I bring Darlene over for dinner. I said, "We'll see."

Life at home improved. My old man and Solomon quit accusing me of being a fairy. I overheard Solomon telling his friends that I might even get my "dick wet" if I played my cards right with Darlene. My old man took me aside and advised me to pull out before I came during sex to avoid pregnancy. As crass as it was, they were treating me like a man, and I relished it.

Darlene evaporated six weeks later. The temperature hit 106 degrees that day. By night, it had only cooled to 79. In the movie theater, I sat through the run of the feature movie twice to avoid the humid heat outside.

"Where you been, boy?" my old man asked as soon as I walked through the door.

"Darlene and I took in a movie," I said, unaware that I was being entrapped.

The old man sat at the kitchen table, skinning an apple with his pocketknife. "Which one?"

"*Treasure Island*." I spotted the first oddity: It was half past ten, and Mama wasn't in the shack.

"You buy her popcorn?"

"Yes, sir. Where's Mama?" I asked, making my way into the kitchen for a glass of tap water.

"Out with her prayer circle."

That explanation satisfied me. Mama's prayer circle did gather at all hours when an ailing member of the church neared their great reward, and since All Saints First Baptist had plenty of elderly congregants who were overdue for their appointments with salvation, I thought nothing more of Mama's absence.

"You sit with Darlene in them back rows?" he asked. "You get your fingers under her skirt?"

I coughed up the water I was drinking and almost dropped my glass. My old man was crude, but he hadn't dragged Darlene into his vulgarity before. I was also struck by the jagged edge in his tone. I sensed anger and realized that I was being mocked.

"She's not that kind of girl," I said.

Solomon came racing through the front door, huffing and sweating. When he closed the door, he leaned against it and crossed his arms. He and my old man looked at each other, and Solomon shook his head.

I suspected the jig was up. My father, my brother, and possibly my mother, who might have been out praying with other church ladies for my lost soul, had uncovered that Darlene was my fabrication. But what response could have saved me? To hold on to the lie as if it were the truth seemed like madness. My old man and Solomon would knock the teeth out of my mouth until I confirmed what they already knew.

However, to readily admit that I'd invented a girlfriend, her family, their history, and their daily lives would earn me no lenience. My old man and Solomon would then demand to hear what drove me to peddle such a pathetic tall tale—and in their bones, they were well aware of what drove me to create Darlene. If I confessed to this web of lies, I'd (finally) be pleading guilty to their perpetual charge of faggotry. My father and brother could have murdered me for that offense, and no one in town would have objected.

I had less than a couple of seconds to choose my course.

My old man placed the skinned apple on the table and stood up with his pocketknife pointed at me. "Solomon done followed you three times after you gone out on your dates. Ain't seen hide nor hair of no girl. Whatcha gotta say for yourself?"

"He's lying," I pleaded. "He'll say anything if it's a mark against me."

"I spoke with our postman," my old man said. "Had him check out if there's a Brown family that just come to Dovencourt. He say there's three Brown families. None of 'em new to town."

I thought fast. "Her family's lodging."

Neither of them bought it. Solomon approached me slowly. My old man held his ground. I was being cornered in the kitchen without a window to throw myself through. My eyes darted around for a knife, a pan, a rolling pin, anything I could use as a weapon. At my disposal was the glass in my hand, a dirty spoon in the sink, a dishrag, and the coffee kettle.

I made one last attempt to dodge the fight. "I can still catch her before she leaves on the bus. I'll bring Darlene here tonight. Solomon can go with me. You'll see her with your own eyes. Please, Daddy."

He turned his head to the side like the sight of me stung his eyes. "There was a morning I caught you starin' at me wrong when I was changin' and you was little. . . . I should've snapped your sissy neck and buried you in the yard."

Solomon rushed me, and that cocky jackass smirked as he drew near. His evil mouth revealed to me what he imagined: the assured steps leading to my death. He and the old man planned to make easy, quick work of me. Solomon had shoved, smacked, and punched me for years, and I'd only ever fallen to the ground in a ball, begging him to stop. He intended to dominate me like always, and force me prone, so our father could slit my throat like a hog in the slaughterhouse. They were counting on my weakness.

Rage saved me. Delivered me. Call me blasphemous, but I must tell it as it was. The most spiritual experience I ever had occurred while I fought for my life. A holy ghost of fury filled my body. It was glorious.

When Solomon got within striking distance, I swung my right arm and smashed the drinking glass against his jaw. The shards cut him along the side of his head, and one flew into his eye. He hollered and fell to his hands and knees. I kicked him in his mouth, and his neck snapped back, and he made a raspy choking noise.

The old man was caught off guard. Solomon was wheezing on his belly, and I stood tall, if now unarmed. The old man still held the pocketknife but looked less sure of himself.

With a scream, I leapt over my brother's body and pounced onto my father. He managed to raise his pocketknife, and I grabbed his wrist as I knocked him onto his back and landed on top of him. The knife was between his chest and mine. The blade was pointed at me.

I held myself above the sharp edge and twisted the old man's hand. Up closer to him than I'd dared to come before, he looked pockmarked, weathered, and small. I pressed the pocketknife down. He shook his head, and his eyes bugged out. He feared me, and I fed off it. I plunged the blade into his rib cage. He yelled, and I savored the sound. The only reason I didn't kill him and my brother was I wanted them to live knowing that I'd whipped their asses.

Taking eight dollars from our family emergency fund, my toothbrush, and a change of clothes, I left the old man and Solomon in the shack, and I walked the ten miles to Cincinnati through the night. I stayed near the tree line along the main roads in case the cops came looking for me. No manhunt ever materialized, and news of a murder in Rufusville didn't hit the papers. I figured Mama came home from her prayer circle and got her husband and elder son the medical attention they needed. Neither man would be much inclined to tell folks how they came by their injuries.

My first morning in Cincinnati, I waited outside the Douglass Branch Library until the head librarian, a Mrs. Finley, opened the doors at nine o'clock. She fixed me a free cup of coffee and let me straighten up in the restroom. I asked her if there was a military recruitment office in the area, and she gave me directions to one four blocks south. She couldn't recall which branch of service the office represented.

The recruitment office was navy. Had it been air force or army or marines, I would have walked through the door all the same: prepared to listen to the recruiter's pitch, to claim I was eighteen, and to sign the papers put in front of me. A way out was a way out.

3

REMEMBER, YOU ASKED FOR THIS

Until I joined Uncle Sam's navy, the farthest I'd traveled from Rufusville was a trip to Toledo for the funeral of my mama's great-auntie; I couldn't have pinned Korea, North or South, on a map; and my notions about what I'd be experiencing on a carrier were shaped by World War II movies like *Minesweeper* (1943) with Richard Arlen in the lead role and *Dive Bomber* (1941) starring Errol Flynn.

In quick succession, the navy brought me jet lag, a crash course on race problems in the military, and a test of my tolerance for boredom. The jet lag passed within a few days. The other two challenges proved intractable and intertwined.

From the newsreels I'd seen in theaters, I honestly believed the military was leading the charge in equality. Right before the start of *Mighty Joe Young* (1949), there had been a two-reeler with footage of white soldiers and Black soldiers intermingled in a squad doing jumping jacks during basic training, and as the short film continued, a faceless announcer with a soothing baritone had said, "No matter the color of a man's skin, we're all brothers in the foxhole." Sitting among a crowd of impressionable moviegoers, I ate that pap like it was popcorn.

There was, I learned, a wide gap between the lofty ideals of regulations and the lowly practices of the governed. For instance, even though President Truman had desegregated the armed forces in 1948 by executive order, the great majority of white men aboard the USS *Stevens*, stationed in Misawa in Japan for the Korean War, resented with open contempt having to serve alongside me and the ninety-five other Negroes on our Essex-class aircraft carrier.

A Black man's rank determined how much scorn and abuse could be heaped upon his back. I was a seaman third class, the rock-bottom rank. There was only a single-bar insignia on my uniform. Mops and brooms were considered more essential than seamen third class and certainly received more respect.

In every movie with sailors at war, the expanses of the volatile ocean and the fateful sky loomed constantly in the frame. I'd assumed the sun would turn me three shades darker, because I'd be out on the deck of the carrier from dawn to dusk. Below deck was where men went to sleep, to eat chow, and to escape the cruel unpredictability of open-air combat.

My first two months on the USS *Stevens*, I slaved in the belly of the carrier for days on end, and my work exhausted me to the point that I didn't have the strength or inclination to climb the stairs to the deck. I might as well have been on a submarine.

With glee, a white petty officer gave me one of the worst jobs to be had, but as he explained my assignment, I didn't recognize the hell I was entering. I got placed in the pot locker. Our carrier had two, one on each end of the kitchen. Cooks dumped used and filthy skillets, griddles, fry pans, stockpots, braisers, saucepans, broilers, double broilers, soup pots, multi-pots, deep skillets, and the occasional French oven down a metal chute. The cookware slid and splashed into the scalding water of a wide sink in the pot locker, which was where I stood on a slick floor in a suffocating room the size of a double closet.

All I had to do was wash the pots and pans—for fourteen-hour shifts that included two fifteen-minute breaks and a half-hour lunch. Wash the pots and pans—as I baked in a hot box where the temperature topped one hundred degrees. Wash the pots and pans—with singed hands, aching arms, a sore back, throbbing feet, and threadbare rags and disintegrating sponges. Wash the pots and pans—while the solitude and monotony lobotomized me. Wash the pots and pans—to the satisfaction of the white cooks, who would hurl the same skillet or broiler down the chute a half dozen times just to fuck me over. There were nights I missed Ohio.

My growing fear became that the enemy wouldn't have to kill me, because the navy was going to see to it before long. The other Black seamen and petty officers told me that my lot might improve gradually if I achieved promotions, but advancement was a fickle mistress to Black sailors. Sixty days into my deployment, and I'd lost ten pounds from sweating in the pot locker and the runs I got from the gruel that passed as food among the enlisted. I felt doomed, and everyone around me just advised me to get used to it.

Then I saw Lieutenant Horace "Hornet" Dixon.

One afternoon, while I was taking my lunch in the mess hall, the fighter pilot came in, kicking up a storm. I'd only ever heard of Horace, because his rank and duties kept us in different orbits. He had private quarters. I slept in a common area among forty men. His lunch was brought to him on the deck, if it wasn't too windy, or in his room, if the weather was inhospitable. I wolfed down my food in the mess hall, which could be so overcrowded that it took most of my lunch break just to get myself a tray of slop.

I knew he had two confirmed kills and was on the verge of becoming an *ace*. One more kill would do it. A Black ace would be a boon for the navy's image and the war effort as a whole. If Horace's reputation was to be believed, the twenty-six-year-old Chicagoan was already throwing his weight around as if he were an ace.

Horace had a commanding figure. His head was shaved cue ball bald, and his prominent nose and thick lips gave him the profile of a pharaoh. His dark skin appeared unblemished. Horace stood a mere five foot eight and weighed 165, but he was the first person I met who possessed what was deemed in Hollywood as *star power*. I was drawn to him. And that was before he started berating a white man.

Horace came into the mess hall because his aide-de-camp, petty officer third class Shane Foley, had made a mistake. The freckled, brawny sailor was eating pea soup with his buddies when he spotted Horace charging straight to him, and he could tell he was about to get bawled out. He got up and tried to avert the scene.

"Whatever I done now," Foley pleaded, "let's talk it over somewhere else."

Horace's voice boomed above all the chatter in the mess hall. "Did I walk onto your plantation? Am I standing in your big house?"

The rest of the sailors and I quit talking as Horace took center stage and Foley got stuck with second billing. It was like opening night for a new movie, and I had a front-row seat, watching from a table behind where Horace stood. I was close enough to see how Foley's bottom lip quivered.

"No," he said.

Horace folded his arms across his chest. "Then why aren't you addressing me as *Lieutenant*?"

"Sorry, Lieutenant. Won't happen no more, Lieutenant."

"I ordered you to clean my flight goggles, didn't I?"

"I did clean 'em, Lieutenant," came the whimpered reply.

"Did I order you to fuck up the straps on my goggles?" Before Foley could answer, Horace continued. "What if I had been called up? I'm counting on my tools and instruments to be as I had them. You got me in the air fuckin' around with the straps on my goddamn flight goggles. You got me distracted and agitated. You got me blown out of the muthafuckin' sky."

"Lieutenant, I'm sorry."

"That's day-old news. I was promised you were smarter than the last fuckup." Horace wagged his finger at Foley like that white man was a child. "Don't touch my tools again unless I'm watching you do so. Understand me, boy?"

"Yes, Lieutenant."

Horace turned on his heels and walked out of the mess hall with white sailors parting to make way. Foley retreated to his friends to grumble but not too loudly. I hung my head straight down at my plate to hide the smile I couldn't suppress. Once my face returned to neutral, I looked up and searched out several other Black sailors. With the slightest of raised eyebrows or upturns at the corners of our mouths, we acknowledged and celebrated what we had witnessed. Horace scored one for our side when he cracked the whip on a white subordinate for all to see.

Back in the pot locker, I compulsively replayed the show Horace put on in the mess hall. A couple of realizations were clear from the jump: I admired Horace's swagger, and I found him sexy in an authoritative manner that was novel to me. The more valuable revelation took days to formulate: I envied Horace's status as an officer and fighter pilot; it protected him from the indignities and grunt work that were draining me. Initially, I wished I could somehow be him. Eventually, it dawned on me that the achievable goal was to become indispensable to him.

My first attempt to speak with Horace failed. One night, I waited in the hallway that led to his quarters until we crossed paths, and I said, "Good evening, Lieutenant Dixon." He kept walking as if I didn't exist. He ignored me a day later when I greeted him on deck and again the following evening when I attempted to join him during a smoke break.

However, the third brush-off gave me the start of an opening. Horace smoked Dunhill cigarettes, a British brand that could be tricky to get on our carrier's black market. So I decided to make getting a Dunhill pack impossible.

It took me three days to track down our carrier's seven plugs, and it cost me a week's pay to corner the market on Dunhills. Since I couldn't take possession of the packs—there was nowhere I could hide them—I agreed to let the plugs sell the cigarettes once I lifted my embargo. So, they'd earn twice the money in the end, an irresistible bonus that rendered them completely uninterested in what they assumed were my harebrained reasons.

Four days passed before Horace smoked through his last pack, and Foley explained to him that he couldn't secure another Dunhill for love or coin. I wasn't there to see it, but word spread that Horace grabbed hold of Foley and had to be pulled off him. There was fear he was going to throw his aide-de-camp overboard. Horace made it another four days bumming cigarettes off other pilots and officers, and I dipped into a second week's pay to maintain the blockade and stash a few packs away for the coup de grâce.

Fighter pilots, almost to a man, were superstitious about their planes and missions. They placed stock in good luck charms and strict adherence to routines. With unwavering insistence, Horace ate the same breakfast (buttered toast, scrambled eggs, and a glass of orange juice), lunch (turkey sandwich with lettuce and sliced tomato on white bread, a bowl of vegetable soup, and a cup of coffee), and dinner (a hamburger with pickles and mustard, fries, a canned peach, and a glass of milk) when on the carrier. He always circled his Sabrejet twice before approaching it. He always rubbed the plane's nose before entering the cockpit from the left side. In his cockpit, Horace tucked away a picture of his mother, a Buffalo nickel that he won at a county fair as a child, and a cowrie shell.

He considered these practices and elements of his surroundings to be nonnegotiable. Without them, Horace wasn't just unsure that he'd succeed in the sky when called on to perform. He felt doomed. He believed he was as good as dead. Another essential piece of Horace's readiness ritual included smoking five Dunhill cigarettes a day.

Two days without a single Dunhill at his disposal, and Horace wasn't speaking to Foley or pretty much anyone else. He looked forlorn. I imagined he was afraid of getting sent out on a mission, although he'd never have admitted so.

After I finished my shift, I showered, put on a white T-shirt and my blue trousers, and sat right outside the door to his quarters. He couldn't miss me. An hour later, he came down the hallway, and he furrowed his brow when he spotted me. I held up a pack of Dunhill cigarettes. Horace stopped in his tracks.

"Are these legit?" he asked.

"If you doubt it, smoke one."

He took me up on the challenge, lighting a cigarette and enjoying that first drag. I stood up, and in the narrow hallway, we were practically chest to chest. I tried not to stare at his lips, which were thick and inviting.

I said, "Now you know. I came through."

"I was told they was out of Dunhill and couldn't say when they'd get any again."

I played it cool. "Officially, there are none to be had. But you should be getting whatever you want. Your aide ought to make that happen."

Horace scratched his chin. "What you trade for these?"

"What do you care so long as you got what you need?"

"Good point," he said. "Step aside."

I moved to the right, and Horace opened his door and entered his room. I stood in the hallway, unsure of my next move. Was he done with me? He hadn't invited me in. But the door hadn't closed yet. So, I caught the door before it shut and slid inside.

Horace's back was toward me. He'd already unzipped his flight suit down to his bare navel, and when he turned to face me, he looked at me like I'd crossed a line, which was fair, because I had. The sensible part of my brain told me to apologize and scurry out of his room. A bolder voice inside me suggested that Horace might respond well to my brashness.

"Lieutenant Dixon, I want to be your aide-de-camp."

Horace stepped toward me. "Who the hell are you?"

"Seaman Aaron Toussaint."

"You bring me a pack of cigarettes and expect a job from me?"

I figured this was my one shot. I had to go for broke. "I can do more than that, Lieutenant. Unlike the aide you got now, I care if you live or die. It means something to me if you become an ace. I want to see you get there. I'd be honored to be a small, small part of your story. I'll give you my all."

Horace openly sized me up. Despite being three inches taller than he was, I struggled not to wither under his gaze. I became self-conscious of how I might look to him. I'd rushed out of the shower and sat in the muggy hallway, waiting for Horace to arrive. My T-shirt felt sticky along my back and against my stomach. My pants were a size too small (and my request for a size up languished unanswered). I hated my latest haircut, buzzed close on the sides with thin waves on top, because I thought it only accentuated my boyish demeanor. My attempt at mimicking James Edwards's stoic manliness in *Home of the Brave* (1949) was crumbling in front of Horace, a legit Black war hero.

I bowed my head and said, "Please, Lieutenant." I paused. "The pot locker is killing me."

Horace clapped his hands together, threw back his head, and laughed. "Now you make sense to me. Now I get why you've been mooning around me."

I felt a pang of embarrassment to be described like a schoolgirl with a crush. "I also meant what I said before."

Horace removed his arms from his flight suit. "If those were your only reasons, I'd think you were screwy in the head. It's gotta be to your advantage to help me, or it just don't add up. Understand me, Aaron?"

"Yes, Lieutenant."

He unlaced and kicked off his shoes. "You grow up with your daddy around?"

"Yes, Lieutenant."

He stepped out of his flight suit. "Was he a mean son of a bitch?"

"Yes, Lieutenant."

Stripped to his boxer shorts and socks, Horace cracked the knuckles in his left hand. "Then you're used to being pushed hard? You can withstand scrutiny and demands? Because I am not a gentle man. Understand me, Aaron?"

"Yes, Lieutenant."

"Remember, you asked for this." He bent down, picked up his damp flight suit, and flung it at me. "Have that one washed. Be outside my door at zero-six hundred."

"Thank you, Lieutenant."

Horace put his stamp on me overnight. He told the brass that it was unbecoming that his newest aide-de-camp was a seaman third class, and I was thereby promoted to seaman first class. I received a new uniform, and it fit. Suddenly, half the crew greeted me with a nod when I walked past. Many of them addressed me by name. Others referred to me as "Lieutenant Dixon's boy."

Day one as his aide-de-camp, I reported for duty at Horace's door at six in the morning. He glared at me in my new uniform and yelled, "Where the fuck is my breakfast?"

"You didn't say anything about bringing you breakfast," I sputtered.

"Why else would I want to see your godforsaken face at this hour?"

True to his word, Horace was a taskmaster. Over the next few weeks, he broke me in by correcting my errors, most of which could have been avoided if he'd provided me with complete instructions. He insisted that I needed to learn how to anticipate his needs. I viewed it as a test he was administering to see if I had the will to stay with him.

Horace required a daily weather report. I knew that he wanted me to provide more than the temperature's highs and lows. So, I included the time of sunrise and sunset, the wind direction, the average wind speed, the wind chill, and the visibility. Even still, Horace bawled me out in front of everyone within earshot on the deck for not knowing the cloud coverage, the chance of rain, or the barometric pressure.

Another time, one of the cooks put mayonnaise on Horace's turkey sandwich. When Horace tasted the offending condiment, he spit out the bite and swiped the sandwich onto the floor. He screamed at me for my carelessness while I cleaned up the mess before running to get him his correct order.

I also had to tend to a map of the war zone pinned to Horace's wall across from his bed. He expected me to move the red and blue tabs to reflect the position of our forces and the North Koreans'. This meant I had to read the battle reports sent to Horace, which he forbade me to look at until he'd finished with them. Sometimes he'd let several days go by, read them all at once, then blow up at me for allowing his war map to fall behind. I couldn't point out the obvious problem in this system. I just had to swallow his anger.

Horace taught me how to spot-check his fighter jet in less than a minute. To no one's surprise but his, I failed to catch all the finer points of the process. As part of his regiment, Horace spot-checked his Sabre three times a day. He had me do it first, then he followed up behind me. If I didn't flag debris caught in the spoke of a tire, or a small dent in the metal of a wing, or a smudge on the windshield, he'd accuse me at the top of his lungs of attempting to murder him.

He would have been unbearable if I hadn't been turned on by the tenor of his voice when he was full-throated furious, if the smell of his soiled laundry hadn't become what I brought to mind when I beat off in the latrine, and if I wasn't convinced that he was also getting pleasure out of us working together. He reached for me often, clamping his hand on the back of my neck or patting my back. Once, he took the cigarette out of my mouth and commandeered it. He inhaled a long drag and blew the smoke in my face. "From now on," he ordered, "you don't smoke." I promised to obey, and he smiled with smug satisfaction.

Within a month, Horace only had cause to holler at me once or twice a week. Usually for mishaps with his laundry or his mail; things far outside my control. I'd discovered a key to keeping Horace satisfied.

I had to tell him what I was doing for him before he got the chance to tell me what he wanted me to do. I implemented new practices to make his life better. I decided he should sleep under fresh bedsheets every night like he was staying at a fancy hotel. I insisted he get a daily copy of his hometown newspaper, the *Chicago Tribune*, even if it was nearly a week old by the time it reached our carrier. After having his flight suits cleaned, I personally ironed them, making him smile at the sharpness of the creases.

We finally found our rhythm. He loosened up, joked around with me. He started to ask me about my crummy childhood in Rufusville. He confided in me that although he claimed Chicago as his hometown, he'd only moved there from Orville, Arkansas, to live with an older sister when he was ten years old. Opening up was difficult for him, it seemed, but he was doing it inch by inch with me. His touch told me more than his words. Sometimes his hands would linger on my hips, knees, or once the back of my head. Occasionally, out of the corners of my eyes, I'd see him staring at me the way I'd take in the sight of guys I longed for. There was something between us.

Or I was lonely and seventeen and naïve enough to misinterpret these fleeting moments. By all outward appearances, Horace was a red-blooded, straight man. He had pinups of Lena Horne and Dorothy Dandridge in his quarters. He mentioned having sweethearts in his past. He'd given me nothing definitive to conclude that he was a queer like me.

It wasn't until two days after Christmas that Horace and I both got what we wanted most. He flew a mission into enemy airspace, where he and Lieutenant Wayne Vogel provoked two enemy fighter jets and entered a dogfight. It was a pitched battle for fifteen minutes. Then Horace downed a North Korean fighter jet in view of Lieutenant Vogel, making it a confirmed kill. Horace returned to the USS *Stevens* a flying ace.

Every Black sailor dropped what they were doing to congratulate Horace when he landed on the deck and hopped out of his Sabre.

There were plenty of white folks in the mix, too, but it was a bigger occasion for us. I'd never seen Horace happier. He shook every hand. He hugged me.

He shocked me because he kept repeating, "We did it, Aaron! We did it!" His kindness in that grand moment overwhelmed me, and my sensitive side slipped out. My eyes welled with tears. I retreated from the celebration on the deck and went to the only place I could think of getting privacy: Horace's room. He found me there sitting on his bed an hour later.

"What you run off for?" he asked with a curious smile.

I stood up to explain myself. Horace moved closer. I opened my mouth, but I couldn't speak. He reached out and put his hand on my forearm. Another vague signal. I was too worked up to play it cool, and I felt one of us had to make a clear move. I kissed him on the mouth.

4

PLAY THE SACRIFICIAL LAMB

My heart wasn't to be trusted. It chose arousal over prudence. It confused risk with romance. It ignored the doom inherent in self-sacrificing gestures. It believed regret was a burden that other people carried. My heart acted as if I were still a kid. By April of 1958, I had grief, a job, a mortgage, and a wife that said otherwise.

I was working for Skyline Motion Pictures as a security agent of studio affairs, and since I was the studio's only Black fixer, I had first dibs on the Black stars. But I could decline to take them on if my roster was full, which it was when Xavier C. Barlow signed a two-picture deal with Skyline, announced on Wednesday, April 9.

I read the news in *Daily Variety* while I drank my morning coffee at the studio commissary, and I was torn about the prospect of working with him. I knew my immediate boss, Callum McManus, the studio's chief of security and studio affairs, would put the question to me as soon as I reached my desk. If my answer was squirrelly or if I asked for time to think it over, that would give rise to suspicion. Never a good idea around a fellow fixer. We are essentially private investigators, and the last thing I wanted was McManus digging for a link between Xavier and me.

The case against becoming Xavier's handler could be boiled down to six words: *He had the goods on me*. We'd jerked each other off in the basement men's restroom of the Dunbar Hotel four years earlier. There was a chance he wouldn't remember me. However, if he did recall, he'd possess information that could ruin my private and professional lives. The balance of power between security agent and star would be erratic.

Ideally, I'd establish and maintain authority in the relationship. Skyline security agents initially met with their stars over coffee on the studio lot in Santa Monica. We used a special office at the top of the studio's white stone Garten Watchtower. Even the coolest of actors lit up like giddy children when they realized we were entering the very watchtower featured in the logo at the start of every Skyline movie. The Garten Watchtower stood six stories and provided a panoramic view. On a clear day, it offered breathtaking views of Malibu, Westwood, Venice Beach, and the curvature of the Pacific Ocean.

That vista served as the backdrop as we grilled stars about his or her moral lapses. We called this practice *giving 'em the jump*, and a lot of agents got off on it. The goal? Speed past niceties and badger the star into confessing his or her sins in detail. Booze, pills, sleeping around—the garden-variety vices were expected, but when we gave a star the jump, we were demanding the particulars: name the favorite drinks and watering holes of choice; name the crooked doctors writing the prescriptions or the dealers supplying the junk; name the illicit lovers, the rendezvous spots, the whorehouses.

Whatever the stars copped to, we'd spell out how their dirty faults would lead to ruin. The money, the fame, and the work would end with breakneck abruptness. Being stripped of the spotlight and banished from Hollywood would make it impossible for them to return to their quaint hometowns. A special hell would await them as the whirlwind of scandal knocked them out cold and scattered them to the wind. Within a year's time, they'd wake up running a gas station outside of Tulsa (like silent film swashbuckler Arnie Gamson, who opposed the US entering World War I), cocktail waitressing on the wrong end of Miami (like screwball comedy queen Bonnie Buckingham, who abandoned her husband and newborn for an affair with a priest), hawking insurance to housewives on a Dust Bowl route (like Academy Award nominee Irving Schafer, who during a live radio broadcast called FDR a dictator after his second reelection), or tossing themselves from a tall bridge (like budding starlet Claire Hollis, who was exposed as a Mexican passing as white) or in front of a moving train (like adventure serial daredevil Dale Yearwood, who never shook allegations that he murdered his second wife).

The star's only hope was to clean up their act . . . or to be discreet when they strayed and to alert us at the first sign of trouble. They could trust no one—not their costars, not their reps, not even their relatives, and certainly not the cops—above us.

Instilling a sense of dependency was key to the relationship. How could I ever accomplish that with Xavier if he also held my fate in his hands? I shouldn't be his handler. Simple as that.

Except, and these sentiments ran deep, I had spent the years since our first encounter following Xavier's movie career, and I knew what he meant to our people, and I believed he had the potential to become one of the greats. We needed more Black stars who did us proud, and Xavier had already cultivated millions of fans in our community.

He managed to be memorable from the start. That was in early 1955, and I went to the movies at the Lincoln Theater on Central Avenue with my then-girlfriend (later wife), Kimberly Pinkens, to watch MGM's *The Battle of San Juan Hill* starring James Edwards as the leader of a regiment of Buffalo Soldiers. Xavier showed up onscreen while their side was under fire, and I jumped in my seat, spilling popcorn onto the floor.

"You all right?" Kimberly asked.

"Yeah," I lied. "My back seized up a little, but I'm fine."

We returned our attention to the movie. Xavier's character had maybe a half dozen lines and was shot dead within three minutes of his appearance. Edwards rallied the rest of his men to fight like hell to honor Xavier's character. I thought Xavier's brief performance was endearing, and seeing his face in a close-up on a silver screen fifty feet wide and twenty-one feet tall stirred me in ways that were better left unspoken with my date.

Yet it was Kimberly who said unprompted as we exited the theater, "I wonder who that tall young man who died was. I wouldn't mind seeing more of him."

She got her wish a few months later when we took in United Artists' *Downtown Dreamers* at the Centinela Drive-In near Inglewood. Sidney Poitier played the lead, Michael, and Xavier got substantial screen time portraying Michael's kid brother, Laurence. Sidney acted like Sidney always acted: dignified, enunciating with impeccable diction, and above the fray. Xavier came across as funny, natural, electric, and alive. His Laurence was a young man who enjoyed poking fun at his stuffy older brother. Kimberly gasped and squeezed my hand when Laurence got swindled out of his meager life savings by a con man and fled town ashamed.

After the picture ended, I teased Kimberly about having a crush on Xavier C. Barlow, and she said, "No sister could blame me," and laughed mischievously.

I genuinely liked seeing that side of Kimberly. We'd met through our church, First African Methodist Episcopal Church of Los Angeles (FAME), and she upheld the standards of a pious Christian woman. She didn't curse, smoke, gamble, drink to excess, or engage in premarital sex. During the beginning of our courtship, she still lived with her parents despite being twenty-four years old and working as a music teacher at Coliseum Street Elementary School. Bawdy talk or even insinuations of carnal urges hadn't been the sort of thing she shared with me. Then Xavier came along, and she admitted an attraction. Her fandom gave me cover to enjoy Xavier's movies, too.

Together, Kimberly and I bought opening-weekend tickets to

Columbia Pictures' *Midnight Falls* (1956), an Eartha Kitt vehicle where she toyed with Xavier's schoolboy affections, only to discard him for Nat King Cole; to Skyline's *Orange Blossom* (1956), a high jinks–laden comedy set in a small town where Butterfly McQueen was the sensible governess to the mayor's children and Xavier played her flighty son; to Universal's *The Coos Bay Express* (1957), in which Sammy Davis Jr. assembled a cutthroat crew to rob a train loaded with gold bullion, and Xavier was the first thief to be fatally betrayed; to MGM's *8-Ball Corner Pocket* (1957), a pool hall melodrama with Xavier shining in an ensemble cast but his character still meeting a tragic end when he can't pay his gambling debts to Woody Strode's loan shark; and to Twentieth's *The Etiquette of Homicide* (1958), a Vincent Price murder mystery that introduced Xavier to his widest audience before his character (one of the dinner guests) was axed to death at the top of the third act.

As we discussed Xavier following each film, Kimberly and I developed the theory that in addition to his talent, the plight of his characters was part of Xavier's appeal. I distinctly remember sitting in the Lincoln Theater when Xavier came on-screen for the first time in *The Coos Bay Express* and a fellow in the audience shouted out, "That poor brother don't never make it!" From the crowd, there was a burst of laughter, recognition of the truth, and head-shaking sympathy. That poor brother of ours.

Collectively, Black moviegoers had realized that this striking young man kept suffering movie after movie. He lost at love, his dreams were thwarted, and he was double-crossed brutally—like so many of us looking up at the screen. Xavier struck a chord that resonated differently from Sidney's. Sidney was aspirational. Xavier tapped into present frustrations.

Black audiences came to identify with Xavier, and picture by picture, they were rooting for him to overcome. Like female audiences had done with Joan Crawford. Like families had done with Shirley Temple. Like the world had done with Charlie Chaplin's Little Tramp.

I'm certain the Hollywood studios hadn't intended to build up Xavier in this fashion. None of them had his career trajectory in mind. They simply needed a Black actor to play the sacrificial lamb in this or that movie in their pipelines. Since his name didn't appear on the poster, Xavier wasn't a casting decision that a studio boss reviewed. Because he didn't get his own trailer during filming, he wasn't even one a director deliberated on too hard. He was low enough on the call sheet to be a casting director's choice, and Xavier had stayed in the good graces of casting directors. By this accidental alchemy, Xavier developed a large Black fan base that was eager to see him in the lead. He was primed to be a major Black star, and Skyline was set to be the first to cash in on him.

My interest in Xavier was a matter of the heart. He was positioned to be a new type of Black hero to a younger, more hardened, and more militant slice of our community that rolled their eyes at the sight of Sidney Poitier. These were the brothers and sisters organizing politically outside of their parents' churches, and they deemed Sidney too polished, too model-Negro, too white-pleasing, and too detached from their struggles. He was thirty-one and already an old man to them. Xavier—age twenty-three in the press releases, and twenty-one in reality—was one of their own.

I wanted to see Xavier become his generation's hero, and if anyone else handled him, his homosexuality would be leveraged against him. His wings would be clipped. If I were his fixer . . . if he didn't remember me from the Dunbar . . . or if he did, and I managed to neutralize that threat . . . and if I could keep his secrets hidden from my colleagues in particular, the industry at large, and the public at all costs . . . and if a litany of complications I couldn't yet imagine were subdued year after year after year, I could protect him. I could shepherd him to the top. Maybe. Possibly.

All right, from the start, I knew in my gut that I didn't have a sensible plan. I chose him anyway. Solidarity had to count for something.

Besides, I told myself, if Xavier turned into an albatross, I could always cut him loose.

I was skeptical that Xavier would be candid about his current homosexual habits if I gave him the traditional jump in the Garten Watchtower. So, shortly after sundown on Friday, April 11, I set up shop outside Xavier's Westwood apartment building in a dark Lincoln Cosmopolitan. A standard issue from the studio's fleet. While I penciled my way through a book of crossword puzzles, I heard the Platters sing "Twilight Time" five times over the radio as the heavy clouds that had been threatening to rain since noon blocked out the moon.

At 8:30 PM, Xavier, dressed in a navy-blue suit, white shirt, and yellow tie, exited his unit. He hopped into a silver Mercury Montclair convertible, also courtesy of Skyline, and he drove with only one hand on the wheel. I followed three car lengths back.

Xavier pulled into a parking garage in downtown LA near Pershing Square and tossed his keys to a Mexican attendant. The two of them were backslapping and laughing for a few minutes. Then Xavier slipped a couple of dollars into the front pocket of the attendant's white, short-sleeve dress shirt. Whatever Xavier's plans for the night were, he had the finesse of a regular. I parked across the street, and I stayed on the opposite side of the boulevard from Xavier, walking parallel to him.

Downtown LA rivaled Times Square in those days. It still had a vibrant variety of gambling halls, massage parlors, greasy spoons, backroom brothels, dance clubs, strip joints, porn shops, and dive bars. Had Xavier ducked into one of those establishments, I wouldn't have interfered. But he strolled onto Eighth Street and into the Crown Jewel, a bar for faggots.

I just about swallowed my tongue. Such a move struck me as either stunningly ignorant or reckless, and I had to know on what side Xavier resided. Was he sincerely unaware that he was running the risk of getting *fairy dusted*?

I always despised how cops said those two words like they were a hilarious punch line: *fairy dusted*. The frivolity of the name belied the severe repercussions of the practice. Bill Parker, better known as Wild Bill Parker, was the LAPD chief from 1950 to 1966, and his police force operated like a band of slave catchers. They stalked, entrapped, beat, captured, and sometimes killed their targets. High on their list of enemies were sex perverts—namely, homosexuals. California law shared the cops' foul-breath disgust of gay men. Anal sex was a felony in the Golden State, and a sodomy conviction could earn the offender a life sentence. Plenty of men served less time for murdering their wives.

Gay men could also go to prison for lesser offenses than penetrating a forbidden hole. California State Penal Code 674 outlawed soliciting, loitering with intent, and/or engaging in lewd or dissolute conduct. Anyone convicted under Code 674 had to register as a sex offender for the rest of his life. Countless homosexuals were left so humiliated and ruined in the aftermath that they killed themselves.

It was just a sick game to the cops. They raided gay bars, arresting scores of men to charge with breaking the broadly defined and subjective anti-sodomy laws, and they came up with that clever term for it, *fairy dusting*. Police departments also deployed *wax fruit*. Those were undercover police officers who posed as gay men, lying in wait to be sexually propositioned or proposing lascivious acts. The wax fruits often made the first moves and struck up suggestive conversations with unsuspecting homos. Because no matter who mentioned the unspeakable deeds, it resulted in the arrest of the unlucky mark who demonstrated an interest in fooling around with another man.

I took my wedding band off and secured it in the fold of my wallet. Then I darted through traffic to cross the street. The Crown Jewel had blacked-out storefront windows on which its name was stenciled in gold lettering. I checked my reflection in the glass, buttoning the top of my blue dress shirt and refastening my gray necktie. Technically, the bar wasn't whites-only anymore, but Blacks were held to a higher dress code and could be denied entry for not meeting it.

I'd learned that the hard way nearly two years earlier when Montgomery Clift was under my watch while he costarred in Skyline's *Autumn Marigolds* (1956) with Jan Sterling. It was Monty's first full picture following that gruesome car accident he got into after enjoying more cocktails than food at a dinner party thrown by Elizabeth Taylor. He'd undergone reconstructive surgery on his face, especially the left side, and he was insecure about his looks. Swilling his painkillers with vodka, Monty would sneak out of his room at the Hollywood Roosevelt Hotel and stumble into a taxicab that deposited him in front of the Crown Jewel, where he'd beg to be recognized by fawning queeny men. I rushed in after him once without a jacket and in scuffed dress shoes, and I was refused entry. Monty shut the bar down that night.

Up to snuff to retrieve Xavier, I opened the green wooden door and stepped inside the dimly lit establishment. The air smelled of pineapple rinds and nicotine, and the rumble of men talking low was rendered unintelligible by a piano player who struck the keys hard and fast. It took a few moments, but I recognized the song was "Happy Days Are Here Again."

With its brown leather booths, its large bar along the left wall, and its jacket-and-tie policy, the Crown Jewel could have passed itself off as a gentlemen's saloon on the level. It was the proximity among the patrons that gave the game away. The men were too close to each other. Hands lingered. Mouths almost brushed with ears. Knees kissed under tables.

I spotted Xavier sitting at the far end of the bar. He was gently cradling a drink in his hand while chatting with a muscly Guatemalan busboy wearing a black dress shirt and red tie. Even perched on a green swivel stool, Xavier was half a head taller than the butch young man, who cleared empty glasses from a deserted booth nearby. The sweep of Xavier's eyes along the busboy's big ass told me that he was flirting. I wasn't sure if the busboy had the hots for Xavier or if he was shining him on while doing his job. He didn't glance back at Xavier as he carried his bin of dirty glasses into the kitchen.

No one else paid their brief encounter any attention. Patrons of the Crown Jewel made a point of not observing the faces or actions of their neighbors. Yet I made note of the rising star's choice to engage one of the men least likely to be aware of his Hollywood identity.

I then scanned the room for undercover officers as I closed in on Xavier. The cops assigned to impersonate homosexuals always had a strained, constipated expression. To my relief, I didn't spot any.

"This seat taken?" I asked of the padded stool next to him.

"Depends," Xavier said, without looking up from his drink. "You buyin' me a round?"

"Sure. We'll call it the price of company. What are you drinking?"

He turned his head, made direct eye contact, and smiled. "A gin gimlet."

I was studying his face for a hint that he recognized mine. Nothing in the lines of his forehead, the squint of his eyes, or the shape of his mouth pondered for even a split second, *Do I know you from somewhere?* We were strangers once more meeting for the first time. I flagged the bartender and put a dollar next to Xavier's glass.

"I've never seen you before," I said. "You new to these parts?"

I was curious to see how familiar Xavier would get with a man in a place like the Crown Jewel. I'd only need a minute.

"I bounce around," Xavier said. His tone guarded. A promising sign.

"I understand how that goes. I work the rails."

"You a conductor?"

"Nah, a porter," I said.

"That must be good bread. Plenty of tips."

"I do all right. What line you in?"

"Me? I'm a pool player," he lied. "I follow the action from city to city."

A welcome relief. He had a cover story. I had one more test.

"My name's Lou," I said.

"Curtis."

Thank goodness. An alias. He was daring, but no dummy. The waiter arrived and took our drink orders. Gin gimlets for each of us. I had no intention of drinking mine. I was about to reveal that I was his Skyline security agent and that we needed to exit the bar immediately. Xavier had other ideas.

"Lou, do you like movies?" he asked.

The question, oddly enough, turned me on. He was challenging me. I'd said I didn't recognize him, and he was probing to see if I was lying. I played along.

"Nah, they haven't been worth a nickel since Paul Robeson quit makin' 'em," I said before sipping my drink.

Xavier laughed. "Robeson. He's well before us—unless you really outrunning Father Time."

"Nah, I'm only twenty-five," I said, thinking fast. "My papa's Elks Lodge had a print of *The Emperor Jones*, and they showed it once a year. Robeson walked on-screen and grabbed hold of me."

"He had you, huh? The first man you wanted to be . . . with."

He added that last word in sync with the piano player's clamorous rendition of "On the Sunny Side of the Street," so it was drowned out by a run on the keys, if the listener selected to ignore the word, or could be explained away as a miscommunication if the listener was offended by the word. I elected to hear it.

"The darker, the bigger, the better," I said, appraising Xavier openly.

He swiveled on his stool to square up with me. He placed his legs on either side of me and straightened his posture to rise to his highest above me. His cologne smelled like burnt cinnamon, and I didn't have to pretend to feel sexually attracted to him.

Xavier put a hand on my shoulder, "What's the last movie you saw?"

Another test. A simple question that should have elicited a quick answer. I hesitated, however, because I wasn't sure how far back to set the end of my movie knowledge. I almost said *Treasure Island*, but that felt too long ago. *Carmen Jones* sprang to mind but hit too close to home.

"*The Jackie Robinson Story*," I said.

Xavier leaned forward and whispered in my ear, "Liar."

"No, that was the one," I protested.

"Liar," he repeated.

I pulled back from him, but he kept his face close to mine. His lips were pursed, and the hoods of his eyes hung low. He reached down into my lap and gave my hard cock a squeeze. I'd been made.

"Xavier," I said, "we should talk somewhere else more private."

5

BLACK ANGEL OF DEATH

Horace kissed me back, all right. He bit and nibbled at my bottom lip until I winced. I tried to pull away, but he didn't let me, and what I'd started between us in his quarters on the USS *Stevens* immediately escaped my control. If I'd been older or wiser, I'd have been scared.

He pushed me onto his bed and climbed on top of me, he undid me, he moved me to his will, he pleased me, and he hurt me. He fulfilled desires I was too embarrassed to voice. I saw no reason to question the terms of my fortune.

From the start, our relationship was our shared secret, but Horace called the shots. He decided when we would kiss, and where he would touch me, and how long I would go down on him, and at what hour I had to slip out of my bunk to go sneak into his room, and when I was allowed to make noise as he finished me off. I learned that my submission turned him on, and his dominance was my kink. Was that the queerest part of us?

We also got a charge from the danger we were courting. Uncle Sam had spelled out in chapter and verse the levels of his intolerance for sodomites among his fighting men. In 1950, Army Regulation 600–443 established three categories of homosexuals and three corresponding separations from service: Class I applied to *those deemed aggressive* (they were subject to court-martial); Class II suited *those considered active but nonaggressive* (they could dodge a court-martial if they accepted a dishonorable discharge, or resigned quietly, if they were an officer); and Class III fit *those who have not violated the sodomy statute but exhibit homosexual tendencies* (they could be removed under a general or even honorable discharge, provided they didn't make a fuss about it). All told, a Joe could have been a raging fucking faggot, a mellow fucking faggot, or a non-fucking non-faggot who acted like a sissy and got himself booted out of the army.

Clearly, Horace had more to lose than I did, and it was chiefly to protect his accomplishments that I kept my affections in check. It was difficult to keep secrets on a carrier, but I learned to avoid ugly rumors by making a show out of being Horace's smart-aleck whipping boy. Unlike the aides preceding me, who were afraid to defy the temperamental Black lieutenant even in their private thoughts, I got away with rolling my eyes in his presence. I made cutting asides to my peers, and on a few occasions, I mimicked Horace in the mess hall.

Horace allowed my antics because they gave him fodder for disciplining me behind closed doors and because he recognized how they served as cover. The white sailors assumed I resented Horace for his arrogance like they did. The Black ones sensed there was no venom in my ribbing and considered me a leavening agent for the navy's newest ace fighter pilot. None of them, I thought, had a clue that Horace and I were Class I homosexuals.

Once Horace ascended into the Aces Club, a certain amount of press was to be expected, given that the navy had only about forty aces (more or less, because some claims were disputed), and a Black inductee was a rarity in any of the military branches. Front-page coverage in *Stars and Stripes* was assured.

The joker in the deck turned out to be the White House. It was President Truman's press secretary, Joseph Short, who made Horace a patriotic headline story that ran across the wire services. He gave

Lieutenant Horace "Hornet" Dixon the nickname that he never liked. Short made him the country's newest Black war hero, and by god, was Truman's administration keen to champion Horace since the nation's previous Black war hero, Ensign Jesse L. Brown, was killed in action in North Korea, less than a month earlier, on December 4.

The day after Horace became an ace, President Truman sent him a congratulatory telegram: "Lieutenant Dixon, you are a credit to your nation and a credit to your race." In countless newspapers from coast to coast, the message ran alongside a harrowing account of the Hornet's third confirmed kill and a hastily staged photograph (taken by a United Press lensman) of Horace in his flight suit standing in front of his fighter jet.

The following Sunday on *The Ed Sullivan Show*, Ella Fitzgerald thanked President Truman for taking notice of "one of our brave colored boys fighting for freedom in a faraway land." Lady Ella recounted the legend of Hornet Dixon for an audience of sixty million people and sang "God Bless America" in his honor. Horace was subsequently interviewed for a feature article in *Life* magazine. Every step in that public relations campaign was arranged by the Truman White House.

Horace reveled in the fanfare. He had me post his press clippings on the common crew bulletin board. He recited flattering passages from the articles to his fellow fighter pilots. In a shocking breach of protocol, he asked our carrier's rear admiral when he could expect a promotion to commander, a leap from his current rank as an O-3 to an O-5.

Within a week of the *Sullivan* show, Horace started receiving bulging letter bags from admirers, most of them Black teenage girls. He read every letter or had me read them to him. He ate up every compliment served to him; his appetite never flagged. He cherished those letters, and each one got a reply, dictated to me by the Hornet himself.

Mind you, I also enjoyed seeing the limelight shine on Horace, but I was equally intrigued to learn how fame could be a manufactured good. Until then, I'd thought notoriety was a matter of fate—

a happenstance of genius, infamy, or beauty catching the world's eye. It spun my young head to witness how fame could be cooked up like a stack of flapjacks. However, the discovery didn't dismay me. I was sort of impressed and only more so with time. The mythmaking of Washington proved to be as swift and as potent as the stagecraft of Hollywood.

Horace attributed his rise to powers greater than politics. He shared the details with me a few days after New Year's while we were out one night in Misawa on a special pass. We ate in a cramped, noisy restaurant with a low tin roof and walls constructed out of rusty sheet metal. We didn't speak the language, so we ordered by pointing at the meals and booze being enjoyed by other customers. The Japanese locals blatantly stared at us for several minutes before they resolutely ignored us at our table for two in the back corner.

Once we'd eaten our fill of ramen and seafood, Horace kept buying whiskey shots for the two of us. Soon he was soused, and it shaded him sentimental. He abruptly steered our conversation about his newfound celebrity into delicate territory.

"My mama would be tickled pink if she could see me now," he said, then paused and shook his head. "She'd be mighty pleased."

"Any mother would be. You just about the most popular Negro outside of old Jesse Owens."

Horace drummed the table with his fingers. "I wish I had a photo of Mama. She was queenly, Aaron. Beautiful, graceful. In her prime, Josephine Baker coulda played her in the movies. They had the same eyes."

I had to razz him. "Too bad you didn't get any of her looks."

Horace continued reminiscing like I hadn't spoken. "Her voice was like music. She'd say my name, and coming from her, it sounded like a song."

From the fleeting occasions on which he had spoken about his mother, I'd gathered that she was long dead, but still I broached the subject gently. "How did she pass?"

He turned his head and stared at a corroded orange streak on the metal wall to his left. "Negro sharecroppers and white farmers would come from all over Arkansas down to Orville and pay the one and only Madame Johnnie Mae to read what the cowries had to tell about their next harvest. She saw the floods, the hard winters, the droughts."

"She was always right?"

Horace snapped his fingers to get the waiter's attention. Then he lifted his empty shot glass, signaling for another. "She was always right, but the men didn't always listen. She warned my daddy against rabble-rousin'. He got a group of Negroes to go with him to the votin' booth on Election Day. They let him vote to avoid a scuffle." He gripped the side of the table and drew a ragged breath. "Before long, they had my daddy swingin' from a tree. . . ."

I moved to place my hand on top of his, but I caught myself. Just because no one appeared to be looking at us didn't mean we weren't being watched, and I didn't want to do anything that could invite hostility. Under the table, I pressed my knee against Horace's knee. He pressed back.

"I'm sorry," I said. "That's horrible."

He nodded and fought off the tears brimming in his eyes. "It broke Mama." He snapped his fingers again for the waiter. "She saw that comin', too. Whenever the awfulness she'd read came to pass, she'd cry, 'Bein' ahead of ya time ain't no good for ya.'"

The waiter finally came over to our table with a bottle of whiskey. He poured Horace a shot and began to move along.

"Where you off to with the bottle?" Horace asked too loudly. "Leave the bottle!"

The waiter frowned at us.

"Please," I said politely, miming the action of placing the bottle on our table, "we'll buy the bottle."

The waiter handed me the bottle, and I thanked him.

"My schoolteacher, Miss Hogan, sat me down and told me my mama was dead, too," Horace said. "An accident, she called it. What did I know? I wasn't nothin' but ten."

"What happened?"

He was sealed off in his memories. "They wouldn't let me see her before the funeral. I was shipped off to be with Gladys the next morning."

Horace bowed his head, unable to look me in the face. He had nothing to be ashamed of, and if one of us had been a woman, I could have crossed our rickety table in that shabby restaurant, put my arms around him, and told him as much. But we were men, and I remained in my seat and he in his. I said nothing until he stifled his pain.

In a way both acute and anew, I felt the pinch of our miserable lot as homosexuals. Horace and I were made small by our circumstances, and while those who hated us always intended to diminish us, they had failed on that score when it came to me. I wasn't a tortured homo who cried alone wishing I were otherwise, and funny as it sounds to the radical and liberated, day-to-day, I didn't chafe against the constraints on our affair. The sneaking around to be with Horace and the lying to stay safe were survival tactics I picked up along with the rest of my child's play. I accepted that the strictures set down in Army Regulation 600–443 and Leviticus 20:13 were as immutable as the laws of gravity, and I made do without sorrow. Yet I pitied us, sitting at a corner table too bound up to express anything that would give us away.

Horace drank another shot. "Mama read the cowrie shells for me. It's why I've never been afraid in a dogfight." A faint grin crept onto his face, and he leaned forward so only I'd hear him. "She predicted I'd be a great warrior."

I was thankful we'd reached a rosier topic. "You came through for her. You made good."

"That wasn't the half of it." He grabbed the whiskey bottle and refilled my empty shot glass. "She said my 'story will be seen by millions upon millions.'"

Having grown up without experience or faith in fortune-telling, I was unsure how to interpret the message that Horace believed was clear. And I can't say I bought into his mother's prophecy that night. However, my curiosity outweighed my skepticism, and, to please Horace, I acted like a true believer.

"What's that mean?"

"Can't be but one thing. 'Seen by millions upon millions.' Not sung. Not read. Not told. Only possibility is a movie."

I laughed to needle him. "What're they gonna call it?"

"*Horace the Conquering Hero*," he proposed.

"More likely *The Black Angel of Death*."

"That'd be fine by me, too."

We spent the rest of the night fleshing out his Hollywood hopes, and the dreaming came easy to me. Unlike the meaning of cowrie shells, I was something of an expert on movies, especially compared to Horace. I'd seen more pictures than he could name, and I kept up with the star reports in newsreels, radio shows, and fan magazines. So, he found me useful as he plotted out how being a Black ace would lead to fortune in Hollywood.

"You know, you could do more than sell your story to a studio," I said as we were paying the check in that metal trap restaurant. "You could star in the picture."

He lit a Dunhill. "The hell I know about acting?"

"The hell you know about flying until you put your mind to doing it?"

He blew me off until I mustered a solid, simple case on the walk back to the carrier.

"Lesser men have done it," I began. "Look at Audie Murphy."

Squinting for a moment, Horace drew a blank on the name, and I explained how, coming out of World War II, Second Lieutenant Murphy was parlaying his combat record in the army and a Medal of Honor for valor into a career as a movie actor. Murphy went from having a bit part in United Artists' romantic comedy *Texas, Brooklyn & Heaven* in 1948 to nabbing top billing in Allied Artists' wayward-youth-rehabilitated saga *Bad Boy* a year later. Plans were underway to turn the book he wrote about his war stories into a movie in which Murphy would play himself. (They came to pass with the release of Universal Pictures' *To Hell and Back* in 1955.)

I reasoned that Horace had more going for him than Murphy, who stood five foot five and looked as plain as a picket fence. The number of Black folks who would buy tickets to see one of their brave fighting boys on the silver screen had to exceed the number of white people who lined up for the sparkless Murphy. With his bald head, full lips, and prominent nose, Horace was dashing and distinct like stars used to be, and in the New Year's glow of 1951, Hollywood looked as if it was opening up for Black, male actors. Rex Ingram (Jim in *The Adventures of Huckleberry Finn*), Willie Best (Andy Jones in *Half Past Midnight*), and James Edwards (Private Peter Moss in *Home of the Brave*) were going strong. Why not a Horace Dixon?

As we reached the USS *Stevens*, Horace promised to consider aiming higher in Hollywood, but we spoke no more about it for weeks. Then the gifts started to arrive. I'd learn years later that between the burst of publicity surrounding Horace and the initial overtures from the movie studios, film executives had already pressed writers to type up script treatments on the newspaper accounts, and production executives had whipped up budgets for war movies of varying scales, and distribution teams had taken a head count of how many theaters (particularly in the South) would run a movie with a Black lead if the movie was wrapped in red, white, and blue. The initial signs were positive. Hollywood doesn't approach unless it is confident success is in the bag.

Warner Bros. sent Horace a sterling silver cigarette case monogrammed with his initials. RKO's package contained a custom pair of gold-rimmed aviator goggles. A meticulously replicated desk model of Horace's fighter jet came from Skyline Motion Pictures. Columbia Pictures mailed him a Hamilton wristwatch worth more than I earned in a month. MGM gave him a brass compass in a leather-bound box. By chance, Twentieth and Paramount had Louis Vuitton Président attachés delivered, and Horace let me keep the extra one. United Artist sent a fancy straight razor shaving kit.

Each gift came with a card thanking Horace for his service. The presents were his to keep, no strings attached. He was encouraged to skip the courtesy of replying with an acknowledgment of receipt. After all, he had a war to win.

6

IDEAL COMPANIONS

Xavier and I walked side by side down South Olive Street, and the first beads of perspiration were sprouting on my forehead. I wanted to wipe them away, but Xavier would notice the gesture, and if he turned to look at me, what other tells might he spot? I couldn't break stride. I had to move like I was in control if I hoped to reassert command.

For his part, Xavier was playing cool, as he had been since he finished his gin gimlet while I settled his tab at the Crown Jewel. There he'd kept up a friendly patter with me as if we were chums. "I forgot all about Felix's party," he said. "If we hustle, we'll make it before Maggie cuts the cake."

As I dropped a five on the bar, I had to give Xavier credit for creating an excuse for our hasty exit, in the event anyone should ever question the bartenders about us. I had intended to mention, for the staff to overhear, that we were running late to the premiere screening of Skyline's June Allyson weepie *Pressed Flowers* at Grauman's Chinese Theatre. Xavier's cover, however, did the job. Someone had taught him how to salt the earth against the seeds of rumors.

Once he and I stepped outside, he said, "Let's talk in Pershing Square Park."

It was three blocks away. He strolled in silence like a man unburdened, and I put one foot in front of the other, feeling my clothes cling to my damp skin and calculating the magnitude of the troubles ahead. I'd cruised and jerked off the actor that I was supposed to intimidate with an iron fist of moral rectitude, and the actor hadn't forgotten the fleeting tryst. He could inform the studio, and the studio would protect him and fire me. He could attempt to blackmail me by threatening to inform the studio. He could run a version of those scenarios with my wife as the target that he'd enlighten, breaking up my marriage. As the green lawn and twin fountains of Pershing Square came into view, I wrestled against the indefensibility of my position. I'd been assigned to bring Xavier to heel, and he had at his disposal a half dozen options to ruin me.

"You smoke?" Xavier asked while he fished a cigarette out of a pack of Old Gold.

I quit smoking in the navy, because Horace forbade me; I restarted the habit on the night that Horace and I parted ways; and I quit cold turkey at Kimberly's insistence once she and I got engaged.

"Yes," I answered, counting on the nicotine to soothe my nerves.

Xavier stopped at the base of a lamppost, gave me a cigarette, and torched me with a thin copper lighter. I made eye contact confidently when I thanked him. But my brow was sweaty. He noticed.

"You could stand to bum a handkerchief, too."

"I've got my own," I snapped, finally able to wipe my forehead dry.

At that hour of night, the park was mostly a thoroughfare. Friends, lovers, and loners unattentively crossed the lawn to live out plans in another destination. Maybe a dozen people—elderly or derelict—planted themselves on benches. Several feral men in tight pants walked the perimeter at a deliberate pace.

Xavier pointed at the stately park restroom facilities built out of smooth, painted concrete. "See the johns. The city's cleaned them up, but I remember when you could find the hottest action in those stalls. Businessmen and street boys and college beatniks and biker dudes would stand in front of the urinals or wash their hands or comb their hair until someone turned the lights out." He took a deep drag from his cigarette, and I mirrored him with mine. "Then everyone would be all over everyone else. Looks, money, power—didn't matter. In there, men wanted men. Simple and pure. Taught me how to step outside myself, how to become someone else in an instant."

Pershing Square wasn't my stomping ground, but I knew it was part of "the Run" in downtown LA. Once a circuit of spots that tolerated the cruising of homos, the Run included the park; the men's restrooms in the Subway Terminal Building; the back stacks and private reading rooms at the Central Library, and the men's-only bar at the Biltmore Hotel. Every Hollywood fixer and vice cop was clued in to what it meant if a young actor was arrested for loitering in any of those locations, and so long as the right people were paid under the table, the matter could vanish from the record.

My boss, McManus, told me the Run had been operating since the Roaring Twenties, and it was considered an orderly, discreet area in which to contain and monitor the sodomites of the city. Better homos gather in a designated ghetto than roam and pop up anywhere and everywhere. Periodically, the police would raid the Run to show they were cracking down on perverts. Examples were made out of a few, and the many continued to frolic in the shadows.

That quasi-permissive approach was vanishing under the watch of LAPD chief Parker and Los Angeles mayor Norris Poulson. I've already told you what a callous son of a bitch Parker was. He found a simpatico partner in Mayor Poulson, who defeated the incumbent mayor and fellow Republican, Fletcher Bowron, by pledging during the election race to not only fire city employees with Communist ties but to terminate those who refused to answer questions about their political leanings and activities. There was no room in Parker's or Poulson's good society for people who even entertained deviant ideas.

While Communists and Black militants were at the top of the list, the effort to rid LA of undesirables inevitably zeroed in on the faggots along the Run. But the push to remove homosexuals from the park didn't rely heavily on raids. The queers were displaced by a beautification initiative. More lampposts were installed, banishing the dark patches that sheltered lurking hustlers. Trees and bushes that once shielded men rutting on their knees, on their backs, or on all fours were pruned or uprooted. Wooden lavatories with clear windows and creaky doors that offered warnings were demolished and rebuilt with concrete walls, open stalls, and frosted glass. Upping the number of benches throughout the grounds attracted more visitors, many of whom were too innocent to know that the park had a history of being frequented by pansies.

"I caught on when the rules changed," Xavier continued. "I moved on. A lot of guys got hauled in because they kept coming back thinking the last sting was an aberration."

I blew smoke out of the corner of my mouth and spoke dismissively. "I see. You think you're too clever to need a fixer."

He got his back up. "I've been looking after myself since day one. Don't have a stain on me. Not even a smudge."

This was my opening to assert myself. "Yesterday and every yesterday before that, you weren't famous enough for *Confidential*, *Hush-Hush*, or *On the Q.T.* to cover you with a wet dishrag." I took a step toward him. "Congratulations—that's gonna change real quick, and they'll pay a Guatemalan waiter to lure you into a back room and pull your cock out for a close-up."

Xavier scoffed and looked off toward the fountains. I'd managed to knock him off-kilter by clocking his brief flirtation in the bar. One of the feral men stalking the edge of the park drew near us and hissed to attract our attention.

"Keep it pushin'," I told him.

He was a gaunt, glassy-eyed white guy in his late twenties, his corduroy was dingy, and his brown hair was greasy and matted to his forehead. He wore a ratty blue jacket that I'd bet covered the track marks on his arms. Still, he licked his lips and leered at a bona fide movie star and me like we would be lucky to have him. He represented the remnant of the gay scene in Pershing Square: the junkie-male prostitutes on the margins.

The hustler walked out of earshot, and I went in on Xavier. My line of attack was taking shape in my hands. I couldn't establish control over Xavier, but I could demonstrate need.

"Your problems are more complicated than you realize," I insisted. "You think if you don't step in shit, you'll be okay, but I swear to you, if someone isn't guarding your shoes the moment you take them off your feet, someone else will steal your shoes, smear shit on the bottom of them, then tell the world that you are a sicko who gets off on stepping in shit. You've gotta have a brother protecting you, looking out for you from all angles."

Xavier flicked the ash from the tip of his Old Gold and looked at me with naked doubt. "Why should I be impressed with you? You lied to me at the bar, and I saw through it. You claim you'll keep me out of jams, but I've got you nailed to the wall. I'd venture no one at Skyline knows you're a tearoom queen."

I tossed my cigarette on the ground between us, then put it out with the heel of my brown Clarks. "That sword cuts both ways. The Skyline brass will exercise the first option out of your contract if they get wind of how you blow."

"It won't be news to Lowell Garten, and he's all the protection I need."

My words caught in my throat. Lowell Garten was the vice president of Skyline studio operations and the only son of the studio's boss and founder, M. K. Garten. Eager to gain status in the motion picture industry and throughout Los Angeles, Lowell was thirty-six years old and recently married to a niece of Norman Chandler, the publisher of the *LA Times*. Young Mr. Garten attended the Hollywood parties and charity galas that his father disdained, and with his silky charm, he was an excellent schmoozer. His major drawback was that he had a penchant for cutting side deals that he didn't bother to inform my department about, driving Skyline fixers to distraction when we found ourselves at odds with assurances he made.

After a hard swallow, I asked, "What exactly is your arrangement with Lowell?"

"He said if I run into trouble, I should call him first, and he'd straighten it out with the press and the police."

"He isn't going to be enough to save you."

"He's practically running the studio now. Soon as his old man dies, he'll have everything."

"At Skyline." I eased my tone to sound concerned. "Skyline is protecting you today, but what about down the road when you're under contract with a rival studio? Hell, even today, some other studio could stick it to you because it will hurt Skyline, and Lowell will have to weigh protecting you against his other interests. I'm offering you my services, my loyalty across the board—no matter what studio you work for."

"Because I've got you by the short and curlies."

I was sincere when I said, "Because I'm a fan of yours."

The air of defensiveness came out of Xavier in a huff, and his shoulders dropped. He smiled. It wasn't the guarded and symmetrical one that graced movie posters. This was his real, unabashed smile. The one I'd seen in the basement bathroom at the Dunbar Hotel.

For his first picture under contract, Skyline tapped Xavier for a supporting role in the church comedy *A Curious Note*. Filming started in July and took place on the SMP studio backlot in Stages 8 and 9. The movie starred Hazel Scott, who returned from political exile in Paris to make her last picture to date in the US after her problematic testimony before the House Un-American Activities Committee.

Hazel portrayed the best singer in a gospel choir who was chosen to perform for (and ultimately duet with) Mahalia Jackson, playing herself, when the legendary songstress swings through the small town to visit an old friend. Before Mahalia arrives, Hazel's character must survive sabotage and other tomfoolery from a young upstart who wants to sing in her place. The upstart role belonged to Diahann Carroll. Xavier played a farmhand so besotted with Diahann's character that he did her bidding, no questions asked.

Diahann and Xavier had natural comedic chemistry that drew off their love for one another. They'd met years back in a makeshift actors' troupe in Inglewood. The troupe invited agents, managers, and casting directors to see the plays they put on in the social hall of a community center. No more than five people ever attended a show. The troupe disbanded within three months. Xavier and Diahann remained friends.

She brought him to the Dorothy Dandridge party as her date, and he slept on the couch in her apartment for several weeks when he was between spots. She knew he was gay; she didn't care. I think she enjoyed the male attention without the pressure of having to satisfy the male desires. Whenever her interim boyfriend or husband wasn't available, Xavier was her go-to escort.

Standing together, they made for a stunning pair. He was as tall and tapered as she was elegant and petite. And they were even more mesmerizing in motion. At nightclubs and parties, they'd dance, and the floor would clear. Xavier would swing Diahann around and dip her with confidence. He'd hold her close, and she'd melt into his chest.

Beyond their combined allure and kinship, their divergent bedroom habits also made them ideal companions in the public eye. Diahann didn't speak to the movie fan or Black magazines about how she longed for Xavier to make an honest woman of her. And Xavier's manly pride wasn't wounded when Diahann strayed from their dates for assignations with Sidney Poitier. (Diahann and Sidney's nine-year affair was an open secret in Hollywood, and now that it is safely behind them—along with the marriages they disrupted with their passion—I feel no shame disclosing its existence, because it shaped Xavier's life, too.)

Yet if I had to identify the fuel in the motor of Xavier and Diahann's bond, I'd say it was a mutual respect of talent. They were initially drawn to each other in those acting classes in Inglewood because they detected spectacular ability in one another, and they were committed to sharpening their skills. Over the years, Diahann and Xavier spent hours discussing the roles they were cast in and the approaches they were considering. They marked up each other's scripts scribbling in notes on motivations and subtextual messages. They didn't just run lines together; they rehearsed scenes, providing one another space for experimentation. I adored and admired the loyalty, commitment, and warmth of Xavier and Diahann's closeness—when it wasn't adding to my workload.

"How quickly can you get us out of that wax museum?" Diahann asked me as she changed behind the golden folding screen in her dressing room. "I have a 5:30 AM call time tomorrow."

I'd just been led into the room by Xavier, who immediately went to fix himself a scotch and soda at the bar cart. Diahann and Xavier were two weeks into filming *A Curious Note*, and normally, I'd leave them be, but Skyline Motion Pictures was celebrating its fortieth anniversary with a gala at the Coconut Grove in the Ambassador Hotel. Xavier and Diahann were under orders to put in an appearance, despite having worked a fourteen-hour day on set.

I was accompanying Xavier to carry out an aspect of my unique agreement with him: We were curtailing his time at the party because one of my duties was to facilitate his sexual escapades, seeing to it that they remain anonymous. Xavier had obviously shared with Diahann that I was extracting him from the festivities, a breach in protocol that ticked me off. Diahann figured that since I was already running an evacuation mission, she could use me to help her escape, too, a presumption of obedience that galled me. Yet I'd been ambushed, and I was piecing all of this together as I came through the door, and yelling at Xavier would gain me nothing, and Diahann's voice was sweet and helpless.

"If you make a point of congratulating Old Man Garten and Lowell shortly after we get there," I said, "I can make you disappear half an hour later."

Diahann squealed with delight from behind the screen. "You're astonishing! Just like Zay-vee assured me."

Xavier turned around from the bar cart and raised his drink at me. "We owe you."

I took a seat on the green velvet sofa. Diahann stepped out into view wearing a peach chiffon dress and went to her makeup chair. Xavier joined her and leaned over her, bringing his head down next to hers.

They looked at their exquisite faces in the vanity mirror. He checked hers, and she inspected his. He advised her to apply a touch more blush. She used her eyebrow brush to separate and curl his lashes. They were scrupulous about their beauty. And they'd forgotten I was in the room.

7

STILL NO WORD

Should anyone dig up the letters, it will appear as if Horace became pen pals with Jack Warner, Louis B. Mayer, Barney Balaban, Harry Cohn, M. K. Garten, Darryl Zanuck, Arthur Krim, and Howard Hughes. From 1951 until his honorable discharge three years later, he wrote to these studio heads about his continued success in the war (two more confirmed kills) and his expanding Hollywood dream (to star in the movie about his life), and the presidents, founders, and chairmen replied with warm congratulations and buttery appeals for him to sign with their respective studios. Ever coy, Horace always insisted that he was too consumed with serving the country to make a decision about the movie business.

Three to six months would pass between letter exchanges, and not all suitors stuck with the campaign. Mayer was forced out of MGM in August of 1951. Hughes's correspondence got spotty in 1952 and stopped abruptly in 1953, during which time the survival of RKO was in jeopardy. Warner dropped out in '52 because of Horace's insistence on playing himself. Cohn went silent at the end of the same year as rumors surfaced that he was recovering from a mild heart attack. In '53, Zanuck's attention got diverted to Twentieth's failed attempt to release every one of its movies in wide-screen CinemaScope. By

1954, the race was down to Balaban at Paramount, Garten at Skyline, and Krim at United Artists.

The trove of letters between the war hero and the studio bosses was diplomatic and cordial, and I suspect fraudulent on both sides. I wrote and signed Horace's missives. His only instruction was to keep the film executives interested without committing to them. I peppered them with questions about salary, accommodations while the movie was being produced, a starring role, and subsequent projects. I complimented Zanuck for Twentieth's Best Picture win at the Academy Awards for *All About Eve* in '51; Garten for Skyline's Oscar win for *A Fire in the Bluegrass* in '52; and Balaban for Paramount's victory for *The Greatest Show on Earth* at the twenty-fifth annual ceremony.

The responses were polite and cagey. Paragraphs of flattery that concluded with the assertion that the finer points could only be hammered out once Horace signed a preliminary agreement to sell his life rights. I gathered from the repetition and the stiltedness of the language that a lot of what was included in the letters was boilerplate. The handiwork of flunkies. Within a year, I concluded that Warner, Mayer, Balaban, Cohn, Garten, Zanuck, Krim, and Hughes weren't writing or dictating their letters either. So, an aide-de-camp was negotiating with business affairs executives under the names of their bosses. On the carrier, it struck me as absurd, but I would come to discover it was a common practice.

Unlike the tabs on his war map, Horace didn't stay abreast of his standing in Hollywood. One studio was as good as another so long as it met his demands at the highest price possible. To my growing dismay, Horace had also adopted a smug attitude toward the future since becoming an ace. The achievement and its subsequent notoriety validated his mother's prophecy. He considered his triumph in the motion pictures industry to be preordained.

I, however, had strong preferences among the studios. The financial turmoil surrounding RKO, for instance, had it on a constant deathwatch, and I was weary of the studio before Hughes quit responding.

Nearly all the others were a mixed bag of clashing sensibilities and track records. The one studio I did favor wholeheartedly was Skyline.

I'd grown up watching enough Skyline pictures to be familiar with its award-winning niche: true-life stories of doomed sacrifice and heroism rendered lavishly—or, as critics complained, melodramatically—on the big screen. The Skyline signature came about because studio founder M. K. Garten didn't trust that original ideas were reliable at the box office. Asking audiences to follow a story they'd never heard of before was too demanding, in his opinion. Instead, he ordered Skyline writers to scour ancient history and the latest headlines for tales of men and women who demonstrated the best of human potential under duress.

The daring touch, however, was that Skyline pictures didn't feed their audiences saccharine endings. While the lovers in MGM musicals danced into happiness and the women in Warner Bros. weepies were triumphant by the time the end credits rolled, the final minutes of a Skyline picture were spent at the side of a deathbed or a grave. Virtue was always extinguished. Crowds ate it up.

A prime example: Portraying World War I fighting ace Lieutenant Frank Luke Jr. in 1945's *The Arizona Balloon Buster*, a young Gregory Peck spends the entire film dying near a river behind German lines after being shot down in his SPAD S.XIII. He fends off German soldiers by firing bullets from his pistol, and with the bang of each bullet, the film flashes back to pivotal events in his daring and brash combat record. After an hour and a half, he shoots his last slug and dies before the Germans can capture him.

I was twelve when *The Arizona Balloon Buster* opened. I ran the projector for its run at the Emerson Palace, and I found it enthralling. During the final reel, I always cried at the same spot: when Peck puts his hand over his heart before closing his eyes to die. I wasn't alone. Men—veterans, even—wept during this film. Such unchecked emotion was allowed in a movie palace.

When I advocated for Skyline, Horace remained unswayed. He

planned to make his choice shortly before he was discharged, and he anticipated that a sign would show him which studio was meant to produce his film. I argued that maybe I was the sign telling him what to do. He snickered, closing the discussion.

There was a part of the future outside of his mother's prophecy that did become a recurring question between us. Horace was the one to raise it in the spring of 1951. He'd just landed on the carrier after an air battle with no kills on either side. He was sweaty and exhausted, and I stood by on the flight deck with a canteen of cold water and a flask full of gin, both for him. He climbed down from his bird and his brow was knitted in deep thought. I expected some strange report from the mission.

Instead, he asked, "Whatcha gonna do with yourself once you get off this tin can?"

Being a smart-ass, I said, "Hell if I know, maybe I'll re-enlist."

"You can't stay without me," he said, as if I would re-enlist under any circumstances.

"Since you know best, what do you think I should do when my time's up?"

"Come with me to Hollywood."

"And do what?"

He took the canteen and the flask from me. "Be my boy."

I was caught off guard by the request and by the tenderness in his voice.

"Think it over," he said, and strolled off for the showers.

I watched him go. He took a swig from the flask. Then he poured the cold water over his bald head. He continued on as if his proposal wasn't consequential.

When I had envisioned life after my enlistment, I had tried to be adult about it. No childish daydreaming, no romantic fantasies. I assumed that Horace and I would part ways. He'd go off and be welcomed in Hollywood with fanfare, and he'd attract the representatives necessary to make him a star. I'd move to a city like Chicago or Detroit, where I could blend into a sizable Negro community of transplants who also left larger families behind. And with any luck, with enough Black men around, I could find another one like Horace.

I'd purposely restrained myself from entertaining the idea of joining Horace in Los Angeles. It seemed too adolescent a suggestion for me to float. It would have opened me up to his ridicule. Even worse, he could have rejected the idea with a swat of his hand.

But if he wanted me to go with him to Hollywood, I'd go. I just needed us to be clear about what we expected from one another—and I wanted it to be noted that he was inviting me. He asked for this.

Later that night, in Horace's quarters, I was folding his laundry when I broached the topic. Horace had just finished typing a letter to his sister.

"What did you mean by 'be my boy'?"

He yawned loudly. "Huh?"

"What did you have in mind for us in LA?"

He studied me as if I were confused. "Look, you can come or not. It's up to you."

He turned back to his fold-out desk and began typing an essay for the *Chicago Defender* paying tribute to former Chicago-area congressman Oscar De Priest, who'd recently died at age eighty. On Horace's bed, I sat slack-jawed like an idiot, folding his socks. I let the subject drop.

That Thanksgiving, we'd gotten drunk along with half the crew. Horace pulled me into a supply closet, spun me toward the door, shucked my pants to my knees, and fucked me while I held the latch in place so no one else could enter. Seconds after we climaxed, he said, "It'd be a shame to give this up."

Months later, I was kidding around with the other enlisted men of my rank about how Horace expected me to be his aide-de-camp when we left the navy. A twisted version of my words was relayed to Horace. He chided me on the flight deck for depicting him as a slave driver.

"I wouldn't bring you to LA to be a butler," he said.

I dared to ask, "Then what are you bringing me to be?"

"Christ," he groaned, "you want my letterman jacket? A promise ring? You want to play house? Will you take my last name?"

"Fuck you," I said before walking off the deck without his dismissal.

I waited for Horace to come find me and—not apologize, that would be out of the question—show a hint of remorse, but I didn't see him until the next morning. We didn't speak about our argument, and I abandoned the notion of moving to Los Angeles with him. He couldn't sort out his feelings, and I wasn't going to beg him for an invitation. I dedicated myself to seeing him through the rest of his service and to guiding his selection of a proper studio for his story. We kept having sex, but we were not lovers.

On Thursday, March 12, 1953, in Misawa, Japan, sunrise was 6:07 AM; the temperature high was 39°F and the low was 27°F; with 4 mph winds from the northeast, the windchill made the temperature feel 33°F; visibility was good for 12–16 kilometers, with moderate cloud coverage; there was a 25 percent chance of precipitation between 9:00 AM and 1:00 PM, otherwise zero; the barometric pressure was 29.7 inches of mercury; and sunset was 5:35 PM. At 2:13 PM, Horace separated from his squad in pursuit of a North Korean combat plane. He entered enemy territory, where he soon lost radio communication. Before he went dark, Horace's last transmission was, "I'ma catch this bastard."

Back on the carrier, I was gabbing in the mess hall when I got the news, and in my head, I cursed Horace's name. His recklessness was uncalled for. Another confirmed kill wouldn't add a noticeable shine to his legend. I could only assume his arrogance and his mother's predictions had him under the delusion that he was invincible. I knew better, and I resented the instant aching fear that Horace's disappearance stirred in me.

Under the watchful eyes of dozens of sailors, I also hated the public demand it placed on my shoulders. Superstitious thinking was sometimes the only kind of thinking that occurred on a ship, and while I didn't subscribe to any of that, I couldn't buck it either. Tradition held that if a pilot flew out of range, his aide stood vigil on the deck as a beacon for his safe return.

I took up my position and stared out onto the horizon. An hour passed. Then another. I refused to consider the worst. Other crew members observed me but didn't approach me. When I got the urge to relieve myself, I found I couldn't move my feet. The old superstition had snagged me, too. What if I abandoned my post and that was when word came down that Horace had been lost? I'd be responsible for killing him. I resolved to keep watch.

Shortly before sunset, petty officer third class Preston Walsh approached me. We were both aware that within the hour, Horace's fighter jet would run out of fuel. He'd come to prepare me for that grim marker fast approaching.

He said gently, "Still no word."

I clung to my new religion. "He'll come back into range before long."

Walsh nodded. "You two sure are *close*. . . ."

I heard the implication in his voice and kept my eyes on the retreating sun.

"If you should ever need it," Walsh continued in a hushed tone, "I could be there for you, too. Day or night."

My hands were clasped behind my back, and my interlaced fingers tightened like the knot of a noose. Here was Walsh, a white man with brown sleepy eyes and a sharp jawline, daring to make his leaning known to me. Here he was, this affable, handsome twenty-six-year-old, who had on occasion been stripped naked by my mind while I was alone seeking release from my lust. For I had indeed wondered if his sensitivity and quiet demeanor spoke to a homosexual nature. I had my answer. I had seen what I suspected.

Of course, I had also been seen. Walsh was on to Horace and me. We must have gotten careless during the years of our affair. Horace playing grab ass with me in the halls or planting a kiss on my forehead when he was sloppy drunk. Me mooning over him or tending to him with too much affection. Or maybe Walsh possessed a talent for spotting another marked card.

Curiosity alone nearly led me to reach out to Walsh. My lips parted to acknowledge the unholy kinship between us, and for a moment, I could imagine the relief of talking to someone who shared my perspective. I had many questions about the mechanics of sex and love with another man. Walsh could have opened up a world for me.

That very idea—the world suddenly privy to my business—was what scared me off. If Walsh had figured out that Horace and I were lovers, who else had? Had Walsh shared what he'd pieced together with others? How many Walshes were on this carrier anyway? My fears smothered the opportunity for fellowship.

I told Walsh, "I'll manage. . . . Horace is on his way."

Walsh walked off.

Ten minutes later, Horace's bird blipped on the radar. I stopped breathing when I spotted him in the sky. Only when my lungs started to cry out did I gasp and resume the practice. In the delirium of the moment, I believed that I had willed him back to me.

Horace landed on the USS *Stevens* to a hero's welcome. Hell, even the white officers who were jealous of him joined the Black sailors and whistled and clapped when Horace removed his helmet and lofted it. Tested and favored by the gods, he looked magnificent. I wanted to kneel before him, to kiss him from head to toe, and to wring his neck for the anguish he'd caused me. The other men swarmed him, and he was hoisted into the air. The cheers were deafening, and I couldn't tell if I was trembling or if our commotion was rumbling the ship.

I stood back, afraid of what I might do if I touched Horace, but before I could collect myself, I saw him on his feet and cutting through the crowd to get to me. The air grew thick and hot. He cupped the back of my head, and to my shock, I found myself smiling and crying without restraint. He pulled me into a tight hug, and I buried my face against his shoulder. Given the circumstances, no one thought it queer, and I realized I was in love with him.

That night, in his quarters, I told him how unbearable the thought of losing him was. I didn't use the word *love*, but Horace understood me. He handled me gently in bed, and he didn't upbraid me for being emotional. When I said, "I need to be with you in Hollywood," he agreed that I should join him, and conclusively, the matter was settled. I don't recall when we came up with my business manager title. But I remember my first act in the role: Lieutenant Horace "Hornet" Dixon signed a contract selling his life rights to Skyline Motion Pictures.

8

THE ORIGINAL STARS

I never cared for the Coconut Grove. The nightclub had no restraint in its décor, in the proportion of its meals, in the obsequiousness of its staff, or in its pricing. Planted throughout the dining area, there were dozens of towering papier-mâché palm trees—allegedly bought from Paramount Pictures after they were used in 1921's *The Sheik*. To add to the spectacle, there was an indoor waterfall. Some nights, parrots had free rein to squawk, fly around, and land on guests' tables. None of those touches spelled fine dining to me.

But Lowell chose to throw Skyline's anniversary party at the Coconut Grove as a nod to his father, who championed the club and the Ambassador Hotel when they both opened in '21. Back in the heyday of silent films, M. K. Garten drank nights away with Rudolph Valentino, Douglas Fairbanks, and John Barrymore—all three stars long dead by 1958. (As part of his lore, the elder Mr. Garten took credit for having convinced Fairbanks to leave Broadway for Hollywood.) Soon Mr. Garten would join two of his chums, Valentino and Fairbanks, at Hollywood Forever Cemetery, and he looked it. Wizened, speechless, and milky-eyed, he sat propped up at the head table next to a pair of white frosted cakes. One shaped like a four, and the other like a zero.

People lined up to shout, "Congratulations!" at the old man. They were really saying, "Goodbye."

Xavier, Diahann, and I entered the party at 7:50 PM. The studio's vice president of publicity, Edmund Woodham, noted the time next to Xavier's and Diahann's names on his clipboard. His PR minions were stationed by every exit to dissuade any of the young stars from leaving before Lowell's speech and the cake cutting, which were scheduled for 9:30.

Skyline fined actors under contract for failure to meet public appearance obligations. Uncooperative stars could also be denied plum roles or assigned a supporting part in arduous shoots for a picture like *The Wizard of Oz* (1939), in which the actors cast as Dorothy's dearest friends and main enemy suffered in cumbersome costumes and through daily applications of pancake makeup. To avoid the studio's punishments, I needed to sneak Xavier and Diahann past its zealous enforcers.

Diahann was itching to leave upon arrival, but Xavier began to think differently once he saw what segment of the Hollywood population prevailed among the seven hundred guests. It wasn't big stars, because the likes of John Wayne, Marilyn Monroe, Jimmy Stewart, Audrey Hepburn, Frank Sinatra, and Jayne Mansfield got away with sending gifts, well-wishes, and their regrets that they could not attend. Most of the guests belonged to the silent movie era.

Xavier nudged Diahann. "See that woman in the mink shawl? That's Vilma Bánky."

"Who?" Diahann asked.

"She was a goddess of silent film. *The Night of Love* with Ronald Colman. *The Magic Flame* with Ronald Colman. And the one where she falls in love with a man building a dam to divert the Colorado River and there's a huge flood that—"

"With Ronald Colman," she teased.

"Yes, missy, with him again. They were paired like Tracy and Hepburn."

Xavier pulled out a red-backed chair for Diahann, and the three of us settled into a table for four on the outskirts of the ballroom. An all-white, seven-piece swing band played without zest from the stage. Diahann observed Vilma, who waited in the receiving line to greet Messrs. Garten, father and son.

Wearing a yellow, sleeveless evening dress and her mink from the 1930s, the former leading lady hadn't made a picture in a quarter century. Her career ended when talkies came into vogue and her thick Hungarian accent rendered her unemployable. During her prime, Vilma starred in two successful Skyline silent films: 1924's *Darling of the Riviera* and 1927's *East of Orange Rock Mountain*. I assessed her under the soft lights of the Coconut Grove. She was in her late fifties, her black hair was swept into a tight ballerina bun, and her bearing was elegant.

Diahann said, "She's a stunner for an older woman. She dyes her hair too dark, but she's kept her figure, and her eyebrows and mouth are perfection."

"I can't believe I'm in the same room with her," Xavier gushed while lighting a cigarette.

"You watched her from the rooftop?" I asked, even though I knew the answer.

"Yeah. Thursday nights at Merv's Drive-In, they'd run the silent flicks for half price. But I wouldn't pay—'cause there was no need, since I could see the screen just fine sitting out on Miss Campbell's roof and the title cards were giant enough to read."

The three of us laughed at Xavier's fond childhood memory. He didn't have many. His life story, after it was condensed, sanitized, and fabricated by Edmund Woodham and his ilk, had only a fleeting reference to his upbringing in Gary, Indiana: *Xavier was orphaned at a young age before being raised by a loving aunt*. The reality was starker.

When Xavier was six, his father was robbed and stabbed to death leaving a pool hall late one night. The murderer was never found. At the age of eight, Xavier lost his mother. She died on the job along with seven other women in a fire at a food-packing plant. Upon his mother's passing, no relatives stepped forward to claim him.

Xavier was moved into the Blair Orphanage for Boys, where he racked up quite a record for breaking curfew, fighting other boys, and attempting to run away. At fifteen, he landed a job on the assembly line making televisions for DuMont Labs. With his wages, Xavier qualified for release from the boys' orphanage and rented a room at a boardinghouse run by Peggy Campbell. She doted on him, baking him pastries and cakes for free.

Diahann's attention drifted to Vilma once more. "What do you think she's doing here?"

"Taking a bow," Xavier said. "I read Skyline purchased the land for the studio lot off the profits of her first film with them." He turned to me. "What was it called?"

"*Darling of the Riviera.*"

"Right. She should have a chair at the head table."

"But she doesn't," Diahann countered. "She's a has-been I'd never heard of. Only movie fanatics like you two remember her or her work. She didn't come expecting flowers."

I asked, "Why did she, then?"

"Same reason girls stand outside the gates with their headshots and résumés in hand. She's an out-of-work actress looking for an opportunity."

"She wouldn't," Xavier blurted. "She'd have her pride. She was right up there with Garbo."

"But Garbo made the jump." Diahann crossed her arms in front of her chest the way she did when she was sure of herself. "I'm telling you, Mrs. Bánky painted her face and put on her best dress. She is presenting herself."

If true, she wasn't the only one. The agents, managers, actors, and actresses of yesteryear twisted their spines to preen and grovel before Lowell and M. K. Garten. They mentioned past glories and pitched stalled projects. Lowell listened and nodded. M. K. recognized no one.

I stood beside Xavier when he and Diahann joined the tail of the receiving line. She cursed under her breath about how slowly the procession moved. Xavier shuffled along in awe of the original stars in the Hollywood firmament.

As we inched forward, he'd whisper in my ear, "It's Bessie Love. . . . That's Clara Bow by the bandstand. . . . See him with the pipe. He was Richard Barthelmess. . . . Over there. Hurts to see what's become of Louise Brooks. . . . My god, look—Harold Lloyd. He made me laugh harder than Chaplin."

Yet it was the vixen who enchanted Ronald Colman from movie to movie that led Xavier to tell Diahann, "Hold my spot."

"Where are you going?"

"I'ma have a word with Vilma Bánky."

"Zay-vee, please."

"I'll never get the chance again, and she's heading for the door."

"She's likely to think you're a waiter."

"All the same, give me a minute."

Xavier made a beeline for Vilma. I followed behind him, maintaining a respectable distance as he introduced himself to the flattered ex-star. She smiled and cradled his hand in hers. Xavier stooped to make eye contact with her. He was her last true fan. They spoke for a few minutes. I couldn't make out exactly what they were saying, but from what I could overhear, Vilma would not be mounting a comeback. Her Hungarian accent was still too thick for the movie business.

Xavier and I resumed our places in line, and Diahann asked, "Did she dazzle you?"

"She was shocked anyone our age had seen her films. She wondered if I'd seen her in *The Awakening*."

"Had you?"

"No, never even heard of it."

"She said Victor Fleming directed her in it. She thinks it's her best work, and she's hoping there's a print somewhere in the country. As it is, the film is considered lost."

Diahann covered her mouth with her hand. "That's horrible. See, these studios can be so careless with our work. They buy a picture, sell a picture, and let a picture rot. Her best work. Gone because a bean counter didn't want to spend the company's money to preserve it properly."

Xavier rubbed her shoulder. "You're more fired up than she was, missy. Vilma seemed resigned to fading away. That's why my recognizing her sent her over the moon."

"I disagree," Diahann said.

"She looked genuinely happy," I insisted.

"Not with that part. I'm sure our Zay-vee lifted her heart. I don't think any performer is ever resigned with fading away. We give too much to earn our positions to be sanguine when it slips from our fingers."

Xavier attempted to argue. "What about—"

"Garbo? You're gonna toss out Garbo." Diahann scoffed. "Stage fright brought the curtain down on her. If she could manage her nerves, she'd still act."

"She's a recluse," he countered.

"Not hardly. She plays peekaboo with photographers all over the world."

Xavier laughed and conceded, which was the best way to settle a disagreement with Diahann. She took him by the arm and rested her head against him. We were nearing Lowell and his father.

Diahann batted her eyes at me. "Have you hammered out how you're gonna spring us?"

"Yes, and I think you'll enjoy my idea."

"Do tell."

"Let's get through this first."

The swing band was doing injustice to "Strings of Pearls" when we were called forward for our audience with the Skyline founder and heir. A studio photographer was positioned off to the side to capture the encounters. I made sure to stand out of frame.

Upon closer inspection, M. K. Garten had been dressed in a brown three-piece suit that was several sizes too big, and his left hand was curled into an unnatural approximation of a fist. Lowell wore a black tuxedo with dark boots to bring his height up to six feet. His chestnut-blond hair owed inspiration to James Dean: long and wavy and a tad unruly on top, but neat and combed back along the sides. Although carrying a slight paunch, Lowell balanced the staunch image of a studio boss with the vitality of a modern man.

"Congratulations!" Diahann beamed.

Lowell kissed her on the cheek. "Glamorous as ever. How is the shoot going?"

"Wonderful," she reported. "Mrs. Scott's a dream. Shame she wasn't invited to be with us tonight, seeing as you are short on Black talent. I've counted only Xavier and myself." Over her shoulder, she tossed an aside to me: "No offense, Aaron."

I took her point. Not counting stung a little, nonetheless.

Lowell bristled. "Diahann, you know Hazel's difficulties with HUAC and Congressman Powell make her a tricky photo partner. Besides, I climbed out on a limb no one else would when I put her at number one on the call sheet."

"That is appreciated, Lowell. But it doesn't explain why Xavier and I are the only colored stars at your party."

"Sidney's tied up doing publicity for *The Defiant Ones*."

"I didn't ask about him. And there are plenty of others who could be here."

"Conflicts and excuses. I did my best. Sammy swore he'd try to stop by and sing a number before the night's out."

"Goodie," she said. "You'll be up to three Negroes."

"You're impossible." He kissed her on the cheek again and ushered her aside. "Xavier!"

"Congratulations, Mr. Garten." He and Lowell squared off like boxers before breaking the stance and shaking hands.

"You look like you're enjoying yourself."

"I met the film starlet that lit the fuse to my stick of dynamite when I was a boy."

Lowell guffawed. "Good heavens. Who is she?"

"Vilma Bánky."

"You're pulling my leg."

"Not at all."

Lowell scratched his chin and asked, "You think anyone would pay to see her these days?"

A loyal devotee, Xavier said, "I do. She's captivating. She'll never lose that."

After Xavier and Diahann concluded their face time with Lowell, we returned to our table. Xavier saw the comedian Ed Wynn entering the ballroom and wanted to go speak with the enduring vaudevillian. Diahann refused to be detained any longer.

"Let's break out now," she said.

"Go over near Edmund Woodham," I instructed Diahann, "and faint. Xavier and I will be right there to tend to you, and we'll help you walk out and get you home. I'll explain that you didn't eat enough and you're working too—"

"Wait," Diahann said, "you expect me to faint—in this dress, on that floor."

I assured her, "Yes, trust me, it'll work. They won't want a scene. They'll want us to make sure you're well. You might even get tomorrow off."

"This is unseemly and ridiculous."

I confided, "I worked with Debbie Reynolds on a picture. She does it all the time to get out of jams. It never fails."

Lips pursed, Diahann was not going to faint for me, but Xavier knew how to get her in action.

He said, "We can think of something else, if you don't feel you can play it convincingly."

9

COSTLY GAME

A limo awaited Horace and me on the tarmac at a private airport in Santa Monica. Our driver, Tobias, was a baby-faced Black man. He took our bags and told us to help ourselves to the limo's minibar. Horace polished off a tiny bottle of scotch. I drank a small ginger ale. Horace was giddy with excitement, and his mood made him playful to the point of acting juvenile.

In the back of the limo, he kept ribbing me and whispered, "Ask Tobias if he wants to help us unpack."

"Quit it," I said. "Nothing's changed. We can't be obvious."

Horace put an arm around my shoulders. "Relax. This ain't the navy. It's California."

I wasn't convinced the distinction would protect us. We were living on Skyline's dime, which meant M. K. Garten held the purse strings. Far as I was concerned, what the white man giveth, the white man can taketh away. One slip, and we could kiss goodbye our room and board, our chauffeured car, and Horace's $325 weekly salary. (As his business manager, I received $75 a week from him.)

The drive across Santa Monica to the studio lot took less than ten minutes. Horace and I lightly punched and poked each other like boys roughhousing. Tobias paid us no mind. I rolled down my window when I spotted the Garten Watchtower. Its white stones contrasted against the cloudless blue sky. That was when it sank in for me: Horace and I were entering the Dream Factory.

We were waved through the security post at the front gates, and the limo snaked past office buildings and soundstages, making tight turns on the narrow streets and stopping to let crew members pass. We reached a cul-de-sac of bungalows in the northwest corner of the 120-acre studio lot, and I gasped when I saw Ruby Dee exiting a yellow bungalow. I nudged Horace, and he saw her, too, before she hopped on a golf cart and was spirited away.

"She's an itty-bitty thing," I said.

"Maybe she'll play my girl, too."

In Eagle-Lion Films' *The Jackie Robinson Story* (1950), Ruby Dee portrayed the baseball great's wife, Rae Robinson. I wondered what girl Horace had in mind for Ruby Dee to play. I didn't want to spoil the moment by asking.

Tobias did bring our bags into the lime-green Fairbanks bungalow. We unpacked them ourselves. Our new digs came with a fully stocked kitchen, two bathrooms, and two bedrooms. Every touch, from the furniture to the fluffy towels, was first-rate.

On the kitchen island, there was a large bucket filled with ice and a dozen bottles of beer. Attached was a note from M. K. Garten: *Welcome to the family, boys. Rest up, Horace. We're going to work hard to turn your life story into a sensational picture. When the world sees it, Jackie Robinson is going to be jealous of you.*

Horace shook up a beer bottle and opened it, spraying me with the fizz as he whooped and hollered. M. K.'s note spelled out Horace's Hollywood wish. He'd star in his biographical movie just as Jackie Robinson had in his. A stipulation in Horace's Skyline deal was that he be given a screen test.

Soaked with beer suds and needing to refresh from the flight, I went to take a shower. I let the water rain down on the top of my bowed head and baptize me in its heat and steam. Breathing through my mouth, I closed my eyes and lost track of time.

Horace joined me in the shower stall, but I didn't register his presence until he put his hands on my hips. He pulled my body against his, making his intentions clear, and my hands worked the bar of shea butter soap into a lather. Then I reached behind me to stroke him. I bent forward to line him up, and I began to press back. I gritted my teeth to bear the initial pain, but Horace stopped me.

He clung to me, kissed me behind the ear, and said, "We ain't got to hurry."

Those five words struck me like a revelation. The sex between us had been nothing if not hurried. Naturally, there had been the need to act fast to avoid detection on the ship, but if I'm being honest, I was also turned on by the way we rushed, because it felt intoxicating to be taken by a man so hungry for me that he couldn't wait to fully undress.

Our shared impatience spoke to the relief we gave each other during sex. Cursing and brutish, Horace pinned me against walls and thrusted into me like he was possessed, and I matched his frantic rhythm. If sex between two men could run another course, we didn't have the luxury or the inclination to explore it.

Until now. I turned around and faced Horace. We kissed, testing every variation of technique and intensity. I learned him anew. I took the time to not only taste him but to savor him. We stayed in that shower until we used up the last of the hot water.

Once we toweled off, Horace and I fell into the king-size bed. My head rested on a plump pillow encased in silk. Horace was on top of me, and sheets made of Egyptian cotton draped over his shoulders. We made love and dozed off with our limbs intertwined.

Thanks to the studio boss, we were given three days to acclimate before Horace's initial meeting with the writers. We ordered our meals from the commissary, and waiters delivered the food to our bungalow door on silver trays and under silver domes. We roamed the lot at our leisure.

There was an outdoor set for westerns, with pioneer houses, a general store, a saloon, and a white clapboard church; each one was nothing more than a façade. We swam in a private saltwater pool reserved for stars, and once, Esther Williams joined us for a dip. Outside Stage 15, I strolled past nuns and showgirls lounging in beach chairs, trading dirty jokes, and smoking up a storm until lighting was ready for the next setup. Those early days did a number on me. I confused them with real life. I forgot that the creative madness and bubbly frivolity were the by-product of a hard-nosed business.

Horace began meeting with the studio's writers in the Farnham Building. He'd arrive at 10:00 AM on the dot as instructed. The writers straggled into the office sometime between a quarter past ten and noon, which is when they collectively took a one-hour lunch break. Two or three of them each day called out sick. What a sorry sight these writers were. I'd never laid eyes on white men so weathered by time, booze, cigarettes, and circumstances. There was a dozen of them, and not a single one of them knew how to stand tall with his shoulders back or how to sustain eye contact.

I sat alongside Horace for the first week to help him recall names and dates about his military service. Among whichever writers turned up during the workday sessions, one or two would take the lead and interrogate Horace while he sat in their bullpen. Six to seven hours a day, five days a week, for nine weeks in the first cycle of the contract. The collective haze of their unfiltered Dunhills and Pall Malls would grow thicker as they prodded him to go into more detail about whatever memories they felt might shape a script.

Watching Horace recall the most painful moments of his life and then sit silently as the writers debated the quality of the material was maddening. Should the picture begin with the death of his father or with the time his aunt took him to the county fair to watch the first air show he'd ever witnessed? How many minutes should be spent depicting the poverty in his childhood? Maybe that entire part of his life could be jettisoned, and the film could open with him enlisting. To the writers, this was shoptalk. To Horace, this was torture. His most intimate and sensitive memories were being handled like scraps that were going to be stitched into a quilt if they could first prove they belonged in the design.

There was only one significant slice of his past that Horace withheld: his mother's gift for reading the cowrie shells and her predictions about his life and legacy. I thought it was a mistake to keep these facts from the writers. They were desperate for a template, and I'd enjoyed Claude Rains in *The Clairvoyant* (1935) and knew that a fortune teller angle could help draw the moviegoers into the story. Once and only once, I voiced this opinion to Horace while we sat alone in the men's sauna at the private Skyline gym.

"If it doesn't work, then it doesn't work," I reasoned, "but at least let the writers mull it over."

He tried to dismiss me with a harsh, "Nah."

"Why are you so set against it? You've already told them all kinds of awful, upsetting things. This is beautiful. Your mama's been proven right."

"They're not gonna let it stay beautiful. I'm on to them." He used a ladle to pour water onto the rocks. "I see how they twist what I tell them. They'll have my mama shakin' her ass, dancin' the black bottom in a dirt hut. Drums beatin' while she talks gibberish in tongues. I couldn't stomach it." Horace stood up, tightened his towel around his waist, and exited the sauna.

A month into the deal, Horace soured on his sessions with the writers, and he told me to stop attending them altogether. He called it a waste of my time, but that wasn't why he wanted me nowhere around. His composure was becoming harder for him to maintain. As the writers pressed him for more specifics about the loss of his parents, they cornered Horace into confessing that his mother probably committed suicide. He left the room to weep. The writers attempted to plumb the patriotic depths of his time in the navy, and instead, Horace's temper flared when discussing the cruel hazing he took during pilot training. They wanted him to crow about the women he'd bedded, and he got bashful when describing the early dalliances with sweethearts named Louzelma and Harmony. I'd never heard of either woman before we reached Hollywood, and Horace wasn't keen on discussing them with me around.

Five weeks into our stay in a Skyline bungalow on the studio lot, and the novelty that captivated us upon arrival now felt like an elaborate tourist trap. It turned out that the studio's private saltwater pool was manufactured by the kitchen staff, who occasionally oversalted the concoction, making it a gritty gruel that clung to my skin as I swam in the heat. The lemons and oranges in the trees on the lot grew plump but never quite ripe. When I cut them open, more often than not, I was greeted by spider mites.

As the summer temperature climbed, Horace's sessions with the screenwriters continued to show no signs of promise. *The story's not taking shape* became the writers' refrain. Horace started drinking with the writers before lunch. By the time he returned to me, he needed a nap, and he woke up groggy, claiming that he'd done all the talking he could stand in a day.

One afternoon, a couple of writers came to our bungalow to question me about Horace's service. I told them about the time he flew out of range, and I stood on deck keeping watch in accordance with navy tradition. I described how the entire crew cheered his safe return. The following day, the writers followed up with Horace about the story. He'd never mentioned the incident to them.

Horace stormed into our bungalow furious with me. I'd betrayed his confidence. I had no right to talk behind his back. I blocked out much of what he said because it was so hurtful and ugly. What stuck were my marching orders: "Get out of my face before I put you through a wall."

I went to the commissary and used the courtesy telephone to call the studio's transportation department. I inquired if Tobias was on duty. Ten minutes later, Tobias was chauffeuring me in a silver Chrysler Windsor.

"Where to?" he asked.

"This is your city. You tell me where I can go unwind."

He took me to Dynamite Jackson's, a jazzy cocktail lounge on Central Avenue. The owner, Ernest Bendy, was an ex–heavyweight champion of California, and he bestowed his ring name onto his joint. He was Black, tall, imposing, and a soft touch. Dynamite just wanted everyone to have a good time, and he put rounds on the house and he paid musicians top dollar to keep the crowds smiling. I don't know how he stayed in business.

I had to squeeze through the packed lounge until I secured a seat on a stool against the mirrored back wall. Onstage, Ben Webster was wailing on the sax with Oscar Peterson on piano, Harry "Sweets" Edison on the trumpet, and William Douglass holding it down on drums. A devilishly attractive waiter in a black jacket and bow tie took my drink order and subsequently brought me a strong old-fashioned.

At a table toward the front, Dinah Washington and Redd Foxx were drinking and taking in the show. In the navy, I'd listened to her tunes over Armed Forces Radio, and I'd laughed hard at his party records when they were smuggled onto the carrier. I couldn't stop staring at them at first. Then I noticed that no one else was. Dinah and Redd were Black stars, and among their people, they were allowed to be human. I paid them the same respect, and my eyes focused on the band.

I downed two more drinks and left around midnight. Tobias drove me home. We didn't talk much, but I noticed him using the rearview mirror to eye me. He turned away bashfully when he realized that I'd caught him. He wasn't my type. Too boyish for me. But I got a charge from discovering that I was fascinating to him. I tipped him a dollar once he let me out on the lot.

When I entered the bungalow, the door to the bedroom that I'd been sharing with Horace was closed. I slept in the second bedroom. The next morning, Horace and I spoke like coworkers. He didn't ask me about my night.

I went out to Dynamite Jackson's several more nights that week. Dinah Washington wasn't there, but I did spot Sarah Vaughan, Dick Gregory, Sugar Ray Robinson, and even the Brown Bomber, Joe Louis. Redd was there every night.

Tobias chauffeured me to and fro. On the rides back to Skyline, I was tipsy if not flat-out drunk. I was angry at Horace, and the Dynamite waiters revved me up sexually. Still, I had no excuse to toy with that young man. But I did. Night after night, Tobias spied on me in the back seat, where I slumped over, feigned sleep, and groped my erection outlined in my pants. Through the slits of my eyes, I watched Tobias struggle to breathe and drive simultaneously. It was a pointless and costly game.

During lunch the following Monday, I was eating alone in the commissary when a squat white man in his late forties helped himself to the chair across the table from me.

"Mr. Aaron Toussaint, I'm Callum McManus, head of security and studio affairs."

"Have I done something?" I asked.

"No, but I'd like you to." He placed a hundred-dollar bill on the table and slid it over to me. "You enjoy Dynamite Jackson's. Go live it up on Skyline and pocket the change."

I let the money lie on the table. "And in exchange . . ."

"Tell me what Redd Foxx gets up to."

Callum explained that Redd's representatives were positioning him to be a comedic movie star, and they were insisting that his raunchy stand-up persona was merely an act. The real Redd was a wholesome family man of unimpeachable character. Callum wanted to verify whether this was true, but every one of his security agents was white and couldn't slip unnoticed into Dynamite Jackson's or any of the other Black establishments along Central Avenue that Redd might visit.

"Can you be my eyes and ears? You don't have to start nothin' or stop nothin'. Simply tell me what you witness. Hell, you'll be there anyway. Let the studio pick up the tab."

Made sense to me. I saw no harm in it. I pocketed the hundred.

10

BEEHIVE

I sat behind the steering wheel while Xavier walked Diahann to the door of her upscale apartment building on Wilshire Boulevard. They kissed goodbye, and she warned us not to get into too much mischief. Afterward, I drove Xavier to his first-floor apartment in Westwood. He went inside and changed out of his suit and into a skintight pair of dark blue jeans, a black T-shirt, and sneakers. I turned off my headlights and slowly steered my Ford Thunderbird into the alley behind Xavier's unit. He crept out his back door and climbed into my car.

We drove to his favorite sex spot, one that he had introduced me to: Griffith Park. We went once or twice a week, avoiding the high-traffic nights on Friday and Saturday. Our routine had no kinks in it. I was prepared for all contingencies.

These excursions forced an intimacy upon us. It was a long drive from Westwood in those years before the expansion of the Ventura Freeway. Xavier passed the miles trying to pry open my private life. My tone was friendly, my answers succinct.

He once inquired if Kimberly and I had weekend plans, and I told him, "We're hosting a dinner party on Saturday for some of our church friends." No elaboration.

When he asked me what became of Lieutenant Horace Dixon, I said, "He's all right. He's a test pilot outside of Chicago." No emotion.

I believed it vital that I keep a buffer between Xavier and me. If I allowed him to get too familiar, then he would be able to seduce me emotionally (and possibly physically), and if he seduced me, he would be able to manipulate me, and if he could manipulate me, my judgment would be shot during a crisis when I'd have to oppose him or even deceive him for his own good.

Opening up about my wife or especially my ex-lover felt dangerous. Talk about Horace could naturally lead to what I desire in men, and to my discomfort, Xavier would become aware of how many boxes he ticked off. I was determined to hold the line. As it stood, my feelings for Xavier ran hotter than what was ideal.

So, I upheld my end of our conversation by mentioning old movies. Xavier and I were both what the French called *cinéphiles*. It wasn't a question of whether we'd heard of a flick. That was too easy. We tested each other on what year a picture was released, by which studio, and who was the third lead. As he demonstrated at Skyline's anniversary party, Xavier's expertise was silent films. I had him beat when it came to Oscar-winning and -nominated movies.

Despite my efforts to keep our discussions clean, whenever we got within a few miles of the park, Xavier began talking about his sex life. With a fair amount of justification, he was proud of his conquests, and if he could astonish me with the details, that was a sweet bonus for him. Meanwhile, I did everything in my power to act unmoved by his escapades—even though I lived vicariously through his exploits and often committed his words to memory for replays in my shower.

The scene at Griffith Park has been derided as a senseless free-for-all of men fucking men in the woods with abandon. The reality was quite different and impressive. The whole operation possessed defensive layers like a beehive.

Finding the cruising zone was the opening test. There weren't a lot of streetlamps in Griffith Park. I never would have made my way to the correct spot with my headlights off if Xavier hadn't guided me, and he wouldn't have been able to show me if he hadn't been led there by another gay man. In this way, all the homos in the park could be mapped together in a queer family tree. Branch after branch taking initiate by initiate into the past until you reached the founding faggots of the scene.

Xavier learned the lay of the land from none other than Sal Mineo. Sal, if asked, probably won't bother to deny it. He's a maverick by nature. The Italian pretty boy made his name as a fey teenage boy lusting over James Dean in *Rebel Without a Cause* (1955), and no one in the business thought he was doing that much acting.

On a typical night, we'd snake along Vermont Avenue into Griffith Park and glide into the secret dirt lot. At least half a dozen cars would already be parked. A score of bicycles would be abandoned on their sides in the grass. My first night on the scene, it appeared haphazard, but there was an order at work.

After a few visits, I watched the others at play and caught on that the men who wanted car sex sat behind their steering wheels, waiting to be approached by the male prostitutes who dotted the perimeter of the woods. This was the earliest level of give-and-take. Johns, who insisted on doing the deed in their vehicles, had to negotiate through their rolled-down windows. Most pros preferred to perform behind trees or on picnic tables, because they didn't want to get trapped in a car with a john who could get violent and drive off with them. Johns dreaded such setups in the open, because they were left more likely to have their jollies interrupted by a policeman's flashlight.

Money and familiarity dictated the terms. A john willing to pay double could score in his car. Those short on cash took their chances on the edge of the woods. The exceptions were the regulars, who brought trinkets and fast food for their favorite hustlers and proved as repeat customers that they could be trusted. Regulars earned the privilege of car service.

What I came to respect was that either by original design or through trial and error, the gay men in the park had arranged themselves into a two-way protection system. It was rather genius. Before he came with me, Xavier had been present for a police raid, and he explained how the officers tipped off their approach to johns and pros in the dirt lot, just by using the headlights on their squad cars.

The men along the tree line decoupled when the high beams sliced through the dark before reaching the secret turn. Only cops and newbies would do such a thing, and I imagined newbies only did it once. The hustlers would certainly castigate the uninitiated for being ignorant of the customs and for panicking the scene.

As the cops rolled into the dirt lot, Xavier said the pros scattered. Some took off on their bicycles. Others hid in the woods. The fleeing hustlers oinked and whistled loudly as they vanished. The piercing noise traveled across the park, warning men deep in the woods and beyond the hiking trails. The use of open-air communication made it next to impossible for the police to catch men in the act of fornicating with other men.

Xavier ran to the hiking trail and raced to high ground, where he watched the cops hassle johns in the dirt lot. To his amusement, several of the experienced johns got out of their vehicles, popped opened their trunks, and showed that they had telescopes with them. He was confused by the coincidence until he realized the telescopes were meant to corroborate a shared excuse. For when the cops questioned these men as to why they were in the park in the middle of the night, there was only one sensible answer: *I came to stargaze*. The police issued several tickets for loitering, then left.

The night of the anniversary party, I parked my car away from the pack as usual. I didn't want Xavier mixed up in that meat market, because hustlers remembered faces, attempted to establish relationships, and sold their stories to tabloid reporters for hot meals and loose change.

I got out of the car to conduct my sweep, leaving Xavier to sit tight and smoke cigarettes. I ignored the furtive glances from the johns and the hissing from the pros as I crossed the first line of trees and reached the official hiking trail. I turned right walking along the path uphill for thirty yards. Then I went left, leaving the trail and descending a rather steep, rocky slope. Once I got to flat land again, the woods were dense, and weaving through them was like making my way through a maze with multiple offshoots and dead ends.

This maze belonged to the masturbators, who silently roamed the grounds alone or paired off in groups of two or three. Occasionally, they would circle up if a show pony of a man presented a prized endowment. I wandered the maze until I was confident I'd seen every participant.

Then I'd pass through the other side of the maze into a clearing that led to the jagged base of Mount Hollywood. If a man stuck close to the mountain, no one on the trails above could see him or what he was doing with partners in the folds along the base. In that area, I received my share of passes, some quite aggressive. But I wasn't there to engage.

I was looking at faces, seeing if I recognized anyone connected to the movie business. Once, I saw a cowboy star's stunt double giving a blow job in the maze. Another time, a costume director shoved me aside to get in on an orgy against Mount Hollywood. I'd also seen actors, studio executives, and a producer or two. In such cases, it was Xavier's choice to wait until the threat left the park or just go home. Usually, he'd give it an hour to see if he could have his turn.

I was also on the lookout for Black men. I felt that they were all but certain to recognize Xavier as a star and would be likely to tell someone about the encounter. Enough anonymous homosexuals singing the same tune would eventually catch the attention of a gossipmonger, and fighting rumors stirred up by a faceless horde was always a losing game. Especially when the rumors were true.

Xavier strongly disagreed with my assessment of the threat. He believed Black gay men would feel obligated to protect him. They were brothers, and they were brothers. The two bonds made betrayal a remote possibility, and Xavier cited my loyalty to him as evidence of his wider faith.

I told him that he was being too trusting, and this was an area in which I imposed restrictions on him. I simply refused to budge on this point. If other Black men were in the park, Xavier could not go into the park. He could wait them out or leave. He grumbled, but my rule prevailed. Xavier took solace in the fact that cruising in the woods wasn't popular among Black queers. They tended to congregate in small mob-owned bars and twenty-four-hour coffee shops.

I finished my sweep in under half an hour and gave Xavier the green light. He walked briskly. His height attracted attention, but his color turned off more than half the men. White men dominated the scene, and gay white men generally held the same racist prejudices as straight white men so that they'd have something in common to trade on when they were passing in mixed company. I trailed behind Xavier.

Mount Hollywood was his destination, but first he primed the unseen crowd. He paused in the clearing, removed his T-shirt, and squeezed part of it into the back of his jeans—not that there was much room between his flesh and the denim. The men by the mountain and in the maze sized him up, and the bold ones stepped forward into the clearing in the hopes of being the first to touch him that night. Xavier got to have his pick.

I held my position on the edge of the maze. Xavier disappeared into the base of the mountain. I remained on high alert while Xavier enjoyed himself. A Mexican bodybuilder in a tank top and gym shorts approached me. I wagged my finger to decline. He lowered his shorts to show me what I'd be missing out on, but my answer didn't change. Several white men walking a loop through the maze circled by a couple of times, paying me no mind. A curly-haired brunette kept a respectful distance and jerked off while eyeing me. I didn't see how I could object to that. He wasn't touching me, and I was on his turf.

I was also flattered and frankly turned on. The entire environment had a hedonistic pulse that got mine racing. Just knowing that sex was unrestrained in an assortment of flavors was like an aphrodisiac.

I had wedding vows and professional standards restricting me, but I discovered pleasure in not partaking since, in the park, my abstinence was the taboo. Maintaining it was my minor fetish.

It was 11:30 PM when I heard Xavier's distinct moans echo off the base of the mountain and ring across the clearing. We'd be leaving soon. I'd counted more than three dozen men throughout the park. An average night. Nothing special.

"Basher!" came a scream from the base of the mountain. "Basher! Gray shirt! Blue cap!"

I was relieved that the voice wasn't Xavier's. I watched the clearing, and a sandy-haired white boy in his mid-twenties came sprinting through the clearing. His chest and arms were stacked, but he had pencil legs. He plucked the blue baseball hat off his head and threw it into the grass, a move that drew attention to him. Two, four, seven men gave chase from the shadows of the mountain. One of the men running in pursuit of the basher was Xavier. I ran from the edge of the maze into the clearing.

The basher's pencil legs gave their all, but Xavier and a young white guy with a buzz cut were gaining on him fast. The basher began to run in an evasive zigzag and pleaded, "I'll give it back!" He tossed the wallet he'd stolen from the gay man he'd assaulted.

There was no deal to be made. The buzz cut guy leapt and caught hold of the basher's left calf, bringing him down onto all fours. Xavier pounced onto the basher's back, knocking him flat. Within seconds, three other men piled on top of the crook. I had never seen gay men fight like this. Wasn't nothing pansy about it. They beat the pulp out of that basher. Xavier landed a few punches before I dragged him away.

"Get off me," he said.

I didn't let him stop moving as we entered the maze. "You caught him. They're beating his ass. We're going."

He yanked his arm free but hurried alongside me to the car. We both smoked Old Golds as I pulled out of the dirt lot with the headlights off.

I didn't chew him out for getting involved in the fight. He'd acted on honorable instincts, and he didn't go too far.

Plus, I admired the instant solidarity on display in the clearing. I hadn't thought it possible. I'd seen small groups of homosexuals loaded into paddy wagons after bar raids. They'd hid their faces and gave no resistance. I'd seen gays cursed at and humiliated by drunk straight men on street corners, and not a single sodomite in the passing crowd ever stepped forward in their defense.

On our drive back to Westwood, I spoke first once the adrenaline in my veins died down. "Bad roll of the dice for that crook," I said. "He picked the one night a gang of scrappers was out cruising."

Xavier cocked his head at me. "He'd have caught that ass whoopin' any night. We're not gonna stand for abuse in our own house."

"What house? And who's 'we'?"

"In our bars or wherever we're gathered. Homophiles are going to rise up same as Negroes."

I scoffed. "Who told you that?"

"I thumb through more than scripts these days. I've read Kinsey, Murray, and Kepner. We're on the cusp of a new age."

Alfred Kinsey's last name rang a bell because his report on sex was notorious, but I had not yet heard of or read Pauli Murray's *States' Laws on Race and Color* or your work, Mr. Kepner, for *ONE Magazine*. Of course, I wasn't going to concede to Xavier that he had a more thorough political education than I did by asking who the hell you and Murray were. I didn't want to learn. I wanted him on the defensive.

"A new age," I prodded. "What's it supposed to look like?"

"It's simple. We quit pretending," he explained. "Just like we know whites are no better than Blacks, we stop acting like gays are any worse than straights. Shit, it'll be easier to deal with the gays, because we're already integrated with the straights in schools and at work. You ain't gotta bus homos nowhere. We're everywhere as it is. They just gotta accept what's already around them."

"Sounds dandy. Problem is politics aren't about right and wrong," I said. "It's all about power and gathering enough people to force a change. Now I can half see it for us Negroes. We got church leaders, we got NAACP lawyers, we got momentum. I don't think sissies have much in their corner."

"Why are you talking like you're not one of us?"

"Because for faggots, there is no *us*."

"How can you say that? You just saw us take action in the park! We can fight back!"

I didn't raise my voice to match his. "Beating up a wallet-snatcher is a far cry from changing how the country feels about cocksuckers and butt-fuckers. Ninety-something percent of the people in the world would stone every single faggot to death if they could. Believe me."

We drove a mile in silence.

Xavier couldn't let it go. "It'll take some years," he said. "All movements do. You can already see signs of it in Hollywood. Tony Perkins finally got himself a smash hit with *Psycho*, and Sal is gonna win trophies for *Exodus*."

"Sure, but neither of them is going to be a top-dollar draw like Cary Grant. And both of them better watch how much they let on that they're queer."

"You're missing the point." Xavier sighed. "Tony and Sal are what they are, and it isn't getting them blacklisted. It's a god-honest fact that our business can't operate without gay talent. Everyone knows it. So, we can drop the charade. We can let people be what they are."

"Do me one favor," I said.

"Name it."

"Let the white boys test the waters before you jump in."

Xavier shook his head and grinned. "Deal."

Reassured, I clicked on the radio and focused on the road. Xavier closed his eyes and fell asleep. I filed our conversation away in the back of my mind. It didn't seem momentous. I assumed the new age was idle talk.

11

EXIT CLAUSE

Hilarious as he was profane, Redd Foxx indulged in indecent habits that involved illicit substances and the flesh of painted women. He made no attempts to disguise his behavior despite the efforts of his representatives to repackage him as an entertainer who would appeal to straitlaced audiences. I shared what I witnessed with Callum, Skyline didn't offer Redd a role in a film, and I'd argue I didn't harm Redd's career one iota. He continued along his natural path, headlining in Vegas up and down the Strip with his brilliant, blue nightclub routine. Not everyone's meant to be a clean household name.

Callum was pleased with my work and asked me to attend Juanita Moore's church to "gather a sense of her." This was half a decade before the second making of *Imitation of Life* (1959), so Juanita was an unknown, and I declined. I hadn't gone out of my way to surveil Redd at Dynamite Jackson's and down Central Avenue. Church, however, wasn't a part of my Sundays, and I couldn't figure out how I'd square it with Horace that I suddenly wanted to start attending services.

Besides, in the sixth week of our stay, Horace took his screen test. He allowed me to walk him over to Stage 7, and I managed to loosen him up by reciting some of the jokes I overheard Redd tell his friends at the lounge. Horace didn't want me inside watching him during the screen test, and I understood.

I waited outside hoping that Horace's effortless charisma would shine through. When he was relaxed, he possessed command presence and sex appeal. And if Skyline could use him as a utility player in their lineup, then it would ease the pressure on turning his life story into a film. Maybe Horace could just portray soldiers and gunslingers in war movies and westerns.

My thoughts were interrupted when a group of animal trainers led five giraffes into Stage 11. I'd never seen a giraffe outside of a picture book or a movie, and to see them with my own eyes stunned me. Their height and beauty were overwhelming. I smiled at them like an elated child. Once the giraffes were loaded into the stage, I looked around and took in the bustle and traffic of the studio lot. The Hollywood spell had taken hold of me once more.

Horace walked out of his screen test happier than I'd seen him in weeks. It had gone great. Everyone said so. He'd felt confident. The lights and camera didn't intimidate him. I wanted to hug him but didn't.

"Congratulations, Lieutenant."

"Let's go out and tie one on," he said. "Take me to one of your nightspots."

It was an order I was glad to oblige. That night, I introduced Horace to Central Avenue. We downed our first rounds at Dynamite Jackson's, where the ex-champ recognized Horace and insisted we drink for free. Other patrons crowded Horace, eager to shake hands with the war hero. He'd never met his fans face-to-face, and he fed off their pride in him. Big Mama Thornton and doomed Johnny Ace were onstage that night and called Horace up to take a bow for his service.

A strapping longshoreman chatted me up, and on his invitation, Horace and I dropped in on a huge party at the Elks Temple. The hall was jumping, and Horace swing danced with dozens of women. I got out on the floor a few times, but I was content to see Horace living it up.

The longshoreman saw to it that my glass wasn't empty for long, and he peppered me with questions about the war in Korea and how I was acclimating to Los Angeles. Nothing of note was divulged. I got no sense that he was hitting on me. He was a nice-enough-looking fellow, but his name didn't register in my head. I was already forgetting him as Horace and I bid him good night and climbed into the back seat of the Chrysler.

Tobias was our chauffeur. He peeked at Horace and me in the rear-view mirror, and I glared at him. There'd be no more games. Problem was Horace was drunk and jovial. By the time we reached the Skyline gates, he'd wrung twenty-three-year-old Tobias's life story out of him, from his birth in El Paso to his joining the transportation department at the studio eleven months ago.

Horace unlocked the front door to our bungalow, and I was curious if our fun night out meant that we could share a bed again. Before I could open my mouth to ask, he grabbed my necktie and hauled me into the bedroom and began to undress me, tearing at my buttons and tugging at my sleeves.

He leveled an accusation. "You like that burly motherfucker sniffin' your ass."

"What?"

"Clyde the longshoreman."

"I didn't want nothing with him."

Having stripped my upper half bare, Horace unfastened my belt. "Funny that 'cause you was takin' drinks from him and makin' eyes at him."

"You took drinks off everyone."

"Yeah, everyone. You just took it from one man."

I couldn't read if Horace was mad at me. His voice was stern, but he was fondling me as he lowered my pants and underwear.

"All right, what if I did like him?" I dared. "What's it to you?"

"That's how you act when you go out?" He lifted me up and threw me onto the bed. "You make men sweet on you?"

Horace flipped me onto my belly and pinned me down. We'd stumbled into a new territory of foreplay. I egged him on, pretending to be enthralled with a guy who was utterly forgettable to me. Horace reclaimed me with a passion that I'd missed.

The next night, we ventured farther down Central Avenue and dropped in on the Bird in the Basket. Erroll Garner held court on piano. Horace basked in the adoration of Black civilians, and I searched for a man I could use to stoke Horace's jealousy and possessiveness. I talked to several men, but nothing of interest took hold. Still, Horace and I had a ball drinking on other people's dimes.

Shortly after 1:00 AM, Tobias was driving us to our temporary home. Intoxicated, Horace dozed off and his head slumped onto my shoulder, and he placed a hand on my thigh. I quickly nudged him off me and looked to see if Tobias had noticed. His eyes appeared to be on the road.

I roused Horace once we were on the lot, and he was talking dirty as we walked into our bungalow. One of the advantages of our accommodations was that late at night, only the security guards and stray cats walked the studio grounds. The guests in other bungalows were actors with predawn call times. We had relative privacy.

Horace had my shirt unbuttoned and his mouth on my neck when we heard a knock at our front door. I told him to stay in the bedroom while I sent whoever it was away. I left my dress shirt undone since I didn't think it would be suspicious that I'd been undressing for bed. I looked through the peephole, and there standing prettified was Tobias.

I opened the door. "We leave something in the car?"

He was breathing hard, and he didn't answer.

"You all right?" I asked.

In my peripheral, I saw Horace leaning against the bedroom doorframe. Tobias charged forward, pushing me onto my heels. I opened my mouth to speak, but he grabbed the side of my face and tongue kissed me. He tasted like peppermint. I didn't resist him. I thought for a second, given the turn in our dirty talk, that Horace might welcome the company. But he didn't want to make that fantasy real. Horace ripped us apart, shoving Tobias onto the floor.

He stood over the quaking young man. "You out your mind?"

Tobias pointed at me. "He been coaxin' me. Feelin' himself up and whatnot, and the two of yous was snugglin'—"

Horace smacked Tobias hard across the face, and it rattled me to see it.

"Only thing you need to know about me is I done killed men," Horace said. "Don't let me catch you talkin' about me or him."

"I wouldn't. I ain't."

"Get gone, faggot."

Tobias scurried out of our bungalow on his hands and knees. Horace slammed the door behind him. Then he turned and glared at me. My throat tightened, but I acted as if there wasn't a trace of fear in me.

"That boy's crazy," I said.

Horace took a step forward. "Was he now?"

"I wouldn't cross the street for him. You know what I like." I bowed my head as if I were submitting before a deity.

Horace walked over to me and brushed his thumb across my lips. "How'd he kiss?"

"Weak," I said.

He grinned, threw his arm around my shoulders, and led me to bed. He was dominant, and I fell into my role. Hours later, when he was asleep next to me, I found myself wide awake, haunted by the sound of the slap, the chill of Tobias's fear, and the ferocity of Horace's hatred. Without fully admitting it to myself, I recognized that I needed to protect my interests from the man lying next to me.

The next morning, while Horace was meeting with the writers, I opened a local bank account, deposited my off-the-books pay, and arranged for the funds in my military account to be transferred over. I took notice of rooms for rent in the weekly *California Eagle*. My bags weren't packed yet, but I'd be damned if I was going to find myself on my hands and knees on the wrong side of Horace's favor.

Two nights later, Horace and I attended Twentieth's party at the Dunbar Hotel. (Tobias was not our driver; he avoided us at all costs.) Part of the way through the bash, Horace discovered me out of sorts and scrambling to fasten my pants in the basement men's restroom, and I no longer had the presumption of innocence on my side. My stripes were showing. Thankfully, with a cool demeanor and some warm flattery, Xavier stopped Horace's suspicions from turning into anger. But when we got back to our bungalow, Horace didn't make a move to have sex with me. I thought, at the time, he was exhausted from all the socializing. Maybe he was preparing to cut ties, too.

At the end of the eighth week, we were invited to lunch with the almighty studio boss, M. K. Garten. We dined on the large terrace outside his office on the top floor of the Pober Building. The coastline glimmered along the horizon.

In his mid-sixties and fond of insidious power plays, Mr. Garten was a dapper man who sat under the shade of a royal-blue canopy while we baked in our seats under the naked sun. He made a show of having his manservant bring us water; there was ice in Mr. Garten's glass of water, unlike ours. He called us by our first names; we'd been instructed by his secretary to refer to him as *Mr. Garten*.

He didn't say much while we ate our salads. He encouraged Horace to tell him war stories, and he asked me about the nightlife I'd enjoyed among the stars. He nodded as we talked. Yet his eyes stayed vacant, and he laughed at none of our jokes.

I studied Mr. Garten from across the table. He was aging in a mold that he must have cast more than thirty years ago. He wore a vest, a starched collared shirt, and a wool suit that was all the rage during the Harding administration. His receding hair was slicked back and parted on the left, a style choice that I imagined hadn't changed since he landed upon it as a college student. The only difference, for the old man, was that his strands had thinned and gone from black to snow white. In total, the studio founder struck me as a proud man defiant to changes in the culture. He liked what he liked. He knew what he knew. Modernity wouldn't infect his thinking.

The temperature only got hotter during this lunch that lacked an agenda, or at least one we were aware of. Finally, Mr. Garten's eyes lit up as if he'd just noticed we were at the table with him. He cleared his throat, and with a thick Lower East Side, Manhattan, accent—which he tried to conceal by speaking in a whisper—he said, "We ain't gonna move forward," ignoring his *r*'s whenever he crossed one in a word.

Horace leaned in over his plate of poached salmon. "Move where?"

"With the picture."

I gripped the side of the table as if holding on to it would keep our dream from slipping away.

"Yeah, what about it?" Horace asked.

"There's no heartbreak. No setback. No story."

Unaccustomed with the prelude of defeat, Horace turned to me. "What's he sayin'?"

I couldn't look at him as I translated. "They're not going to make a movie based on your life."

"Bingo." Mr. Garten pointed at me and added, "Ya business manager gets it."

Horace got his back up. "Why the hell not?" he asked me before turning to the studio boss and asking even louder, "Why the hell not!"

"None of my story boys can crack it," Mr. Garten explained in a hush that was drowned out for a few moments by an airplane flying over the ocean. "Ya go from success to success. No dips."

Horace looked at me again.

"He's saying your life won't make for a good movie," I explained, "because you haven't been knocked on your ass. There's not enough struggle in your story."

"Horseshit." Horace swiped his cloth napkin off his lap and tossed it onto his plate. "Y'all wasn't listenin'. I told white boy after white boy about my upbringin'. A mob of crackers done lynched my daddy when I was knee-high. My mama lost her mind and killed herself, leaving me to go live with my sister. When I joined the navy, the white folks gave me hell up in there the second I said I wanted to fly a plane. I done nothin' but struggle in a white man's world."

"Can't sell tickets to a race picture," said Mr. Garten. "Now, let's say, if you'd overcome polio or gotten shot down during the war, that would sell."

I was taken aback. "If he'd gotten shot down, he'd be a dead war hero."

Mr. Garten whispered, "I could sell that, too."

Horace poked the table with his index finger. "What about my money? I signed a six-month contract."

"The contract includes an exit clause after nine weeks," said the studio boss. "We're exercising the clause. You'll be paid through next Friday."

"What about my screen test?" Horace pleaded.

Mr. Garten shrugged. "It wasn't up to par."

It wasn't a vicious criticism, and it wasn't delivered with venom, but Horace couldn't fathom why it was being directed at him. He'd proved himself exceptional in the navy during war, and he'd spent the last several years lauded as a national hero and pursued by the titans of Hollywood. This casual dismissal must have been a mistake. Yet he'd heard the old man clearly.

"You can also have your life back," said Mr. Garten.

"What does that mean?" I asked. "How does he get his life back?"

"The rights. His life rights. We're releasing our hold. He can sell them to another studio."

The heat was stultifying, the light reflecting off the ocean caused a glare, the studio boss drank his ice water in the shade, and there weren't any counterpoints worth screaming. We were vanquished. Horace stood up and walked away from the table.

Mr. Garten set his gaze upon me. "If you want to eat the rest, take it with you."

I got up and went after Horace. I reached the elevators and saw him inside one as the doors closed. He saw me, too, and he made no attempt to hold the elevator for me.

Horace got to the bungalow first, and he was already packing his two suitcases when I entered the bedroom. I wanted to reassure him that he'd done nothing wrong, to remind him there were plenty of other movie studios, to encourage him to fight for his story, to fight for us. The words *We can't quit* danced on my tongue. They got no further.

To advance and succeed, Horace would have needed to recast rejection—likely multiple ones—as nothing more than pockets of turbulence. Instead, he viewed his stint at Skyline as a failure, and to him, a single setback was fatal. His service record of excellence, of defying odds, of never taking a direct hit, made him unequipped to survive in Hollywood. So, there I stood with this wounded man and our tattered dreams of a life together, and nothing I said would have made a bit of difference.

"You fucked this town for both of us," Horace said, carefully folding his clothes before stacking them neatly in his suitcases.

Confusion joined the swarm of emotions swirling in my mind. "Me?"

"You think it's a coincidence?" he continued. "That driver rolls up in here kissing you and making assumptions about me. He didn't get those ideas in his head from nowhere. And if he was onto you and smeared me for being next to you, other people were bound to do the same."

"Horace, no one's said anything about us being gay."

"They wouldn't, would they? They'd give other bullshit reasons."

I realized the story he was cooking up was more palatable than the possibility that he was a lousy actor and storyteller. He wasn't going to accept this as his failure. It had to be mine.

I didn't want to wade into those waters, so I tried to reason with him along another tack. "Mr. Garten doesn't have to be the last word on whether—"

"I shouldn't have let you tag along. It was stupid," he said. "It couldn't have gotten much further anyway. Hell, you ever seen two Negro men shack up and play house?"

I blinked back the urge to cry. "Let me tag along. You asked me to come with you."

"No, I didn't. You begged me the day I flew out of range. I wasn't thinking straight, and I gave in to you when I knew better all along."

I opened my mouth to argue, but suddenly, I wasn't sure of my ground. Hadn't he said that he couldn't make it in Hollywood without me? My mind raced to recall which one of us was correct. We were back in his quarters. My face was wet with my tears. I was overjoyed that he was alive. . . . Goddammit—I *did* ask to join him. I asked for this, too.

"Skyline's just one studio," I said softly.

"I can't do this with you. It would only be more of the same. You sneaking off like a cock hound to get nasty with other twisted homos in bathrooms and parked cars and back alleys or wherever else you can get it." He looked me in the face with the same disgust he'd shown Tobias. "I need to regroup. I'm headed to Chicago. Gladys will take me in until I find honest work and my own place."

"What about your mother? Her prediction?" I asked.

"It'll just have to wait."

Despite hearing the click as he locked one suitcase, I said, "But we can stay for another week."

"There's an evening train."

"C'mon, stay the night," I pleaded. "You don't have to hightail it out of town."

"The sooner I put this damn city behind me, the sooner I can get back to being the man I'm meant to be."

It wasn't just the city that Horace wanted to put behind him, and the slight cut me to the bone. How soon did he plan to forget me? How quickly would he write me out of his story?

"I won't see you off to the train station," I said. I had my pride, too.

He nodded and clicked the other suitcase shut. Then he walked slowly toward me, approaching me cautiously. I extended my right arm, offering to shake hands. He swept my arm away and pulled me forward. He kissed me. I gave nothing back.

He left.

I fell onto the bed. The bungalow was mine and mine alone. I don't know how long I wept, but when I stepped outside, the sun had set. I told myself that the throbbing pain that kept rhythm with my heartbeat would pass. It had to be this way. It had to be this way. For the likes of us, it had to be this way.

12

FOR LACK OF A BETTER PLAN

On the Monday of my ninth and final week as a resident of the Skyline studio lot, I ate pancakes for breakfast in the commissary. The heartache of being ditched by Horace still weighed on me, but I had more pressing concerns that didn't allow me to wallow in misery. I was going to be homeless and jobless come Saturday if I didn't piece my life together before then. So, with a pad and pencil, I assessed who I was without Horace. My concentration was such that I didn't look up when the men taking the seats across from me leaned their rifles against the table.

The studio's Civil War drama *My Brother's Blood* starring Kirk Douglas and Burt Lancaster as General Ulysses S. Grant and General Robert E. Lee, respectively, was filming in the woodlands of the backlot. Most of my fellow diners were extras dressed in the blue and gray of Union and Confederate uniforms. In the moment, their attire and prop weapons didn't register with me as remarkable. People were always going about their business in one costume or another. I'd grown used to it.

Blocking out the noise of pretend armies, I made a list of what I had going for me as an employee. I was twenty-one; I was a combat vet; I could type forty words a minute; and I was reliable, discreet, and personable. Then I scribbled down the things limiting my prospects of landing and keeping a job: my race; my sexual proclivities; my loathing for repetition and mindless manual labor. My appetite waned as creeping despair expanded in my chest. I wasn't cut out to be a factory worker, a day laborer, or a pencil pusher. That wiped out the lion's share of the jobs for men in 1954.

I was at a loss until I went walking between the grid of sixteen soundstages. Outside Stage 3, I noticed an actor sneaking a swig from a flask at 8:30 in the morning. Later, I spotted a married director driving a golf cart with one hand while his other hand disappeared up the skirt of a C-list actress. I knew a spoiled child actor had thrown another tantrum, because filming was on hold on Stage 10. My mind automatically kept tabs on the stars around me, and if quizzed, I could name every film shooting on the backlot and the top-line talent for each project. I was already prepared for the job that suited me. Skyline was my beat.

I headed directly to Callum McManus's office, located on the studio's exterior Main Street. I walked through the door of the police station façade to enter the two-story brick building that housed Callum and his dozen security agents.

He welcomed me with a handshake. "Sorry to hear the flyboy's picture isn't going to work out at Skyline."

"Don't be. It could be to your advantage." I rolled the dice. "I'm available for hire. You've already had a trial run. You know I can deliver. Let's make our arrangement official."

Callum smirked. "And if I pass on this marvelous opportunity . . ."

"I go to Twentieth or Paramount or MGM and share your bright idea to have a colored man keep an eye on the colored stars. One of them is bound to take me up on it. But I figured I'd give you first dibs since this approach is your brainchild."

Now, I didn't know a soul at the other studios, and I was petrified that Callum would call my bluff. But I stood in front of his desk like I had nothing to lose. I even managed to imitate the cocky grin that

Horace flashed whenever he believed that he had someone over a barrel.

"Take a seat," Callum said. "Let's talk terms."

I was hired as a security agent at a salary of forty-five dollars a week, plus incurred expenses. It was a pay cut from what I earned as a business manager, but I'd bank more than I needed to cover my bills. Callum's secretary typed up the job offer on Skyline stationery, and I used the letter to secure a one-bedroom apartment in a Black neighborhood called West Adams.

I barely got a chance to furnish my new place, because Callum immediately assigned me to shadow and shepherd Nat King Cole while he filmed Skyline's rag-to-riches bandleader comedy *Follow That Rhythm* in Lake Tahoe. Nat was the opposite of most stars that I'd deal with down the road. He didn't seek out trouble or bad company; those wicked things pursued him. He was almost an innocent who had to be shielded from men out to trade on his fame and women eager to trap him in bed. Ever gracious and inviting, Nat could turn no one away, which kept me busy working as a third wheel for five weeks.

When I returned to my apartment building in West Adams, the other renters said good morning and good evening when they passed me in the halls. Yet the familiarity went no further. I didn't get invited to dinners or out for drinks. My irregular work hours made it even harder to strike up friendships with other bachelors, and my lack of a wife and kids set me too far apart from the young families as well. And where the other gay Black men were hiding was a mystery I couldn't seem to crack.

Not that I had a lot of spare time to contemplate my social life. James Edwards was shooting the bank heist caper *Silent Alarm* in Stages 11 and 12 on the backlot, and he liked to unwind after a full day of filming by playing marathon games of bid whist. When I wasn't with him, I was called on to help get Sammy Davis Jr.; Tony Curtis; and Barbara Payton out of separate jams. The three entertainers were attached to movies in development with Skyline, and while I wasn't the primary fixer for any of them, sticky situations often demanded the talents of several agents.

I mailed a letter to Horace in Chicago by way of general delivery, informing him of my new address and job. I wrote as if we were just two chums who had served together. Nothing heartfelt or incriminating. I assured him that I was happy in Los Angeles. No two days on the clock were the same, and I loved meeting stars and solving problems. A month passed before I got a short letter from him, informing me that he'd taken a job as a flight instructor and reconnected with a childhood crush named Harmony. I ripped his letter up into tiny pieces.

Despite my desires, I was as celibate as a monk. My duties unexpectedly changed my condition when I was sent to the airport to intercept a male heartthrob and the mobster's daughter that he had absconded with. Their flight from San Francisco was delayed by fog, and I found myself at a Pan American gate with an hour to kill.

LAX wasn't what it is today. During the 1950s, we were using *intermediate facilities* while design disputes and soaring constructions costs delayed the birth of seven new terminals and the Theme Building. Built quickly and meant to only last for a few years, the four temporary terminals were not vigilantly maintained. Small disrepairs lingered since no one saw much value in spending money to fix up a place that would be left behind in the near future. As it happened, the intermediate facilities remained in operation for fifteen years.

I'd never been to LAX until my assignment to fetch the heartthrob and the mobster's daughter. One thing that struck me as I walked into the airport was how it afforded me the paradoxical chance to be anonymous in public. The employees were consumed with the unrelenting demands of their jobs. The travelers, a great many of them running late, were focused on catching their planes before they taxied away from the gates. The people there to meet arriving loved ones only had eyes for their kin. There was no security to speak of. No checkpoints.

The only places I couldn't go were onto an airplane without a ticket or out onto the runway under any circumstances.

It was a relief in and of itself to be invisible around that many white people. Nobody called me "boy" or worse. Nobody questioned my right to be where I was. Since I wore pressed dress pants, a blue collared shirt, and a suit jacket, the white folks who paid me a fleeting glance probably assumed I was somebody's personal valet or driver.

Once I discovered the arriving San Francisco flight was delayed, I bought myself a cup of coffee, and I perused a newspaper stand offering the latest headlines from *The New York Times*, the *Chicago Daily News*, the *Miami Herald*, the *Daily Mail* (two days behind from England), the *Asahi Shimbun* (a day behind from Japan), and dozens more in every language under the sun. As I tried to make sense of the foreign headlines, I noticed that the newsstand blocked the view of a men's restroom, and a couple of white gentlemen exited the bathroom looking flushed and shifty. Another man glanced about before entering the restroom. Curiosity got me. I finished my coffee and decided I needed to relieve myself.

When I pushed the door open, it creaked loudly. A light fixture with a single bulb, where three bulbs should have been, flickered in the center of the ceiling. It gave off a weak yellowish light. The smell of bleach was strong, and it stung my nostrils. One of the urinals gurgled nonstop. Two others were marked Out of Operation.

The working urinals were occupied by loitering white men. I went into one of the stalls. Its partitions were made of wood, and the toilet paper dispenser was broken, leaving a soup-can-size hole between my stall and the next. A roll of TP sat on the lid of the toilet tank. When I saw the hole in a bathroom partition, nothing lascivious came to mind. Like the light bulbs that needed replacing, I assumed the broken toilet paper dispenser was toward the bottom of a lengthy list of airport repairs.

In the next stall, a handsome German got onto his knees and his mouth appeared in the hole. "Feed me," he whispered with his hard accent. "Feed me the cock."

Absurd as it was, my head swiveled to see if he was talking to me. The German licked his lips. I was alone in my locked stall and quickly considered the risk. I was concealed. The squeaky door would warn me if anyone else entered. The other men in the restroom were holding their positions, waiting for action of their own. The German offering his mouth and throat was a stranger I was unlikely to cross paths with again. This was my opportunity.

I was fully aroused before his lips touched my skin. The German was no novice. He pulled me in, and my chest pressed against the partition. He was swallowing me to the root. I saw stars. I put my hands over my mouth to quiet my moans. The German fellated me for several minutes before I came. He left while I regained my bearings.

I washed my hands and walked back to the Pan Am gate. No one looked at me as if I were wearing the mark of Cain. When the heartthrob and the mobster's daughter got off their plane, they argued against going with me, but I convinced them that they'd be in far less trouble if they cooperated with the studio before they were tracked down by the mob. My tryst in the men's room had been without downside.

When my schedule allowed it, I returned as often as three or four times a week to the special lavatory near the Pan Am gate. My partners were European, and from what I caught of their accents, I drew a few conclusions. The English were efficient and tidy. The French preferred to make the pleasure last. Spaniards acted as if they were doing me a favor whether they were servicing me or I was servicing them. Greeks had the stamina and steel to last for multiple rounds. Scandinavians played it coy, but their skills belied their modesty. And the Germans, who showed me the way, always greeted me with a carnal hunger.

I felt safe and desired in that dim, pungent, windowless room. I got a kick out of watching white men light up when they saw that I was

Black and game. I loved having white men drop to their knees for me. Was it twisted? I didn't care. It was a room where the rules of race and sex were rewritten in my favor. I just enjoyed the uncomplicated exchange: Men blew me; I blew men. Forgive me if it sounds sordid, but the release restored the part of me that needed to be accepted and wanted. It might have been vain of me; I am certain that it was human.

Outside of my work for Skyline and recreation at the airport, my days were empty. I tried making friends at the restaurants and bars I frequented, but none of those connections took root. With Thanksgiving approaching, my loneliness was growing acute. I needed to plug into a community somewhere somehow.

For lack of a better plan, I turned to church. The First African Methodist Episcopal Church of Los Angeles (FAME) was thriving on Eighth and Towne Avenue with a congregation of three thousand on Easter and Christmas. Surely, I figured, I'd find a way to join a circle of people there. Never mind that I'd been raised Baptist. My faith was weak enough not to notice much of a change.

For the first couple of services, I sat in the back pews, keeping to myself and singing along to the hymns I recognized. An usher with the deepest and most adorable dimples I'd ever seen made a point of getting my name and complimenting my voice. She urged me to audition for the choir. I begged off until she sweetened the pot by promising to fix me a home-cooked meal if I tried out.

So, I did, and the fussy choir director rejected me after two songs. He claimed that they already had too many lyric tenors in the group. I didn't know enough about music to argue with him. It was news to me that I was a lyric tenor. I told the usher that I'd failed, and she said, "I'll just have to enjoy your singing from where I stand."

The usher's name was Kimberly Pinkens, and her radiant smile made you offer your own in return. She had a playful spirit. It made me feel jovial, which was practically a new sensation for me. Kimberly was also observant, kind, and honest—a rare combination of virtues. I was drawn to her immediately, despite how it might appear to cynics. I didn't fake my affection for Kimberly. Anyone could see that she was beautiful and marvelously outgoing, and I genuinely enjoyed her company.

She lived with her parents in Exposition Park, and we ate on the back patio under the spying eyes of her father, who didn't leave his den to greet me but peered through the green curtains to monitor us outside. (Her mother was attending Bible study.) Kimberly paid her daddy no mind as she served chicken à la king and cheese rolls. The meal was delicious, although I admit that I'd hoped for more to drink than water and milk.

Kimberly, however, was thoroughly churched. All eight of her great-grandparents were founding members of FAME in 1872, and she was of royal lineage among the congregants. The pastor gave her birthday gifts, and her opinion was sought out whenever church elders planned initiatives for young women. She could even let it be known that she disagreed with the biblical interpretation of deacons. Had I designs to be a church leader, Kimberly would have made for an excellent partner.

I was drawn to how well she understood and gamed the social hierarchy of FAME. She knew the personality, politics, and history influencing every interaction at her church, and in me, she found someone eager to learn everything she had to teach. I was fascinated by the conflicts and alliances that were generations long, and Kimberly shared these stories with gusto. I told her that she should be a writer during our first dinner together, but she swore that she could never put everyone's business out in the world for everyone to see. That would be vulgar.

She asked me about my family and upbringing, and I explained that my father and brother had hated me since I was a boy and that they attempted to kill me when I was on the cusp of manhood. Kimberly was so shocked by the violent nature of my tale that she nearly cried herself. She accepted that I had run away from my kin and not looked back.

Often, she imagined what her life would be like if she could cut ties with her family, although she was always quick to stipulate that she loved her relatives. She just wondered how liberating it would be if they didn't exist. She shared what it was like being raised in Los Angeles with strict parents who didn't let her watch movies unless they were approved by the church's ladies auxiliary board. Her teenage rebellion consisted of sneaking into theaters to see *Mildred Pierce* and *The Lost Weekend* (both 1945).

Unwed at twenty-four, she was aware that she was considered an old maid. (Even I had wondered, at first, why a trim, beautiful woman like herself didn't have a husband.) It was not as if she were a homely spinster. She'd had two serious boyfriends, who didn't propose in a timely enough manner to please Kimberly's parents, who pressured her to end the romances. She resented them for it but complied.

Kimberly had recently attempted to move into an apartment building for single women. Her room would have been on the second floor of a converted Gothic mansion in Leimert Park that restricted men to the common rooms and came with a live-in chaperone to enforce the policy. Kimberly's mother deemed the proposed relocation "one step from prostitution." Marriage was the only acceptable way for Kimberly to get out from under her parents.

I took a risk in teasing her. "You talk about getting married the way inmates discuss escaping Alcatraz."

She cut her eyes at me, grinned, and said, "If it were as easy as breaking free of the Rock, I would have done it years ago."

We both laughed loudly. I adored her dry humor and her decision to meet what frustrated her with jokes instead of tears. Her father chastised her for making light of sad situations. I considered her approach to be a salve.

Kimberly even spoke wryly about a sensitive subject that I'd been skirting: She walked with a pronounced limp and the aid of a cane. I hadn't figured out how to mention it politely. I didn't want to embarrass or upset her. That evening on the patio, she caught me eyeing her cane.

"I have a top hat that goes along with it," she said with a defiant grin. "Give me a presto tempo, and I can tap in step with the Nicholas Brothers."

I was speechless until she guffawed. Her irreverence relaxed me. She made it safe to discuss thorny circumstances. I could be jocular with her.

"Will you tell me the truth," I asked, "or do you want me to make three guesses?"

Kimberly reached across the table to pat my hand. "Polio. It swept through our neighborhood before I was old enough to walk. Killed a cousin of mine. I made it. My parents credit the prayer circle at church, and I believe prayer played its part. . . ." She let her voice trail off; she wanted to be pressed into continuing.

"But," I obliged.

"My aunts tell me that before I got sick, my parents were capable of having a good time." She shook her head. "I'm the miracle they're still working to pay off. It's front of mind for them, not for me."

Her attitude was more than lip service. She moved with an assurance that made her limp a matter of course, and she persuaded me that while her disability was a part of her, it was not a leading characteristic. As far as she was concerned, her condition gave strangers a misguided notion of what she was like, and she didn't want to be saddled with their pity before she met them. So, when I described her to people who hadn't met her, the limp and the cane didn't make the first cut of important information.

Polio had, however, caused a lasting consequence that mattered to her suitors.

"I was young when I got sick," she explained. "My pelvic bones didn't form right. The long and the short of it is I can't bear children."

In that moment, my heart melted for her. I calculated instantly what her condition had cost her. I knew the minds of men, and while Kimberly would never say so, I was certain that her beaus didn't get down on one knee and offer her an engagement ring because she could not give them children. My bet was that she'd learned to disclose this truth early when she liked a man. See if he bolted. See if he could have feelings for her anyway.

I interlocked our fingers on the table and told her honestly, "I've never been keen on kids."

Within months of our courting, Kimberly and I became a favored couple in the church. We attended three or four dinner parties a week when my schedule allowed me to go with her. I went from eating Chinese takeout alone in my bachelor pad to touring the living rooms and dining rooms of the newlyweds and newly parents of the FAME congregation. Kimberly and I prayed and broke bread and gossiped and played backgammon and listened to Moms Mabley records and drank a nightcap or two.

People just adored having us over, and I loved who Kimberly and I became together. She got me to lighten up. I boosted her confidence. We just fit. When she'd sit on my lap, I'd see our hosts marveling at the ease of our rapport.

In short order, I got chummy with Kimberly's eight aunts (three on her daddy's side and five on her mother's side) and their husbands and their children. During the Christmas season, Kimberly's mother knitted me a stocking to hang on the mantel. Being embraced by a family was a novel experience. My own kin surely didn't care for me like Kimberly's relatives. To swim in all that approval and goodwill gave me comfort and purpose. I wanted to be the man they saw in me. In many ways, I was.

Yes, there was no denying that the physical aspect of my relationship with Kimberly was limited, and that relieved me to a great extent. Sex outside of marriage was unthinkable to her. Our hands didn't wander underneath our clothes, and no kisses traveled below the collarbones. When we necked, I closed my eyes and didn't overthink it. I reacted to what I felt and responded, secure in knowing that we couldn't go too far. We were almost always in the company of church people.

On Valentine's Day of 1955, I knelt on one knee on the Pinkenses' patio, presented Kimberly with a gold wedding band that cost me a month's pay, and asked her to be my wife. (I'd requested and received her father's blessing a week earlier.) Kimberly said, "Yes," with a happy squeal that startled the birds out of the trees.

Invite Horace to our wedding. Kimberly's mother, Bernice, was the one to suggest it. I didn't heartily agree or push against the idea. A lot of names got mentions as the guest list for our nuptials grew as thick as my hometown's phone book. For a while, Kimberly's father proposed inviting A. Philip Randolph because he'd spent three days at a conference with the labor union boss and the two had hit it off; they had not crossed paths in the intervening fourteen years.

Part of this predicament was my doing since I'd flouted my ties to Horace when Kimberly was introducing me to her family. "He was the aide to Hornet Dixon" was my shorthand biography, and the goodwill that Black people held for Horace was bestowed upon me. I told war stories to the men in Kimberly's family, and Horace had a leading role in each account. I gave the impression that we'd remained friends following his departure. Outside a handful of perfunctory letters, I had no reason to believe that Horace gave me much thought.

Yet given how I'd run my mouth, Kimberly's father assumed Horace would be my best man, and Bernice latched onto that notion. She believed that if Lieutenant Horace "Hornet" Dixon attended the ceremony, it would elevate the entire affair, and she was certain that with Horace by my side, *Jet* magazine would run a picture of Kimberly, me, and our wedding party above a gushing caption. Kimberly didn't care for all that fuss, but she wanted to please her mother. So, my fiancée leaned on me to reach out to Horace.

He and I had not seen each other since he fled Hollywood. We needed two thousand miles separating us. Or at least I did. My attraction to Horace hadn't diminished even though our life together was unworkable. He remained the perpetual star of my sex dreams. I often fantasized that the men I coupled with in the airport bathroom were really Horace. I couldn't shake my desires, and his hold over me would return with him. I knew if he was near, I'd betray myself.

Kimberly hounded me for Horace's address. I lied and claimed repeatedly that the task of hunting it down slipped my mind. When she told me not to bother because she'd look it up herself, I felt helpless. There seemed no way to stop the invitation from going out, and I was afraid that Horace would indeed fly out to Los Angeles to see me get hitched. I imagined that he'd take perverse pleasure in watching me pledge my heart to a woman while stirring my longing for him. *You asked for this*, he'd taunt.

Kimberly got Horace's address and added it to the mailing list. The thought of having Horace as a guest at my wedding started waking me up at night. Kimberly, her mother, and her aunts had a dinner party during which they stuffed, sealed, and stamped 358 wedding invitations. The next morning, I had an unrelenting headache. The invitations remained at Kimberly's parents' house in her father's den, and I contemplated how I could smuggle Horace's invite out of the stash.

I tried calling Horace's home telephone number, but a woman always answered, and I couldn't bear to speak. I must have hung up a half dozen times. I considered writing Horace a letter, begging him not to come. But I couldn't think of how to explain my reasons without revealing our past and endangering both of us if the letter fell into the wrong hands.

It was on a Sunday that the stress forced me to speak up. The invitations were going to be mailed the next day. We'd spent most of the morning and afternoon at FAME. We were due for dinner at her Aunt Eileen's place at six.

Kimberly came with me to my apartment to help prepare the way for when she moved in once we were man and wife. By her estimation, I'd incorrectly arranged everything from the pots and utensils in the kitchen to the towels and toiletries in the bathroom to the clothes in my closet. She was going to reorder it all. She planned to start with the medicine cabinet, but I led her to the couch.

I had trouble looking at her, and my words got wedged in my throat. Kimberly saw me in distress, set aside her cane, and cradled my hands in hers.

"Aaron, what's wrong?"

"Horace can't be invited," I said.

"Why not? You and he are so close."

"Too close," I said, startled by my candor.

"How's that?"

I started to heave. My headache became blinding.

"Honey, what's wrong? Should I call a doctor?"

"I've done things," I said. "Things you'd be disgusted by."

The grip of pain surrounding me lessened a little when I let the truth spill.

"What things?" she asked.

"In the war. It started then."

Kimberly rubbed my back. "Tell me. Let it out."

"I'll understand if you hate me—if you want nothing more to do with me."

"Don't you go deciding what I will and won't do," she said softly. "Now, go on."

"Horace and I . . ."

She thought she knew where I was headed. "Killing is a part of war. You and Horace did your duty, no matter how gruesome."

I wished that her version were accurate. I even considered adopting her storyline and spinning a yarn about some horror of war that I witnessed. But lying wouldn't end my suffering. And it wouldn't be fair to Kimberly. I forced myself to look her in the face. She was beautiful inside and out, and I loved her as best I could, and she deserved honesty.

"He and I . . ." My voice sounded separate from me. I didn't feel the words passing my lips but heard them filling the air. "We did what men aren't supposed to do. We were lonely. We became lovers."

Kimberly stiffened, and she withdrew her hands from mine.

"It's over now. We broke it off, and I never want to see him again."

"Tell me something else," she demanded. "Not this, not this wretched . . ." She covered her mouth like she might vomit.

"I'm sorry. What I did, though, is in the past," I said. "I'm different with Horace out of my life, and you in it. I love you, Kimberly."

She leapt to her feet without the use of her cane. "You slept with a man. You're one of those sinful fairies."

"I'm more than what I did with him," I insisted.

"But he's who you want. Him, not me." She looked as though she was fighting off the urge to scream. "You've been lying to me since day one."

"No, I haven't. Everything I've felt for you and the love I've shown you are genuine." I reached for her cane and handed it to her. "I'll be a husband to you. Care for you. Protect you and provide. Make love to you when you want."

"Don't do me no favors," she said.

"That's not what I mean." I took a deep breath and added no sugar to my assessment of us. "We both lack what others would require of us. We can't deliver on perfect, and we shouldn't hold out for it either. Think on how I've treated you. It can go on like it has been if you can look past my faults."

Kimberly thought over the divergent paths before her: marry me or stay with her parents, praying for another man to spring her from captivity. Her eyes remained bone-dry. She refused to cry. She refused to run away. I wanted to hold her but knew better than to try.

"If we go through with the wedding," she asked, "how can I trust that you won't backslide and fall into sin like you did with Horace?"

"Because he's the only man I've ever gotten entangled with, and I'll stay away from him forever. You have my word or may God strike me dead."

"Men have urges." She shook her head and continued, "Yours, I can't satisfy."

I promised her, "I will be faithful to you—like all husbands should be with their wives. I can control my urges."

"And what if it goes beyond that?" she asked. "What if you do fall in love with another man? What if you meet a different Horace?"

"To fall for the first one, I had to be trapped with him on a ship during a war." I stood up and walked over to Kimberly. "It won't happen again."

Kimberly nodded. She told me she needed time to think over what to do about our pending nuptials. When she returned to her parents' house, she took to her bed, claiming that she felt run-down and dizzy. The wedding invitations weren't mailed on Monday. Two days passed without a word from Kimberly, who remained in her room.

Then she emerged. We spoke, and I reaffirmed every pledge I gave her during my confession. Horace's invitation was plucked from the bunch. We told her parents that Horace was carrying out a special assignment for the navy and sent his regrets.

Kimberly and I were married at 2:00 PM on a radiant June Sunday, before a thousand congregants at FAME. Five of Kimberly's male cousins served as my groomsmen. Our church friends filled in for my absent family and sat in the first few pews on my side. Kimberly walked down the aisle, her cane in her right hand and her father linked to her left arm. There were no hiccups or hesitations.

Only after we returned from our honeymoon night in the newlywed suite of the Dunbar Hotel (Kimberly's choice) did we discover a wedding gift that was mailed to us with no return address and no card identifying the sender. We opened the present, and there was a brass compass in a leather-bound box. Kimberly couldn't imagine who the sender might be. I said I was stumped, too. But I recognized that brass compass. It had been given to Horace by MGM during the war. Now it was mine. A reminder from Horace that he was keeping an eye on me even from afar. I was comforted to know that I remained under his watch.

PART II

13

LOCK THE DOOR

By the fall of 1961, Kimberly thought Xavier could do no wrong. After numerous encounters with him at movie premieres and Hollywood parties, she'd gone from fan to zealous defender. If I complained about Xavier being a pain in my side, she recited his perceived virtues. Over the years, my wife's increasing idolization of the biggest star in my stable amused and saddened me. I was glad she adored him, because her feelings were surrogates for my own, but I was aware that her heart would shut him out if she knew Xavier was a practicing homosexual.

Kimberly was giddy because she and I were sure to see Xavier that night at a debutante ball organized by the local Links chapter and bankrolled by Nat King Cole. Nat's adopted daughter, Carole, was one of twenty-eight girls coming out to society in great style at the Beverly Hilton Hotel. Along with the boldfaced names of Black Hollywood, Kimberly and I made the guest list because we were among the crooner's closest five hundred friends.

I had my trepidations about going to the party. There was a studio matter that I'd taken it upon myself to fix. I hadn't notified my boss, because my tactics wouldn't have been approved. If I succeeded, my efforts would have to remain anonymous. If I failed, I'd be fired.

"I wonder what table Maria is going to place us at," Kimberly said as I locked the front door of our two-bedroom Craftsman house. "Or do you suppose someone else made the seating arrangements?"

I replied, "Whoever did it will segregate the stars from the commoners."

"But Xavier will swing by and chat with us."

"You mean flirt with you."

Kimberly beamed. "I can't help it if Xavier enjoys the company of a sanctified lady. He needs to let me introduce him to a few of our church sisters. It's getting to be high time he settled down."

I left that subject alone as we walked to the car. Forty minutes passed with the Miracles, the Marvelettes, and the Shirelles singing to us over the radio before we reached the striking hotel with its name writ large on the side of the building. I knew the ins and out of the Beverly Hilton because Brock Peters had it included in his contract that he could stay in a room there for the duration of filming when Skyline brought him out from New York and loaned him out to Columbia Pictures to film 1959's *Porgy and Bess* for Sam Goldwyn.

Outside the hotel's main entrance, the stars walked a red carpet lined with jostling photographers. Kimberly and I drove to a side parking lot, and I handed my car keys to a Black valet attendant. He stared, mouth agape, at Kimberly's cane as she walked toward the hotel.

He said, "Ma'am, it's quite a ways to the ballroom. I can run and fetch you a wheelchair to make it easier on—"

"I'll manage," Kimberly interrupted cheerfully.

I took her left arm in mine and whispered to her, "I didn't care for his tone."

"He was just angling for a tip."

"Well, talking to you like you're one hundred and three wasn't the ticket."

"Let it pass."

"I suppose."

"What's got you on edge?" She squeezed my arm. "Is there going to be funny business tonight?"

I couldn't divulge details, but my silence told Kimberly that she'd figured correctly. Nat had unwittingly set the stage for me to strong-arm Sidney Poitier to Xavier's benefit. Xavier would have objected if he'd known my intentions, but I was sick of Sidney's posturing. He was abusing his power and silently bullying Xavier. And bullies must be confronted.

The task fell to me, since Xavier would never have done it, because he was desperate to avoid a public spat with Sidney. Xavier wanted audiences to think that they were simpatico, although the relationship between the rising Black prince and the reigning Black king of Hollywood had always been fraught. They'd gotten along fine while acting together in *Downtown Dreamers*, but Sidney kept Xavier at arm's length. I'm not sure if it was a conscious decision. Career preservation probably made Sidney instinctually wary of a handsome, talented Black actor in his mold and ten years younger than he was.

Sexual land mines also made the ground between Xavier and Sidney dangerous. Sidney was still married to his first wife and years into an affair with Xavier's closest friend, Diahann. Countless were the nights that Xavier served as a cover date for Diahann so that she could sneak off with Sidney, and many were the mornings that Xavier listened to Diahann's tearful complaints that Sidney wouldn't leave his wife for her—especially after she ditched her first husband to be with Sidney.

Xavier found the back-and-forth between Diahann and Sidney exasperating, and he placed the blame on Sidney. Xavier considered him a romantic coward. Once, he said to me what very few would have dared say about Sidney: "He's no braver than a scared schoolboy. He's petrified of being scolded, and he'll do anything for a pat on the head."

I only ever dealt with Sidney as it related to his affair with Diahann. I'd arranged to have a few pictures destroyed and blind items spiked when she was shooting for Skyline. I was even quite bold with Diahann and Sidney while they filmed 1961's *Paris Blue*. They were playing lovers in the movie and allowing their affections to show off camera, as well. I sent a bucket of ice to each of their hotel suites with the same note attached: *Cool it*.

Diahann let me know that Sidney was furious with me. He and I never spoke about it. We did no more that nod and smile stiffly when in passing. He knew who I was and what I did, and my knowledge of his disreputable behavior negated any hope of us becoming chummy. I imagined I unnerved him, and I meant to make use of that tiny fear.

I'm not certain how much Sidney ever knew about Xavier's homosexuality. Xavier wouldn't share such a dangerous secret with a rival, and Diahann wouldn't betray Xavier's confidence. But Sidney wasn't stupid. He must have wondered why Xavier was platonically devoted to a woman as sexy as Diahann. He likely recognized that the dating rumors surrounding Xavier were always with his costars (Cicely, Kim, Marpessa) and the romances fizzled shortly after the movies opened in theaters. If Sidney did deduce that Xavier was gay, it would have been another reason to keep his distance from the upstart. Any man who was friends with Xavier would have his sexuality questioned should Xavier's homosexuality ever be exposed.

The cordial if frigid posture that Xavier and Sidney took toward one another kept them out of open conflict. Then in the summer of 1961, a Brazilian producer came to Skyline with the rights to a sensational script called *House Money*. It was a film noir about a Black private investigator named Jonah Bledsoe, and Lowell, having assumed sole control of the studio upon his father's death in 1959, wanted Xavier to star in the movie. Xavier was hungry for it, too. He saw *House Money* as his golden ticket to break out of cookie-cutter love stories and to sink his teeth into a role that would show more of his range as an actor.

The hitch was this: The Brazilian producer would accept Xavier, only if Sidney passed on the part. Sidney received the *House Money* script in July, and within a week, he deemed it "intriguing." He sent word that he was mulling over whether to star in the picture, leaving the project in limbo. Xavier was in anguish. He couldn't fault Sidney for seeing the upside of portraying Jonah Bledsoe, and he restrained himself from putting any kind of pressure on Sidney to make a decision.

However, I was convinced that Sidney really didn't want the role and knew it in July and that he'd only been hemming and hawing to keep Xavier from making the most of this opportunity. Months had already been squandered; Lowell was losing patience and was threatening to remove Skyline from the deal; and Xavier was on the verge of being assigned to another romantic comedy. Meanwhile, the Brazilian producer loved the idea of having Sidney in his picture, and he was willing to wait until Sidney slammed the door shut on the possibility. The whole situation appeared hopelessly logjammed until one recognized that the only piece that had to be moved was Sidney.

Kimberly and I entered the ballroom to the sounds of a six-piece band providing a soulful take on sock hop music. A parquet dance floor belonged to the debutantes, their gangly dates, and the prim chaperones. Surrounding them at circular tables were the everyday Black folk, who drew their local status from the time and toil they devoted to their fraternal, sororal, and religious orders. And at an outer table were Black men and women, who drew worldwide fame from the characters that they pretended to be. There at a table for ten sat Sidney, Diahann, Xavier, Harry Belafonte, Sammy Davis Jr., Lena Horne, Ruby Dee and Ossie Davis, James Edwards, and Eartha Kitt (eight months pregnant).

We weren't in the ballroom for longer than ten seconds before Nat broke away from four other guests and greeted Kimberly with a kiss on each cheek.

"Aren't you a doll," he said before gesturing at me. "You even managed to clean this one up, too."

I protested, "When have you seen me less than sharp and polished?"

Nat puffed on his cigarette and grinned. "You looked a little harried the night you had to speed me out that county before the sunset laws went into effect."

"That was close. We had a sheriff on our ass."

Kimberly slapped my shoulder lightly for cursing.

"Sorry, dear, but it was a jam. I couldn't go over the speed limit with the sheriff tailing me, but I had to cross the county line by six o'clock."

"We just made it at five fifty-nine," Nat bragged with a hearty laugh that Kimberly and I joined in on.

"God was with you," Kimberly said. "After all you've done for the struggle, it would have been a tragedy to have lost you then."

Nat put a hand over his heart and took a deep drag from his cigarette. "Kimberly . . ." His eyes welled up. "Thank you. You're too kind."

Nat excused himself to greet other arriving guests, and Kimberly and I found our seats at table 23. My wife thought Nat was a sweet soft touch to be so moved by her compliment. I believed he was uplifted by evidence that the rap against him had been rewritten. People forget, but for years, Nat was not a foot soldier in the battle for civil rights.

He readily agreed to perform in front of segregated audiences, claiming he could do nothing about the seating policies of the venues he sang at. He didn't change his tune until 1956, after he got tackled onstage by three white men in Birmingham, Alabama. The violent racists were part of a much larger plot to kidnap and murder Nat, all on account of someone passing around photos of him hugging up next to several white female fans. At first, Nat tried to shake off the assault and return to his apolitical ways, but the bell had been rung. He was a Black singer, not a singer who happened to be Black.

Roy Wilkins, head of the NAACP, drove the point home in a telegram to Nat: *That attack upon you clearly indicates that organized bigotry makes no distinction between those who do not actively challenge racial discrimination and those who do. This is a fight which none of us can escape.*

Nat got on the right track, and our people enthusiastically embraced him like he was a wayward relative who belatedly accepted the invitation to the family cookout but brought delicious ham hock and pickled collard greens to boot. It was a full transformation. Nat went from singing at the Republican National Convention for President Eisenhower to cutting it up with Frank Sinatra during a performance at President Kennedy's inaugural party.

Nat's old stance was washed clean. From Kimberly, he got the version of himself that he preferred: a champion of the struggle. To his credit, he worked hard to live up to that title. Earlier in the evening of his daughter's debutante ball, Nat sang during a special concert at the Hollywood Palladium for President Kennedy, who was in Los Angeles for a string of political fundraisers. Nat had raced straight from the Palladium to the Hilton, looking no worse for the wear.

Xavier came to our table to greet Kimberly and me. He kissed her and shook my hand. He was wearing one of those new collarless Cylinder suit jackets from Pierre Cardin. I couldn't argue that Xavier looked bad in anything, but the jacket was too hip for my taste. It appeared incomplete.

He asked Kimberly, "Will you dance with me tonight?"

"Sure, if my husband doesn't forbid it."

"She's all yours," I said all too quickly to get a fake rise out of Kimberly.

Xavier and Kimberly went right ahead gushing over each other while I scoped out Sidney from across the ballroom. He was in the middle of an animated debate with Harry, and his hand was placed too low on Diahann's back. He'd been dodging Xavier for months, and I'm sure he was insisting that tonight wasn't an appropriate time to talk business, but I'd hit upon an idea that would force the issue.

Sidney and Harry's conversation ended with them wagging their fingers at each other, then waving each other off. Bickering was just part of their friendship. I managed to catch Sidney's eye and mouthed the words, *Follow me*. Surprised, he straightened up and pointed at himself. I nodded.

"I need to freshen up," I told Kimberly and Xavier, who were engaged in their banter and hardly noticed me.

I walked to the men's restroom located at the right corner at the rear of the ballroom. Sidney followed me. When I entered, I washed my hands until a couple of men exited, and Sidney walked in. The two of us had the room to ourselves.

"Lock the door," I ordered as I dried my hands.

"Do you work for me, and I don't know it?" he asked in his crisp baritone.

"Lock the damn door. We don't have all night."

"Or do I work for you, and nobody informed me?"

He was acting unflappable, so I responded with cynical indifference to his coolness.

"You can be clever, or you can save your career. I get paid the same no matter what you choose."

Sidney fidgeted with his wedding ring before locking the bathroom door. "I don't take kindly to threats."

"I'm not threatening you. I'm laying out your choices." I swallowed hard. There was no turning back. I gave voice to an audacious lie. "Lowell Garten wants Xavier for the lead of *House Money*, and he's willing to burn you to clear the way for his star. Are you ready for the country to learn that you're a dog?"

"That's not a threat?"

Someone pushed against the bathroom door. When they discovered it was locked, they knocked against it.

I shouted, "We're cleaning up! Find another john!"

Sidney jabbed his finger in the air inches from my nose. "I want to speak with Lowell, not a flunky."

"Mr. Garten isn't going to sit down with you. You'll make a stink, and he doesn't want to be accused of dictating terms to a cherished Black star."

"But that's what he's doing, and you're the Tom carrying out his orders."

He was baiting me, but I remained unflinching. He wasn't exactly a model of brotherhood either. "I happen to agree with Mr. Garten. Xavier should have the lead. The only reason he doesn't is because you are boxing him out. And why? Because you love being America's favorite Negro and can't let the competition shine."

"To hell with you and this nonsense."

Sidney raised his fists to hip level, and I contemplated the ramifications of getting into a fistfight with a bankable leading man. Leaving a mark on his face could cost me every dime I had. Plus, I'd be exiled from Hollywood and large swaths of the Black community.

"Bow out," I said, "and you can go on with your halo intact."

"Tell Lowell I won't be blackmailed. Release what you got." He turned to inspect his reflection in the mirror. "Bogart quit his wife to marry Betty, and everyone loves them."

"There weren't pictures of Bacall in the nude on top of Bogart."

"Wait a minute," he fumed, "don't drag Diahann into this."

"Ball's in your court, Sidney. Pass on a movie you don't actually want or set a torch to everything you and Diahann have worked for."

He shook his head. "Xavier's got no qualms about screwing me and Diahann for a part?"

"He doesn't know. Besides, it's not his call. This comes from the top," I lied. "Congratulate Xavier tonight. You'll be the big man, the hero you play so well."

"You are a snake," he said.

"We have an agreement?"

"He can have the damn movie." Sidney glared at me.

He unlocked the door and exited. My legs went weak, and I grabbed the sink to hold myself up. I'd pulled it off. I'd bluffed Sidney and cleared the deck for Xavier. The excitement and residual fear of the gambit flooded my body.

I bummed a cigarette from one of the men who came in to use the restroom and enjoyed every puff. Then I chewed two mints to mask the smell. I walked out of the bathroom just as the trumpet player in the six-piece band began a solo rendition of "Hail to the Chief." That song could only mean one thing.

The debutantes and their dates quit dancing, and the adults stood at attention. President Kennedy strode into the ballroom and was met with thunderous shocked applause. He'd decided to make an impromptu visit to give Nat's guests a thrill, or so it seemed.

I'd never seen President Kennedy in person before. His magnetism was stunning. He moved with a confidence born of power and wealth. He raised his arm to wave at the crowd, and the cheers only grew louder. That toothy smile of his beamed.

Everyone's attention was fixed on the president except for mine and that of three other people. I noticed that Kimberly was staring intently at the table of stars. I followed her sight line and landed on Sidney and Xavier having a private chat off to the side of their peers. Xavier was shaking Sidney's hand and bowing slightly. Sidney upheld a tight-lipped smile. When I returned my gaze to Kimberly, she met me with pursed lips and a raised eyebrow.

I went over to my wife and attempted to blow past her consternation. "Can you believe the president is here? Your mother and aunts are gonna be beside themselves when they hear you've seen him in the flesh."

"Yes, they will indeed." Kimberly flashed a cautious smile. "My gosh, he's handsome. He could've been in movies."

President Kennedy greeted Nat and the debutantes first, and a photographer snapped a picture of a dark-skinned girl in white evening gloves curtseying to the commander in chief. It was an irresistible photo to the press. After a few minutes, Nat guided President Kennedy to the star table. No photos were taken, and that tipped me off.

The president took a seat between Harry and Lena. He began to talk with them, the most famous Black actors and actresses in motion pictures, and their pretty faces hardened against him. I was too far away to overhear their conversation, but Ossie was talking fast, and Eartha put in her two cents. Sidney and Lena followed suit. President Kennedy tapped his index finger against the table as he made his points in response to them.

Kimberly noticed the tenor of the exchange, too, and said, "He's getting an earful."

"But he's not surprised," I noted. "He didn't just turn up on a whim, and Ossie, Ruby, and the rest of them didn't come here to shake hands with debutantes. This was orchestrated."

I had no proof to back my claim, but it was a sensitive time in the struggle. The Interstate Commerce Commission had issued a ban on segregation at travel facilities and on buses on November 1, and segregationists like Chief Laurie Pritchett had already circumvented the ban by arresting Negroes on trumped-up charges of disturbing the peace, since white patrons would go ballistic when Blacks behaved as equals. President Kennedy and his brother the attorney general Robert Kennedy lauded the ICC ban as a victory, and political Negroes argued that the ban was pathetically ineffectual. It was a hot-button issue that the president had to both address with key members of the Black community and to avoid being dragged into publicly. I think the debutante ball served as a cover.

Before I could share my theory with Kimberly, Xavier tapped me on the shoulder. He could hardly contain his joy. I acted as if I didn't know why he was happy.

Doing my best to seem stunned, I asked, "You walked away from an audience with the president?"

"I'm not gonna outtalk the others at that table," he said. "Can I have a word?"

"Excuse us," I said to Kimberly.

"Of course," she said, suspicion returning to her eyes.

Xavier and I went off and huddled to the left of the bandstand.

"Sidney's dropping out of *House Money*," he reported. "Says he's hot about another project. His agent sent him the advance copy of a book about a Black handyman and a bunch of nuns or whatever. But *House Money* is mine."

"Congratulations."

Xavier hugged me, catching me off guard. I hugged him, too, thinking nothing of it.

"I should thank Lowell," he said.

"Why?"

"Sidney said that Lowell's been backing me hard. It's another reason he's stepping aside. If Lowell believes in me so much, Sidney said I oughta have this chance to shine."

I allowed Sidney to play the good guy, and I convinced Xavier to send Lowell a box of Cuban cigars and a thank-you note and to leave it at that. Within the hour, President Kennedy waved goodbye to the crowd in the hotel ballroom, and the debutantes and their gawky dates went about their night as if the president had never stopped by. Xavier and Kimberly danced to a couple of songs. Before we called it a night, Kimberly and I talked with Nat's wife, Maria, and briefly spoke to Diahann, Xavier, and James Edwards.

It was a quarter to ten, and we were a couple of miles from our house, when Kimberly turned off the radio. She'd been quiet during the ride. That wasn't unusual on nights out when she'd had a couple of glasses of wine. At the Beverly Hilton, she'd downed three.

"I realize your work can call on you, now and then, to be rough with people," she began, "but I always figured it was the kind of people who brought trouble on themselves."

"It is," I assured her.

"Hard to believe Sidney is a lowlife." She folded her arms across her chest.

I sighed. "You don't know his business like I do, and you're better off for it."

Too appalled to look at me, she turned her head away from my direction and watched a street lined with aging Victorian houses go by. "You have no misgivings about putting the screws to Sidney?"

"Where is this coming from?"

"I can put two plus two together. He met you in the men's room. When he came out, he was fit to be tied. Then he pasted on a different face to go make Xavier's day. And you must've done something that had you shaken afterward."

"Shaken?"

She scoffed. "I can smell the cigarette under the mint."

"I'm sorry I smoked. I shouldn't have—"

"You need to watch yourself," she warned.

I glanced at her and nearly rear-ended a truck that stopped at a red light. "What do you mean?"

"You obviously went to great lengths for Xavier's sake."

"That's my job."

"Whatever you did to Sidney doesn't strike me as run-of-the-mill. Otherwise, it wouldn't have distressed you so."

"You're right," I admitted. "I took a risk tonight, but it paid off, and you don't need to waste sympathy on Sidney. It all worked out, I swear."

I often ended our marital spats by agreeing and apologizing before regrettable words were spoken. Kimberly took a deep breath. I thought I was in the clear.

"Still, you . . ." She covered her mouth before dropping her hand into her lap. "Your loyalty to Xavier could be misconstrued."

I honestly wasn't following. "How's that?"

"I saw him hug you, and you . . ." She tilted her head toward the roof of the car and closed her eyes. "Only way I can describe it is you melted into his arms."

Had I? I didn't recall doing such a thing, but I couldn't dispute her. She saw what she saw. I felt embarrassed.

"You promised me that you'd never—"

"I haven't," I snapped.

"If you're not careful, you could—"

"I won't."

Kimberly reached out and turned on the radio. Bobby "Blue" Bland was singing the final refrain of "I Pity the Fool," and the lyrics cut like a knife, but neither of us moved to quiet him. Our house came into view.

"I'm not afraid to leave you," said Kimberly.

14

KISSED THE FLAME

The events in *House Money* were written to take place on the outskirts of Las Vegas, but to save on production costs, Skyline had the movie filmed in Palm Springs. It was a six-week shoot, and Lowell personally ordered me to keep a close watch on Xavier because he felt stars "go wild in the heat of the Devil's Playground." This was not hyperbole to Lowell. He recalled that even a class act like Tyrone Power gave in to tawdry temptation in Palm Springs.

Xavier and I were assigned adjoining rooms at the Foxtail Lodge. He got the bridal suite, and I got a junior one. Every room in the Foxtail smelled of suntan oil and cigarette smoke, offered air-conditioning if you could stand the continual roar and clang of the unit, and sported orange carpet and lime-green walls. The accommodations were a reminder that Skyline's investment in Negro films fell short of what the studio spent on the white talent making white movies. Sean Connery or Audrey Hepburn would have stayed at the chic Del Marcos Hotel or the reclusive Ingleside Inn. We got the old Foxtail.

By the second week of filming, we were shooting more night for night than originally scheduled, and along with the rest of the cast and crew, Xavier and I fell into a blurry nocturnal existence. I blamed the movie's director, Lenny Winters, a white man who enjoyed that studio bosses interfered with his cuts less when the stars were Black. Lenny felt it fed the film's noir tone to stage scenes outside of small churches and around lit pools at night, and he changed multiple locations in the script to have even more pages under the moon.

His schedule scrambled our body clocks. Xavier reported to hair and makeup at dusk. Shooting got underway at 8:00 PM, and we'd film until the break of dawn ruined the dark sky. Amped up from acting, Xavier couldn't think about climbing into bed until noon. Not that turning in a few hours earlier would have made it easier to catch a wink. The curtains in our hotel rooms weren't blackouts, and the cleaning ladies barged in despite the Do Not Disturb signs dangling from our doorknobs. Plus, Xavier's nerves kept him obsessing about what was shooting the next night, and he suckered me into running lines with him.

During the third week of shooting, our waking hours took on a dreamlike haze, complicated by the strange effect of watching a film get made. The scenes that got shot added a hypnotic layer of reality for my mind to contend with: a lived experience as outlandish, vivid, and unbelievable as any dream. A fiction that both happened and didn't happen. Mix sleep deprivation into the equation and the line between real and the unreal vanished. I started to spend more and more time trying to sort out what was a memory and what was a figment of imagination, and I got to a place where I didn't trust my eyes.

Did I see a Vegas showgirl stab her abusive boyfriend and shove him into a swimming pool? Yes, because that was meant to be a quick scene to pick off, but the director was dismayed when the fake blood turned unmistakably purple against the artificial blue water. The blood had to be triple-dyed red to read for the camera.

Did my hotel room catch fire? No, but I repeatedly awoke with a start, convinced that the flames were lapping at my arm as it hung over the side of my bed. It was a fear born of the way sunlight knifed through the yellow curtains and reflected off the orange carpet; the persistent smell of a thousand snuffed cigarettes; and the rising temperature that turned my room into an inferno in the early afternoon if I forgot to turn on the loud air conditioner before I hit the sheets.

Was I dreaming that Xavier, wearing nothing besides blue swim trunks, had come into my room while I lay in bed? Did I open my eyes to find him standing over me in the atomic yellow of the early Saturday morning light? Yes, but it was all too real.

"No one's called you with the news?" he asked.

Groggy, I rolled onto my side. "What now?"

"The studio asked me to make a statement. Uh, see, Horace was in a terrible accident at an air show outside Chicago." Xavier trailed off as he added, "It'll be over the wires soon."

I managed to rouse myself enough to sit up and begin to take in what I was hearing. "Why'd Skyline want a statement from you?"

"Every studio is asking every Black star to pay tribute."

My eyes stopped burning, and Xavier's face finally came into focus. His brow was wrinkled with sorrow and pity. His mouth kept drawing his lips inside. He didn't want to utter the line he'd entered my room to deliver.

I said it for him. "He's dead."

"Yes," Xavier whispered.

I didn't cry or scream. I went numb. I held out the slim hope that I was in the middle of a hallucination.

Xavier asked, "Is there anything I can do or get you?"

My mind turned to morbid details. "Did Horace burn?"

"No, the biplane didn't catch fire. It was torn to pieces on impact."

"Did they say what went wrong?"

"Mechanical failure."

"The engine? The landing gears?"

He shrugged helplessly. "No one said all that. 'Mechanical failure' is the only answer I got."

"I hope he wasn't cut to ribbons," I said. "I'd like to see his face."

I telephoned Kimberly and broke the news to her.

She gasped, then leaned on faith. "God bless his soul. He's with the angels now."

I wondered if she believed Horace was in heaven. Didn't the God of FAME segregate sodomites to hell? Or were war heroes granted waivers? Of course, I kept my questions to myself. There was no sense in interrogating Kimberly, especially in light of my request.

"I want to attend his funeral."

"You should," she responded quickly. "I can put in for days off with the school."

"I want to go alone," I said. "This feels like something I need to do—"

"Without me."

"Yes, if you don't mind."

Unprepared to object, Kimberly gave me her blessing to attend Horace's funeral, but Skyline did not. My direct boss, Callum, made it clear that *House Money* was going to continue shooting, and Lowell wanted me to stay with Xavier. I was too flummoxed to argue in the moment. My back-channel phone calls to Lowell's office received no reply from him. The studio boss had a habit of making himself scarce when pressed to justify an unpopular edict.

I tried to accept the decision, but I grew steadily unnerved by the prospect that I wouldn't lay eyes on Horace before he was lowered into the ground at Arlington National Cemetery. I drank a bottle of scotch from the hotel minibar, hoping it would calm me and slow my racing heart. No dice. I attempted to clean myself up, but my hand trembled while I was shaving, and I cut myself. I had to call on Xavier to finish the left side of my face as I staunched the bleeding on my right cheek.

"You nicked yourself pretty good," Xavier said.

"I'm lucky it wasn't my neck."

"Hold still." He shaved along my jawline. "You gonna pull it together, or do I need to sit on you?"

"I'd be fine if I could go. It's like . . ."

"It's like what?" Xavier prodded.

"I'll never be sure he's dead unless I see him in his casket."

"You've got to go, then. Damn what Lowell says."

"Will you pay my bills after I'm fired?"

Xavier grew pensive as he finished shaving me. I thanked him and rinsed my face. He stood in the bathroom doorway and watched over me. He was scared to leave me alone, and I think his judgment was sound. In my head, I tried to devise several schemes to sneak off to Horace's funeral while others kept up the ruse that I was on set. Nothing worked.

Around noon, Xavier and I were in his suite's living room, drinking scotch on the rocks and listening to Duke Ellington's *Such Sweet Thunder*. The ploy began to crystallize as I rattled the ice in my glass. It would require an audacious lie. Yet, if played correctly, it could fly.

"What if we go together?" I suggested.

Xavier frowned. "That'd be even harder to swing. I film on Monday."

"What if you're too distraught to work, and you want to pay your respects to an old friend?"

"I only met Horace once, and that's not a story worth repeating."

I said, "The ending is all we need."

Xavier cocked his head at me. "What do you mean?"

I finished the final sip of my drink before explaining, "You and Horace took that picture sitting next to each other up onstage. You look like pals. Now, if you pick up that phone and say that you were pals, you're giving Lowell a story he can run with. The press will just eat it up. The Black star honors the Black war hero. And I'd go with you."

Xavier downed his drink as he considered my plan. He'd asked if there was anything he could do for me, and the favor I concocted would force him to fake grief for Horace. The effort required was arduous and the scope of the lie was sacrilegious. Still, Xavier contemplated the role.

"They'll expect me to tell stories about him—to know him," he said.

"You can use my memories."

Xavier ignited his lighter and kissed the flame to a cigarette. "You do deserve to be there," he reasoned.

On the phone with Lowell, Xavier gave a measured performance. I listened in on the kitchen line and could see Xavier acting in the living room. His speech was halting. The words he managed to utter were weighed down with sorrow. He spoke of his formative friendship with Horace with such pathos that it spurred Lowell to deem Xavier in no condition to continue working on the picture come Monday.

Only then did Xavier mention a desire to attend Horace's funeral. Lowell fell silent. I assumed he was sizing up the pros and cons, but since we couldn't see his face, Xavier and I stared at each other in anticipation.

"You'll have to mourn him in the papers," Lowell warned. "This will be a story. Can you handle that?"

"Yes," Xavier said, "and if my going to honor Horace reminds people of his life and sacrifice, that's to the good, ain't it?"

"Indeed," Lowell replied, although I doubted his motivation had anything to do with promoting Horace's legacy in and of itself.

Filming on *House Money* was temporarily suspended. The cast and crew groused. Their lodging and meals were covered by Skyline, but they weren't paid for the days the picture was on hold. The rescheduling amounted to an unpaid vacation in stifling heat.

Xavier and I flew in the studio's private plane to Washington, DC. The overnight flight took us from a scorching desert to a snowy district. When the cabin door opened, a blast of cold air assaulted me, and my eyes watered in shock. The sunlight reflected off the white winter landscape, creating a strong glare. Thanks to advance notice from Skyline's publicity department, reporters were waiting on the icy tarmac.

I followed Xavier as we descended the stairs and walked toward the scrum with their snapping cameras and microphones. Everyone's breath turned into thin clouds. No one wanted to hear from me, but my throat tightened all the same.

For what it was worth, Xavier looked dashing. Skyline's costume department took the liberty of packing Xavier's bags for this trip. He wore a gray suit, a black overcoat, a charcoal scarf, and a black fedora. He put his gloved hands into his pockets and addressed the welcoming press with a short, prepared statement:

"Good morning. I have traveled across our great country to mourn the passing of Lieutenant Horace Dixon, a courageous man, a proud patriot, and a model Negro. He befriended me during his time in Hollywood, and I was made the better for it. He was a true American hero. Thank you."

Every reporter yelled out questions, but it had already been arranged that the first turn would be given to a United Press reporter, and he asked, "What does the loss of Lieutenant Dixon mean to you and to the country?"

Xavier looked up to the heavens like he was searching for the right words to convey his thoughts. In truth, he'd learned his lines on the plane:

"Lieutenant Dixon's guidance and encouragement, in those early days and throughout my career, gave me confidence and the strength to persevere through any manner of hardships. I will miss him tremendously. As for our beloved country, Lieutenant Dixon's death is profound. He had so much more to give our beautiful nation. We will have to console ourselves with his legacy as a war hero. A legacy that is honorable and eternal."

A female reporter asked, "Will you be a pallbearer at the funeral?"

I winced at the thought. Xavier wasn't meant to play a featured role in the funeral service. The plan was that he and I would sit several rows back from the relatives in the front pews. We'd blend in with the regular mourners. The only nods to Xavier's star status were to be this brief press conference at the airport and a candid graveside snapshot at Arlington National Cemetery, taken with a long-lens camera by an Associated Press photographer. Some quotes and a solemn picture to run in the newspapers and magazines alongside the old photo of Horace and Xavier (and me) on the stage at the Dunbar Hotel.

I didn't want Xavier to give more. We were already blasphemous for breaking from the truth of Horace's life. My stipulation, unstated and unenforceable, was that Xavier and I keep the lies it took to justify our presence to a minimum.

"I'm not a pallbearer," Xavier said, "but I'm willing to do whatever Horace's family asks of me."

It was an innocent ad-libbed answer to a question that caught him off guard. I don't blame Xavier. Yet the second he said it, I felt the door had been opened too widely. We were inviting trouble.

15

BORROWED MEMORIES

The funeral was the following morning, and we were flying back west after the service concluded at the cemetery. The rest of our hours were meant to be spent holed up in the Mayflower Hotel. Xavier and I had separate suites on the tenth floor, and I drew the velvet curtains in mine, prepared to meet sleep, anguish, Horace's ghost, or whatever grabbed hold of me in the dark.

I stripped down to my boxer shorts, and I pulled back the blankets on my queen-size bed. Then Xavier knocked on our shared door, and I opened it to find him still dressed in his traveling clothes.

"Gladys Dixon left a message for me with the front desk," he explained.

"That would be Horace's sister."

"Yeah, well, she's staying at the Statler Hilton and wants me to meet her there."

"Don't go," I said. "Don't even call her back."

"Too late," Xavier blurted. "I rang her up to be polite and to tell her how I'm exhausted after the long flight, and she . . . steamrolled me."

I groaned.

"Feel however you want, I've gotta go now. I gave her my word, and I don't want to cross her."

"Fine, go charm her."

Xavier stepped into my room. "You're comin' with me," he insisted. "If I say the wrong thing, and she catches on that I'm full of bull, we're both fucked."

He was right. The Hollywood star couldn't stand up the sister of the dead war hero. That would find its way into one gossip column or another. News that the Hollywood star fabricated a connection to a dead war hero would make front pages, and Xavier would be eviscerated. People would think he was a heartless opportunist who lied for free publicity.

I got dressed in a navy-blue sweater and tan slacks that I bought along with a suit in a rush at a Bullock's in Palm Springs. Xavier peppered me with questions about Gladys. I told him what I remembered: She was Horace's older sister, and after their father was lynched and their mother committed suicide, Horace was shipped to Chicago to live with Gladys, who had struck out on her own at seventeen.

"Gladys was one of Madam C. J. Walker's sales reps. She went to damn near every Negro church and beauty parlor demonstrating how the hair products worked," I said to Xavier as we walked along Connecticut Avenue. "When she sold, they ate. When she didn't, they starved."

"Did they settle on a church for themselves?"

"Yes," I answered before the name came to me. "First Mount Zion Baptist.'"

Xavier nodded. "They believed in that old-time religion."

"Horace was ten, maybe eleven, and she whooped his little hide until he passed out because she caught him listening to *The All-Negro Hour* on the radio. In her opinion, comedy promoted sloth and wayward thinking."

Xavier asked over his shoulder, "Can I borrow any good memories between Horace and his sister? Any stories he told you that I can use with her?"

Borrowed memories. The oddity of our conversation pinched me hard on the bridge of my nose, and I squeezed my eyes shut to fight off the pronounced pang. Xavier was asking me to remember a time when Horace recounted a memory about him and his sister so that Xavier could memorize the details and share them with Gladys, who we hoped would remember the incident with her brother. How twisted. We were grave robbers, but instead of pulling gold rings off fingers, we were stealing a dead man's memories.

There was, however, no way to turn back now. "Horace enjoyed her singing. Gladys was in the choir, and she got solos."

"What songs?" Xavier asked eagerly.

"'Down by the Riverside' and 'Keep Me Every Day' were Horace's favorites."

Xavier breathed easy. He had another arrow in his quiver. I trudged behind him, wondering how I would react when I met Gladys, the savior and boogeyman of Horace's childhood. Gladys, the spinster sister and the last survivor in her immediate family. Gladys, the one Horace chose to return to in Chicago, instead of forging a life with me in Los Angeles. I never imagined I'd meet her, and now Xavier and I were entering the Statler Hilton.

I'm grateful that I spotted Gladys before she saw Xavier and me. Seated alone at a table in the hotel restaurant, she was a short, frail woman wearing a black dress with a hem that swept at her ankles, sleeves that cuffed her wrists, and a collar that climbed her neck. I rocked back on my heels.

"What?" Xavier asked.

"Her face . . . She and Horace came from the same mold for sure."

The resemblance, however, seemed contained to the harsher features. The brow set in skepticism. The mouth prematurely turned down at the corners. The eyes searching for weaknesses in what they beheld. The complexion and shapes of the nose and jawline were also identical, but what stood out was the face's default message: *I suffer no fools*.

Xavier plucked a stray thread from my sweater. "You ready?"

"Ready as I'm gonna get."

Gladys stood to greet us. She might have been an inch or two taller than five feet. Her hands were bony and her skin dry. She greeted us with the voice of a stern schoolteacher. Xavier and I took our seats after offering our condolences, and a Black waiter poured coffee for Xavier and me. Gladys drank herbal tea. She stared at me for a beat, and I had to look away because her resemblance to Horace was too strong for me to handle.

"You were my brother's footman in the navy."

I forced a smile. "That's not quite the term for it."

"I don't care whatcha call it on the ship," she said. "Point is you was at his beck and call. He mentioned you."

I repressed the urge to grin wide. "Is that so? What did he say?"

Gladys turned her attention to Xavier. "He didn't mention you far as I can reckon."

Unfazed, Xavier leaned forward and lowered his voice like he was confiding a secret to Gladys. "No surprise there," he said. "Your brother made a much larger impression on me than I would expect I made on him. I was a kid, standing at the edge of the party while Lieutenant Dixon held court."

"He liked admirers and hangers-on," she said, tossing a glance at me. "Vanity. He couldn't shake it."

"There was more to Horace than that," I challenged.

She cut her eyes at me.

Xavier shielded me with a fresh lie. "Lieutenant Dixon looked after folks and didn't make a big show of it. He attended a showcase a group of us young actors put on, and he made it clear to everyone else in the audience that he was having a good time. My agent signed me that night."

Gladys pointed at me. "You must've been with him at that show. Seems Horace rarely took a step out west without you tagging along."

"Is that how he told it?" I asked, sounding much too indignant.

"And then some," she said. "It's fitting that all these years later, you've hitched your wagon to another handsome stud full of potential."

I raised my hand and pointed at her. "Lookee here—"

Xavier squeezed my knee under the table and spoke as if he were introducing me to Gladys. "Miss Dixon, Aaron proved his loyalty to your brother during the war."

"I'm no sponger," I added.

She locked eyes with me and curled her lips like her brother did before he cursed. "Then what are you? In your tight sweater. What are you?"

Gladys wiped her mouth and looked down into her tea. Apparently, I wasn't the only one at our table battling with truths best left unsaid, and her feelings had won the latest round. An insinuation laid bare and unretracted.

I assessed my position. Gladys hadn't raised her voice and created a scene. Yet I felt humiliated. She hadn't outright charged me with being a homosexual, but my skin burned as if the letters *F-A-G* had been branded onto me. I wanted to belittle her in turn. Or explain that I'd bought the sweater without trying it on first. Or tell her in lurid detail how her brother lusted for me.

Instead, I said, "You must be sick with grief. You hardly know what you're saying."

"Perhaps," she allowed before pivoting to Xavier again. "The word *friend* means one thing in Hollywood and something different everywhere else. Did you know Horace or simply drink on his tab?"

Xavier assured her, "I knew him, ma'am. Although maybe not in the ways you'd prefer."

Gladys's mouth tightened, and I fixed a worried gaze on Xavier, unsure where he was headed.

"I didn't figure I'd have to paint it to you plain," he continued, "you being a Christian woman. But I stayed with Horace to the end of the night in many bars. Leaving the navy was rough on him, and Hollywood wasn't the gold mine he'd dreamed it would be. I won't tell just anybody, but I'll be straight with you. Your brother drank a lot. Most people called it a night after two or three drinks. Not him. Even Aaron would pack it in, and your brother would still be going. I'd stick with him, and that's when he'd get to really talking.

"These aren't the sort of stories you can share in church. I heard what the Klan did to your papa and how it broke your ma. He spoke of sleeping hungry. He spoke about you and the way you raised him. He told me that he thought of running away some nights, but you know what kept him from it?"

Gladys shook her head.

"He didn't want to miss out on hearing you sing in church come Sunday. 'Down by the Riverside'—I believe that's the one he liked best."

The tears appeared and fell from Gladys's eyes in a single instant. She put one hand over her mouth and another hand on top of Xavier's forearm. He'd pierced her heart in less than ten minutes. She cried quietly for a few more, and Xavier gave her the white silk pocket square from his suit jacket.

I also felt the urge to cry swelling inside my chest. Doing so would have condemned me further in Gladys's eyes and spoiled Xavier's efforts. With a trembling hand, I picked up the butter knife, and under the table, I gripped the dull blade in my palm. Not hard enough to draw blood, but tight enough to hold back tears.

Once Gladys composed herself, she patted Xavier's arm and said,

"I was afraid you were a poacher. I've already had to chase off one or two."

"Poachers?" I asked.

"Horace rarely said a word about how we grew up," she explained to Xavier. "Few people have any idea what we went through. They only know him as the war hero. I don't want the whole of tomorrow to be nothing but boasting about men killing men."

"He was more than that, too," Xavier said.

"I intended to send you packing," Gladys revealed. "I don't care for the movies or movie people. That dark one the girls fuss over. Sidney something. He called offering his sympathies—and asking if he can buy my brother's life story. I hung up on him."

Xavier said, "I'm here to pay my respects, nothing more."

"Yes, I see you are moved by a righteous spirit. I'd like you to speak at the service tomorrow."

"I couldn't," he was quick to insist.

"You must. My brother in Hollywood was a man in the wilderness. He was at his lowest, but he still shepherded you in brotherhood. I want folks to hear about that man. He's closer to the Horace I loved before that ugly war in Korea. When we had next to nothing, he wasn't full of himself. He didn't have to play the hero everywhere he went."

I opened my mouth to object but realized nothing good would come of it.

"You want me to deliver a eulogy?" Xavier clarified.

"Eulogy, testimonial." She shrugged. "Let the Lord guide your words."

I dropped the butter knife onto the floor.

Xavier attempted once more to decline. "While I'm honored that you'd think I could—"

"Good, it's settled. You'll speak after Pastor Stewart."

I excused myself from the table. The men's restroom was too far away for me to maintain control over the swelling in my chest. I looked for cover and spotted a row of telephone booths in the hotel hallway, and I ducked into one, sliding the door closed and turning my back to the glass. I held the phone to my ear so anyone walking by would think I was in the middle of an important conversation. I wept silently. Horace was dead, and I now understood the irrevocable cost of attending his funeral under false pretenses: I was to be drawn into blistering circles of hell.

16

DON'T QUESTION

When Xavier and I reached his hotel suite, I fixed myself an Irish coffee. I was desperate for warmth and relief. After a couple of sips, the whiskey eased the ache in my shoulders and neck. Xavier smoked another cigarette in the chain he'd started since we bid Gladys goodbye.

He huffed. "I don't know what to say."

Since I was responsible for our predicament, the burden was mine to shoulder. "I'll write the eulogy for you."

"No, don't put yourself through that," he advised.

"You can't get away with boilerplate remarks," I insisted. "The press is gonna get wind of this, before or after, and they're gonna demand a copy of your speech. This might put you on the front of *Jet*."

Xavier slumped onto a leather couch. "You're playing to my vanity, but I haven't forgotten that we're in DC for you. You need to make peace."

"I will—through you."

He shook his head. "Is there any way I can stop you from tearing yourself up?"

I sat on the armchair perpendicular to Xavier. "You wowed her with the material I gave you. I just have to do it one last time."

I went back to my suite and sat at a small mahogany desk, where I held a fountain pen and stared at blank pages of Mayflower stationery. My instinct was to write a simple tribute. Talk about Horace in his quiet and vulnerable moments. Chip away at the hero myth that his sister despised. Xavier would add the right mix of charm and pathos to elevate my words. And everything would be under control.

I wrote two drafts. Each was a ball of tangled platitudes. I ripped them up and tossed them into the brass trash bin. Xavier knocked and told me it was lunchtime. I wasn't hungry but mixed a whiskey and soda and returned to the small desk. Hours passed.

A sentence came to me: *In the sky, Horace was sure of his every move, but on the ground, he tripped and stumbled like the rest of us*. Not a gushy opening to a eulogy. I almost crumpled up this false start, too. Then I made another whiskey and soda, and as I drank the final sip, it hit me that Xavier's gifts as an actor would soften the blow of whatever I wrote.

I followed that first line, and I described Horace, not as he appeared in headlines or in citations but as he sweat and breathed. I honored his drive, which could be admirable or cold depending on where you stood with him. I acknowledged his struggle to find a place for himself in Hollywood. I touched upon how he found it difficult to love other people and to accept the love given to him.

The booze had my head rocking on a gentle tide when I returned to Xavier's room. He ordered room service for both of us, and we ate a late dinner in his suite. I poured myself a glass of red wine. I handed him the pages, and he set them aside. I tried not to prod him. I got as far as two bites into my lamb chops.

"You should read it."

"You should get some food in you," he said. "I'll study it before I go on tomorrow."

"You should read it in case I need to rewrite any of it," I said. "I might have gone too far, and we don't need anyone wondering if you and Horace were . . . lovers."

"Lovers?" Xavier dropped his knife and fork and went to retrieve the pages. "Did you write a tribute or a confession?"

"You tell me. "

Xavier leaned against the wall as he read the remarks silently.

"It's damn fine work," he said. "Better than the lines I'm usually given. There are some sentences I'd nix."

"Which ones?"

Xavier read in a neutral voice, "'His affections were sweeter because he could be so withholding. . . . I miss his anger as much as his tenderness. . . . You can only be your true self with a handful of people, and you're lucky if you get to meet even one of them.'"

I stopped him before he could force me to hear another line. "Got it. Cut what you like."

I helped myself to another glass of red. Xavier put the pages on the table next to his half-eaten lamb chops. He reached for his wineglass and emptied it with a gulp.

"You're blocked up," he said.

I was tipsy enough to assume that he was talking about constipation. "No, I'm regular."

"Not that kind of blocked. It's a problem in acting and life. You feel several strong emotions at once, and you judge yourself for feeling them, and you try to suppress certain feelings because you've decided they aren't appropriate. Basically, you tie yourself into knots. You're blocked."

"Is this that New School, Brando, Method shit?"

"No, that's bastardized Stanislavski," he explained as he took a seat to my left and pulled it close to me at the circular dining room table. "This is Stella Adler's technique, which is more in line with Stanislavski."

"You sound like a televangelist."

"Listen, this could help you." His earnestness made him ever-more handsome, and the combination of the cologne and the cigarette smoke clinging to his skin was alluring. "To unblock, you need to play the scene without judgment. Don't question what you say or do. Just react. Give yourself over to the circumstances."

Uneasy, I laughed. "What circumstances?"

"You've got feelings you need to get off your chest—beyond what you wrote." Xavier clasped the side of my neck and massaged it gently. "You need to speak with Horace."

Now my head was swimming through choppy waters. "Whatever this is, stop."

"C'mon, say what you've got to say to Horace. Close your eyes if you need to, and I'll play him for you."

"Xavier—"

"Try. Just try."

His grip on my neck got firmer, and he looked adamant. I was drunk, and I didn't have the wherewithal to argue with him. Complying seemed like a faster and tidier solution.

"All right," I said. "How do we do this?"

"You'll talk. Whatever comes to mind, let it out. And I'll answer as Horace."

"How will you know what he'd say?"

"I've got a good handle on who he was. Anyway, whatever I say, don't get hung up on whether he would or wouldn't say it. People say things all the time that we can't believe came out of their mouths, and we don't question it, because we heard it. It is what it is, and we react. Do that with me."

I closed my eyes, and Xavier put his other hand on my thigh. He leaned closer, and his body heat warmed the air between us, and my face began to tingle. I could feel his breath on my skin.

"Your sister hates me," I said, and I loathed how whiny and aggrieved I sounded, but I pressed past my disdain. "She can only know me through you. You tell her I was some gay puppy dog you couldn't kick hard enough to get to quit following after you?"

"She could never understand what we were to each other,"

Xavier replied in an even tone. "She's got no monopoly on the truth."

I sobbed and pressed my forehead against Xavier's. "But why couldn't you just tell her I was a good friend? How did I end up being the one to blame? I didn't ruin us in Hollywood."

The calm voice replied, "I was angry when I left you. I thought awful things, I said awful things. That's what happens after a breakup. How highly did you speak of me?"

We were talking into each other's mouths.

"I didn't say a word about you. There was no one I could tell. You left me with no one."

With no pity, the voice said, "You made out fine."

That was the Horace I knew. He brooked no bellyaching. My survival was proof to him that he'd done me no real harm.

"You bastard." I latched onto his forearms, and with my eyes shut, I might as well have been in our bungalow on the last day I saw him alive. "You can bad-mouth me to whoever you like, but what do you tell yourself?"

Horace said, "I loved you as far as I could."

"Bullshit. You got scared and ran."

"Doesn't mean I didn't love you."

"You wrote me letters that revealed nothing."

"Did you write me anything better than what I gave you?"

"You sent me a wedding gift but couldn't put your name on it."

"What did you ever send me?"

"You never reached out for a visit."

"Neither did you."

"It wasn't on me to bridge the distance. You were the one who walked away. You failed to come back to me."

"Doesn't mean I didn't love you."

"You broke me, and you're the only thing that can heal me, and you're gone."

"I'm right here."

He was. I believed with total conviction. Horace held me by the neck, squeezed my thigh, rested his forehead against mine, and shared breath with me.

"I'm here for you," he said.

I closed the gap between us and kissed him. He drew me in with his hands, and we met on our knees as our chairs tumbled to the side. I groped him, and his cock was as rigid as iron. I went to unbuckle his belt, and his hands stopped me.

"Aaron . . ."

I opened my eyes, and I was startled to find Xavier before me. Yet the craving that had been ignited inside me didn't mind the difference in partners. It would accept a substitute so long as its demands were satisfied.

Xavier's lips were still parted, and he edged toward me. Both of us had lost hold of the reins. Slowly, we met with another kiss. He let me unfasten his belt. He wanted to provide relief in any manner of my choosing, and my mind was running on a blistering combination of grief, whiskey, arousal, and wine.

There might as well have been three of us on the dining room floor of the presidential suite. With my pants caught around my ankles, I fulfilled my taboo fantasies of sex with Xavier, and whenever I elected to imagine that I was reunited with Horace, my body reacted as if that were the case. I gave myself to both men that night. The hurriedness of the hard fuck belonged to Horace, and the kisses and stroking to climax were Xavier's doing. It was the most intense and electric lay of my life, and I didn't begin to regret it until I awoke alone in my hotel bedroom the morning of Horace's funeral.

17

GRIEF AND AROUSAL

The heater in my room conked out during the night, and I shivered awake at dawn. My head and my ass were already aching and throbbing in sync with my heartbeat. The hangover reminded me not to drink spirits and wine during a bender. My rear end notified me that before the previous night, nearly eight years had passed since I was last sodomized. (I had been faithful during my marriage, quitting my trips to the gay men's bathroom at the airport.)

From under my bedsheets, I used the telephone on the nightstand to call the front desk to report the broken heater and to order aspirin, coffee, and a bowl of oatmeal. I dragged myself gingerly to the shower, and with every step, my physical discomfort was raging, and I wished it were a hundred times worse.

I deserved to be obliterated. I'd betrayed Kimberly; I'd prostituted Xavier; and I'd violated my professional duties. I'd sullied myself and everything I touched. And I didn't see how I could make amends.

A waiter and a repairman arrived at my door shortly after I finished dressing in my gray suit and vest. I swallowed the aspirin with scalding coffee, and I ate my breakfast, deciding what was less cruel—confessing my affair to Kimberly or keeping it from her.

The repairman got the heat working and practically refused to leave until I gave him a tip. It was 7:30 AM, and I debated whether Xavier would still be in his bed. We were supposed to meet the limo driver in the lobby at nine, and the funeral service was scheduled to begin at ten. Xavier wouldn't need more than half an hour to get himself up to snuff. I crept down the hall and pressed my ear to the door of his suite. I heard no movement.

I retreated to my suite, wondering how Xavier felt about the jackrabbit sex we'd had. Quick but gratifying. We came in tandem. "It's all right," he repeated as we pulled up our pants and I headed for the door. Although he had shepherded me through our encounter, he appeared dazed in the aftermath. His innocent exercise in channeling had gone awry. Maybe he worried that he'd taken advantage of me. Or perhaps the way he saw it, I'd abused him, and his *It's all right* mantra was something he'd said to soothe himself.

When it was almost nine o'clock, I peeked through my peephole and waited until I spotted Xavier walking past en route to the elevators. I held back for a few seconds before stepping out into the hallway. I hurried to his side.

"Good morning," I said.

"Morning," he replied with no emotion and no eye contact.

"Last night—"

"Shouldn't have happened and won't happen again."

"Agreed."

He pushed the button to summon the elevator.

"I'm sorry."

"So am I."

The elevator arrived, and we stepped inside. There were three other hotel guests already aboard. I was grateful that we couldn't continue to talk more about our mishap. If he harbored no hard feelings, I was eager to resume our roles as good-humored brotherly pals.

Of course, I was wishing for a whole helluva lot. We'd taken a bite of the forbidden apple, and it whetted our sexual appetites. That was the wicked allure to our temptation: We recognized the act was wrong, but there had been unmatched pleasure while we transgressed. No one accounted for how delicious the apple tasted.

Xavier and I didn't speak and barely looked at each other during the limousine ride to the Nineteenth Street Baptist Church. Xavier studied the eulogy I wrote, and I stared out the limo's tinted window and watched the snow powder the streets and buildings. As we neared the stately church with its two steeples and arched windows, our limo was stopped by foot traffic.

Black people came pouring from every direction. The sidewalks couldn't contain the crowd, forcing many to cross and walk in the street. The women donned dark mourning hats and were wrapped in fur coats. The men wore black suits or, if they were veterans, their service dress blues. A handful of children were dragged along in their Sunday best.

"We'll get out here," Xavier told the chauffeur.

Xavier opened his door and stepped outside into the falling snow. The limo had already caught the attention of pedestrians. A few had even shaded their eyes with their hands and peered close to the back-seat windows to see if they could make out who was inside. Once Xavier emerged from the limo, his height and his beauty made him a focal point. I got out of the limo on my side, and no one took the slightest notice, as was natural.

Someone shouted, "That's Barlow!"

The information and the ensuing excitement spread like ripples from a stone dropped into a placid lake. Murmurs of "Xavier," "Barlow," "star," and "Hollywood" overlapped and crescendoed until everyone on the block knew who the famous mourner was. Xavier pressed forward through the crush of bodies that clamored for his handshake, his wave, his passing glance. I struggled to walk in his wake. A reporter from *The New Crusader* climbed onto the hood of a parked car to snap photographs. Xavier didn't offer a smile. Instead, he nodded somberly to his fans and made his way toward the church steps.

Word of Xavier's arrival had reached the folks gathered inside Nineteenth Street Baptist, and Gladys greeted him outside the front door of the church. Her stoic face was just visible behind the veil of her black, wide-brimmed hat. Xavier brought her hand up to his lips and kissed her fingertips. A reporter from *Jet* caught the moment from over Gladys's shoulder with Xavier's face in the foreground and I in the sea of Black mourners behind him. It was the photo that ran on the cover of *Jet* a week later.

Xavier said, "My condolences, sister."

"God bless you," Gladys replied. "Sit in the pew behind the family. I'm eager to hear your tribute."

"I'll do my best, sister."

Gladys kept her hands at her side while I offered my condolences. Then she bowed her head and gestured with her eyes that I should move it along. She remained outside to welcome others. Xavier and I entered the church, and he shook hand after hand until I realized we weren't headed to our seats.

We were in the viewing line. Horace's cherrywood casket was open and lying in state before the pulpit. Catching glimpses of him through the people ahead of me, I couldn't make out his features, but light gleamed off the top of his bald head. I reached for a funeral program from an usher, and I rolled the program up, squeezing it tightly. I stopped moving forward.

Xavier noticed, turned to me, and said, "You came this far."

I mustered my courage and walked behind him. Xavier continued to attract attention from pastors and congregants alike. He was unruffled by the bombardment. I focused on watching him as we came to the foot of the coffin.

I braced myself before looking at Horace. He was wearing his dress blue uniform. His placid face appeared more lined and tauter than I anticipated. The mortician had done his best to conceal lacerations on the forehead, nose, and chin with makeup. I shook my head. This wasn't Horace. This was an imitation. The guys in the props department fabricated this wax figure.

My irrational doubt was squashed when it was my turn to stand before Horace and say my last words to his face. Up close, despite the toll of death, I couldn't deny that my first love was in repose. The urge to kiss him led me to bend forward. I stopped myself before I caused a scandal.

Instead, I whispered, "We should've stuck together."

I made it to our row behind Horace's family before I started to cry. Xavier lent me a spare handkerchief. He moved his arm as if he was going to drape it over my shoulders, only to rethink the implications and retract his limb. Not only might such a gesture be misconstrued by onlookers, but he likely worried that touching me would give me the wrong ideas. So, quietly, I wept, aware that I was to receive no physical comfort.

The senior pastor began the funeral service acknowledging Horace's extraordinary deeds and tragic demise. He led us in prayer. He introduced the first selection from the choir. The organist played the opening of "How Great Thou Art," and from her seat in the front row of pews, Gladys proceeded to outsing the choir's soloist during the verses. Gladys's voice was powerful if unpolished. She reminded me of those big-tent revival singers.

The senior pastor read a long passage from Psalms. I was wedged between Xavier and a stout, older man, and the warmth inside the packed church swaddled me. The senior pastor's cadence and timbre rocked me into a stupor, and I lost the meaning of his sermon. But he delivered two lines like thunderclaps: *Oh, that I had wings like a dove! For then would I fly away and be at rest.* After another half an hour, the pastor tracked down his conclusion.

The choir sang "In My Home Over There." The senior pastor read a citation honoring Horace from Walter Tobriner, president of the board of commissioners, the closest thing to a mayor the district was allowed to have by Congress and the White House. Then a representative from the navy was called forth: Chief Petty Officer Preston Walsh.

The mention of his name transported me back to the deck of our carrier scanning the horizon for Horace's missing bird. I used my will that day to reject the very possibility of Horace's death. What I would have given to have those powers.

Walsh walked into the pulpit and adjusted the microphone, causing a squeal of feedback. Time had treated him well. He looked older and a bit heavier, but still attractive. He wore his service dress blue and a wedding band. I hoped that he was happy.

Walsh said, "I requested to be the navy rep for this sorrowful occasion, because I served with Lieutenant Dixon during the Korean War."

The congregation applauded and shouted out praise to God and for Walsh.

"To this day, Lieutenant Dixon is the best fighter pilot," he continued, "that I have ever had the honor of brushing shoulders with. He was fearless, confident to the utmost, and effective."

Walsh looked up from his notes and spotted me. I was barely capable of holding his gaze, but we shared a moment. Then I lowered my head.

"Lieutenant Dixon was a true-blue patriot," Walsh concluded, "and, personally, I will never forget how he rid me of my prejudice toward Negroes. May he rest in peace."

The other Black mourners inside Nineteenth Street Baptist applauded the repentant former racist. I wondered how Horace, who was unabashedly arrogant and mercurial during the war, could have led any white man on our ship to think better of colored people. Was

Walsh intentionally rewriting history, or had time and death sincerely softened his recollection?

One of Horace's nephews delivered a eulogy on behalf of the Dixon family. The young man's resemblance to Horace was too distracting for me to listen to him. I felt guilty that I found him sexy. I was discovering that my grief and arousal were intertwined. To cool down, I stared at the funeral program and read Horace's short obituary over and over.

Finally, the senior pastor asked Xavier to come forward and offer his remembrance. The congregation clapped and shouted as Xavier walked the aisle and climbed the stairs to the pulpit. He left my handwritten pages lying in his seat, and I pocketed them.

Having seen how the sunshine filtered through the church windows to light the previous speakers, Xavier positioned himself half a foot left of center to the microphone. His dark skin was bathed in golden rays, and the effect was majestic. He looked like an angel of the Lord.

Xavier said, "I appreciate being asked to speak about the great man that we are sending off to be with the Lord our God."

My chest tightened. He was improvising.

"I want to honor him, and to do so, I must be candid. Horace didn't mince words, and I feel he'd insist I'd do the same, especially in a house of God."

The congregation encouraged him, stomping their feet and yelling, "Well!" and "Amen!"

Xavier took in the whole of his audience, then turned his gaze to Horace's coffin. "In the sky, Lieutenant Dixon—Horace—was sure of his every move, but on the ground, he tripped and stumbled like the rest of us. Out of uniform, he wasn't a hero. He was a man."

These words were mine. Xavier had memorized his lines, making it appear as if he were talking extemporaneously from the heart. I relaxed in the pew.

"And he was not always an easy man to be around, particularly in Hollywood. That peculiar town didn't know what to make of Horace's talents, and he grew frustrated with the empty promises and fair-weather partnerships of that business. Yet even as he was struggling to find his footing, he rescued me from my despair. He noticed me and took me into his heart. We spent quite a few late nights in bars. Usually, nothing God would approve of happens in a bar."

The congregation shouted and stomped with knowing affirmation. Even Gladys clapped her hands. This was as close to truth-telling as anything spoken thus far at the service.

"But Horace used that time to talk to me about the war and to share what he'd learned about being a man and about leaving your mark on this world. I will always treasure the time he gave me. We didn't know each other long when you consider the span of a lifetime, but he reached me. His guidance and approval led me to believe in my own worth, and I still try to carry myself in accordance with his strong judgment. He molded me as a man."

I observed the church ladies, the pastors, the choir members, and the laymen, and they looked upon the bond that Xavier was describing with wholesome joy. The essence of what Horace and I shared pleased this saved community of earthly saints, so long as no detail of sex between men was mentioned. Gay love could be accepted as a chaste tale.

It struck me as ridiculous to praise the spirit of a love and reject the carnal expression of that same love. Yet I reveled in how they received my words. This was an unexpected gift: to have my relationship recognized and voiced, even if the messenger wasn't me.

"He taught me that the world owed me nothing," Xavier said, "which is why it's a blessing to cross paths, if just for a little while, with someone whose soul speaks to yours. Thank you, Horace, for walking the road with me until our courses pulled us in different directions. Fly with the angels, my brother."

Gladys beat the rest of the churchgoers to their feet, and Xavier basked modestly in the rapture of a standing ovation. I stood up and applauded. The release I sought began, and the heaviness weighing on my soul started to relent. I felt lighter as Horace's coffin was closed and carried out of Nineteenth Street Baptist and loaded into the hearse. Lighter still when we arrived at his open grave site at Arlington National Cemetery. When the senior pastor finished the final prayer and Horace's casket was lowered into his plot, I believed that I, too, could bury him in the recess of my memory.

During the limousine ride from the cemetery to the private airport, I thanked Xavier for playing along in this grand deception that allowed me to pay my respects to Horace. He told me to consider it repayment for the latitude and protection that I'd provided him over the years. Because the chauffeur could hear us, our conversation was surface level, devoid of incriminating details, and I was unable to question Xavier about what our ordeal had been like for him.

We spoke some more during the flight to Palm Springs, but with studio handlers surrounding us, again we kept it light. Xavier was cordial, occasionally funny. I thought we were returning to our routine.

I was mistaken. Filming resumed on *House Money*, and the change in my access to Xavier was immediate. We kept our adjoining rooms, but the door between them was locked on his side. We shared meals and drinks together, but not just the two of us like before. Xavier invited his costars to join us. Our private connection was gone, and he maintained a professional posture that gave me no grounds to complain to the studio about his behavior. As long as he kept his nose clean, I couldn't exactly write Xavier up for refusing to be my pal. I was checkmated.

House Money wrapped. It was released in July to glowing reviews and robust box office receipts. Xavier landed a Golden Globe nomination for Best Actor in a Motion Picture. He lost at the 1963 ceremony to Gregory Peck for his performance in *To Kill a Mockingbird*. Diahann Carroll, whose divorce from her first husband was finalized, was Xavier's date to the award show. They made for a smashing couple in photos.

Although there was no Oscar nomination for his work in *House Money*, Xavier's career took a major leap forward. Anthony Riley, a film agent at Lew Wasserman's MCA, signed Xavier as a client. With a bare-knuckle style that endeared him to few, Riley managed to break Xavier's contract with Skyline Motion Pictures, and he signed Xavier into a lucrative two-picture deal with MGM. Xavier was a bona fide star. He was also no longer under my watchful eye.

18

BE LESS THREATENING

After Xavier signed with MGM, I spent the next five years at Skyline looking after the likes of Ivan Dixon, Flip Wilson, Cicely Tyson, and Diahann. At industry galas and parties thrown by and for Black celebrities, I bumped into Xavier periodically. He and I kept our conversations surface level. I complimented his latest film, and he sent his love to Kimberly. In this fashion, we were like distant old friends who preferred to keep our relationship at a remove.

He had his work to keep him busy, and I had mine. Skyline showed interest in plenty of young Black talent for me to vet, and the studio even signed deals with a slew of hopefuls. But I was surprised that more of the aspiring Black stars I worked with didn't become famous. They had the goods but weren't groomed and promoted by the studio like their predecessors were. In fact, Xavier was the last star I saw advanced film by film in the reliable, deliberate manner that made him bankable.

It seemed to me that the studios got skittish about turning actors and actresses into household names once stars got entangled in politics that split the audience—a shift that caught the industry off guard. You see, we were all rowing in the same direction during the Second World War when John Garfield and Bette Davis organized the Hollywood Canteen as an oasis for the visiting enlisted and when the beloved Carole Lombard lost her life in the campaign to sell war bonds.

Then came the congressional effort to purge Communists, ex-Communists, and Communist sympathizers from government, universities, television, and the movies. A lot of prominent executives and producers in the film industry agreed with the aim of the House Un-American Activities Committee (HUAC), if not its tactics. In the opposing corner were the actors, writers, and directors supporting the Hollywood Ten, who were held in contempt for refusing to testify before HUAC. The clash resulted in a blacklist that barred hundreds of actors from appearing on screens, silver or small, and the ban quietly persists for some to this day. Worse still for the bottom line, moviegoers began to factor in whether a star's politics matched their own before buying a ticket.

The political calculus got even more complicated for Black stars as the struggle for civil rights dominated the evening news and front pages across the country. If they didn't take a stand, they alienated a significant number of their Black fans, and if they did take a stand, they lost a lot of white fans. It was a moral test for the stars; it was a financial liability for the studios.

Xavier and other Black stars tended to join marches and protests in groups, so as not to be singled out. Xavier, along with the likes of Diahann, Sidney, Ruby Dee, Ossie, Harry, and Nat, participated in the March on Washington for Jobs and Freedom in 1963; the St. Augustine Movement; and the Selma-to-Montgomery march in 1965. Although it had to be kept out of the press, I know that on his own, Xavier met with and gave money to Malcom X, members of the Afro-American Association, and leaders of the Communist Party USA. He was daring.

Studios were not, and the safe solution for them as the issue of civil rights ran hotter was to mint fewer Black stars. Simple arithmetic pointed the way. Why would any businessman spend hundreds of thousands of dollars developing Black talent that could render his investment worthless with one brash comment from the actor condemning the South or charging Northern whites with hypocrisy? The smart money bankrolled white actors and actresses who were under no obligation to offer an opinion on the latest acts of police violence against peaceful Black marchers. So, between 1962 and 1966, the town did not nurture another Xavier.

Not that *the* Xavier C. Barlow would have noticed the competition. His post-Skyline years were plum, and he proved, in my opinion, to be a better actor than Sidney. (Sidney remains the better star of the two.) Xavier was the lead in *Harlem Justice* (1963) and *Forgive and Forget* (1963) for MGM; *A Pound of Flesh* (1963) for Paramount; and *The Left-Handed Gunman* and *Card Shark* (both 1964) for Columbia Pictures. He garnered two more Golden Globe nominations in the lead actor category in 1964 for *Harlem Justice* and in 1965 for *Card Shark*. The Hollywood Foreign Press chose the nominees of the Golden Globe Award, and they appreciated rakish charm.

Nominations, however, were not trophies, and Xavier still hungered for recognition from the Academy Awards. Unfortunately, his silver screen image missed the sweet spot. Building upon the success of his portrayal of a morally questionable private investigator in *House Money*, Xavier's subsequent roles continued along that antihero line. He completely negated the early roles in which he was the dopey younger brother who got scammed at every turn. As a leading man, Xavier exuded cunning and danger. No one got the better of him without paying a price, and that went for his enemies and his expendable love interests alike. Audiences adored seeing Xavier outsmart corrupt politicians, bankers, cops, lawyers, and factory owners, but Oscar voters didn't go for tough guys in the noir style.

If Xavier's goal had been to mimic Sidney Poitier's persona, he lacked the inherent refinement and admirable dignity that Sidney brought to his parts. In short, American white moviegoers needed Xavier to be less threatening. After all, Sidney did break the color barrier for Black actors at the Academy Awards, winning the Oscar in 1964. But it wasn't for playing the rudely ambitious son in *A Raisin in the Sun* (1961); it was for portraying a compliant handyman who single-handedly builds a chapel for an order of nuns in *Lilies of the Field* (1963).

Nuns could only light candles and pray for the characters Xavier embodied. He was in camp with the uneasy appeal of Robert Mitchum in *The Night of the Hunter* (1955). Mitchum, whose only Oscar nomination (Best Supporting Actor)—to date, which came when he played a doomed soldier in 1945's *Story of G.I. Joe*—remains a box office draw more than two decades later, but his nails aren't clean enough for the Academy.

Of course, with the right picture, an actor could be reborn in the eyes of the industry. In March of 1966, Lowell Garten thought he had the role that would earn Xavier the respectability and accolades he craved. Moreover, Lowell was willing to bestow the best release date and the largest budget on the Xavier film. It was quite a reversal for Skyline Motion Pictures, which had trimmed its output and pinched pennies during production for the last couple of years.

Lowell had proven to be a stricter and more hands-on studio boss than his late father. He dropped in on sets in the middle of production and watched the filming over the shoulders of the directors. He summoned writers to take notes on the "setups" and "golden threads" that he expected them to weave into riveting screenplays. He recut movies in editing.

It was routine for people in the business to gripe that Lowell was power drunk. I considered that a lazy take. Lowell had waited decades to exercise the authority that befits a studio boss. He was no more or less aggressive and capricious than Richard Zanuck was at Twentieth or than Robert Evans would be at Paramount, and those men are celebrated in the trades.

When Lowell's secretary called and informed me that I was wanted in Lowell's office immediately, my initial thought was, *Diahann and*

Sidney have gone off and eloped. Both were, at last, divorced from their first spouses. The runway was clear.

Instead, Lowell met me at the door to his office with the order, "You need to go speak to your old friend. You still have his number, don't you?"

"Depends. Can I get a name?"

"Xavier. No one else is right for this picture. This is the golden opportunity I always knew would come his way. Tell him I'll pay top dollar, and there will be something in it for you, too."

I followed Lowell outside onto the terrace. The sun was directly overhead. I squinted as I looked at the sparkling ocean.

"Boss, you've got me in the dark. What picture?"

"You being coy?" He put his hands on his hips. "I figured the family was keeping you abreast of our negotiations." He smiled triumphantly. "We bought Lieutenant Dixon's life rights back. Closed the deal myself last night."

I forced a smile, realizing that Lowell would be confused and disappointed if I was anything other than exuberant. I just pressed my teeth together and opened my mouth wide. I even pushed a laugh out of my throat. My face probably looked pained and maniacal, but it did the trick. Inside, I felt sick.

"His sister resisted selling the rights for years, but I finally talked her into it," Lowell continued. "I sort of assured her that Xavier would play her brother. If I don't deliver him, the life rights revert to her, and she'll keep a hefty chunk of change."

"It will all work out," I said cheerfully. "Xavier will leap at the chance."

"His agent, Roaring Riley, didn't seem keen on it. Could be bullshit to raise his quote. Could be real. You can get a read on Xavier for me, right?"

"Sure," I croaked. "I'll reach out."

Lowell patted me hard on the back. "We get cameras rolling, and I'll sweeten the pot for you. I figure an extra three hundred dollars a week can come your way as an accuracy consultant. Make sure the lingo is correct and that those fags in the art department don't turn the carrier into a dollhouse."

He laughed, and we shook on our side deal. Lowell's secretary interrupted with the news that Natalie Wood was on line one. The secretary led me out while Lowell hopped on the phone. In the lobby of the Pober Building, my stomach seized, and I ran to the men's room. I reached a toilet just in time to vomit. A dozen years after our failed attempt, Horace's story was going to grace the silver screen at last.

PART III

19

POLITICAL THINKERS

The number for Xavier's answering service hadn't changed, and I left a message with the lady in the call center. Xavier rang me at my office within the hour. He knew I was reappearing on his radar because of the Horace movie, and he didn't want to discuss it over the phone. He invited me to his house on Coronado Terrace in Silver Lake.

I arrived at 4:00 PM, and the front door of his Craftsman house was ajar. The opening drumbeat and horns of "Uptight (Everything's Alright)" paraded through the air. I walked in and closed the door behind me just as Stevie Wonder started singing. The record player was spinning in the living room.

I removed the needle and shouted, "Hey, Xavier! I made it!"

"I'm in the library!" he answered.

I followed the sound of his voice through the dining room and past the kitchen. The house was decorated tastefully, but without a trace of showbiz glitz. You'd never have guessed a Hollywood star lived at this address. I walked down a hallway and entered a converted guest bedroom.

Xavier had lined the walls with floor-to-ceiling bookshelves, and a small-town librarian would have envied the number of books in his possession. Xavier sat in a yellow, upholstered wingback chair. He tucked a bookmark into the middle of *City of Night* by John Rechy and put the novel on a side table. He didn't rise to greet me, and I stood awkwardly in the doorway.

His sex appeal hadn't waned. Xavier the actor was thirty-one years old, while Xavier the man was twenty-nine, but by either count, he was aging glacially. His dark skin banished wrinkles and sunspots. His tall frame remained fit. The boyishness of his early years had hardened into a lean masculinity. He appeared camera-ready in his red polo shirt and his cream-colored slacks.

We'd last seen each other the previous September at a memorial service for Dorothy Dandridge held inside Forest Lawn Memorial Park's Great Mausoleum. Nearly every Black star who sang for her at the Dunbar party in her honor—the one she failed to attend—came to pay their respects. The noticeable exception, of course, was Billie Holiday, who had passed away in 1959 from heart failure brought on by cirrhosis of the liver. Billie had been only forty-four.

Diahann had insisted that I attend Dorothy's memorial even though I'd never met her. She wanted to mend the rift between Xavier and me. But he and I didn't discuss our issues. Instead, we shook hands and echoed the same lines of regret that the other attendees voiced: *What a shame. Dorothy taken out by an overdose. What a loss of talent. She was only forty-two. We can't lose another star like this ever again. Someone should check on Frankie Lymon.*

Out from under the pall of that dark episode, I whistled and made a show of admiring the hundreds of books in Xavier's library. "You read all these?"

"No, but I will someday." He sized me up. "You here of your own volition? Or did Lowell send you?"

"Lowell asked me if I would come talk to you, and I decided that I wanted to."

Xavier smirked. "It took him to get you to call on me. Nothing I did moved you? You couldn't send a telegram congratulating me on a performance or mail a Christmas card."

"Okay, you're not pussyfooting around." I braced myself; my visit might be brief. "I didn't come around because you didn't want me around. We fucked, and we never should've, and you cut me dead."

"We fucked?" Xavier shot up out of his chair and onto his feet. He jabbed his finger in my direction. "See, that right there. That's what stings. It was just a fuck to you?"

I was astounded. He stared at me like a wounded animal. I'd managed to hurt him deeply, and honest to God, I didn't know how.

"I didn't mean to cheapen it," I explained. "I don't know what to call what we did."

"Well, it wasn't sordid."

I wasn't trying to argue, but I felt I had to state the facts as I saw them. "We did screw on the floor with most of our clothes still on."

He huffed. "You wanted *Pillow Talk* with Doris Day and Rock Hudson? By the by, I could tell you a thing or two about Rock Hard Hudson."

"Don't bother," I said. "The files on him have their own cabinet."

"Point is that straight romance shit ain't nothing but a lie. You think we're dirty faggots because we didn't make it in a canopy bed surrounded by burning candles. But all that matters is the connection, the release we give each other. Doesn't matter if we do it on the floor, in the woods, or in some alleyway."

"If that's how you see it, why'd you give me the cold shoulder?"

"You iced me out," he protested.

He told me the story from his side. He recalled that throughout most of our encounter, when I moaned, I alternated between using his name and Horace's. Then as the pace quickened, I insisted that he was Horace. I ordered Xavier to be rougher with me, and when he hesitated, I begged, "Please, Horace." Xavier complied, acting more forcefully than he'd like.

Still, we orgasmed. Xavier was proud of what we'd shared. He tried to wrap his arms around me and hold me close. He wanted me to revel in the release. I pulled away. Shame cut off my afterglow, and I hiked up my pants and ran for the door like the room was on fire. Xavier attempted to soothe me, to slow me down, to rid me of my shame. "It's all right," he insisted. I wouldn't hear it.

"You were spooked, so I backed off." He gestured for me to take a seat in a rocking chair while he returned to his yellow wingback. "I was also mad. I thought we'd done something special, even beautiful. To see you recoil . . ."

"I didn't realize."

"It's not all your fault. You were brainwashed."

"How's that now?"

"The hete notions on courtship and love set us homos up for dissatisfaction."

"Which of these books told you that?"

Xavier smiled. "It's not just books; there are movements. Black, homophiles, women, migrant workers, pacifists—we're all breaking from the old order."

I was out of my depth in a political conversation with Xavier. I got my news from the *Los Angeles Times*, *Hollywood Reporter*, *Daily Variety*, *Jet*, and Walter Cronkite. I supported Rev. Martin Luther King Jr., and Kimberly and I were among the forty thousand at Wrigley Field when he spoke during the Los Angeles Freedom Rally. I also was a member in good standing with the NAACP and the Urban League. But I despised the college students burning their draft cards to dodge service in Vietnam, I didn't trust Communists, and I thought Malcolm X and the Muslims were rabble-rousing separatists. I considered myself a mainstream Black American.

Since the nights when I drove him out to the secret dirt lot in Griffith Park, Xavier was beyond me—he would say he was *ahead* of me—when it came to the latest political thinkers and trends. Xavier read *The Nation*; Frantz Fanon's *The Wretched of the Earth*; Simone de Beauvoir's *The Prime of Life*; *ONE Magazine*; and countless other works of ultraliberalism. He was confident of progress that was unthinkable to me.

I didn't have the knowledge to spar with Xavier, and I wanted to end the rift between us. So, I laid down my sword. I agreed to ideas that I didn't understand.

"You're right. I shouldn't have acted cold or ashamed," I said. "I still have a lot to learn."

"To unlearn," he stipulated.

"Yes, that, too." I stood up and spread my arms into the air to invite a hug. "I'm sorry, Xavier. Please forgive me."

He embraced me like the old days. "Apology accepted."

Xavier insisted that we eat some of the chili that he'd made a few nights before. He reheated it on the stove. I perched on a stool next to the pony wall that divided the kitchen from the dining room. We each had blood and sand cocktails within reach. The aroma from the chili made me keen to chow down.

"You on board for the Horace film?" he asked.

"Yeah, and I'm surprised you aren't. This part—"

"I'll kill it. I've got no worries on that end."

"Then what's the holdup?"

Xavier used a ladle to fill two bowls with chili. "I'd be chiseling a big, fat lie in stone. I pretended to be Horace's friend to get you through the funeral, a couple rough days. We skated by with the press. But the publicity for the movie is going to see to it that even Luddites hear that Horace and I were tight. They'll want cute anecdotes I can share with Mike Douglas in the morning and risqué ones I can tell Johnny Carson after midnight." He added chunks of pepper jack cheese to the chili. "Shit. Keeping the lie alive will be more work than acting in the film."

Xavier's reluctance wasn't a negotiating tactic, and the idea that he'd pass on this movie stirred a frenzy in me. The film, if it came to be, offered an enticing coda to my relationship with Horace. I could see through the mission that brought us to Los Angeles. His mother's prophecy would be realized. His legacy would live in eternal celluloid glory, if I got Xavier past his misgivings.

"I can take a lot of that load off your shoulders," I said. "We have the photo from the Dunbar, and I can corroborate any story we work up for you. As for other witnesses, Diahann adores you. She'll play ball."

Xavier carried our chili bowls to the dining room table, and I joined him there.

"Aren't you the one who taught me that the last thing you want to do is let in more people on a secret?"

I amended my rule. "You don't share a secret with anyone who doesn't have skin in the game. Diahann would be on our team."

"An accomplice," Xavier said before eating a spoonful of chili.

He didn't flinch. Therefore, I tried the chili with no warning as to how hot it was. The heat didn't set in until I swallowed a bite, and everything coated by the chili burned. I opened my mouth to inhale cool air, only to be reminded that fire feeds on oxygen.

I screamed, "Milk!"

Xavier ran to get me a glass. My eyes were watering, and my nose was running. I stopped breathing to keep my throat from flaring up again.

"Here!" Xavier shouted.

I drank the milk in grateful gulps, and once I regained the power of speech, I said, "There are gentler ways to murder me."

"I thought you'd like it," he said. "I guess I've built up a tolerance to the habaneros."

Then he laughed, and despite the burning sensation still putting up a fight in my mouth, I started laughing, too. Xavier cracked up so hard, he slapped the table repeatedly. I stomped my feet under the table. We egged each other on like cutups in the back of class.

Xavier was the one to say what I didn't dare: "It'd be good to have you around again."

"You've been blazing quite a trail without me."

He nodded and grinned. "Hardly anyone mentions it because they don't want to offend King Sidney, but my movies are making more money than any other Black star's. No jive—look it up."

"I believe you."

"Funny thing is, though, when I left Skyline for MGM, everyone at Metro bowed down to me from the start. 'Mr. Barlow, is everything to your liking?' 'Mr. Barlow, let us know if we can get you anything.'"

I teased him, "You complaining about star treatment?"

"No, I love it from just about everybody, but I'd like a couple people in my trailer to call me 'Xavier.'"

"And check you on your bullshit."

"To see through the fame." He took a sip of his cocktail. "I don't expect pity, but hear me out. Success is lonelier than typical folks can imagine. I tried to keep up with the actors from my old classes and the ones I used to see at the cattle calls. It breaks down. I'd listen to their problems and have nothing to say except, 'Hang in there.' They'd hear my problems and wish they had them. I didn't know how to tell them about my day without bragging. In '63, I was at the Venice Film Festival and bumped into Jimmy Cagney. I idolized him when I was a kid, and he told me he's a fan of mine."

I was duly impressed and said sincerely, "Holy shit."

"Right? Cagney quoted my lines from *House Money*." Xavier threw his head back and looked to the heavens in awe. "Try dropping that story in a bar with three brothers competing for the same nonspeaking role in a television commercial, where all they get to do is hand a basket of laundry to Gail Fisher."

"Goddamn."

"This is a mean business. The starving and the fortunate can't be friends."

I brought my glass of blood and sand to my lips, and Xavier snapped into hosting mode. He cleared my empty milk glass and bowl of chili from the table. From the kitchen, he asked, "Seeing as the chili was a bust, can I fix you something else to eat?" I ordered a plain turkey sandwich on wheat bread with lettuce and mustard.

Xavier returned with a harmless turkey sandwich, and I asked him, "What else is keeping you from accepting Skyline's offer?"

"They don't have a locked script."

I gritted my teeth to stifle a scoff. Actors, as a class, always come up with new demands, and an emerging trend among big stars was a fixation on having a "locked" script before filming started. In the history of film, this was a recent and impractical stipulation.

From the dawn of talkies in the late 1920s straight through into the 1950s, when our business worked with the dependability of a factory assembly line, actors were assigned to the films in which they appeared. At its most efficient, actors finished a picture on Friday, they received the working script to their new film over the weekend, and they started shooting that flick on Monday.

Working script in our lingo was a shade shy of redundant, because it went without saying that there would be rewrites. A part written with Bette Davis in mind would need adjusting if Bette was out on loan and got replaced by Barbara Stanwyck. Directors got fired and replaced on pictures quite routinely, and the new man behind the bullhorn would dictate story changes to suit his sensibilities. Even Mother Nature could force revisions in the script by raining on plans for exterior shoots or by demolishing outdoor sets with a fierce storm.

Rewrite chaos could still lead to classics. The script for *Casablanca* (1942) required the filming of two endings—one where Ilsa gets on the airplane alone, and another where Rick flew away with her. You see, scripts were malleable. Insisting otherwise amounted to a fool's bargain: The locked script was either ninety pages of lies or it failed to capture the creative adaptations that elevated great movies.

"There's no such thing as a locked script," I said, "until the print is running through the projector at the premiere. Besides, Horace's story is straightforward. He joins the navy, shoots down enemies, and dies in a tragic crash."

Xavier tilted his head down and fixed his eyes on me. "He did more than that."

I appreciated the acknowledgment, but I remained a realist. "Ain't no way our private affairs were ever gonna make the cut." My voice caught in my throat as I continued, "What is possible is an uplifting picture that every Black man, woman, and child can admire. Horace can be a legend."

"A credit to our race."

"That is worth something," I said, "and you'll reap rewards, too."

"I hear you. I see how it could all play out."

"But?"

"My agent is pressuring me to take another picture. John Frankenheimer wants me as the main rival to James Garner in a racing movie."

"You'd pass up a lead to be a costar?"

"It could be an international hit," he pleaded. "A Black war hero movie won't pack houses overseas."

He had a point, so I pivoted. "You know if you turn down the part, Lowell will call Sidney. You want to see him on-screen eating up a role that could have been yours?"

He howled. "You're using the sharp knives!"

"I'm spelling out a scenario. It's Oscar night, and you're watching at home, and Mr. Poitier is accepting his second bald statue."

Horace took a deep breath and stared up at the ceiling for a full minute. Then he raised his last hang-up. "There's no love story in Horace's picture. It's a war flick, pure and simple. Heroic, Americana."

"What's wrong with that?" I asked.

"You really don't mind?" He searched my face for signs of discomfort or ambivalence.

I had none. "Horace left Hollywood after M. K. Garten convinced him that his life couldn't be made into a profitable movie. I'd like to prove the old bastard wrong. I'd like Horace to be brought back to life by you."

20

ACUTELY UNSEEN

Lowell put *Hornet's Hellfire* on the fast track for his 1966 slate, and he announced Xavier's casting with a level of spectacle that set a new standard for Hollywood. Industry reporters were invited onto the Skyline studio lot for an evening outdoor concert by the official navy band. Then-senator George Murphy, who sang and danced in a couple of Skyline musicals in the 1930s and parlayed his mediocre acting career into representing California in Washington, DC, spoke about the importance of movies that celebrated patriotic virtue and military service.

Lowell took the stage next and introduced Xavier as the star of the film. He bragged that he'd first discovered Xavier and that Skyline was the studio that birthed Xavier's career. "It is only fitting that he should carry our flag in what will be a glorious victory."

Xavier shared a heartfelt letter supposedly penned by Gladys blessing the film, and he spoke briefly about how honored he was to be portraying a man he knew and admired. The event ended with a roaring flyover by a half dozen navy fighter pilots.

The pomp and pageantry wowed the jaded press. A movie that studio executives and politicians could support was a welcome development for those opposed to the spread of the counterculture's growing influence over music, literature, and film. The early buzz was that *Hornet's Hellfire* was unassailable and a surefire hit, and that Lowell had arranged the elements to achieve a groundbreaking first for the industry—a Black film that transcended colored audiences and captured white moviegoers, too. Lowell was already counting the box office profits.

Kimberly joined me for the kickoff concert. She was thrilled that Xavier and I were working together like old times. I hadn't told her what transpired between him and me at the Mayflower Hotel, and to her, Xavier and I were never estranged. His work for other studios had taken him out of our orbit.

I didn't pay much attention to it, but during Xavier's remarks, Kimberly got a faraway look on her face. I figured she was thinking through some problem with one of her piano students. I squeezed her hand, and she shook off the momentary trouble.

Once his movie star duties were done, Xavier hurried over to greet Kimberly on the lawn of the studio's Small Town Square standing sets. Reporters snapped photos of them despite not having a clue as to who Kimberly was. I shooed the press away while my wife and Xavier got reacquainted.

"This is such a blessing," she said after they broke their embrace, "that you and Aaron get the opportunity to honor Lieutenant Dixon through this movie."

Xavier said, "We certainly will—if we get a good script."

"Don't harp on that," I said.

"It's not an insignificant detail."

"The script will be ready any day now."

"I heard that last week," he said. "Are they having troubles?"

"They can't be. The story writes itself."

Kimberly stopped our bickering with an inconvenient observation. "Xavier, I wasn't aware that you palled around quite so often with Lieutenant Dixon while he was in LA."

I scrambled to make light of her comment and to breeze past it. "Honey, of course he did. That's why he spoke at Horace's funeral."

She wouldn't drop it. "Yes, in your eulogy, you talked about crossing paths while you were out drinking. Today, it seems like it was more than that. You and Horace were friends."

"I think our friendship meant more to me than it did to him," Xavier said modestly.

"See now, I could just strangle Aaron." She studied Xavier with sharp focus. "Because he must have been around when you and Horace were buddies. You all would have been like the three Black musketeers."

Kimberly, Xavier, and I laughed, but I was uneasy with the direction of our conversation.

"To think, when we started dating, Aaron and I would go see your movies, and he didn't mention that he knew you—that he'd spent time with you on numerous occasions."

She held her smile while Xavier and I stood tongue-tied.

"Well, I didn't want to brag," I said. "Besides, we met so many people during that time who came and went."

Puffed up with pride, Lowell interrupted, "Flawless, wasn't it? The press is in the palm of our hands."

Xavier said, "One hundred percent. I won't say it too loudly, but you outdid your old man."

"Well," Lowell crowed, "it's all right if you say it a little louder."

Xavier and I chuckled. Lowell smiled. Kimberly did neither. She gripped her cane and used it to twist a divot into the manicured grass.

When we got home, Kimberly heated the teakettle on the stove. A hot cup of lemon ginger tea helped her sleep on restless nights. I almost retreated into our bedroom, but I couldn't bear the thought of the silent tension that traveled with us in the car, making itself at home.

I leaned against the refrigerator. "Come out with it."

She gathered her cup and saucer and tea bag like usual. "You've been lying for years, and there's only one reason I can come up with for why you didn't mention knowing Xavier in the early days. You, him, and Horace sinned together, hopping in and out of bed with each other. A trio of sodomites."

I laughed; it was an uncontrollable burst. I didn't mean to be cruel. It just struck me funny that Kimberly was right (I had been lying for years) and wrong (Xavier wasn't a friend of ours in 1954) and right (Xavier, Horace, and I were homosexuals) and wrong (Horace and Xavier never had sex with each other) and right (I'd had sex with both men).

Kimberly flung the empty cup at my head. I ducked to the right, and the cup smashed into pieces against the refrigerator. The shards of porcelain skidded across the floor.

"I'm a joke to you!" she screamed. "You said Horace was the only man in your past."

"I wasn't laughing at you," I said, "and Xavier wasn't friends with Horace. They happened to take one picture sitting next to each other. The rest we made up so I could go to Horace's funeral."

The teakettle whistled, and Kimberly moved it to an unlit burner. "And now you're lying more for the movie?" she asked.

"Yes. This is showbiz."

She gathered her thoughts for a few moments. "But that's not everything there is to it. You're always holding back a piece or two. Always retelling the story with a change here or there."

"There are things I can't reveal—to keep other people's confidence and for your sake."

"Don't give me that. You don't do anything for my sake." She headed to our bedroom. "Clean up this mess and sleep in the guest room."

I fixed myself a rum and Coca-Cola before tending to my chore. Then I swept up the broken cup and dumped the shards into the trash can. Kimberly and I had never fought like this. I'd never been banished from our bedroom. I didn't know how to begin to repair the damage.

After finishing my drink, I contemplated making a second one. There was nobody around to disapprove. I'd put fresh ice in my glass when I heard the slap of a package landing on our porch. I opened the front door and nearly dropped my glass. At my feet was an envelope marked "Confidential." I knew immediately what its contents were. This was the shooting script for *Hornet's Hellfire*.

Even before he secured Horace's life rights from Gladys, Lowell had already gone through four writers, who worked on a half dozen drafts of what became *Hornet's Hellfire*. The shooting draft that I received bore the credit of L. K. Bradlee and Rodrick Nelson, a writing team with a reputation for being dependable and fast. Their big hit was MGM's 1959 *Gimme Tit for Tat*, the last film to costar Judy Garland and Mickey Rooney.

Since then, Bradlee and Nelson wrote four to six movie scripts a year on average. The creative hallmark of their output was a rapid-fire banter that they applied to sly variations of the boy-meets-girl, boy-and-girl-can't-stand-each-other, boy-and-girl-can't-help-but-fall-in-love-with-each-other romance formula. *Hornet's Hellfire* was their first venture into the genres of war movies and biographical pictures.

I brewed myself a pot of coffee to counter the drowsiness of the late hour and the liquor in my bloodstream, and after rolling back my shirtsleeves, I began reading the shooting script at the vanity table in the guest room. The story started where I thought it might:

Horace is flying in the fateful air show that would be his last, and he's performing tricks in a biplane. He radios ground control that he's going to do a climbing spin. Ground control advises against the idea since the maneuver is difficult and he's never flown this biplane before today. Horace disregards ground control with jovial confidence. The crowd will love it, and he can do it!

As far as I knew, this dramatization was accurate; based on eyewitness accounts and an after-action mechanical investigation. I prepared myself for the first revelation the script was building toward: Horace set the chain of events in motion for his untimely death by insisting on an aerobatic stunt that he was cautioned against doing. The news accounts of the accident never spelled out what went wrong in the sky. The movie was giving me an answer. I took a deep breath and turned to the next page:

Horace goes into the climbing spin. The biplane struggles, but Horace perseveres. He gets his way and feels triumphant. Then at the top of the climb, his engine catches fire.

It wasn't clear to me why a climbing spin would cause an engine fire, but I kept reading. Maybe that would be explained in the radio communication between Horace and ground control. It wasn't. Instead, the first major irrefutable deviation between reality and the movie appeared:

It is revealed that the air show is taking place over the Navy Pier in Chicago. Horace radios ground control that he can't keep the biplane in the air long enough to return to the landing strip. He could attempt an emergency landing on Grand Avenue, endangering the lives of civilians. Or, to make sure no one else is hurt, Horace valiantly nose-dives the biplane into Lake Michigan.

This was horseshit. The air show was in Cicero, Illinois. Horace crashed in a field. Now, I understood the film would take dramatic license, but this seemed out of line. I scribbled notes in the margin since it was my job to provide meaningful consultation. The story continued to deviate from the truth:

After the title card and credits, we are introduced to seventeen-year-old Horace, who convinces his sister, Gladys, to sign his parental consent form as if she were their mother. Gladys objects, then relents. Horace is in a hurry to leave home for the navy, but on the way to turn in his enlistment papers, he runs into a pretty sixteen-year-old Black girl named Harmony.

Harmony pines for Horace and is sad to hear that he is leaving town. She promises to pray for him while he's away. Horace is attracted to her but begs her not to waste her prayers on him. He plans to be a fighter pilot and is prepared to die in service to his country. Chances are they will never see each other again. Harmony insists that her heart will only yearn for Horace, and to spare her from spinsterhood, Horace is harsh with her in an attempt to keep her from waiting for him to return.

Between you, me, and God, the truth was Horace forged his mother's signature on the parental consent form to join the navy. Gladys was horrified and angry when she learned that he'd done so. And I can't stress this enough—Harmony was not a girl that Horace was serious about. They'd gone to dances together in high school, and he reconnected with her after Los Angeles, but they never got engaged or married. She didn't even fly out from Chicago to attend his funeral in DC.

To be clear, I saw the purpose of Harmony as a device to round out Horace's character. He was driven, charming, and certain that he was destined for greatness. Also, he was impatient, he was bossy, and he could be terse in order to be kind. That all came through in the scenes with Harmony. I wouldn't suggest cutting her out of the picture. Just prune the laughable sappy sections. For example, Horace never recited poetry to anyone. The notion that he'd memorized "If You Should Go" by Countee Cullen was ludicrous. I read on:

The time between Horace's enlistment, his pilot training, the start of the Korean War, and his first mission as a fighter pilot is breezed through in roughly five pages. Everyone starts calling him "Hornet" incessantly. Horace receives no hazing and no harassment in the navy. His race causes no conflict for anyone in the navy. Horace is, however, told by his flight instructor that if he is captured by the North Korean or Chinese armies, he will be mistreated as a prisoner of war because he is a Negro. He is encouraged to kill himself before he can be taken alive.

In between missions, which seem to be written with no knowledge of aerial combat, Horace reads letters from Harmony. She pours out her heart in her missives, revealing that she's loved Horace since they were kids in Sunday school. He writes letters in reply but doesn't mail them. As he explains to his good buddy Petty Officer Walsh, "Harmony's a sweet girl, and she shouldn't be gettin' her hopes up for a soldier who might not make it home." Harmony does not take the hint. She maintains a steady barrage of one-sided correspondence, updating him on characters we didn't meet or hear mention of on the home front.

Halfway through the script, comic relief arrives. . . . Petty Officer Aaron Toussaint reports for duty, and he is to the navy what Gomer Pyle is to the marines. Toussaint is a simpleton far too innocent to realize that he is the butt of Horace's wisecracks. Everyone on the carrier has a laugh at Toussaint's expense. He is, to his credit, devoted to Horace and can follow basic instructions. He's like an amusing dumb dog.

My coworkers in the Studio Security Department, my casual friends across the Skyline lot, my brothers and sisters in Jesus Christ our Lord and Savior at the First African Methodist Episcopal Church of Los Angeles, my in-laws, and my wife would see this depiction of me and deem it harmless and endearing. Who isn't naïve and socially embarrassing when they are young? If cast with the right wide-eyed, baby-faced actor, the film version of me could endure in the hearts of moviegoers for generations, and those around me in the real world would expect me to be a good sport about my on-screen alter ego.

I hated it.

Worse still, I was cornered, and my resentment had no hope of being released. I couldn't defend myself in my notes without looking thin-skinned. Nor was there an alternative characterization I could even propose.

The script presented Walsh as Horace's best friend and confidant, a savvy choice that invested a white role (and white audiences) with a sense of self-importance and a reason to care about Horace as a human being. The rest of the sailors were used to reinforce the imperative of winning the war and the heroic significance of Horace's achievements. The film's story was in danger of being unbearably earnest and humorless. Cue the clown. The balance "Petty Officer Toussaint" brought to the picture was undeniable. Even I could see his utility.

Nonetheless, I felt both acutely unseen and overexposed in an extraordinary way that can only occur when Hollywood turns episodes from your life into a movie. The very process of taking a real person and rendering them as a character is maddening for the original subject. Man and his myth are not meant to exist simultaneously, which is why we should stick to deifying the dead. Caught alive in the spinning of a folklore, I found myself forced to accept the truth and a lie as two valid versions of singular events. My mind strained like I was violating a law of physics.

I was to be projected on-screen in name, but not body. Words and deeds were to be attributed to me although I didn't say or do much of what was scripted. And those were the disconnections that I had expected. That was the standard Hollywood treatment. What surprised and pained me was how the shape, tenor, and depth of my working relationship with Horace were set aside to transform me into a buffoon. The truth wasn't simply ignored. It was mocked. It was warped into a crude parody.

My indignity over the intended use of my personhood was compounded by what I'd forfeited from the beginning—the weight of my meaning in Horace's life. Its scope couldn't be captured, because our love affair wasn't fit for a general-release film. So, I was very aware that I'd be greatly diminished in the movie, and I'd anticipated being shown, at best, as a loyal kid brother to Horace, or, at worst, as a nondescript, competent functionary who carried out his orders. Instead, I was written as a grotesque perversion; I was my unacknowledged lover's public laughingstock.

I wished I wasn't in the picture at all.

I finished the rest of the script without stopping:

Harmony finally writes a letter informing Horace that she intends to start dating an older man who can provide for her. Presumably, all the young men worth their salt are serving in the military. Horace writes a letter begging Harmony to marry not for security but for love. Yet, he can't bring himself to mail it to her. Lovelorn, Horace volunteers for a dangerous mission, and when he disappears from radar, he is feared dead. Walsh and Toussaint keep the faith and pray together for Horace's safe return. The Lord answers their cry, and Horace comes back into range and lands on the carrier. When Horace's enlistment ends (seemingly the next day), he bids farewell to Walsh and tasks Walsh with passing on his goodbye to Toussaint.

Horace returns home the night before Harmony's wedding. At his sister's insistence, Horace pays Harmony a visit. He enters her parents' house and spies on her in her wedding dress while her mother makes final alterations. Harmony is a vision of beauty, and she seems happy. Horace leaves without interfering. Harmony goes through with the wedding.

Years pass. Horace trains pilots for an airline. He catches up with Walsh and explains why he hasn't moved on from Harmony: He's found no woman half as wonderful as she is. Unbeknownst to Horace, Harmony's husband is deathly ill. With his last words, he urges his soon-to-be widow to pursue Horace. Tragically, at that very hour, Horace is participating in the air show over Lake Michigan.

Horace survives his watery crash long enough to be taken to the hospital. His prognosis is dire. Gladys and Harmony keep watch by his hospital bed. (Presumably, Harmony steps away from Horace's bed to attend her husband's funeral.) To Gladys, Harmony cries, "If only I could know that he felt about me the way I feel about him." Gladys retrieves the unmailed letters that Horace wrote to Harmony and delivers them to the young widow. Harmony reads the letters, and we hear them in Horace's voice. Harmony pledges her love to Horace, and he gains consciousness long enough to whisper, "I love you, Harmony." Then he dies while she weeps at his side.

Damn the writers Bradlee and Nelson. Damn Lowell. Damn Hollywood. In eighty-seven pages, a war hero's journey got twisted into a romance weepy. I'd thought such a transfiguration would be impossible, but the screenwriters overcame the narrative challenge. What is the suitable love story for a man who doesn't confirm his heterosexuality by getting married, shacking up with a woman, or fathering children? A doomed romance foiled by circumstances.

21

NO CONTEST

I slept in past nine, and Kimberly was at work by the time I opened our closet for a change of clothes. I'd just come out of the shower when the telephone rang. I answered it dripping wet.

"You read the script?" asked Xavier.

"Yeah. Are you disappointed, too?"

"No, are you kidding? This is a ripe plum."

"Did we get the same script? What I read was sappy mush."

"Come meet me for lunch," he said patiently, "and I'll walk you through how we steal this picture out from under Skyline. See you at Tam's at noon."

An old restaurant, located in Atwater, Tam O'Shanter existed in a dimension of its own making. Built in the 1920s, the exterior looked like a storybook cottage from centuries gone by. The interior was decorated with fanciful Scottish medieval artifacts and coats of arms. Yet the specialty on the menu was Yorkshire pudding. Despite or because of the anachronistic clashes, Xavier loved eating at Tam's, as did Walt Disney.

When I arrived, Xavier whistled and waved me over to a snug booth for two alongside the square bar that preceded the dining room areas.

The lighting was dim, but Xavier's ironed, white dress shirt and his excitement lit the booth like a candle. His right elbow pinned his copy of the script to the table. He'd already dog-eared dozens of the pages.

"Can you keep a secret?" he stage-whispered.

I took a seat across from him. "I'll take it to my grave."

"I've thought a lot about what you said when you talked me into accepting this role. *A movie isn't locked until the print is running through the projector at the premiere.*" He tapped his finger on the script. "I see ways to push this to the limit. We can add a subtext for those in the know. You see, I've been pulling strings of my own."

"What have you done?"

His eyes darted around the bar to see if anyone was close enough to eavesdrop. Then he leaned forward and spoke softly. "It'll be announced in the trades next week, but I set up the meeting between Lowell and our director, Nicholas Ray."

"*The* Nicholas Ray is directing a Black movie?"

"After the egg he laid with *55 Days at Peking*, he needs to show the town that he can finish a movie and deliver a hit."

Despite his questionable health and his recent misfires at the box office, I considered Nicholas Ray a huge get for the film. He'd bring the project gravitas, and the top white movie critics would review his work. I also suspected that I could guess exactly why Xavier had championed the director of *In a Lonely Place* and *Rebel Without a Cause*. Ray had gotten great performances out of Humphrey Bogart and James Dean, two actors Xavier idolized.

"How did you rope him in?"

"I shared with him my angle on the character and the film," Xavier said.

"Which is?"

"Promise you'll keep your cool."

"Stop messing around."

He grabbed hold of my wrists, pressing them against the table.

"Horace was a clandestine homosexual who would rather die in the air than face life on the ground as a faggot."

It's a good thing Xavier had me in his grip, because on instinct, my hands balled into fists and yearned for a target. "Why the fuck?" I yelled.

The waitstaff and customers looked at us sideways, and I apologized for my outburst. A waiter rushed over to take our order and to make sure we weren't about to become a bigger disturbance. Xavier and I both selected briskets with mashed potatoes and creamed corn.

Once the waiter left us, I asked Xavier, "Why would you tell that to anyone? If word spreads—"

"Nicky won't gossip. He understands the pressure and the power of homosexuality—and bisexuality, too. We spoke for hours."

"How did you explain how you came by this conclusion?"

"I didn't mention you, if that's your concern." He arched an eyebrow. "Did you forget? As far as the general public knows, I was pals with Horace. I implied that he confided in me."

"Very clever," I snapped. "How does revealing this help anything?"

"My angle is what brought Nicky on board. He wants to explore the inner turmoil of a gay war hero."

"Lowell's going to murder you both."

Xavier smirked. "He won't be in any position to object. He's already hyped the movie to heaven, and Nicky is going to bring critical acclaim. Lowell will have to hug this film with both arms, if he catches wise to what we're doing."

"What is it you're even trying to do, playing Horace as a queer?"

"Unmask the heart of the man." He looked at me as if I was daft. "I'm an actor."

"Of course, but . . ." I sighed. "Don't we want to make him a hero? That's our goal, and there's no such thing as a gay hero."

His face glowed with the fire of a zealot. "But there is, and he's coming into clearer view. Monty Clift gave us a glimpse of him showing off how well he could handle another man's pistol in *Red River*. Sal and Dean went just shy of sealing their love with a kiss in *Rebel Without a Cause*. Stephen Boyd queered *Ben-Hur*. Now's my chance to carry the mantle even further."

I was incredulous. "How far you expect to go playing a sissy?"

"You're missing the trick," he said. "I'm not hamming it up like Bert Lahr. The joke won't be on me. I can play the silence and the looks, I can spin the lines just so, that most moviegoers will see the butch hero they paid to see. Those of us with a deeper perception will pick up the signal driving my performance, and as our movement grows, that signal will go further and further."

"This is the fag and the dyke movement you predicted would overcome before the civil rights bill got passed?"

"I was wrong about the timing."

"Your watch is still busted if you think you can queer up this picture with no repercussions."

"Fuck me. Is there any winning with you?" Xavier jabbed his fork in the air only a few inches from my nose. "You begged me to take this role. You said you wanted me to play Horace. Okay, I gave you what you wanted. Now today, you walked in here upset at the hete script with the boo-hoo love story. You want me to make it better, and I'm gonna. But still you're shooting daggers at me because I've come up with a way to actually show some of the truth about Horace. Is there any pleasing you?"

"I just wanted you to play a war hero."

"You've seen my work and how I've grown. Did you think I'd deliver a superficial performance?"

I hung my head and said, "I thought we'd agreed to make a movie Horace would be proud of. He wouldn't approve of this."

"I didn't sign on for Horace. I barely met the man. I signed on because you asked me to, and you said this was my chance to make an everlasting mark on the silver screen, and that's what I plan to do."

As the picture continued to take shape, the star and the director held sway over casting, though their choices didn't necessarily seem to serve their aims. To play Walsh, Ray brought on Tab Hunter, a fading actor who lived in a glass closet; he wouldn't come out, but everyone could see him in there. It was a curious pick, because while he was gay, Tab was not a boat-rocker. In the late '50s, he and Tony Perkins were an undercover item for years until Paramount pressured them to end the relationship. Tony kicked up a fuss; Tab didn't.

I just couldn't imagine the clean-cut blond buying any of Xavier's gay liberation speeches, so I doubted that he was in cahoots to infuse his role with a gay sensibility. Plus, and I don't mean to be snide, Tab was a medium talent. He owed the lion's share of his limited success to his beachboy looks, not his acting skills. He could be serviceable in a light comedy or musical, but I didn't see how he was going to size up as an acting partner against Xavier.

For the part of Harmony, Xavier managed to get Lowell to okay hiring Rosalind Cash, a theater actress Xavier admired. He'd seen her in a Broadway revival of the musical *Fiorello!*, and she stole his heart. At Xavier's insistence, Rosalind was flown out to Los Angeles, and from her screen test, you could tell she possessed stage presence and beauty. However, she had zero film experience. The passion with which Xavier vouched for her was all the evidence I needed to believe that Rosalind was wise to his designs for the movie.

Finally, in a casting decision that didn't get heralded with a press release, an actor championed by Lowell booked the role of playing me. When I saw him, I about fell over. The twenty-year-old kid was a dead ringer for me at that age. His screen name was Wes Malone (born Wesley Mumford), and he'd caught Lowell's eye portraying a gullible student in the 1965 Skyline musical *Wuthering High*, a failed attempt to modernize Emily Brontë's novel in the vein that *West Side Story* updated *Romeo and Juliet*.

Through his agent, Wes extended an invitation to have coffee with me and pick my brain. I put him off with excuses, although I knew I'd have to meet with him before shooting began. Call me yellow, but the prospect of talking to a doppelgänger of my former self spooked the hell out of me.

The rest of preproduction ramped up in April and May. Every interior scene and all the exterior scenes in Horace's intentionally unidentified hometown were to be filmed on the Skyline lot. Exterior scenes on the ship caused a lengthy delay because Lowell wanted the navy to bring a carrier as close as possible to the Port of Los Angeles and allow us to film on the deck. The initial proposal was rejected. Eventually, enough money filled briefcases, and Lowell closed the deal with the navy and the port authority before Memorial Day.

As part of his preparation to assume his leading role, Xavier shaved his head. I knew he was going to do it but got no warning as to when. We'd agreed to have lunch in the studio commissary, and I walked in to find him waiting for me at a table. His dome was gleaming. I couldn't stop grinning. It did make him seem more like Horace.

Preproduction got underway, and with Xavier busy with wardrobe fittings, rehearsals, and pilot training class (even though he would never actually fly a plane during the film), I had time to run background checks on his current circle of intimates. This hadn't been necessary in 1954, when Xavier was at the start of his career, when his ties to other aspiring actors were looser. Diahann being the exception to the rule.

Stars of Xavier's caliber attracted hangers-on. Removing leeches from his back was my official goal, but I was equally interested in neutralizing those who were exerting a political influence over Xavier. His head was full of enough gay lib daydreams. I feared what might happen if other radicals whispered in his ear that he could advance the queer revolution with his fame.

Within a week, my digging turned up a problematic intimate. Xavier had a no-strings-attached lover named Antonio Herrera, and he'd earned quite the reputation. Plenty of barflies were happy to trade stories for drinks on my tab. I must have interviewed three to four dozen people about Antonio. I'd rarely encountered a greater number of eager sources.

Antonio was thirty-four years old, born and raised in Boyle Heights to Mexican parents. He didn't wait long to become notorious. He got expelled from his Catholic middle school when it was discovered that he'd talked other boys into going down on him in a church confessional booth.

By the time he was a teenager, he was a dropout and a jack-of-all-trades in a local tavern. He earned cash as a barback, a cocktail waiter, a bartender, and a bouncer. Antonio had an easy charisma, an intimidating street toughness, and a bodybuilder's forearms and chest. He could do whatever was needed.

Trouble was Antonio also did a lot of what wasn't needed: pouring drinks on the house for his buddies, breaking hearts by sleeping with patrons indiscriminately, selling quaaludes in the bathroom, and indulging a penchant for spotting wax fruit, exposing them to public ridicule, and sparking altercations with them. He hated cops more than unruly drunks.

Antonio came by his ability to sniff out an undercover police officer during his days as a young drinker at Latino gay bars. Between the ages of eighteen and twenty-one, he'd gotten caught up in four raids. His brushes with the law passed as pillow talk with the white, gay college students that he sometimes liked to turn out; the undergraduates were always astonished and petrified at the idea of being arrested by the cops.

If he felt like educating the white boys while he bit hickeys onto their necks, Antonio would explain that during the raids he'd been party to, there had been no tears, gnashing of teeth, or pushback from the Latino men hauled out onto the sidewalks and loaded into police wagons. The processing at the precinct for Latino men like Antonio, who worked in manual labor or the service industry, or who lived in Spanish-speaking neighborhoods, didn't spark the panic it did in white guys with white-collar jobs or on promising collegiate tracks.

As a matter of systematic humiliation and punishment, Antonio's name would be printed in local, English-language newspapers along with the other deviants arrested in the gay-bar raid. For white men who worked in law offices and accounting firms, an outing in news ink led to immediate termination at the office, divorce at home, and ostracization from their heterosexual loved ones. No one in Antonio's circles ever read the *Los Angeles Times* or the *Los Angeles Herald Examiner*. Thus, the intended torpedo missed the mark.

The real snag for Antonio was the fines, which could vary wildly depending on how a case was disposed of. This was not a matter of jurisprudence. Nor was raiding gay bars about maintaining public safety. These were shakedown operations. The sooner one could bribe their way out of the night, the cheaper the price would be.

During his second raid, at the Golden Horseshoe on West Adams, the white cop cuffing Antonio complimented his wristwatch, and Antonio said, "It's yours, please." The cuffs came off. So did the watch. Antonio walked away, leaving behind the other bar patrons headed downtown for booking.

His maiden raid, at the Cellar on Los Feliz Boulevard, resulted in a night in jail and a morning appearance before a judge. Antonio's public defender didn't bother introducing himself, let alone talk him through the courtroom procedures. When asked how he pleaded, his lawyer answered for him: no contest. Antonio's knees almost buckled; he thought he was about to be sentenced to prison.

Instead, the judge gave away the game and griped about the police, "Why did they bother hauling in this lot? They don't have two pennies or pesos to rub together." Antonio was ordered to pay a ten-dollar fine. He didn't have that kind of money lying around, but he scraped it together before the twenty-eight-day deadline.

Antonio's run-ins with the law forced a political education upon him. He was experiencing how race, money, and sexuality shaped legal outcomes. While Antonio was not a political animal by nature, he was working in bars when the queer scene was smaller, and gays and lesbians gathered in the few spots they could regardless of differences in desire, class, or education. Antonio poured drinks for professors, journalists, activists, and others in the know. He couldn't help but learn from them. Within a few years, he became a political radical, too, almost through osmosis.

Mr. Kepner, you must admit that counterculture types like yourself do recruit and indoctrinate new members. Please take no offense. It's an effective strategy. Antonio was turned politically, and he went on to help turn Xavier.

It was on October 12, 1963, at the Biltmore Hotel in the Emerald Ballroom, that Xavier and Antonio met. Xavier was looking for a distraction since the event underway in the ballroom was a premiere party for *Lilies in the Field*, and Sidney had already strutted around as the odds-on favorite to win Best Actor at the Oscars. Xavier kept his smile in place and congratulated Sidney, who was perfectly lovely and gracious in return. Xavier couldn't tell if Sidney was being phony or not, and either way, his jealousy for Mr. Poitier ate him up inside.

Once he'd been photographed with the man of the hour, Xavier had little to say and absolutely no interest in his arranged date, a young chorus girl named Paula Kelly. He gave her use of the studio limo, encouraged her to pursue a fine Black newcomer with whom she'd been trading come-hither stares, and tucked twenty dollars into her palm. "If anyone ever asks," he said, "I was a gentleman and a phenomenal kisser."

Free of his work obligations and his date, Xavier left the ballroom, removed his tuxedo's bow tie, and went to the hotel's secluded men's bar. No beer, no wine, no women. Xavier relaxed into a leather chair against a wall. A waiter brought him an ample glass of whiskey, and he watched the other men come and go. He wasn't cruising, per se, but his eyes were open.

Antonio frequented the men's bar at the Biltmore on his nights off, if he had the cash to spend on the one-drink minimum. The hotel's twin appeals for him were that the staff greeted him, a Mexican homosexual, with unwavering courtesy and that the other men in the bar were reliably clean. Antonio had gotten crabs a couple of months prior from rough trade he came across in the park, and he didn't want to go through the mortifying business again with the rinse shampoo and the tiny comb.

He sat in a chair next to Xavier because it was the first open spot he saw. He hit on the gorgeous Black man because he had a weakness for tall fellas, and he liked the thoughtful way Xavier thanked and tipped his waiter. Antonio could have sex with just about any kind of man except a rude one.

Xavier was receptive to Antonio's pass once he realized that the burly guy with delicious lips didn't recognize him in the slightest. Fame often robbed him of being anonymously desired. To his dismay, Xavier discovered routinely that some men (fanatics) pursued him just because he was a star, and others (actors) hoped that if they proved to be amazing in the sack, he'd grow attached to them and help further their showbiz careers. The terms of such exchanges made Xavier feel used. He missed the pure lust. Sexual gratification in exchange for sexual gratification—nothing less and absolutely nothing more.

Although Xavier had reached a level of celebrity where he was reliably recognized in crowds of everyday Blacks or moviegoing whites, Antonio represented the limits of mainstream Hollywood movies. Unless a film was a runaway hit that permeated all corners of America, Antonio wasn't going to spend pocket change at the movie theater to see it. So, out of a handful of American movie stars he could identify, Charlton Heston was the one at the top of Antonio's list, since Chuck starred in two box-office behemoths that Antonio watched on the big screen: *The Ten Commandments* (1956) and *Ben-Hur* (1959).

As far as Black actors went, Antonio wouldn't have been able to pick Sidney out of a lineup, let alone Xavier. In fact, gun to his head, Antonio knew exactly one Black star by name—Buckwheat.

And technically that was the character's name. The actor was Billie Thomas, and Antonio wouldn't have recognized him as a grown man.

In the men's bar at the Biltmore, a rush to explore each other naked swept Xavier and Antonio out onto the street and into the first complication of their new attraction. Neither wanted to take the other back to their place. Xavier believed that his house would prompt questions about how he earned a living, and he didn't want to lie or share the truth yet. Antonio feared that Xavier was too distinctive a catch to hustle in and out of his apartment building, and his Pentecostal landlady had adopted the alarming habit of knocking on his door when she suspected that he was entertaining a gentleman caller. The lease for his apartment explicitly defined sex outside of wedlock as a "lascivious and immoral act," which was likened to prostitution and grounds for immediate eviction.

So, Antonio led Xavier to the Palace Turkish Baths on East Fourth Street shortly before midnight. Xavier intended to have sex with Antonio and ignore the other men. Once they were inside the Palace, they went to the narrow room that Antonio paid for, and Xavier began to close the door.

"No, leave it open," Antonio said.

"Why?" Xavier asked. "You want guys looking at us when they jerk off?"

He nodded. "It makes me hot."

Xavier not only left the door open, he also pulled Antonio in for a deep kiss. He'd found it endearing and arousing that Antonio could say what he needed sexually without shame. He felt inspired to match his latest hookup's unabashed candor.

"If there's a crowd, I might invite one or two of them in to play," he said.

Antonio's answer became their motto: "Do as you like."

Xavier tested their link that first night. He blew Antonio as three or four men took turns watching the action from the doorway. Xavier topped Antonio and invited other men into their narrow room to touch and lick his body. The link between the two leads was not broken or diminished by the inclusion of others. Xavier found meaning in that. He sensed a connection worth maintaining.

After they'd both cum and put on their clothes, Xavier wrote his phone number down on a scrap of paper. He gave his number to Antonio as they walked down the steep stairs side by side. Xavier said, "I'd like to see you again."

22

SWANEE

Despite my years in the industry, I hadn't spent much time on film sets during production. Work typically kept actors out of mischief, leaving me with little to do between takes. My role as an accuracy consultant, however, gave me unfettered access during the shooting of *Hornet's Hellfire*.

I took advantage of the open invitation, since my marriage was breaking up and I didn't have the heart to face it. Kimberly had moved my clothes into the guest room closet, and she attended church groups and dinner parties without me. There were days when I didn't lay eyes on her although we were sharing the house. When we did talk, nothing I said to her got me closer to regaining her trust or affection. Telling our social circle that I was consumed with the filming of *Hornet's Hellfire* served as a perfect excuse for my absences.

Day one of production consisted of two exterior scenes in the Small Town Square section of the Skyline backlot. Of the main cast, only Xavier and Rosalind were needed. The breakdown on the call sheet described the two scenes thusly: *Horace and Harmony talk romantically*, and *Horace informs Harmony that he joined the navy*. Light work to get the picture off to a smooth start.

Lowell was on hand with a studio photographer, waiting to snap the big moment when Nicholas first yelled, "Action!"

During the marking rehearsal, Xavier and Rosalind strolled along a sidewalk. Their characters discuss an upcoming party. Horace is eager to know if Harmony will attend the shindig, and she explains that her father won't let her go unless she has a proper date, an upright young man who will come to the house, greet her parents, escort her to the party, and bring her home before her curfew. Horace playfully teases Harmony that a fellow would have to be awfully sweet on her to go through the trouble of dealing with her father.

Without missing a beat, she joshes him, "If you're afraid my daddy won't find you respectable enough, just say so."

The bait works. Horace says, "We are a pair, aren't we?" and agrees to be on her front porch, dressed clean and carrying flowers, on Saturday at 7:00 PM. End scene.

To mark their movements for the camera and lighting departments, Xavier and Rosalind walked through the scene twice and recited their lines flatly, saving the emotion for when it counted. Nicholas, in collaboration with the set designer and the wardrobe mistress, had created an arresting way to illustrate the drabness of Horace's hometown. The buildings were painted in light gray and faint browns. The background extras were dressed in dingy white and khaki. Together, the nameless people and location lacked vibrancy. In stark contrast, Xavier and Rosalind wore primary colors. He sported bright blue overalls over a bloodred T-shirt, and she donned a canary-yellow, tea-length dress. The net result was that your eyes were glued to Horace and Harmony. They seemed to be the only two in town living in the modern world and blessed with destinies.

Lowell watched the first take. It was almost flawless. An extra tasked with the business of working under the hood of a black Ford Model A forgot to look up and nod at Harmony as she and Horace passed by him. Nicholas called cut, and everyone went back to their starting positions. Then there was a technical difficulty with a camera, and Lowell bid Nicholas and Xavier goodbye and returned to his office.

Xavier received a touch-up from the makeup girl and beckoned me over. "Watch carefully," he said with a grin.

Just before the second take got underway, Xavier and Rosalind switched positions. Whereas she had been the one walking closer to the street, now he was. Nicholas didn't object, and the change didn't strike me as significant. But I knew that Xavier must have made the move for a reason.

The director shouted, "Action!" and Rosalind gave a different performance from the one Lowell watched.

Harmony speaks with newfound trepidation. There is a sorrowful quiver in her voice. She talks about the party like she is desperate to get out of her parents' house for however long she can justify it. She relays her father's stipulations as if they are hurdles that the old man is daring her to find anyone willing to attempt jumping. Harmony isn't flirting with Horace. She is beseeching him to rescue her from an untold horror inside her home.

Xavier wasn't playing it light and airy either.

Horace gazes upon Harmony with sympathy, but he states plainly that she is asking for a big favor, given the difficulty of dealing with her father. Horace utters an unscripted line: "Your daddy's ornery, and he wants you for himself."

In response, Harmony says, "If you're afraid my daddy won't find you man enough, just say so." There is bite in her delivery, and it sounds like an accusation.

Xavier's Horace and Rosalind's Harmony share a knowing look informed by shared struggles and hard truths. Their bond reminded me of siblings more than lovers. She wasn't trying to win over his heart, and he wasn't toying with her affections. These two already had each other's numbers.

Horace draws a deep breath before he says, "We are a pair . . . aren't we?"

Horace and Harmony walk in silence approaching the man inspecting the engine of his Model A. He's a redbone brother in his early twenties. He wears a newsboy cap, a gray, sleeveless undershirt, and khaki corduroy pants. His muscular arms and shoulders are oiled up. He looks like a pool hall hustler. Positioned closer to the street, Horace eyes the young man and utters three more unscripted words: "Lookin' good, LaMonte."

Startled by being addressed with dialogue and rendered lineless, the extra's eyes went a little wide, and he nervously nodded before glancing toward Nicholas to see if the director would call cut. Nicholas let it roll, and in the rushes, the brief encounter would tell another story: Horace spoke to a strapping young mechanic who was immediately put on edge to be named in broad daylight by him, and the mechanic looked around to see if anyone else had noticed.

Rosalind's Harmony catches the moment and its undertones. She tugs at the arm of Xavier's Horace to bring him back to their conversation. Her side-eye says, *This is no time for you to lust after a trick who can only be turned after several beers on a lonely night*. Horace bows his head repentantly and agrees to be Harmony's date for the party.

Nicholas shot the scene twice more. Xavier and Rosalind gave slight variations on their line readings, but their characterizations and intentions remained set. The extra, however, was never as good as he was on the second take. The element of surprise birthed his best performance.

Once the scene was in the can, Xavier and Rosalind headed to their separate dressing rooms, which were set up inside the façades of houses on the street. Xavier hugged Rosalind and whispered in her ear. She laughed and clapped her hands.

Rosalind's talent could appear effortless, and her beauty was beguiling. Yet she was a very analytical actress, insisting that her character's internal truth could not be set aside to make a film or a play more commercial, and if one assumed that her femininity meant she was a delicate pushover, she'd set that fool straight, then kiss them on the cheek before sending them packing.

She was wary of me. From her viewpoint, I had competing alliances. I was Xavier's friend and Skyline's employee. Rosalind didn't want to say anything around me that might cost her if I passed it along to my boss. I didn't hold her reluctance toward me against her; I respected her for it. She was a clever and gifted sister.

When I joined Xavier and Rosalind on their walk to their dressing rooms, she said, "Good morning, Aaron. You look fine enough to be on camera, too."

"Thank you, Miss Cash. I enjoyed your performance today," I said. "You and Xavier certainly took the words off the page and made them your own."

Rosalind arched an eyebrow and presented a closed-mouth smile. "I'm glad you liked it."

Xavier assured her, "Aaron is down with the plan."

"What plan?" she asked, and before Xavier or I could say another word, she pivoted toward the house with her dressing room inside. "Oh, I'd better go change. We'll be shooting again before you know it."

Xavier and I watched her go. She didn't look back.

"Think she'll ever trust me?"

"Give it a few years." Xavier draped his arm across my shoulders, and we headed to his dressing room. "I've wanted Rosalind to be in every film I've made since *House Money*. She didn't say it, but she thought I was blowing smoke to get her in bed. Only when I told her the score did she start to consider my film offers."

"I meant what I said. You two are far more interesting than what the script gave you."

"I told you, everyone hip to what the squares can't see is going to dig what we're putting into this film."

"Hey, I'm with you, but what is everybody going to say when Lowell and the other suits watch the rushes?"

"Nicholas doesn't allow executives to see his rushes. Only actors and the DP are allowed to see them."

"Okay, when he turns in the first cut, won't Lowell hit the roof?"

"He can get as mad as he wants. He can't bury this picture," Xavier explained. "Nicholas promised him that it's going to nab Globes and Oscars. We'll paint it as artsy and not fruity."

"What's the distinction?"

"Fruity pictures have no restraint. They want cheap laughs," he said. "We're going to sweep audiences away like a riptide. They'll be in deep waters, and only the sharp ones will understand why."

Congenial Tab Hunter was not privy to the subversive plan underway. He was manipulated into duty by Nicholas and Xavier. I was conflicted about how he was used. It did him no lasting harm, but Tab was incredibly openhearted, and that quality was exploited. I winced when I saw his scenes being filmed.

Tab's first day on set coincided with the company's move to Stage 9. I'd been aware that a construction crew was working around the clock on the carrier, but my imagination didn't picture the scope of what they were building. I walked over at dawn when Stage 9's elephant doors were opened, and I just about swallowed my tongue. Inside the massive soundstage, it looked as if the construction crew had dissected the USS *Stevens* with a giant cutter that left three-quarters of the ship's interiors exposed like an open dollhouse.

I stepped inside Horace's quarters. In my mind, I was clear about where I was, but my body responded to the facsimile. The shades of light green and off-white trim on the walls, poles, and pipes. The tightly strung cot, the scratchy blanket, and the thin, ineffectual pillow. The fold-out desk, and the war map with its red and blue tabs. Standing in the room that was not his room but looked like his room brought on a dizzying rush of recall.

I closed my eyes to stop the onslaught, but it only got worse. In the blind, I could feel the heat of Horace's chest pressed against my back; his arms locking me in place; his breath tickling my left ear. The air of nostalgia was suffocating.

"Is it like you remember it?" asked Nicholas.

I opened my eyes and seized on the discrepancies. "Very close—although I can guarantee you, Horace didn't keep a picture of Jesus taped to the wall."

The director summoned an assistant and ordered the Jesus photo struck, and it was removed within the hour. I moved on to the ship's mess hall, which was another haunting re-creation of the original. A dormant reflex was awakened, and my stomach rumbled even though I'd eaten breakfast and never loved the chow on the carrier.

I wandered the rest of the three-story set's rooms, stairs, and hallways. The layout was spot-on, and I didn't need a map to know what was behind each door. Rumor had it that the total cost of the build came in at $500,000. In my opinion, not a dime was wasted.

At 8:00 AM, the elephant doors on Stage 9 were locked shut and the red lights outside the entrances were ready to glow when the cameras were rolling. Tab's scene with Xavier was in Horace's quarters on the carrier. The call sheet description read: *Walsh congratulates Horace on becoming an ace*.

It was straightforward. No subtext. The point was for Walsh to underline for the audience how extraordinary Horace was in the air. Xavier and Tab rehearsed the scene a couple of times. The blocking and marking were a breeze. Xavier announced to the crew that he and Tab would make quick work of the setup and they'd all break for lunch early. I noticed that Tab wrung his hands behind his back. He'd flubbed the same line in both run-throughs.

"Action!"

"You just got your fifth kill. That makes you a flying ace," Walsh states for the benefit of moviegoers in need of the criteria.

Horace begins to relay the story of his latest perilous mission. As he talks, he does something unplanned: He unzips his flight suit down to his waist and tugs his arms free from the sleeves.

Xavier was shirtless underneath, and the exposure of his fit, bare chest provoked an unguarded reaction from Tab. His blue eyes quickly scanned Xavier's torso, and he licked his lips. I doubt Tab was aware of either tell, but they were only the opening notes in the aria of a man trying to suppress his homosexual attraction and failing on two levels. In other words, Tab, a gay actor desperate to pass for heterosexual, was unwittingly portraying a homosexual sailor attempting to come across as straight.

Not that I could blame him, but Tab was incapable of ignoring Xavier's sexiness. A response always managed to surface. Tab blushed, stammered, let his jaw drop, grinned sheepishly, averted his gaze, or stared for a split second too long depending on what enticement Xavier was serving, and the lead actor's efforts to arouse were endless. Xavier would rest his forearm on Tab's shoulder and lean against him, or he'd rub the small of Tab's back while Nicholas explained what he wanted from each scene. He always put his face very close to Tab's face when they were discussing the film.

Sometimes, Xavier would be eating grapes or strawberries from studio catering, and he'd insist that Tab should have a bite. When Tab relented, Xavier made a point of feeding them to him. While they were filming, Xavier found any excuse he could to disrobe or play the scene in a tight-fitting T-shirt or boxers. Even in group scenes, Tab wasn't safe. More than once, I saw Xavier goose Tab with a pinch to the ass below the camera frame.

Tab never complained, as far as I knew. He was eager for praise from Xavier and Nicholas. He probably assumed that Xavier's handsy affection and razzing were all in good fun. Tab, in the end, was delighted that none of his scenes were cut from the movie.

Wes, the young actor cast to play me, would have killed for the affirmation or physical affection that Xavier slathered on Tab. The twenty-year-old admired Xavier, and Xavier kept that kid on ice. Granted, at the read-through before production commenced, Wes did commit a cardinal sin in the delicate relationship between a supporting actor and a lead actor. Wes told Xavier that he'd loved Xavier's work ever since he sneaked into a movie theater with his teenage cousins to watch *Midnight Falls*—when Wes was ten years old. This memory was offered as a compliment, but no actor should ever age another actor in this manner.

Xavier did not take Wes into his confidence. Instead, he knocked the kid off balance during preproduction by quizzing him about how he thought their scenes should be played. Wes answered with all the confidence and limited experience he could muster. Then Xavier would say nothing, considering the supporting actor's ideas with a pronounced, excruciating silence. Finally, Xavier offered the mildest "I see," refraining from criticizing what he'd heard and from praising it.

By the time he arrived at the studio lot for his first scene in the picture, Wes didn't know which way was up. His call time was 11:00 AM, but he didn't shoot until after the lunch break. I watched Wes fix himself a full plate and eat nothing except a few saltine crackers. He was so in his head, he couldn't follow the conversation taking place around him.

I hurried over to Xavier's dressing room, where he was keeping to himself, I suspect, to further isolate Wes, and I called Xavier out over his treatment of the actor portraying me. "You're riding him too hard. You should see him out there. He's sick to his stomach."

"Good. I'm getting him into the right mindset," Xavier said.

His dressing room had an extra-long daybed for him to stretch out on and take naps. He wrapped himself in a thin sheet and fluffed his pillow. I got the message but didn't want to drop the subject.

I took a seat in his makeup chair. "You're withholding. You're treating him how you think Horace treated me."

"Say I am. Wouldn't it be good if that showed in his performance?"

I objected, "It's too slanted. You're giving him nothing but the stick."

Xavier sat up in the daybed. "You proposing I give him the carrot?"

"Don't get crude. You're missing the tenderness that was between me and Horace."

"I'll handle that when we're rolling. My top priority is to beat the clown out of that boy. I can't have him cutting up like Don Knotts in blackface."

I couldn't argue against an attempt to eliminate the vaudeville bumpkin shenanigans scripted into the role of Petty Officer Toussaint. Xavier turned onto his side on the daybed and slept for twenty minutes. I debated whether I should take a walk during the shooting of Wes's scenes. I wasn't certain I could act cool and unbothered if I saw aspects of the performance that grated at my sense of self.

Curiosity won out. I stood behind the lights aimed at the chow hall set. Seventy-five extras teemed in the background while the cameras focused on Xavier and Wes. *Horace selects Aaron as his aide-de-camp* was the one-liner. The scene was supposed to begin with Aaron dancing on a table singing "Swanee" like a minstrel to entertain his fellow sailors. Then Horace summons Aaron over, sizes him up, and asks if he'd like to be his aide. Aaron happily accepts. Check the camera gate and move on.

After Xavier and Wes rehearsed and marked the scene, Xavier pulled his supporting actor into a corner. I was too far away to hear what Xavier said, but I saw him stuff a pack of cigarettes and a lighter into Wes's pocket. Xavier's face was stern, and he was talking fast. Wes nodded obediently.

"You boys ready?" asked Nicholas.

Xavier answered for the both of them. "Yeah, boss. Frame us loose. We're going to try a couple new things."

"You got it," said the director, shutting down any complaints about to be voiced by the camera crew, lighting guys, or the script girl who just went through a marking rehearsal to cement the action and dialogue of the scene.

"Action!"

Aaron stands on the table and sings "Swanee," but gone are the shuffling feet, the apish grin, the hammy Al Jolson impression. Instead, Aaron sings in a dignified baritone at a slower tempo, and the lyrics about separation from home and loved one ring true for this room full of wartime sailors. No one laughs at him.

Horace enters the frame earlier than rehearsed and lets the power of the song wash over him. He starts to applaud, and the other sailors follow his lead. Horace waves Aaron over and places a hand on his shoulder. He asks Aaron where he's from and who's waiting for him back home. Aaron reveals that he doesn't have much family to speak of.

The script girl was frantically scribbling down this new stream of dialogue so the editors would be aware of what to expect in the footage.

Horace says to Aaron, "Sounds to me like you're an orphan."

Aaron shrugs in bashful agreement.

"Got a smoke I can bum?" asks Horace.

Aaron fishes the pack out of his pocket. The brand is Dunhill.

"Those are my favorites," Horace says. "I thought no one could get their hands on these anymore."

"You can get anything," Aaron explains with a pregnant pause, "if you know where to look."

Horace puts a Dunhill between his lips and issues his first order to Aaron: "Light me."

Aaron quickly produces the lighter and flicks the flame to life. Horace steps in close to ignite the end of his cigarette, and Aaron's hand trembles ever so slightly. Horace, tall and commanding, looms over the petty officer. Bogie and Bacall had nothing on these two men in that moment.

Horace steps back and exhales his first drag like he's in afterglow. He eyes Aaron until Aaron looks down at his shoes.

"Want to be my right hand?" Horace asks.

"It'd be an honor," Aaron replies.

"Cut!"

I was enthralled and slightly aroused by the scene as played, but I thought Xavier and Nicholas would never get away with keeping this scene untouched in the movie. Its homosexual nature was not subliminal. One didn't need to be hip to feel the sexual heat Xavier radiated toward Wes. A pulse and two brain cells would be sufficient. The prigs and prisses at the Catholic Legion of Decency were certainly going to detect the "disordered desires" in Horace and Aaron's on-screen relationship.

For his part, I don't believe that Wes understood while we were in production what Xavier and the director were doing. This picture was his biggest break, and he was trying to please the standoffish lead actor, who was challenging him with last-second changes and improvised dialogue. Subsequently, his performance jettisoned the slapstick mugging and dim-witted caricature that he brought to the read-through and early rehearsals. Xavier was leaving Wes no other choice but to react like an honest human being to what was thrown at him. Wes comported himself well. To the extent that the strain and eagerness to hold his own against Xavier showed, it benefited his character. Wes's Aaron mirrored how I felt during my early days with the real Horace: in awe of the fighter pilot's brilliance and under the gun to give him what he wanted.

23

COSTUME 127

I felt the movie would come together brilliantly, so long as the most flagrant homosexual overtones were cut in editing. For once, the shoot wasn't troubled. Production days didn't tip into overtime. The restriction on who could watch the rushes held up. Cast and crew got along, and the filming progressed with Nicholas and Xavier working in tandem to shape performances.

Yet there were a couple of scenes that unnerved me as the filming approached its final week. Their one-liners summed them up: Scene 48—*Aaron waits for lost Horace to return*; Scene 49—*Horace returns to ship and a hero's welcome*. My presence was required on set for the scenes, and I feared the experience would be overwhelming because, thanks to Lowell, the navy provided the film with the decommissioned USS *Stevens* to shoot the deck scenes.

Just seeing the carrier from the dock caused my chest to tighten. Despite having lived on her during my service, the USS *Stevens* seemed unfathomably larger than I remembered. The navy restricted the cast and crew to deck level, and I was grateful. I started to sweat as I walked aboard my old carrier.

The director's assistant, Oliver, ran up to me on the deck. "Mr. Toussaint, if you come with me, I'll get you squared away."

His words reached me on a delay because my senses were jammed taking in an onslaught of once-familiar details. The smell of metal and oil and the burn of the sun, for instance, reactivated a sense of duty in me. Had I gotten Horace his breakfast? What were the flying conditions for the day?

"Mr. Toussaint," prodded Oliver.

I forced myself to focus on him. "Lead the way."

He took me to the makeshift dressing rooms, where hundreds of extras were getting into navy uniforms, and said, "Ask a wardrobe girl for costume 127."

"Hold on, why would I—"

"Mr. Ray wants you in the wide shot for the hero's welcome in Scene 49."

I didn't see how I could argue with the director, and it wouldn't have mattered if I tried, because Oliver walked away and one of the wardrobe girls came over to me and requested my number. When I hesitated, she grew cross, and I coughed it up.

I wore a navy officer's uniform for this one and only occasion. The necktie proved trickier than I'd expected. After three attempts, I failed to make the knot the correct size, and a wardrobe girl fixed it for me. She also informed me that I needed to be on standby all morning, because Nicholas decided to shoot Scenes 48 and 49 without cutting between them.

The setup had to be intricately coordinated and could only be run twice, according to scheduling and budgetary constraints. It would begin with Wes staring out into the ocean at an empty sky, while a retired navy pilot in Horace's old Sabre was flying a swing route toward the carrier. The fighter jet wouldn't appear on the horizon for three to five minutes, which would signal Wes to break his trance and cue the extras to start gathering. The retired navy pilot would land and hurry out of the cockpit. Xavier would climb into the cockpit, count to five, then climb out of it like he had just landed. The crowd of a hundred extras and Wes would swarm and congratulate him.

I was shown my position and blocking by one of the second assistant directors, but he had to repeat himself because I was transfixed by the sight of Horace's fighter jet. It appeared smaller than I recalled, and its paint was faded. I had the urge to spot-check the bird, but access to it was restricted, too. I stood on my mark for an hour while everyone else was placed. Xavier waved at me as he went to his temporary hideout behind the camera.

"Picture up!" Nicholas yelled through a megaphone. Then he chewed the nub of his thumbnail. The director had four cameras operating, little room for error from his principal actors or the extras, and officials from the LA Port Authority and the navy breathing down his neck. I worried that Nicholas's health—he suffered from bouts of exhaustion or a weak heart, depending on who you believed—might give out at this critical juncture. The retired navy pilot took off and began his route. Nicholas's eyes were glued to a stopwatch ticking away, and at the allotted second, he screamed, "Action!"

From my vantage point, Wes had his back toward me. His torso slumped almost imperceptibly to the left, and the index and middle fingers of his right hand tapped gently against his thigh. I didn't need to see his face to know the face was mine all those years ago.

I closed my eyes. The California air was warmer than that day in the Pacific, the noise in the rest of the port caused a ruckus louder than the war, and my costume's snug necktie constricted my breathing. Yet I felt transported back to my carrier. I held vigil, in communion, with Wes. This time, the wait was only two and a half minutes.

The familiar roar of the fighter jet snapped my eyes open. A minute later, the Sabre came into view. Wes took one step forward, and his posture became ramrod straight. Extras were sent out in groups of four and five to gather gradually on the deck. One cluster had to be redirected off the landing strip, but they were corrected with a swiftness, and the misstep didn't spoil the sequence.

I was in the seventh wave of extras. There were rows of men between

Xavier's and my final mark on the deck, and I fought the urge to push my way forward. *He's not Horace*, I reminded myself.

The fighter jet landed, and the pilot swap happened without a hitch. Xavier removed his helmet and held it aloft. The extras cheered. I whistled and clapped. Xavier climbed down from the Sabre, and Horace's triumph was palpable. The allusion became indistinguishable from reality. I cried.

Horace shakes several hands, but wades through the crowd until he reaches Aaron. He pulls him into a hug that I recognize as a lover's embrace. The surrounding sailors go wild. I bow my head and weep. The pandemonium lasts several minutes.

Nicholas called, "Cut!"

The director was so pleased with what he got on the first take, he announced that there wouldn't be a second one. I was relieved. I didn't have another take in me.

The movie wrapped eleven days later. Xavier was so proud of himself at the after-party inside Stage 9. He'd used his cunning and artistry to transform a schlocky, mortifying script into a compelling adult movie. He'd saved my character from mockery, and he'd played Horace more honestly than I'd thought possible. The parts where the homosexual flourishes were too pronounced would need to be pruned, but on the whole, Xavier had orchestrated a rare feat. I couldn't help being impressed and grateful. In all my years in Hollywood, I'd never witnessed an actor manage to beat the industry at its own game.

Lowell was in the dark about how the studio's anticipated masterpiece was coming together. On the handful of occasions during production when I spoke with him in passing, he was ecstatic about the film. He tried to pump me for information, asking me if I was enjoying what I was seeing on set. I told him what he wanted to hear: He was producing the greatest patriotic Black film in the history of motion pictures.

A month after filming ended, Nicholas invited Xavier, Rosalind, Tab, Wes, and me to lunch on a Sunday afternoon at the restaurant in the exclusive Hotel Bel-Air, where he was renting a suite for an extended stay of indeterminate length. The director had taken up residency in a similar fashion at the Chateau Marmont in the 1950s. He rented a bungalow at the château one Friday night, and he remained there for eight years.

As our party was being shown to our table, I thanked Nicholas for including me. "Unlike the actors, I didn't do anything to bring the movie to life."

He cocked his head to the side. "Are you kidding? Without you, there'd be no heart to the story on the ship."

"I'm not sure what that means," I said, "but I'm glad you're pleased."

I'd accepted that the minds of creative types would always be a bit of a mystery to me. The connections they made and the concepts that lit up their talents were beyond me. My exchange with Nicholas was the first signal that registered with me that my interpretation of the footage might not match what the director had assembled.

During lunch with the director, the actors fought the nagging urge to ask him how the movie was shaping up in the editing room. They each gave small-talk updates on how they'd busied themselves since filming finished. Xavier confessed that he'd been a hibernating homebody. He managed to jog once a day, but other than that, he'd been recuperating from the outpouring of energy the film had demanded from him. Tab beamed while he told us about a pair of stallions that he was breaking in on a horse ranch in Santa Barbara.

Rosalind cracked us up with a recitation of the general meetings, auditions, screen tests, and Hollywood parties that her agent sent her on to make the most of her time in Los Angeles. She'd been kissed, praised, sexually propositioned, and assured by countless film industry players that she was the second coming of Dorothy Dandridge. What she hadn't received in the past month was a job offer. In two days, Rosalind was flying back to New York City, where an off-Broadway theater role awaited her.

When it was his turn, Wes didn't have much to report. He'd made enough money from the film that he didn't have to go back to cutting hair in a barbershop. He'd booked a small part on an episode of an ABC police drama called *The Felony Squad.* We congratulated him, but Wes downplayed the gig. He only had four lines.

Xavier tried to buck him up. "Once this movie comes out, they'll be begging you to be the lead in one of those shows."

Nicholas drank the last of his Rob Roy. "Turn them down. You belong on the silver screen."

Wes said, "You two are too kind."

"I'm not being nice," the director insisted. "You'll see for yourself. After lunch, I've arranged for us to have a private screening of the film."

The four actors and I simultaneously said some version of either *wow*, *yes*, or *holy shit*.

"It's just a rough assembly of the movie—no score yet," he warned.

"I can hardly wait to hightail it to Skyline," Tab said.

"You won't have to go that far. I'm editing the movie in adjoining rooms in this hotel."

I was so stunned, I spoke up. "How the hell can you do that? The equipment required, and the people, and the sign-off you'd have to get. It's unprecedented."

"Lowell told me I could have whatever I needed to make the film great," Nicholas explained. "This is what I need. I sleep in my suite, I usually order room service, and I can walk over and work on the picture for the rest of my waking hours."

We returned our attention to our meals, and I'd never seen actors eat quicker. No one took the waiter up on his offer of coffee or tea. We exited the restaurant in a giddy, controlled rush, and we followed Nicholas past the pond and several swans on the hotel property.

Xavier whistled the navy fight song "Anchors Aweigh" into the warm afternoon air.

We reached a ballroom that Nicholas had converted into a screening room. The arched windows were draped with heavy blackout curtains. There was a web of wires that fed into four speakers placed around the room. A projector was mounted opposite a screen that dominated the twenty-six-foot-high wall. For seating, the hotel had provided a half dozen plush red velvet armchairs.

Nicholas ran the projector himself. "Remember, you never saw this."

We were seated close to the screen and had to crane our necks to look up and take in the entire picture. The speakers played at top volume. The bombardment of sight and sound immersed me into the film like I hadn't experienced the hundreds of times before as a moviegoer. On such a grand scale, the images overruled any objections from my brain. Was that Xavier exiting a church façade on the Skyline backlot with Rosalind pressing through dozens of extras to stop him and have a word? No, that was Horace leaving First Mount Zion after Sunday service and Harmony wading through the faithful congregants to speak privately with him.

Swept away, I was tossed and pulled by the story, and I forgot I knew where it was going. Horace's battles in the air had me rooting for his survival, and his victories at war lulled me into viewing him as unbeatable. His reversal of fortune jolted me. Despite having lived it, despite having read the script, despite seeing the scenes shot, despite the vivid opening sequence where Horace's biplane crashed into the lake, it slipped my attention that the hero's death was foretold.

As for the unspoken strain of homosexuality in the bloodstream of the movie, I can't pretend my opinion wasn't biased. I thought it played beautifully, for the most part. What I hadn't picked up on was during filming—probably because I was homing in on Xavier's performance—was that Rosalind's Harmony not only sensed Horace was gay, but she was a lesbian herself. She longed to link with him in marriage to better protect them both, and she married a much older man because his sexual appetite had presumably diminished, if not vanished. I came to adore Harmony to an extent I would have guessed impossible before the screening. She and Horace did have a love story in this film, and it was one I could believe and respect.

While I suspected that the subtext of Horace and Harmony's unconventional bond could have been sneaked by censors and average people, I was convinced that the scenes between Horace and Aaron were too homoerotic. One stolen glance might have been permissible, but Horace undressed Aaron with his eyes almost every time they were together. Aaron, devoted and naïve, doesn't notice the pilot's desire for him. Yet I don't see how anyone in the audience could miss it. I imagined that Nicholas could cut around the moments of unmistakable lust. I even suspected that he was including more incendiary moments than need be in order to trade them away without sacrificing the whole of his intent.

The screening ended, and Xavier and Rosalind led the rest of us in applauding.

Xavier stood up on his velvet chair and shouted, "Goddamn, it's perfect!"

Rosalind wiped tears from her eyes. Tab grinned, happy that no one found fault in him. Wes was speechless; he'd never seen himself on a big screen in such a meaty role. Xavier assured him that his reaction was natural. It was disorientating to see yourself suddenly as giant as the movie stars you grew up worshiping.

"You'll get used to it. You're a citizen of Mount Olympus," Xavier told him.

Nicholas shook hands with each of us. He reminded me of a proud papa accepting congratulations on the birth of a healthy son. He had champagne waiting on ice, and we all drank to *Hornet's Hellfire*. Our joy would be snuffed out the next morning.

24

SWALLOW AN ELEPHANT

The levers of power in Hollywood move methodically when building rising stars up, and they turn swiftly when casting renegade stars out.

Army Archerd had the exclusive in his Monday column, "Just for *Variety*":

GOOD MORNING: *Skyline Studios is scrubbing the release date for "Hornet's Hellfire" due to director Nicholas Ray's fragile health. Insiders say the "Rebel Without a Cause" helmer, who suffered a heart attack in 1962 while filming "55 Days at Peking," is once again ailing. He has fallen behind in editing, and the studio isn't sure he got all the coverage necessary to complete the picture. Reshoots might be in order. So might a new director.*

Our Judas was revealed in a *Hollywood Reporter* headline: "Skyline Pictures Signs Actor Wes Malone to a Two-Year Holding Deal." In the bottom of the short item, Lowell refers to Wes as "the fresh black talent every studio has been searching for since Sidney and Xavier matured past their heartthrob years." The payout for the holding deal was listed as between $1,000 and $2,000 a week.

Both news items were clipped out by my boss's secretary and left on my desk on the studio lot. I was furious at Wes. The fucking rat wasted no time betraying his costars and Nicholas. He must have gone straight from the screening to his agents, who rang Lowell and monetized their client's disloyalty.

To think how we coddled and praised Wes the day before. We assumed he was overwhelmed by the novelty of seeing himself on-screen, when in truth, he was disturbed by the gay attraction that Xavier's character had for his. But he didn't have the guts to confront Nicholas or Xavier about his misgivings. No, he ran behind their backs to report them. He named names.

It was 8:00 AM, and I figured that Xavier must already have been notified by his reps that his movie no longer had a release date. I picked up the phone and dialed his number, but he didn't answer. A few minutes later, I received a phone call from Lowell's office. I was instructed to go see him without delay. I braced myself for termination.

I walked into Lowell's office and found him snoozing in his father's old chair. I closed the door with a bang, and he was startled awake. He rubbed his eyes, then stared at me for a beat.

"I was up half the night because of this faggot nonsense," he said. "Nicholas tried to hold the footage hostage. Said he'd burn it before he'd hand it over. I had to call in favors with the LAPD to get the footage out of that hotel."

"Whatever you did is working. Not a word of that is in the papers or even being whispered in the halls," I said, as if the seizure of the film footage wasn't news to me.

"It's costing us a pretty penny." He yawned. "Listen, I'm going to need your help."

So, I wasn't getting fired yet, which was a relief, because I wanted to find a way to salvage the movie. "Name it."

"I understand that Xavier was at this unsanctioned screening Nicholas held for the actors, and I figure he's under Nicholas's spell," said Lowell. "Wes said Nicholas is like a hypnotist."

To hell with Wes, but at least he hadn't mentioned that I was also in attendance.

"He's filled Xavier's head," Lowell continued, "with the idea that they're going to make the most daring, artsy picture ever seen. But that's not what I green-lit. That's not the script they were handed."

"Have you seen the film?" I asked.

"Yeah, I watched it as soon as we got it back to the studio."

"How bad is it?"

"It starts off all right. Once you get to the ship, it's fag propaganda." He stretched his arms above his head. "I've tolerated Xavier being a fruit since we added him to our roster, and I don't care who he fucks long as I don't get fucked at the box office for it. This picture, though, is out of line. He'll have to do reshoots for another director. Tell him. I can still turn this picture into a winner. Xavier can still nab trophies. He's just gotta play ball."

I drove to Silver Lake and pressed Xavier's doorbell twice before I was greeted by Antonio. He wore a black T-shirt that strained to contain his muscular upper body, and dark, straight-legged blue jeans. He seemed taller than I'd been informed until I noticed he had on cowboy boots. He was smoking an unfiltered Pall Mall cigarette, and he smirked at me.

"Come in," Antonio said in a raspy voice as he walked away from me and into the house. "Xavier's showering."

Although I'd conducted a background check on him, Antonio and I were meeting in person for the first time. His lax attitude worried me. He hadn't asked me who I was or what business had brought me to the house.

"Do you always let in strangers?" I asked.

"Aaron, you're no stranger. Xavier talks about you. Yap, yap, yap. I think sometimes you are his main squeeze."

He said this without an inflection of jealousy, and I couldn't tell if he was joking. Maybe he meant it as a dry observation. Or perhaps he just wanted to make it clear that he knew who I was.

I trailed behind Antonio into the kitchen. "Tell me, what kind of mood is our movie star in?"

He poured himself a cup of coffee. "Steaming like a bull. Not that I blame him. Censorship *es mierda*. It can't be tolerated."

"Movies get edited and changed all the time," I said. "Compromise is part of the process."

He spoke in an unflappable deadpan. "*Compromise* is what a punk calls it when he convinces the john fucking him to cum on his face instead of down his throat."

I was speechless.

Antonio turned to me. "You want coffee?"

I barely managed to gather the breath to answer. "Yeah, I could use a cup."

Talking Xavier into reshoots, with militant Antonio in his ear, was going to be tougher than I'd anticipated. I racked my brain for ways to get Antonio out of the house and out of my conversation with Xavier, but Antonio handed me a cup of coffee and slumped onto the couch in the living room with the languid air of a man with nowhere to go. He grabbed a novel, *A Queer Kind of Death* by George Baxt, off the coffee table and began to read.

From the edge of the kitchen, I asked him, "When did Xavier get word there was trouble with the picture?"

Antonio didn't lower the book from in front of his face. "The director—what's his name, Ray. The phone rings after one in the morning, and it's him screaming and crying. Out of his mind. 'The cops took everything.'"

"How did Xavier take the news?"

"Why interrogate him, when you can talk to me?" Xavier asked combatively, sweeping into the room and crossing it to join Antonio.

The two kissed. Open-mouthed and with tongue. I couldn't tell if this was their normal habit or if they were putting on a show for me. I let them finish without interruption.

"I'm not here to interrogate anyone," I insisted.

Xavier sat on the arm of the couch and stroked the hair on the nape of Antonio's neck. "Then what are you here for?"

"I want to save the movie you made."

"You weren't in on the plot to steal the footage?"

Experience has taught me that fatigue and anger breed paranoia, and the bags under Xavier's eyes attested to the sleepless night he'd had. While he stewed in a void of limited information, I imagine he indicted everyone aware of the covert screening except for Nicholas and himself. His accusation wasn't to be taken personally. It was to be defused.

"I didn't squeal, and I didn't know the studio was going to take it back by force. I loved the movie. You saw how much I loved it," I said calmly. "Wes dimed us out."

Xavier stared at me for a long beat. "You're sure."

"Lowell confirmed it."

"Lowell—he's taken the picture hostage."

"Can we talk in private?" I asked.

Antonio interjected, "I told you he'd try to get you alone."

Regrettably, my temper flared. "Excuse me, do you work in Hollywood? Do you know the first thing about how our business runs?"

Xavier stood up and pointed a finger at me. "Watch it! This is my house, not yours. I call the shots."

"Fine," I said, regaining my cool. "I just don't want you turning a creative dispute into a political crisis. All Lowell is after are a few reshoots to rein in the gayest sections. And even I have to agree, there were places where it crossed the line."

"I thought he said he loved the movie," said Antonio.

"Does he have to be part of this discussion?"

Xavier looked at his lover, then back to me. "Antonio keeps me honest."

"Please . . . Don't be ridiculous. You have no leverage," I said. "You do the reshoots or the movie never sees the light of day."

"You're too wedded to the establishment," Xavier told me. "The old men who built Hollywood are dead or dying. The studios are dead or dying. I'm going to start an outcry for this movie. A movement against censorship."

"What are you talking about? You'll destroy everything that you've built."

He furrowed his brow and spoke to me with grave disappointment in his voice. "You watched me pour my heart into this picture. It's my best work, and I lined up the right talent to be with me, and I pulled great performances out of them. Hell, I should get codirecting credit." He shook his head. "That's what I built, and I'm not carving it up for Lowell or the other squares. He's going to have to swallow the elephant. Because I'm not giving him shit. He can't afford to burn the money he's spent on this movie, and the people won't allow him to censor it."

I thought he'd gone mad. "'The people'? Who the fuck are 'the people'?"

"I have a voice. I have a fan base."

"You're gay. How many fans you expect to have once that gets out? Don't you see? Lowell can burn you."

"Times have changed."

"Not enough."

"Aaron, the politics around gay and lesbian liberation—"

"Why the fuck does this have to be about gay politics?" I cried.

"Because you, a gay man, asked a gay actor to play a gay hero in a movie." He threw his hands into the air. "You and I talked about doing exactly what we've done. What made you think I'd fold at the first sign of trouble?"

My answer was frank. "I figured you'd do whatever it took to win an Oscar. You've been chasing Sidney for so long, and this is your big chance to catch him."

Xavier said, "Leaving an everlasting mark—that's what I'm chasing now."

25

INSIDE MAN

On the drive to Skyline the next day, I considered how to shade Xavier's staunch refusal to do reshoots in a manner that didn't send Lowell onto a warpath. The tumult stirred by the raid and seizure of the footage had Xavier and Lowell operating on raw emotions after a sleepless night. I was confident that the breach between the studio boss and the star could be mended, provided the dispute didn't escalate publicly.

I arrived at Lowell's office, and his secretary informed me that I'd have to wait. Lowell was on the telephone with the showbiz beat reporter from the *Los Angeles Times*. Through the closed door, I heard Lowell raising his voice. His words were muffled, but his displeasure was clear.

Turned out that he was being asked to respond to a statement that Xavier gave to the newspaper: "I completed every scene in the script for *Hornet's Hellfire*, and I stand by the work that I delivered under the direction of Nicholas Ray. Reshoots aren't needed, which is just as well since my commitments to my next movie for Columbia Pictures make it impossible for me to do extra work for Skyline."

Lowell's response was terse: "Stars act in movies, and they go on acting until their studio tells them the picture is finished."

The hope of resolving the matter behind the scenes evaporated. The battle between Xavier and Lowell became a referendum on a host of issues for the industry. Who does decide when a picture is done? The director, the producer, the studio president? Could studios wrap a picture and come back weeks or months later demanding actors perform in reshoots? Was Xavier being a difficult actor? Was Skyline censoring art? All those questions spoke to the eternal rolling debate in Hollywood: Who runs this town anyway?

Early vocal support favored Xavier. The first big name to rally to his side was Bette Davis, who had a history of being repeatedly suspended in the 1930s for her refusal to work for salaries and on films she deemed subpar. Asked what she thought of the "Barlow affair" by an audience member in London during the question-and-answers portion after a special screening of *Jezebel* (1938), Bette recounted her clashes with Jack Warner for twenty minutes.

Then she said of Xavier, "He has my support and sympathies. Studios believe that they make stars and they can break stars. Preposterous! No one makes a star except the star themself." She was interrupted by rapturous applause. "I'm sorry to say Mr. Barlow will have to pay for his convictions, but he is on the right side of things. Actors can't be worked ceaselessly. We're not slaves."

Olivia de Havilland, who had achieved a legal victory against the studio's practice of extended seven-year contracts by adding on the days that actors were suspended to the end of the agreement, spoke out from Paris in support of Xavier. Jimmy Cagney and even the revered Charlie Chaplin sided with Xavier.

As the standoff between Skyline Motion Pictures and Xavier dragged on into the fall, Xavier iced me out, and the weaknesses in the star's position began to show. First off, only actors past their prime (many of them legends) were speaking out on the record for Xavier. Young stars didn't want to risk alienating their relationships with a studio. Black actors, in particular, sidestepped the story.

When questioned about it, Sammy Davis Jr. said, "I don't concern myself with the ins and outs of another cat's deal. That's between the studio, him, his agent, and his God."

After several weeks, Diahann Carroll did break her silence in an *Ebony* magazine interview. She was quoted as saying, "Xavier is a dear friend, and one of our most talented actors, black or white. He knows when he's given his all to a role, and he believes he has done so. The studio ought to release the picture and let the audience decide if it measures up to snuff. My money is on Xavier."

A week after that article hit newsstands, Diahann's film in development at Skyline was scrapped. She had been in talks to portray Queen Nefertiti. Lowell not only stopped the film from moving forward at Skyline, he refused to relinquish his hold on the script so that Diahann could shop the project to other studios. She would never wear Nefertiti's crown.

Before waging its open counterstrike at Xavier, Skyline authorized a series of proxy attacks. Anonymous inside sources reframed Xavier's principled stance as a bid for more money. It "leaked" that the studio was offering to pay Xavier $5,000 a day for the reshoots, but he wanted twice that amount. The greedy-actor angle enraged a lot of movie fans and cost him support among the working-class crew members and junior executives. Ironically, in October, Xavier's agent at MCA did negotiate a deal with Lowell, offering Xavier $8,000 a day, and when Xavier reiterated that his refusal to participate wasn't a ploy for money and he rejected the deal, his agency dropped him.

A separate onslaught of stories fed to the press suggested that Xavier abused drugs and alcohol during the filming of *Hornet's Hellfire*. According to this line of lies, Skyline was protecting Xavier by holding the movie from release. The reshoots were an opportunity for Xavier to rescue his performance if only he would get himself clean first.

With the loss of MCA representation, Xavier didn't have the muscle of a major company to defend him. In fact, getting dropped by his agent fed into the idea that he was troubled. Tabloids put him on their front pages in doctored photos and headlines that exclaimed his downfall. FROM HEARTTHROB TO JUNKIE was typical of the lot. Gossip columnist Dorothy Manners wrote that she had it on good authority that Xavier had been deemed uninsurable, meaning no studio would hire him.

Essentially blackballed from appearing in film and television, Xavier assumed he could argue his case in front of press cameras. He was mistaken. Every major and minor studio banned Xavier from the red carpets at their premieres and parties. Talk show bookers and magazine editors were told that if Xavier appeared on their programs or on their pages, the studios would withhold their other stars. On the advice of a third-rate publicist, Xavier called a press conference for 11:00 AM on a Monday outside his house. Afraid of retaliation from the studios, no reporters showed up.

Less than ninety days was what it took to dislodge a star from the sky. There hadn't been a descent like Xavier's since Ingrid Bergman was roundly denounced in 1950 for her extramarital affair and love child with Roberto Rossellini. It took Ingrid six years to regain her standing as a leading lady. She somehow withstood being ostracized. Cut off from Xavier, as Christmas drew near, I grew concerned that being shut out and defamed could drive him to suicide.

I began calling Xavier's house and letting the phone ring dozens of times before Antonio picked up, took my message, and half-heartedly promised to pass it on to Xavier. Days went by before my home telephone rang around midnight. I answered it in the kitchen, and Xavier was on the line.

He sounded agitated. "Why haven't you been canned?"

I spoke quietly to keep from waking Kimberly in her bedroom. "Because I'm being Switzerland or at least acting like it."

"Fat load of good it's done me."

"If you had kept talking to me, maybe some of this could have been avoided."

"Or maybe not." Xavier muffled his mouthpiece, but I heard him say something in Spanish, presumably to Antonio. "Aaron, if I'm going to trust you, you gotta show me you have pull. I don't need a sympathizer. I need an inside man who can make shit happen."

He hung up before I could reply.

The next morning at the office, I reported to Lowell's secretary that I had vital information about the standoff with Xavier. I was summoned to Lowell's office twenty minutes later. He was surprisingly eager to discuss ways to make peace. Gone were his defensiveness, hurt feelings, and moral outrage.

I wondered what had softened him, but I didn't want to question the first break in the impasse. He listened as I reiterated that he and Xavier did indeed share the same goal: the release of a successful movie. They differed on how the film should be cut, but such a disagreement could be hashed out.

So I proposed to Lowell a modest step toward resolution. He and Xavier would sit down together and screen the film. Just watch it. No talking. No cheering. No harrumphing. After the screening, Lowell would lay out the scenes he wanted reshot and why. Xavier could make the case for keeping those scenes. No decisions would be made immediately, but the parameters of this conflict would be set. A dialogue would be underway.

Lowell agreed to those terms. Over the phone the following morning, I presented the plan to Xavier, and he claimed he was open to it. He asked if I would meet up with him to discuss a few ideas before he committed to sitting down with Lowell. I told Xavier to name the time and place. He instructed me to meet him on New Year's Eve in Silver Lake at a gay bar called the Black Cat.

26

BLACK CAT

We were supposed to meet at 11:00 PM. I arrived five minutes early, and at ten of twelve, I was still waiting for Xavier. He was testing my loyalty. I stuck around to prove myself as a brother.

Given the circumstances, I wasn't feeling festive, which was just as well. The Black Cat Tavern was a new gay bar, only a couple of months old. It hadn't found its groove yet, and no one had broken it in enough to be considered a regular. The crowd in the Black Cat consisted predominantly of Latino men with some Black guys and white boys sprinkled about. There was little excitement for the new year.

Javier Solís's "Regalo de Reyes" blared over the speakers, and the music continued along that vein and at that volume. A bunch of red, white, and blue helium balloons dotted the ceiling, and silver noisemakers were free for the taking at the bar. Three tinseled Christmas trees were shedding what sparkle they had left onto the floor, and pointy party hats with '67 on the front of them were stacked on a side table next to the entrance. Nobody was wearing those hats.

Xavier finally walked into the bar, and I smiled in relief until I spotted Antonio and another friend named Larry Armstrong come in behind him. Larry was a costume designer for drag queens, and in those circles, he was known as Blaque Head. Since I'd requested that Xavier and I speak alone, I hoped that Antonio and Larry would entertain each other while I laid the groundwork for a settlement.

"Sorry we're late," Xavier said, leaning down to speak directly into my ear. "Antonio tried talking me out of coming."

"I can respect that you care for him, but—"

"I love him."

"All the same. He's an idealist, and there's no place for that kind of thinking in our industry."

"Maybe there should be," he said.

Antonio and Larry joined us and shook my hand. Our greetings were perfunctory. Larry, at least, seemed relaxed. Antonio looked around the Black Cat with disdain.

"We should be up the street!" Antonio shouted over the din of the crowd and the music. "New Faces is a better bar!"

Larry tugged at Antonio's elbow. "Let's get drinks."

Antonio went with Larry to the bar. Another dozen men crammed their way into the Black Cat, and Xavier and I moved deeper into the crowd and farther from the door. Xavier fiddled with the zipper on his black leather jacket. His eyes darted around the room, and the usual warmth of his company was absent. I got the sense that he was wary of me, and I was unsure how to put him at ease.

I attempted to divert our minds briefly from his troubles by getting his two cents on the talk of the town for the past two weeks. "Do you think Walt Disney was murdered?"

The animation titan had passed away, at sixty-five, on December 15, and the subsequent details were sketchy. Mr. Disney either died of a heart attack, cancer, or natural causes. His body was hastily cremated, and he was interred at Forest Lawn Memorial Park on the seventeenth in a private funeral. It was not the Hollywood send-off befitting his stature, and the hurried nature with which he was dispatched sparked rumors. A leading one was that he'd been offed by a powerful cabal that was opposed to the plan to build a Walt Disney World Theme Park in Florida. I didn't believe the gossip, but speculating can become sport.

I shared my favorite ridiculous theory. "Word is the author P. L. Travers had him poisoned because she hated what he'd done with her *Mary Poppins*."

Xavier nodded sternly. "If they can get to Disney, none of us is safe."

"I'm joking," I explained. "No one killed him. He was a smoker and—"

A grinning Black dandy in his fifties, done up in a purple suede jacket, had recognized Xavier and weaved through a crush of bodies to lay hands on Xavier's forearm.

"I won't scream your name," said the dandy, smelling of whiskey. "Just know I loved you in *The Left-Handed Gunman*. What was it you said to the evil judge before you shot him dead?"

Xavier was indulgent of his drunk fan. "A bullet's too good for you."

"Yes, there it is." The dandy laughed and coughed and laugh-coughed before concluding with a sigh. "You's one of us. I wouldn't have guessed it."

"Make sure you don't run and tell it," I said.

The dandy's grin faded. "I'd never." He turned to Xavier. "I wouldn't. I swear it on my mama's grave."

He left us to cross the Black Cat and entered the men's restroom. Xavier frowned at me. I could already guess the subject of his grievance. I glanced at my watch. It was 11:57.

"You didn't have to be rude to him," Xavier said.

"I wasn't rude. I was direct. Last thing you need these days are rumors that you're gay hitting the tabloids."

"More like it's the last thing Lowell needs. Because if I'm outed, tell him I'm gonna level this town. I'll share the names of the men I've fucked."

I folded my hands in prayer and implored him, "Don't make threats. You'll only do more damage to yourself than you could ever do to Skyline."

"What is it you worry more about—me or my career?"

I leveled with him. "Way I see it, if one goes up in flames, the other will burn soon after."

"Is that what you suppose happened to Horace once he couldn't be a war hero no more?"

His question sucker punched me. I didn't, in the moment, see why Horace's fate was relevant, and I resented having his misfortune thrown in my face.

There was an edge in my voice. "I'm not here to talk about him."

Xavier ignored my objection. "He's been on my mind, not because of the film but because he helps me understand you. I see you, brother, breaking your back to fix me up. The question is why."

"Ain't it obvious? I'm trying to look out for you."

"There's more than that to it," he said. "You're being pulled in so many directions—past and present. No one can serve two masters."

"You're quoting the Bible now?"

"Point is if you don't know who to serve," Xavier said, "you can't be trusted."

More hurt than indignant, I yelled, "I can't be trusted? I could've ratted you out before the movie started filming! Lowell would have been all over you!"

The music didn't pause for a group of men by the bar who started the countdown with shouts of "*Diez!*"

"I'm on your side! I'm yours!"

Xavier didn't reply as the countdown continued.

Nearly everyone inside the Black Cat had joined in by "*Siete!*"

I noticed a white man in his late twenties, standing alone and not counting the seconds to the new year.

"*Seis!*"

I had a strong and urgent feeling that I knew him from somewhere.

"*Cinco!*"

Was he someone I'd seen on the Skyline lot?

"*Cuatro!*"

Yes—not on the lot, but he was at the port when we filmed on the carrier.

"*Tres!*"

Was he an extra?

"*Dos!*"

No—he was one of the cops maintaining the perimeter.

"*Uno!*"

He was a wax fruit. Fuck. We were standing in the center of a sting operation.

"*Feliz Año Nuevo!*"

I turned to warn Xavier, but he was already wading through the crowd to get to Antonio. I couldn't scream loud enough. The noise in the Black Cat was deafening. Men were banging their fists on the bar and tables. Men were stomping their feet. Men were whistling and cheering. None of that was illegal.

There were men kissing, but not a lot. Most of the kissing was a put-on, a gag. Men were grabbing their buddies by the side of the head or by the neck, holding them in place while they planted one on them and their buddies tried to pull away. In fact, the only two men I spotted sharing a genuinely romantic kiss were Xavier and Antonio. However, intention meant nothing, and whether offense was committed in passion or in jest, the law was unwavering. A man kissing another man constituted lewd conduct. Violations surrounded me.

The white cop I recognized wasn't the only plainclothes officer in the Black Cat. Less than ten feet from me, a stocky Puerto Rican with the build of a boxer planted a kiss on a tall, wavy-haired Colombian. Their closed lips were pressed together. Friends having a laugh.

A white, buzz-cut cop, dressed in blue jeans and a green flannel shirt, yanked the boxer by the shoulder, breaking the kiss. The cop yelled in the boxer's face, and maybe the boxer couldn't hear the cop identifying himself as a police officer, or maybe the boxer just reacted on reflexes. The distinction is lost to history, because the boxer's response gave the cops all the justification they needed to unleash the violence to come.

The boxer delivered a quick, solid jab to the cop's nose. The buzz-cut cop dropped to the ground like a marionette who got his strings cut in a single clip. Three other plainclothes police officers positioned in different areas of the Black Cat rushed the boxer and his friend.

I realized that I was witnessing a police raid in progress, but hardly anyone else in the bar had that perspective. What they saw were white men attempting to jump Latino men. What they saw were men they felt an unspoken connection to in need of help. What they saw was a call to arms.

Mind you, the drinking patrons probably wouldn't have been as keen to fight if they'd realized they were taking on cops. But the plainclothes officers didn't flash badges, and the New Year's commotion made speaking to anyone more than a foot away impossible. So, a dozen of the Black Cat patrons came to the aid of the men they knew and seized upon the white strangers causing trouble in their bar.

The brawl swept the room like wildfire. The fighting was far less choreographed than the ones in westerns like *Destry Rides Again* (1939). This was a sloppy, drunken pile-on. Elbows and knees inflicted more harm than clean punches. The cop I recognized grabbed a bartender by his hair and pulled him over the bar. Cries of pain pierced through the screams of anger. I didn't see who hit him, but the Black dandy in the purple suede jacket fled for the door holding his bloody nose.

I looked toward the bar for Xavier and didn't see him or Antonio. Larry was using a barstool as a battering ram in a desperate attempt to reach the exit. He tripped or was grabbed at the ankles, and he fell to the floor, where a lot of the fights raged on in a mess of spilled beer and cocktails. Bodies rolled about with arms and legs flailing. The brawl was pulling bodies into itself, gathering mass and a frantic energy.

I was nearly knocked down by five men in a scrum: three Latinos and two undercover cops wrestling in a spinning dervish. I had to step on a fallen man's hand to keep my own footing. From the intensity of his holler, I believe I broke a couple of his fingers. I wish I hadn't had to.

I shoved and pushed along a path to the bar. I saw Xavier lifting Antonio upright. A gash on Antonio's forehead bled profusely. Through the chaos, Xavier locked eyes with me and glared. There was no mistaking his message: *Come no closer.*

A ferocious, belligerent roar drew my attention to the entrance. Reinforcements had arrived, and a surge of uniformed cops waded into the melee, police batons out and swinging. One of them came right at me. His first blow struck me on the left shoulder. The next one caught me in the side of the mouth. I tasted my own blood and felt a tooth rolling loose over my tongue. My jaw flashed white hot, then went numb.

The cop cocked back to deliver more abuse. He wasn't going to stop. None of them were going to show any restraint tonight for colored faggots who had the temerity to fight back. If only Xavier could have seen me at this crossroads, but he was carrying Antonio out the back door. My years at Skyline had enabled me to cultivate useful connections inside the LAPD, and I considered putting my hands up in surrender and sorting out my involvement at the station. I wasn't in the Black Cat as a gay man looking to get lucky. I was on official business for the industry that dominated the city.

But as I spit out a tooth, I realized that the cops didn't care about who I was outside the Black Cat. Deals for mercy were off the table. Whatever immunity I thought I had was worthless. I balled my hands into fists and reared up swinging. I stunned the cop with a gut punch and a left hook that struck him in the throat. He bent forward, and

I kneed him in the eye. He stumbled over a body and landed on his side.

More uniformed officers were pouring into the bar. There was a stampede of men headed for the back door. As I passed the bar, I saw a cop beating the bar's manager, a woman he had mistaken for a drag queen. I'd lost track of Larry. I pushed forward. Several police officers turned up to seal the back door, and they managed to nab a few men, but the rest of us broke free into the night, into the new year.

27

SURRENDER THEIR NAMES

I spent New Year's Day having my jaw wired shut. Everything I ate was blended into a thick shake, and a straw was placed through the hole left by my lost tooth. I swallowed painkillers around the clock. Kimberly was horrified by my appearance, accepted my vague answers about what had happened to me, and had enough pity for me to keep my ice packs fresh as I recuperated in the guest room.

Against doctor's orders and despite the pain, I drove to the Skyline lot on Monday, January 2. Only a skeleton crew reported for work at 9:00 AM. Given the holiday weekend, most employees trickled in hours later than usual, if they didn't just take the day off. I turned on the lights in the security office, went to my desk, and began typing a report describing how my talks with Xavier were interrupted by a raid on the Black Cat.

My injuries were evidence of the night's brutality. The other details I gathered over the phone. A source of mine—a Black secretary at the Silver Lake police station—revealed that the fairy dusting resulted in fourteen people being booked and charged with lewd conduct and assault. I'd seen for myself how badly the bartenders and manager had been beaten. It was easily the most violent incident in my life, and I'd served in a war. Yet the straight world had heard nothing about it. At

11:00 AM, my boss, Callum, was taken aback when he came into the security office and saw my swollen and bruised face.

Through my fastened teeth, I managed to say, "I got caught up at the Black Cat."

Callum hadn't heard of the gay bar or the raid. He read the first few pages of my report, and when he caught up to the words I was pounding out on the typewriter, he read over my shoulder. Once I finished, he said, "I'll take this to Lowell. You get out of here and rest up for a few days."

When I returned home, Kimberly was over at her parents' house, so I fixed myself a cup of hot chicken broth. Then I tried to sleep but couldn't get comfortable. The ache in my jaw steadily strengthened in the hour before I was due to take my next pain pill. I stared up at my bedroom ceiling, and my mind fixated on Xavier.

He'd gone quiet since he escaped arrest at the raid. I wondered how many stitches Antonio needed to sew shut the gash in his forehead. I calculated the odds that Xavier had heard about my busted jaw. I fantasized about him calling to check on me.

Then I'd remember the last minute of our conversation and how he scowled at me during the pandemonium. I couldn't take it. I couldn't let it be. Against my better judgment, I used the kitchen telephone to dial Xavier's number. It rang and rang and rang and rang.

Finally, Antonio answered. "He doesn't want to speak with you."

With my constricted mouth, I asked, "How'd you know it was me?"

"No one else lets it ring so long."

"Are you all right?"

"Don't pretend to care for me."

"I'm not asking because I care for you," I said. "Your answer helps me gauge Xavier."

Antonio laughed, which he'd never done to anything I'd said before. "I see. Then I am fine, and Xavier is fine, but he still doesn't want to speak with you."

"Why not?"

"He says you set him up or you were used to set him up."

"Bullshit. Neither happened."

"How do you know?" Antonio asked evenly. "You investigate your own studio?"

I wanted to argue, but a rush of words collided at the locked gate of my wired jaw. I grunted unintelligibly. As I regathered my thoughts, my initial reaction (*It's absurd to think that Skyline Motion Pictures arranged for undercover cops to raid a gay bar to entrap Xavier*) was overtaken by another (*I could see the studio doing just that*).

The key to Hollywood's conquest of the world lies in its devotion to scrupulous stagecraft on and off camera. It's an endeavor with ambitions that well exceed a desire to sell movie tickets. What the founding moguls of motion pictures learned in 1926 when one hundred thousand crazed silent film fanatics mobbed the streets of New York City to catch a glimpse of Rudolph Valentino's casket was that they were presiding over more than a business. They were the purveyors of a newborn religion.

And religions demand sacrifices. Like Xavier, most stars surrender their names at the start of their careers. They typically strip years from their ages. They torture their bodies into the approved proportions. Some undergo surgery. Others need only their teeth straightened. Vocal training erases accents. Rigorous dance lessons instill bearing, if not grace.

And religions demand myths. Childhood stories are tailored to give every star an auspicious beginning. Early failed marriages and bastard children are cut from the star's journey as told in candid magazine profiles. Interests and hobbies are fabricated from whole cloth. Public love affairs and marriages are stitched together between couples with no sexual attraction to each other. Flawed lives are refashioned into impeccable personas.

And religions demand obedience. This last principle was the one that rebel stars neglected to heed. It was the fine print at the bottom of their contracts. They overlooked it because the motion picture industry projects to the world an image of itself as a liberal bastion where anything goes—an unjudgmental business that embraces hedonists and artists. The pose isn't completely phony. The industry allows a host of indiscretions. Murderers, rapists, and abusers have been granted career absolution and permitted to keep working in Tinseltown. Yet a star can offend the gods. Damnation is possible for those who ignore that there's only one sin in Hollywood: Don't expose the rapacious puppet masters who prey on stars and crews and audiences alike.

Xavier didn't come to the phone that day or the next. I drove out to his house and knocked on the door. I heard movement inside, but no one answered. I spent the rest of the week at home, finally sleeping for a long stretch once I decided without my doctor's permission to increase my dosage to a pill and a half every four hours. Time became a blur. I slept; I slurped soups and shakes through a straw; I showered; I slept some more. I don't recall reading the paper or receiving any urgent messages.

I thought I could afford the rest because traditionally no one in Hollywood makes big moves during the opening weeks of the year. I was sorely mistaken, and if I hadn't been hopped up on painkillers, I'd have been able to intervene. I would have charged into Lowell's office once I got wind that he was leaking to *Confidential* a story about Xavier being in a gay bar on New Year's Eve. I'd have reminded him that he'd said that he didn't want the conflict between the studio and Xavier to reach scorched-earth tactics.

I would have driven to Xavier's house and broken down his front door the moment I was tipped off about his counterthreat to Lowell. Xavier said if he was outed, he'd confirm the story and list all the Hollywood players and politicians he'd slept with since he came to town as a seventeen-year-old minor. I'd have warned Xavier that such a move would put a target between his eyes. But I was sidelined by a broken jaw and blindsided by my studio and my dear friend. In my subsequent bitter mourning, I have had to accept that no one was interested in the middle ground that I believed possible.

Yet I must own my share of the blame. For years, Xavier had been telling me and showing me that he was preparing himself to be an openly gay Hollywood star. He understood that by doing so, he'd lose mainstream roles, money, and a large chunk of his fan base, but he believed he'd become a leader in the gay liberation movement and that a queer audience could sustain him. He aimed to be a groundbreaker for gay actors the way Sidney was for Black actors. This was to be part of his everlasting mark on the industry.

I dismissed his dream. I belittled his political views. I downplayed the significance of the books that he read and the company that he kept. I ignored who my friend was becoming: a rare man of character in our industry; a man who would be willing to confirm a story identifying him as gay. He'd practically been waiting for the chance to proclaim his sexuality.

If I'd accepted Xavier on his terms, I wouldn't have begged him to play Horace. I would have recognized the lengths he'd go to show the truth about himself and my former lover. I'd have told Lowell that Xavier had his heart set on other projects. Maybe that would have been the end of the film's development, or perhaps Horace's sister would have accepted James Earl Jones in the role. He would have been magnificent and safe.

I was drinking a bowl of tomato bisque for an early dinner on Tuesday, January 10, when Diahann used the courtesy phone at the restaurant La Dolce Vita to call my house. I answered, and she breathed deeply into the receiver before speaking. She was collecting herself, and her voice was steady while tinged with fear.

"Xavier's car was hit on the street outside the window," she said. "I'm looking at him right now. Zay-vee's unconscious, and he's pinned inside his car. The police, the paramedics—they're trying to cut him out. It's taking forever."

What had transpired was this: In a show of love and loyalty, Diahann invited Xavier to dine with her at a celebrity haunt where the paparazzi would be waiting and would snap photos of the two of them looking fabulous. Diahann wanted those pictures to prove that Xavier was not a pariah and not a drug addict. He was still her friend. They agreed to meet at La Dolce Vita in Beverly Hills at 5:15 PM.

According to multiple witnesses, Xavier was driving along Santa Monica Boulevard when a truck speeding along Walden Drive cut through oncoming traffic and jackknifed Xavier's car on the driver's side. The truck was estimated to have been traveling at a speed of thirty-five to forty-five miles per hour. Broken glass lacerated Xavier's face and neck. His driver's-side door caved in on him, trapping his leg inside a fold of metal. Mercifully, the impact knocked Xavier out; he was still breathing at the scene.

Here's where witness statements conflicted: The white driver of the truck hopped out of the vehicle and fled on foot down Walden Drive. Descriptions of his build range from five foot eight to six feet tall. His hair color was either blond, dirty blond, or black. He was thin or muscular. He was between the ages of eighteen and his early thirties. Most witnesses lost sight of him after he ran. Two witnesses claimed that he hopped into a waiting black car. The truck involved in the accident had been reported stolen in Silver Lake the morning of the crash.

This was no accident. Xavier was hunted down. I'm certain that Diahann was unaware of the setup, but her agent, manager, and publicist knew when and where she'd be meeting Xavier that evening. Any of them or the other secretaries in their offices could have tipped off the people determined to silence Xavier.

Diahann didn't know I was on the outs with Xavier when she phoned me, and she assumed that I could have the studio pull strings to ensure that Xavier got the best care possible at the hospital. I assured her that I'd see to it even though I had no confidence that Skyline would lift a finger to save Xavier. I didn't want to send her deeper into despair.

I rushed to the hospital, where the press was outside on the lawn and Diahann was pacing in the waiting room. My face along the jawline was still puffy, but Diahann took no notice. Nor did she react to my strained voice.

"How is he?" I asked.

"The nurses won't tell me anything," she said, "except that Xavier's in critical condition."

I gave her two nickels for the pay phone. "You know Xavier's number by heart."

"Yes."

"You know who Antonio is?"

"Yes. My god, he doesn't know yet." She covered her mouth with her hand. "I called you and not him."

"Try now."

Diahann nodded. A task gave her purpose and direction. She headed for the pay phone, jangling the two coins in the palm of her hand.

I went to the nurses' station and claimed to be Xavier's brother. I recited his address, telephone number, date of birth, and Social Security number as proof. My genuine concern also bolstered my case.

The nurse said, "Wait right here, sir. I'll notify Dr. Holmes that we have next of kin."

She hurried off, and I stared at the pattern in the floor tile, a checkered beige and white. The floor was cleaned to a fine gloss, and I could see my reflection in the tile at my feet. My mouth was downturned, and my eyelids were heavy. My body already knew.

Dr. Holmes approached like a kindly white grandfather. He'd delivered this type of news before. He led me over to a wall in case I needed to lean against it or punch it.

"The injuries your brother sustained were severe. His left leg was crushed, and his femoral artery was cut. He bled out in the ambulance and was dead on arrival. I'm sorry. I'm truly sorry."

My hand pressed against the wall to steady me. "Can I see him?"

"By all means," the doctor said. "Take your time while we gather the forms for you to claim the body."

Three words never landed on me with more weight than *claim the body*. I went numb. The part of me that just handled problems—the fixer in me—took over. Kimberly and I were friends with Bruce and Valerie Chapman, and his father owned and operated Chapman Mortuary. They would prepare Xavier for burial. My church, First African Methodist Episcopal, would host the funeral. Forest Lawn Memorial Park was the resting place of stars, and Xavier would be buried among his peers.

A nurse led me to an elevator, and we took it down to the hospital morgue. I hesitated at the door. Somehow, in my mind, Xavier wouldn't really be dead until I laid eyes on him. I needed a moment to hold off the inescapable.

"Not much farther," the nurse coaxed.

I braced myself and walked over to the metal table where Xavier's lifeless body lay naked under a powder-blue sheet. The lacerations on the side of his face were visible but had been cleaned. His face was handsome, but his spirit was gone. He didn't appear to be in a beatific sleep. His body looked robbed; his talents, his intelligence, his light were stolen.

28

EVIDENCE FOR A PRICE

Skyline, MGM, Warner Bros., Universal, Columbia Pictures, Disney, and Paramount sent flowers. Diahann sang "Take My Hand, Precious Lord." Sidney, who was in San Francisco preparing to begin filming *Guess Who's Coming to Dinner*, paid for the coffin and the hearse. Ossie delivered the eulogy. I served as head pallbearer. Antonio didn't attend the service.

Although Xavier still looked like himself, Diahann and I chose a closed casket. I, for one, couldn't have borne seeing him during the funeral. Diahann insisted that the ceremony be private. She said that she feared it would be overrun by fans, but I think she suspected, as I did, that if the funeral were open to the public, the turnout would be embarrassingly low. In the end, only a few dozen devoted movie lovers came to place flowers on the steps of the church.

The news reports following Xavier's death impeached his character. Intimations about his homosexuality became less subtle the tawdrier the newspaper or rag. The implication was that gay men naturally had messy lives and untimely deaths. I believe the press was emboldened to paint Xavier any color they pleased because he had no one with the standing to defend him. His parents were dead; he had no siblings, spouse, or children. No one even came forward claiming to be a lost cousin. Xavier's estate fell into probate court, and his property and money were escheated to the State of California.

The circumstance surrounding Xavier's death were also fodder for sensational headlines. The car crash was framed as if both drivers might have been at fault, and Xavier was somehow the guiltier of the two. Speculation about whether he was under the influence of drugs and alcohol ran so rampant that the city coroner's office seized Xavier's body from the funeral home and conducted an autopsy. Trace amounts of alcohol and marijuana were detected in his system, and you would have thought from the headlines that Xavier was driving and behaving like a madman in the hours before his death.

To the extent that the press mentioned the white man who struck Xavier's car and fled the scene, it was used to raise questions about what sort of company Xavier was keeping in his private life. Did he owe money to a bookie? Was he in bed with the mob? *Confidential* magazine went as far as to print that "the driver of the truck could well have been one of Xavier's spurned male lovers."

Furious at the coverage, Diahann asked me, "Why don't they print the lovely things I have to say about Xavier? I've given countless interviews, and they don't use a word of it."

I said, "They never will. Xavier fought the studio, and everything you're reading is part of his punishment."

Xavier's death was meant to be the end of the matter. Hollywood got the final word. The public moved on to following new stars. These things happen. It just didn't sit right with me, and I felt the only way to fight back against Skyline was to find evidence of a more scandalous story than the ones they were having published.

So, I carried on at work like I'd put Xavier behind me. I watched out for Wes in his next picture like he was a nephew I adored. I settled a sticky situation between a young Black starlet and her mother, who was secretly taking risqué photographs of her daughter and selling them to tabloids. On the surface, I was a good little soldier in the studio's brigade. But very quietly, I investigated the murder of Xavier.

It was a painstaking process. As a rule, I didn't bring up Xavier as a topic of conversation, and only when others did could I pry for a scrap of information. To throw off suspicion, I had to cultivate the attitude that Xavier got what was coming to him. My first break in the case came from a conversation with my boss six weeks after Xavier died.

Callum mentioned, "We're bringing on a new agent, and I'll need you to show him the ropes."

"Sure thing," I said.

"He just graduated from one of them all-Negro schools. You'll get on like a house on fire."

The school was Tuskegee University, and the new guy's name was Eric Hill. His surname piqued my interest right off the bat because I'd read the police report for the stolen truck used to kill Xavier. The owner of the truck was Paul Hill of Silver Lake, and within a day of sleuthing through census records and newspaper microfiche, I established that Paul was Eric's uncle. I couldn't buy it was a coincidence, especially since Eric was forgetful, lazy, and utterly unsuited to be a security agent. I smelled quid pro quo.

After uncovering that connection, I spent hours thinking about the motivations to kill Xavier. I remembered how Xavier claimed that Lowell couldn't afford to scrap *Hornet's Hellfire*, and I took one of the two Black secretaries in Skyline's finance department to lunch at a sandwich shop off the lot. She and I had always been on speaking terms, and I revealed that I wanted to talk brother to sister about the Barlow affair. We discussed what a shame it was to lose a Black star as bright as Xavier was to drugs. Then I asked her about the cost of the film and the implications of scrapping it.

She explained, "Frankly, the picture's better off with him dead. When he was refusing to do the reshoots, the insurance company was denying our claim to write off the picture. As long as he could do it, they wouldn't pay."

"Now that he's dead, Skyline can recoup the cost?"

"Yes, but now they don't even have to."

"Why?"

"His death means the guild will let us hire an actor to double Xavier on-screen."

I masked my disgust and changed the topic to the rave reviews Sammy Davis Jr. was receiving for his show at the Sands Hotel. Black audiences were flocking to see him since the hotel was no longer segregated. The secretary and her husband had tickets for the first weekend in March.

As I walked back to the studio, I tried to wrap my mind around the idea that Lowell Garten had orchestrated Xavier's murder in order to successfully file an insurance claim or to recast him with a body double in a film. It didn't square with the Lowell I'd seen in action for the past thirteen years or the Lowell who had championed Xavier's career. He saw the talent and beauty in Xavier before almost anyone else. Lowell was second only to George Cukor.

There had to be more to it, and the answer came into view while I was crossing in front of the Pober Building. I would have to step out of the shadows to ensnare Lowell, and there was no guarantee my ploy would work. But I had to know if my hunch was correct.

I headed up to Lowell's office and told his secretary that I needed to speak to him immediately. She tried to put me off, inquiring about what could be so important.

I lied. "I found Xavier's little black book."

She went into Lowell's office, and less than a minute later, she and five studio executives came out. I was ushered inside. The door was closed behind me.

Lowell looked stricken. "What are we talking about? A phone book? What's a phone book even mean?"

I helped myself to a drink at his wet bar. "It's got more than numbers. There are names, dates, locations, and brief descriptions of sex acts."

"Oh God."

"It's quite a read." I began to drink my whiskey neat.

"Aaron, that's a dangerous book to hold on to. It's gotta be destroyed, and I'll need to see it burn. Otherwise, the men on that list will be—"

"Relax. I'm going to sell it to you."

Lowell nodded. "How much of it did you read?"

"All of it." I locked eyes with him. "Do you want to know what he wrote about you?"

He blanched. "The parties Cukor used to throw were wild. I hadn't settled down yet. Xavier and I only fucked twice."

I had him, and I didn't let up. "When he was seventeen?"

"He lied to us about his age." Lowell glanced up at the ceiling. "How much do you want?"

"Fifty grand in cash."

"You expect me to have that in my wallet?"

"I can suggest some men who would pitch in."

"I just mean I need time to put that kind of money together."

"You have until tonight. Meet me at the Crown Jewel at six," I instructed.

Lowell acquiesced, and I left the studio lot to go prepare for my endgame. I stopped by Longs Drugs and bought a small black notebook. I twisted it and creased it to make it look worn. I purchased a recorder with an attached microphone from Leon's electronics store. My plan was to wear a wire for the handoff, get Lowell's confession on tape, and take the recording and the payoff to a reporter I trusted at the *Los Angeles Times*. If the story broke quickly, the police would be forced to investigate.

I went home, intending to brief Kimberly on the unfolding developments. But she didn't come home after teaching at school, and when I called her parents' house, they weren't sure where she was either. I used two pens, one with black ink and the other with blue ink, to fill in the little notebook as I had described it to Lowell. He would undoubtedly flip through it before we concluded our trade.

I was well aware that Lowell might try to double-cross me. That was why I asked for so much cash and gave him only a few hours to come up with it. The task of assembling the money would eat into the time he needed to concoct a scheme to hurt me. And I felt confident he would turn up with the money because he had to get his hands on the little black book.

Lastly, I put stock in the fact that Lowell wasn't a gangster. He'd offered to buy Xavier's cooperation, and he'd resorted to violence when Xavier threatened to name him as a former sex partner. Lowell was frightened of exposure, and whereas Xavier couldn't be swayed by dollars, I was offering to quietly hand over the incriminating evidence for a price. Lowell was a businessman. He wanted to write checks to make his problems disappear.

The Crown Jewel was crowded with the usual clientele. The gay white men gave me the standard once-over glances as I took a table for two near the back of the bar. The piano player had abandoned early jazz songs for the modern era, but he still performed "Summer Wind" without finesse.

I arrived ten minutes before six. No sign of Lowell. I ordered an old-fashioned. The tape holding the wire against my chest was causing me to sweat, testing the adhesive. It didn't have to work for long. I aimed to keep the meeting short.

Lowell entered carrying a brown leather satchel. He came straight to my table and tossed the bag at me before taking his seat. The waiter brought my drink, and Lowell commandeered it. I asked the waiter to bring over another one.

"Check the bag. It's all there."

I opened the satchel, and there was the fifty grand. It didn't look as impressive as I imagined. Five stacks, each with a hundred one-hundred-dollar bills. The cash didn't even fill a briefcase.

"Fifty thousand bucks," I said for the recording. "I knew you'd come through."

"Give me what you promised," Lowell demanded.

"I want a few answers first."

"That wasn't part of—"

"I have a hard time believing you wanted to do this to Xavier. Was your hand forced?"

"It wouldn't have been," Lowell snapped, "if he'd just done the damn reshoots or taken his drubbing. I held the others at bay until he made it impossible."

I pressed buttons to keep him emotionally charged. "Your father's dead. I thought you didn't have to take orders anymore."

"My old man couldn't have prevented this either. The names you probably didn't recognize in the book, they run this city. LA and Hollywood can't survive unless they are coordinated. Studio bosses answer to politicians." He took a big swallow from his drink. "You know Xavier was like nothing any of us had ever seen. Every hopeful young stud who thumbs it to Hollywood is one of the best-looking guys in his hometown, but you'd forget their faces on the drive home. Xavier was memorable from day one, and then he became the last thing any of them expected—a gifted actor, a star. I saw it in him."

"How'd you know?"

"He was acting when he was at our parties. I spied him once before he stepped out to join the others by the pool," Lowell confided. "I saw him turn it on, and if I hadn't caught that glimpse, I wouldn't have been any the wiser."

The tenderness in Lowell's voice was jarring to hear. He'd been party to Xavier's murder, and he spoke of his victim with awe. I don't know how Kinsey would classify Lowell's sexuality, but if it is possible, I think Lowell was attracted to the magnetism and talent of actors.

I saw the waiter approaching with a drink for me, and I wanted Lowell to incriminate himself beyond question. "Did you put together the plan to kill him, or did you just step out of the way?"

He glared at me. "You don't understand how much he put at risk. I prayed for him to be reasonable. At the end of the day, there was no meeting. There was no vote. Someone acted in our collective best interest. Someone always does."

"Was the Black Cat riot a sting to catch Xavier in a gay bar?"

Before Lowell could answer, the waiter delivered my cocktail. I took in Lowell during the silence. He was a second-generation Hollywood titan, and his left elbow was on the table, and he rested the side of his face in his hand, and his mouth was pouty. He wanted me to recognize that he felt awful about what had transpired and that he was not the real bad guy. It was galling. This powerful motherfucker expected me to feel sorry for him.

"I've said enough," Lowell insisted. "Hand over the book."

"You almost bested your father," I said. "He brought Douglas Fairbanks to Hollywood, and Xavier is not only your greatest find—he outshined Fairbanks. But you didn't protect Xavier, and his legacy and yours will both suffer. You'll just be the guy who inherited the studio from your daddy."

Lowell sat up straight. "Fuck you. Where's my book?"

I pulled the doctored notebook out of my pants pocket and tossed it onto the table in front of him. "You were right about Xavier. He didn't care for any of you."

I took the satchel and left through the back of the bar, making my exit quicker than Lowell could thumb through the book. Once in the alley, I sprinted. My car was parked at a meter a block away. Before I reached the end of the alley, I was struck in the back of the head and fell unconscious onto the pavement.

A deliveryman woke me. I'd been dragged behind a cluster of trash cans. The deliveryman saw my feet as he was passing by and was relieved to find me breathing. I'd been out for half an hour. My head wasn't bleeding, but I had a big knot where I was hit. The satchel and the recorder were gone, and my shirt had been ripped open and the wire removed from my chest. The deliveryman asked if I wanted to call the cops and report the mugging. Since you can't report blackmailed money stolen, I declined.

When I returned home, Callum was sitting on a bench on my porch, and my front door was wide open. Callum had his hand on a pistol lying on the arm of the bench, and my house had been ransacked.

"You got some kinda gambling debt?" he asked.

"No," I said, determined to sound as unbothered as he did.

"Then you were gonna shake down the boss and run?"

"Something like that."

"And the recorder?"

"In case I needed more money in the future."

"The boss burned the bogus notebook," he said, "and he had us search your place for the real one."

"There isn't one."

"So I gathered." Callum sucked his teeth. "I don't see as how I'll ever figure out actors or Negroes. You all will work steady for years and years, then up and go haywire."

Callum stated the obvious: I was fired and banned from the Skyline studio lot for life. Once he left, I began to clean up inside the house, starting with Kimberly's bedroom. I'd managed to hang her clothes in the closet and armoire before she returned from a weekly meeting for a women's group that she joined a month earlier without my noticing. She was upset by the state of the house and by the news that I'd lost my job, but she refused to listen to my explanation.

"We need to consider separate lives," she said.

I cleaned until midnight. When I went to bed in the guest room, I stared into the darkness, balancing the day's gains against its losses. I had some answers that brought me a measure of solace, but justice remained unattainable. I was unemployed and headed toward divorce, but I would be free to pursue honest work and to be an honest person.

Show business didn't mark my departure or adhere to the laws of decency. Xavier was exploited by the studio that murdered him. In June, Skyline Motion Pictures released *Hornet's Hellfire* in theaters nationwide. Nicholas Ray's name was removed from the film at his demand, and the Directors Guild of America created an official pseudonym (Alan Smithee) to use when its members wanted to disavow a movie they'd shot.

Lowell cut the most homoerotic moments and scenes from the picture. To fill in the gaps, the studio used a Black body double and reshot several scenes either from a distance, on the body double's back, or over his shoulder. A white vocal impersonator was paid to say new lines like he was Xavier. It was almost seamlessly done. I could spot the imposters, but the general public couldn't. When the end credits rolled, I wondered if Horace's mother had seen the dark side of her prediction, too.

The advertisement campaign for the film emphasized that it was the final performance from "one of the brightest Black stars of his generation." In a radio interview, Lowell claimed the picture "captured Xavier's gifts before his personal problems overwhelmed him."

Hornet's Hellfire was a box office hit. Topped only by *The Graduate*, it was the second highest-grossing movie of 1967, earning $35 million. Xavier would have been delighted in seeing that the third-place slot went to Sidney's *Guess Who's Coming to Dinner*. More bittersweet accolades arrived when the Academy Award nominations were announced. The film's only distinction went to Xavier, who was nominated for Best Actor.

The Fortieth Academy Awards were scheduled for Monday, April 8,

1968, and I was morbidly curious to see if Xavier would win an Oscar posthumously. However, the world was altered in big and small ways by the assassination of Dr. Martin Luther King Jr. on April 4. The Academy wanted to press on with the ceremony, but Diahann, Sidney, and Sammy Davis Jr. refused to attend out of respect for mourning Dr. King. The date was pushed two days, and the Black stars showed up, hoping that Xavier could win one for the race. Of course, voting for the Academy Awards had concluded weeks before. Rod Steiger took home the Oscar for Best Actor for his role, opposite Sidney, in United Artists' *In the Heat of the Night*.

29

ADAMANT YOUNG QUEERS

Too late for Xavier, the gay liberation movement that he believed was imminent has at last arrived without apologizing for its tardiness. He didn't live long enough to realize it, but Xavier was at one of the movement's inciting incidents. The raid on the Black Cat led many local gay, Black, and Latino activists to unite on February 11, 1967, in a demonstration protesting police brutality.

Two hundred people gathered. No laws changed, but it had lasting impact. A group called PRIDE (Personal Rights in Defense and Education) helped organize the protest and then began publishing a monthly newsletter that evolved into *The Advocate*. That word, *pride*, also began to gain traction among queers.

More than two years later, the Stonewall riots in 1969 rang the bell for a lot of people. Gay pride marches sprang up the following year in New York City, Chicago, San Francisco, and LA. In Xavier's honor, I went to McCadden Place and Hollywood Boulevard to watch the march get underway. Then I started sitting in on Gay Liberation Front (GLF/LA) meetings. I was suddenly surrounded by young activists who adhered to the motto "Don't trust anyone over thirty." I was thirty-eight. On sight, they branded me too cautious and rigid to be of much use to them.

At the third GLF/LA gathering that I attended, Brice, a white college dropout from Santa Barbara, asked me, "At your age, how have you not been arrested at a protest?"

I locked eyes with Damon, a young Black law student, expecting him to share my incredulousness toward a white person questioning a Black person's political credentials, but Damon piled on: "Where were you when our people were shedding blood in the streets?"

"I marched with King," I said.

"How many times?" asked Damon.

"Once," I said, and I became invisible for the rest of the meeting.

I don't know how to say what I believe in a manner that they will understand and respect. As a Black man and a gay man of a certain age, I have my informed reservations about direct confrontation with police, with churches, with governments, with any powers that be. I have seen the militant executed.

I sometimes feel as if these adamant young queers think that everyone older than they are cowered in the face of homophobia because we lacked backbones. They don't realize how our lives were picked apart for an infraction as tiny as a kiss. They don't seem to grasp that the penalty for their brand of civil disobedience used to be death. I can take them to the cemetery plot of the bravest gay man I ever knew. Like everyone else born before a movement gathers critical mass, he was silenced so that his voice could not convert too many others.

The young ones seem to roll their eyes whenever I dare to speak at meetings. Once I started to tell a story about Xavier, and Damon howled, "That closet queen!" The other youngsters laughed. They don't know the truth about Xavier or our lives. I was too angry and frustrated in the moment to argue. Besides, I'd need hours to make my case, and they'd never give me the time. Their great impatience with me might only be equal to mine with them. I am tempted to shout in their faces: *Forgive me if I am slow to join your revolution at your speed. I am haunted by a society that was eviler and crueler than the one you've met.*

Anyway, I keep going to the gatherings. I long to learn and to be heard. I'm not totally sure these kids are worth the effort, but I'm convinced that I owe it to Xavier to show up as he would have. I want to contribute what little I can before I die.

That is why I'm submitting this manuscript to you, Mr. Kepner, and your colleagues at the ONE National Gay & Lesbian Archives. The history of queers ought to include Xavier, and while I have no faith that justice will be served, I hold out hope that eventually the truth can be known. Xavier C. Barlow was a forerunner cut down in his prime. He deserved to live in the liberated world that he sensed was possible if enough people dedicated themselves to the struggle. His killers wanted him disgraced and forgotten. Don't let them win. He died for the revolution to come.

ACKNOWLEDGMENTS

My father took me to the theater to watch my first movie when I was three years old. We saw *E.T. the Extra-Terrestrial* (1982) on the big screen, and I was mesmerized. Afterward, a poster of the brown alien with a glowing finger was taped to my bedroom wall. My mother was with me the first time I insisted on walking out on a movie. It was a special theatrical re-release of *Fantasia* (1940). I was four or five years old, and I didn't grasp the appeal of the film's eight animated segments set to classical music. I finished my bucket of popcorn on the drive home. My passionate relationship with movies runs deep, and I thank my parents for nourishing it.

On our second date, Jonathan—the man who became my husband (2012)—and I sat through the Portuguese-language drama *City of Men* (released in the US in 2008). I don't remember much about what happens in the movie because I was busy holding Jonathan's hand and reading him for signs that he liked me as much as I liked him. Spoiler alert: he did, and he does. His love and support have proven vital to my life as a writer.

When my daughter was a toddler, I'd scoop her up in my arms and waltz with her wildly around our living room during the "Shall We Dance" number in *The King and I* (1956). For my son, I'd imitate Jack Haley's dance routine as the Tin Man in *The Wizard of Oz* (1939). I appreciate how my children bring out the kid in me. JoJo and Max, I love you.

I am grateful to Nadxieli Nieto, who saw the potential in this novel and acquired it for Flatiron, and to Kukuwa Fraser, who served diligently as the book's editor. My literary agent, Jim McCarthy, guided me as always to stay true to my voice. My screenwriting partner, T.J. Brady, continues to encourage me to take these solo flights of literary fancy. They are all *As Good as It Gets* (1997).

For this novel, I drew inspiration from and owe a debt of gratitude to Paul Winfield, Sherman Hemsley, and Howard Rollins, as well as several Black actors I dare not out, and thousands of queer Black artists who never attained the notoriety they sought. The old prejudices against those who are not heterosexual are with us still, even in show business.

I am a research fanatic. I have been studying some of the real-life actors in this novel since I was a child. I knew things about them and couldn't tell you why or how I knew them. But there were several sources that I relied on and wish to thank: *Gay L.A.: A History of Sexual Outlaws, Power Politics, and Lipstick Lesbians* by Lillian Faderman and Stuart Timmons; *The Legs Are the Last to Go: Aging, Acting, Marrying, and Other Things I Learned the Hard Way* by Diahann Carroll; and *Hollywood Black: The Stars, the Films, the Filmmakers* by Donald Bogle.

Finally, I offer my thanks to the legion of authors, booksellers, librarians, archivists, and dedicated readers who have motivated and promoted my writing. I love our community.

ABOUT THE AUTHOR

© Christopher Marrs

Rasheed Newson is the author of the national bestseller *My Government Means to Kill Me*, which was selected as a Lambda Literary finalist for Gay Fiction and was named one of the "100 Notable Books of 2022" by *The New York Times*. He is also a television drama writer, producer, and showrunner. He codeveloped *Bel-Air* and worked on *The Chi*, *Animal Kingdom*, and *Narcos*, among other drama series. Newson is a 2025–26 American Library in Paris Visiting Fellow. He currently lives with his husband and their two children in Pasadena.